ONCE UPON AGAIN

ONCE UPON AGAIN

David Lewis

With Lisa Dugas

Leonard Press

Leonard Press
Bolivar, MO 65613-0752

For other titles, prices, and order information:
www.leonardpress.com

ISBN 0-9769114-4-2
Library of Congress Control Number: 2005937468

Cover Art: Anastasios Kazapedies

ONCE UPON AGAIN

David Lewis

With Lisa Dugas

Leonard Press

Leonard Press
Bolivar, MO 65613-0752

For other titles, prices, and order information:
www.leonardpress.com

ISBN 0-9769114-4-2
Library of Congress Control Number: 2005937468

Cover Art: Anastasios Kazapedies

The brothers Grimm, for their confidence in my stories
Joel Becker, Godfather of the Kosher Nostra
Pam Misner, 800 pound gorilla
Ulva Eldridge, language artist
My wife Laura, for the time, the place, and the space

I owe all of you more than thanks

This book is dedicated to my co-conspirator Lisa Dugas, whose sensitivity, understanding, and dedication are mightier than my pen, and whose slippery mind so challenges my own.

Bread, brie, and thee, Greeb

We are like birds
Who have forgotten we have wings,
Kings and queens
Who have forgotten our royal heritage.
We feel enslaved by conditions
That should have no power to bind us,
And powerless before forces
Over which we have been given dominion.

Marianne Williamson

PROLOGUE

WE ARE BUT RIPPLES on the ocean of existence. During our brief passages here we often take the shallow view, believing life begins with our birth and ends with our death. We assume because we *feel* separate, we *are* separate. We conclude that because we cannot remember other places and other times, there are no other places and times. We see ourselves with narrow eyes and feel ourselves with tiny hearts, frightened of the destination instead of celebrating the journey. Now and again, what we were shows us what we are. Now and again, what we have been calls us toward what we can be. Once upon again, we may be offered the opportunity to discover that we are no more separate from what has gone before than waves are separate from the sea.

> The surf crashes.
> Foam-filled, on sullen shore
> It swirls against the rocks until,
> Content, it slips quietly back to sea.
> The surf crashes.

> Tamiko Asaruka

ONE

Do not believe
Winter to be the end
Of anything.
Within its cold heart
Begins the Spring.

STEPHANIE'S VOICE FLOATED UP THE STAIRWAY and into Lucin's dressing room. "Ms. Montgomery, the car is here!"

"I'll be right down," Lucin answered, checking her lip liner in the vanity mirror and slipping her stockinged feet into her most comfortable pair of Italian loafers.

In the hall she paused to admire a pale peach rose nestled amid a spray of baby's breath in a bud vase at the top of the stairway. It was a nice reminder that spring would arrive soon and removed a bit of heaviness from her step as she descended the staircase.

"I'll just be a couple of hours," she said, shrugging into her wool overcoat. "Please set out the service for lunch. Harrison intends to be home around twelve-thirty."

"Yes, Ma'am," came the reply from the kitchen.

"Oh, and Stephanie?" she smiled. "The rose is lovely. Thank you." She stepped out the side door to find James waiting under the overhang in her new, dark green Jaguar.

The car and James O'Doud were both a compromise. Her husband wanted her to have a slightly stretched Mercedes and a full-time driver. She wanted a Miata and to be left alone. They settled on a Jaguar and James to drive her through the winter, until the streets were more navigable and she better knew her way around Kansas City. She opened the passenger side door before James could get out and plopped onto the front seat.

He smiled at her. "And what is it that ya think you're doin' now? You're supposed to be me passenger, not a co-pilot," he said.

"And you are supposed to be a driver and not criticize the lady of the manor," she countered, tossing her hair.

He chuckled. "At least I don't have to be wearin' a uniform. And where are we off to today, M'Lady and fair?"

Kansas City in winter is a very messy place. Rarely does it stay cold enough to grace the city's fountains and parks with pristine white. Instead, melt usually comes on the heels of snowfall, mud is more common than towering drifts, and the streets become rutted, crunchy avenues of dirty slush. It took about three blocks for the Jag to be covered in a fine film of salty filth, the car's spotless windows transformed into hazy portals to the outside world and smoky reflections of the auto's interior. James hit the windshield washer frequently as he plowed his way toward the Plaza.

A retired firefighter turned limo driver, he jumped at the chance for a few months of full-time employment. Harrison Montgomery paid well, James had his own room, ate at least two meals a day at the house and, in his third winter after Katherine's death, he had no one to answer to and his time was his own. With the extra cash, tarpon fishing off the Keys was closer every day. Plus, it was nice to have Mrs. M as a regular client. He enjoyed kidding with her, and the company of a young woman was pleasant. She and his own daughter were about the same age. He hadn't seen Mary Ruth since Katherine's funeral.

Lucin watched the block-by-block progression of the city as the neighborhood gave way to smaller, half-million dollar homes, shifting to old pseudo-Spanish facades on converted apartment buildings that segued into the neo-Spanish architecture of the Country Club Plaza, one of the nation's most celebrated shopping districts. From Neiman Marcus, Eddie Bauer, and Laura Ashley, to Gap Kids and the Sharper Image, to small exclusive shops and trendy restaurants, the Plaza was continuously crowded and busy. Fox jackets and mink coats shouldered along the slippery sidewalks side by side with Gore-Tex and layered sweatshirts. It was a cacophony of color and culture that cut through the swirling flakes and almost brightened the leaden, overcast day, but it was still Kansas City, and Kansas City was not home. Kansas City wasn't even close to home. It was about as far from Philadelphia as a person could get. Much farther than Lucin ever thought she'd be.

Philadelphia was a comfortable circle of friends, the right clubs, the proper charities, the correct sorority, acceptable volunteerism, and a life she'd been bred for and born to. Hers was very nearly the mantle of royalty. From her earliest memory she'd trained to fill her station. An only child, Lucin's mission was to marry well and continue the tradition of civic responsibility and social example set by her mother and her mother's mother. This generational destiny was firmly in place on the day of her birth, as much a part of her as the color of her eyes. It was her duty, she was told, and duty was all. The obligation of her rank hovered over her and she was never allowed to dismiss her responsibility to her family or her accountability to the conventions of her status. Covered in the commitment of her class, Lucin assumed her place. Now, her place was gone. Removed from the connection to family and Philadelphia, living in an immense house in a totally unfamiliar community, seldom seeing her husband of ten years because of his career demands, and with nearly nothing to occupy her time, she found herself unencumbered by most of the social burdens she had so freely shouldered since infancy. Her world was shaken, and boredom had rattled loose.

James eased the Jag to the crest of the hill on Jarboe Street and into the parking area in front of a row of single-story shops, stopping in front of one bearing a pink and green neon sign proclaiming simply *Nails!* Lucin shouldered her handbag.

"If ya find it agreeable, Ma'am," he said, turning slightly in his seat to face her, "I'll be runnin' a few errands for Stephanie and return in about an hour, traffic permitting."

"That's fine," she smiled. "Enjoy your shopping."

"Sure, and ya know I will, Ma'am," he replied. "Like a root canal."

As Lucin stepped out of the car, she noticed the shop next to *Nails!* In her other two visits to the center, its windows had been covered in heavy, white paper and masking tape, the contents secret from passers-by. Today all that was gone. In the window hung a lovely sign in muted pastels that appeared to have been hand-painted. It showed an elegant white crane balanced delicately on one foot. Beside the crane was a single word. *"Wa."*

The bell above the door jangled as she entered the nail shop and Jolee, the owner and proprietor, came bustling up from the rear of the building.

"Good mornin', Sweetie. I just got here myself." She smiled, then glanced out the front windows. "Lord, look at that snow come down. Take a seat. I got coffee goin', and I brought a Thermos of hot chocolate from home. Take your pick."

"Hot chocolate sounds wonderful," Lucin replied, hanging up her coat. "Perfect for a day like this."

"Honey, there ain't nothin' perfect for a day like this except a good man and a good bed," Jolee said, filling two Styrofoam cups with the pungent liquid. "They got stores full of good beds. I don't know where the hell you find a good man," she twinkled. "But that ain't never stopped me from looking."

"I have one," Lucin quickly responded, taking an offered cup and sitting at a manicure table.

"Not sayin' you don't. There are one or two out there. Hell, most men are good enough if they think it's part of foreplay, or until the sweat dries," she laughed, pushing a strand of runaway red hair off her forehead and tugging at a bra strap.

Lucin smiled in spite of herself. "Do you really feel that way?"

Jolee sat on the other side of the table and examined her make-up in a mirror, picking at a small clot of black eyeliner. "Sweetie, I love men. Always have. I love their smell, I love their taste, I love a good growl in my ear, and I even appreciate a little whisker burn in certain areas, but most of 'em need to lose a couple of hundred pounds of ugly fat and just leave the important parts behind. I can snore all by my-self!"

Lucin giggled. "Any exceptions to that?"

"Every damn one of 'em for a little while," Jolee laughed, pushing a soaking bowl across the table. "I ain't been a virgin for twenty years, and my only regret is that it ain't been twenty-one."

"You certainly seem ... liberated."

"That ain't Latin for easy, is it?"

Lucin blushed. "No! Oh, no. I'm sorry, that's not what I meant at all!"

"Relax, Honey," soothed Jolee. "I'm just givin' you a little shit. No offense taken."

"You just seem so self-actualized about men. So comfortable with who you are and what you want."

"I figured out a long time ago that Fairy Tales are scary. Poison apples, witches spells, long sleeps, dwarves, dragons ... Jesus! Who needs that shit? All of us are just what we are. Some people go through their whole lives denyin' their natures, or worryin' about consequences, fussin' over some useless version of morality, or waiting for Prince Charming to show up, build a picket fence, and mow the yard. Lots a' women spend their days expectin' something to happen instead of accepting what does. You can waste a lot of time expectin'. If you accept, then you don't like it, it's a hell of a lot easier to change the situation or move on, whatever works for you."

Lucin sat quietly for a while as Jolee concentrated on her cuticles, rolling over in her mind what the other woman had said. The plain truth was, Jolee had hit a nerve or two. While Lucin was not dissatisfied about her relationship with Harrison, she was beginning to realize she was somewhat less than totally satisfied.

"You're thinking too much," Jolee commented.

"What?"

"You're thinking too much."

"What makes you say that?"

"I'm psychic."

Lucin gave the other woman a skeptical glance.

"Your hands are tense. When you think too much, your hands get stiff and rigid. Relax, you're making me work too hard."

"Oh. I'm sorry."

"Get out of your head and get into your heart. I can see in the little lines around your eyes that you're not the happiest camper in the park. This is only your third visit here and we don't know each other very well, but I hold hands for a living, Honey. When you hold as many hands as I do, you get to where you can read people a little from it."

Lucin raised an eyebrow. "Is that right?"

"Yeah, that's right," answered Jolee, lifting her own eyebrow. Both women laughed.

"Okay," Lucin said. "Analyze me. I can take it."

"Alright. First of all, you've told me you're new to Kaycee. I'd say you feel displaced, you have no friends here, you got more money than God, you don't have anything to do, you're bored, you live in some big, old, impersonal house, you lack a sense of purpose, and you ain't gettin' enough."

Lucin felt her face redden.

"Gotcha, huh, Honey."

"Can we talk about something else?"

"What else is there?"

In spite of herself, Lucin giggled.

"Don't get me wrong," continued Jolee. "I'm not makin' judgments, I'm not attackin' anybody. Your husband may be the finest man on the planet. None of what I said applies to him. This is *your* situation. If you don't like it, it is up to *you* to change

11

it. Start with the boredom. Volunteer at a hospital, get a job, take up a hobby, start a project. Enjoy. Find something that will charge you up and relax you at the same time. You'll sleep better."

"That's your prescription, huh?"

"Yep."

"Actually I do have sort of a project. There is a guesthouse on our property that is terribly run-down. In the old days it was probably servant's quarters. I've never even been inside it. Harrison mentioned that I might re-do it."

"Your husband's name is Harrison?"

"Yes."

"What do you call him?"

"Harrison."

"Uh-huh. So why don't you fix up the house?"

"I don't know how he would want it."

"What difference does that make? It's *your* project. Do whatever you want. Express yourself, Sweetie. It'll be good for you! Have some fun."

"It would be fun."

"You'd have something to do, a way to be creative, kick the boredom and have something of your own. Sounds great to me." She slid back from the table. "You're all done, unless you want some color on these nails, or American flags and rhinestones."

Lucin smiled. "They're fine just short and buffed."

"No spirit of adventure," Jolee grinned, standing up. Lucin's cell phone rang and she spoke briefly as she retrieved her wallet from her purse and presented a credit card.

"My ride is going to be late," she said. "Maybe I'll go next door and look around. What do you know about the new store?"

"It's an import business for all kinds of oriental stuff. The guy that owns it is named Tommy something. He's Japanese or Chinese and he'll bring a lump to your throat. He's been in here a couple of times. Reminds me of a cat." Jolee displayed a wicked little grin. "Now, Tommy would be a great way to spend a snowy day!"

Lucin laughed. "You're terrible!"

"Just honest, Sweetie. Same time next week?"

"That'll be fine."

"Next time I see you, I want you to have a project or a hobby. Get yourself some way to pass the time and have fun."

Slipping into her coat, Lucin looked at Jolee. "What do you do?" she asked.

Jolee smiled. "Whisker burn, Sweetie. Lots and lots of whisker burn." They laughed together, again.

When Lucin stepped into the store next door, she immediately smelled the scent of jasmine and heard the sound of dripping water. To her left, just inside the door, was a pool surrounded by rocks, a trickle of water flowing in darting pathways down one large stone, weeping onto the rippling surface. She stepped up to it and stood as if transfixed, watching the play of light upon the water, catching an occasional flash of white on orange beneath the surface. She did not notice her muscles relax, her breathing slow, her pulse rate drop. She was not aware of the release of tension in her body, the escape of the mundane from her mind. There was only the water, the sound, and the jasmine. As simple as that, it claimed her.

"Pardon me."

The words pulled her back with a small start and an almost audible rush of reality. Slightly dizzy, she looked to her right. An oriental man regarded her with a level gaze from deep brown eyes. He was dressed in a black turtleneck and pleated black slacks, less than six feet tall with long hair pulled into a ponytail. Slender, he stood with a relaxed poise usually seen only among dancers.

"*Konnichi wa*," he said. "Hello. Welcome to my shop." His eyes glinted with just a trace of amusement.

"Hello," replied Lucin, fussing with her coat and purse, slightly confused and trying to focus. "I th-think your pond is lovely."

"*Domo*," he smiled, "Thank you. You've been standing here gazing at it for nearly twenty minutes. I thought, perhaps, I should come bring you back."

"Twenty minutes? No!"

"Yes," he said, his smile widening into a grin. His teeth were very white.

"Oh, I'm sorry!"

"Sorrow should not be a part of this. I have gained great face. This pond is of my design and construction. Your meditation does me honor. You have paid me a wonderful compliment."

"It truly is lovely," Lucin replied, still reaching for her composure. "I don't know what happened to me. I just went away, I guess."

"In Japan we call it surrender. A person's fate is a person's fate and life is but an illusion."

"You're from Japan?"

"Yes."

"You speak English beautifully."

"I have lived here since I was three. I speak Japanese horribly." He smiled. "Please excuse me. You have been so kind in enjoying my pond, and I am being terribly rude. I am Tamiko Asaruka." He bowed deeply from the waist. In reflex, Lucin bobbed a bit. It seemed to amuse him. "And you?"

"Ah, Lucin Montgomery. It's very nice to meet you, Mr. Uh …"

"Call me Tami. It's much simpler," he replied, extending his hand. She took it almost reluctantly, as if wary of the contact. The handshake was brief, warm, and dry. She felt relieved, but the glint of humor that rose in his eyes at their touch kept her cautious.

Through the window she saw James arrive in the Jaguar. "There's my ride," she said, nearly gratefully. "I must go. It's been nice to meet you Mister … uh, Tami." She started for the door, and he moved beside her, his hand lightly grazing the small of her back. Warmth spread up her spine and settled at the nape of her neck. Slightly shocked, she turned to move away from him, but he stood six feet distant, the hint of a smile on his lips.

"*Dozo*. Please visit me again, Lucin-*san*," he said with a small bow. "I will count the moments until you return."

Tamiko Asaruka watched her rush through the snow to the familiarity of her waiting car and smiled to himself.

"It is good to see you, Child," he whispered, his eyes losing focus with memory. "You have come, and now it begins again. *Yokoso oide kudasareta*. Once more, welcome to my house."

TWO

Nothing can be gained
Without release.
Nothing can be released
Without gain.
Karma is all.

THE JAGUAR FISHTAILED IN THE SNOW as they turned onto Ward Parkway. Lucin silently stared out the window. James watched her from the corner of his eye.

"Sure, and ya hit that seat like you'd just run a marathon," he said. "Are ya alright, then?"

"Yes, James, I'm fine."

"You'll pardon me for sayin' so, Mrs. M, but ya don't look fine to me. Ya look like you're glowin' a bit."

"Glowing?"

"That's right. Horses sweat, men perspire, ladies glow. A lady is what ya are."

She smiled. "Thank you, James. That's nice of you to say. I just don't feel very lady-like right now."

"What do ya feel like then, if ya don't mind me askin'?"

"I don't know. I'm kind of numb."

"I noticed ya comin' out of that shop next door to the nail place."

"I stopped in to see what they had. It was ... very strange."

"Did someone treat ya badly? Do I need to go back and have a bit of a chat with anyone?"

"No," she chuckled, "nothing like that. But it's kind of you to offer. You would go back, wouldn't you?"

"Of course. I'd not be takin' kindly to anyone that brought ya grief."

"James O'Doud, you are a fine and decent man."

"And why wouldn't I be?" he winked. "I'm Irish."

Stephanie was fussing in the kitchen when Lucin entered. She retrieved a bottle of Evian from the fridge and smiled at the young woman.

"What's for lunch?"

"Poached salmon, Ma'am, in a light mustard and white wine sauce, steamed new potatoes in dill and chives, sautéed asparagus with diced yellow pepper, and a lime sorbet for dessert, if that's alright?"

"Alright? That's marvelous, Stephanie."

The young woman dimpled. "Thank you, Ma'am."

"There's enough for you and James?"

"Oh yes. I'll serve James after I serve you and Mr. Montgomery. James and I will eat in the kitchen."

"Fine. Harrison should be home in an hour or so. We'll have lunch about one. I'm going upstairs to change."

In her dressing room, Lucin slipped out of her loafers, jeans, and sweater, put on fresh panties and a new bra, ran a brush through her nearly black hair a few times, and donned a dark green lounging pant-suit in raw silk. Camel colored two-inch heels and small crystal earrings were next, followed by a lipstick touch-up, and a final hair fluff. Leaving through the bedroom, she stopped to look out the window and check the snowfall. When she turned around, there stood Harrison. He appeared rather disheveled.

"Hi, Luce," he said. "You look wonderful."

"Thank you," she replied, moving to present her cheek for a kiss. "You're early."

"My plane leaves at two."

"Your plane?"

"I'm afraid so. Back to Philadelphia," he said, dragging a suitcase out of the closet.

"Oh, no. How long this time?"

"I really don't know. A week, maybe more."

"Since we moved to Kansas City, you've spent more time in Philadelphia than you have here!"

"Lucin, I know it. There's just nothing we can do about it right now. Until the firm gets the new office fully established, I'm gonna be going back and forth a lot."

"I don't mean to complain," she said, watching him pack, "but I thought when you made senior partner, things might even out a bit."

"They will, Sweetheart. I promise. It's just going to take time. I'll be staying at the company apartment, and somebody will always know where I am if you need me. Better yet, why don't you come along? You could see your mother, visit with some friends, make it a holiday."

"That sounds nice, but I'm thinking about starting a project."

"A project?" he asked, gathering up toiletries.

"Renovating the guest house."

"Big job. You're gonna need a hammer."

"I'll borrow one from James," she smiled.

"He'd loan it to you," Harrison chuckled, closing the suitcase and grabbing a carry-on. "Are you serious?"

"I've been thinking about it. With you working such long hours and being gone so much, maybe I need to get involved with something. You know, a hobby."

16

"Renovating the guest house is a hobby?"

"Why not?"

"Darling, if that is what you'd like to do, I can't think of a single reason why not."

"Wonderful!"

"It will work well as a base for garden parties, a place for the family to stay when they visit, and it will give you something to do while I get everything squared away for the firm. I think it's perfect for personal, business, and social reasons. Do you have any idea what you're going to do with it?"

"Not one."

"Well, it's totally up to you," he said, picking up the bags and heading for the door. Lucin followed him downstairs. "Just send the bills to the accountant and have fun. I have a cab waiting outside," he continued, pausing to slip into his overcoat. "Sorry, Luce, gotta run." He kissed her quickly on the lips and opened the side door.

"But what about lunch?"

"I'll grab a sandwich at the airport. I love you." He was gone.

"I love you, too," Lucin whispered.

She ate lunch in the kitchen with James and Stephanie.

It was a long afternoon. The snow dwindled to a stop at about three. Lucin tried Linda Howard, but couldn't maintain interest in the plot. She tried Oprah, but it was a makeover show. She even tried writing an actual letter to her mother, but couldn't think of anything to say. She drifted downstairs, but Stephanie and James had both gone to their rooms. She left Stephanie a note that dinner would not be necessary, trudged back upstairs, filled the tub, added bath salts, lit four or five lavender candles, tied her hair up, lowered the lights, stripped, and slid into the scented water.

She hadn't realized she had been tense until the water began to work on her. Spreading her toes, she felt pain flash through the arches of her feet. Pointing her feet, the pain moved up into her calves. Flexing her calves pushed it into her knees. Tightening her knees drove it into her thighs. She chased the muscle aches up her body for a while, amused at how the discomfort ran from her until she began to feel cool. The tub's thermostat was on ninety-four as always, but today it didn't seem to be warm enough. She turned it up to a hundred and felt the gentle vibration as the circulation pump kicked in.

Leaning back against the bath pillow she began chasing her aches and pains again, feeling herself relax as the temperature rose, watching the flickering candles through the rising steam. There was something so comforting, so familiar about it all. After a time, unnoticed, the small candles burned away, leaving only the quiet glow of a night light out of sight near the floor to manufacture shadows in the darkened room, without any reflections from mirrors that had become steam-frosted opaque panels. Only her exhaled breath touched the surface of the water. Only the slowing beat of her heart disturbed its stillness. From deep in her body, about halfway between her navel and pubis, warmth began to coalesce, a sphere of quiet energy no bigger than an egg. It came on so slowly, with such delicacy, she scarcely noticed it in her languor, did not become alarmed by the new sensation or struggle with it. Instead, something long dormant surrendered to the sphere, and it began to stretch out diaphanous tendrils through her, following her neural pathways, caressing the natural power points in her body, a cobweb of contentment growing through every organ, every tissue, every part of her. Time stopped. Lost in it, she smiled.

When Lucin came back, she came back very slowly. The room slowly gained substance from the void, appearing between her half-closed eyelids as if the walls were returning from a great distance. She found it difficult to distinguish where her body stopped and the water began. Immersed to the chin and completely relaxed, she reveled in the sensation, at length turning her head slightly to look at the clock. One-fifteen. One-fifteen!? Normally she would have bolted from the tub, embarrassed for herself at the time lost, but this was far from normal. With considerable effort, she flipped the lever to drain the tub and lay there, gaining weight and substance as the water flowed away.

God, she felt heavy! It took nearly all of her strength just to sit up, taking the rest of it to actually get to her feet and stumble to the hook where her robe hung. As she removed it from the hanger and the material brushed against her chest, she gave a start. The terrycloth was like velvet sandpaper, deliciously abrasive, and it sent a chill racing up her back. She shivered from it and quickly slipped into the long robe, noticing the weight of the garment, feeling how it lay on her skin drawing the water from her pores, how it brushed against her legs as she slowly walked into her dressing room, how the belt pushed against the small of her back.

She tried to ignore the sensations as she removed a fresh pair of pajamas from the closet shelf, but she was awash in them, the sphere in her belly a glowing marble, pushing gentle heat up behind her navel and down between her legs, creating more dampness there than the bathwater could account for. Thirsty, she crossed to the bedroom fridge and removed a bottle of water. Her first sip could not be stopped, and she drank the entire container in long, greedy swallows. The cold rushing into her stomach battled the warmth in her belly and she pressed her thighs firmly together, gathering the robe tightly across her breasts. Nearly panting, she sat for a moment, then turned down the bed. She dropped the robe and picked up the pajamas, then let them fall to the floor and crawled between the sheets totally nude. Wedging a pillow hard between her legs, she pulled the covers over herself and was almost instantly in slumber, the sphere's glow slowly fading away. Her sleep was dreamless and deep.

Lucin didn't get up until almost ten. Sitting on the toilet she peered owlishly about the bathroom as if she'd never seen it before. Everything seemed excessive. The porcelain was too hard, the lights too bright, the floor too cold, the toothbrush too stiff, the toothpaste too sweet, the towel too rough. The tub called to her, ready to immerse her again in deliciously fluid warmth, willing to remove her weight and give her blessed freedom, waiting to carry her out of herself to who knew where. She resisted the urge, almost fleeing to the dressing room for a sweatshirt, sweat pants, sweat socks and Reeboks. She brushed her hair and pony-tailed it with a scrunchy, then headed downstairs.

James lounged in the kitchen over his third cup of coffee. When she entered, he rose to his feet.

"Top of the mornin' to ya, Mrs. M. I hope ya had a good night."

"Good morning, James," she mumbled. "Coffee. I smell coffee."

"Set yourself down, and I'll get ya a cup. A big one," he grinned, moving to the coffee pot. "Don't be takin' no offense, but are ya sure you're awake?"

"No," Lucin replied. "I'm not sure of anything except that I want cream in my coffee, and that other aroma is driving me mad. What is it?"

"Scrambled eggs."

"That's it? Just scrambled eggs?"

"Sure and that's all. Three eggs, a bit of cream, a touch of pepper, a dash of paprika, a little cheddar cheese, some dill, a modicum of diced onion, a drop or two of malt vinegar, and a sprinkle of sea salt. Stephanie has gone shopping, so I made myself a bite of breakfast." He placed the coffee in front of her. "Could I be fixin' a bit of nourishment for herself this mornin'?"

"God, yes! James, please and thank you! It sounds wonderful."

"Would ya be wantin' a lovely bagel and some blueberry jam with that today?" he asked, opening the refrigerator.

Lucin smiled. "Marry me," she said.

"As sweet as the offer is, it's not necessary. I'll break your fast, no strings attached. I miss the days when I did this for my darlin' Mary Ruth. It's an artist with an egg I am, and I enjoy it, ya know."

"Did you make the coffee too?"

"Sure."

"Where'd you get it? It tastes marvelous!"

"It's the blend ya keep in the pantry, same as always."

"What?"

"That's right," he said, putting a skillet on the stove to heat and adding a dollop of butter. "Took it right off the shelf myself."

"It tastes different."

"Maybe it's not the coffee, Ma'am. Maybe it's you that's a bit different."

"Me?"

"Sure."

"How am I different?"

"Well, ya never asked me to marry ya before."

She laughed. "That's certainly true," she said, blushing slightly.

"Now don't be getting' all self-conscious, M'Lady and fair. There are other things, too. Ya never eat breakfast, just that canned drink of yours and black coffee. Ya never come downstairs in sweat clothes, I've never seen your hair in a ponytail before, and you're not wearin' any make-up. Not even lipstick."

"Wow!"

"I don't hear ya say 'wow' a lot, either. It seems like to me, that you're more casual this mornin', less, uh ..."

"Anal?"

James smiled. "Rigid," he said, adding whipped eggs to the pan.

She returned his smile. "Rigid will do, James."

"So, if ya don't mind me askin', what brought all this about now?"

"It sorta started yesterday at the nail shop." She paused and thought for a moment. "James, will you do me a favor?"

"Without a doubt."

"After breakfast, will you go with me to look over the guest house?"

"That I will."

"Thank you. We can talk more freely then."

"I don't want ya thinkin' that I'm tryin' to pry, Ma'am."

"I don't. I think you care."

"Then you'd be right."

"Will you do me another favor?"

"Sure."

"Will you not mention anything to anybody about my, uh … change?"

"Mum's the word."

"Good," she said, "because it's probably going to get worse."

"Won't that be darlin', now?"

The eggs were perfect.

Early that afternoon, Lucin and James walked through the rapidly melting snow to the guesthouse. The main residence, a six thousand square foot, two and a half story stone structure, faced west. Directly behind and to the east of it, converted from a two-story stable, was the garage. East of the garage about a hundred and fifty feet and separated from the main property by a ring of elm trees, was what had originally been servant's quarters. It was a low, shallow-roofed building sided in weathered, lapped boards, with both a southern and a northern entrance. James pushed open the creaking south door, and they stepped inside.

The smell of mildew was everywhere. Dust covered odds and ends sat about the living room. In addition to the living area, there were two small bedrooms, a tiny kitchen, and a cramped bathroom, complete with an ancient, claw-footed tub. Blinds had fallen from window frames, dead flies littered the sills, paper peeled from the walls, paint flaked from the wainscoting, and grime covered the battered hardwood floor.

"And wouldn't this be a handyman's delight?" James muttered as he poked about. "This place looks like it's been empty for a thousand years."

Lucin grinned. "It's perfect!"

"Have ya lost your mind, then? It's perfect alright. A perfect mess!"

Undaunted, Lucin's grin remained intact. "Let's check out the other side."

"Saints, preserve us."

The north side of the structure was a mirror image of the south. The roof leaked over both bedrooms and down the walls, separating the old horsehair plaster from the lath that supported it, and badly rotting the floorboards. In the bathroom, James found another piece of water damage from a leaking stool.

"Sweet Jesus," he said. "The water's on."

"What's the matter?" asked Lucin, coming in from the living area.

"Ya have some plumbin' problems, too. I don't think anybody bothered to shut off the water. The valve is probably up at the main house. It's a real can a worms you're openin' here."

"What would you do with the place?"

"Pay up the insurance and burn it."

"Let's look outside," she smiled.

"Well, we've come this far."

They prowled through the slush as James looked the place over.

"It could be worse," he observed.

"Really?"

"It could be bigger."

"James!"

He grinned at her. "Now, don't take this the wrong way, Ma'am. I sometimes forget that expense is not a consideration with you. With enough money there are always possibilities. If the structure is sound, all that mess inside is fixable. What ya need to do is get somebody in here who knows more about it than I do."

"Do you know somebody?"

"Sure."

"Will you tell me who, or contact them for me?"

"That I will."

"Thank you James, I mean it."

"I know ya do."

On the west side of the building, an area screened from the main house by a line of trees about fifty feet from the guesthouse, they encountered an old cobblestone patio. As James started across it, a cobble wobbled under his foot, sank into the earth and left him ankle deep in mud. "Matthew, Mark, Luke and John!" he grumbled, "I'm captured by the quagmire. Stay back." He stamped vigorously on a few of the cobblestones, with the same result.

"That's not good," he muttered.

"What's the matter?"

"Five'll get ya ten the water line from the house runs right under these cobbles. Five'll get ya twenty there's a rupture in the line someplace under the stones. I saw a shut-off in the first bathroom out here. That'll do us no good. If there's not a shut-off in the main house, this is like leavin' a hose on twenty-four hours a day. Thousands and thousands of gallons will be collectin' underground. The freezin' and thawin' must have been too much for the pipes. I'll check for a shut-off. If I can't find one, I'll have to call somebody today. We can't let this go on."

"Can it be fixed?"

"Oh, sure. I can't imagine there are any plumbing diagrams available. They'll have to dig out this whole cobbled area, find the break in the line and cap it. The plumbing and all these stones would have to be replaced anyway. Now it will just be sooner instead of later."

Lucin pondered the house and the cobbles for a moment. "James, will you be my foreman?"

"What?"

"Will you oversee the rebuilding of this place? The structural stuff?"

"Ma'am, this'll take months! I stop workin' here in another three weeks or so."

"Not if you want to stay."

"What, continue to drive you around and watch over this place?"

"More watching than driving. Fifty dollar a week raise."

"I'm goin' fishing."

"For how long?"

"Ten days."

"When?"

"May."

"Where?"

"Florida."

"It's on me."

"What?"

"Consider it a bonus for taking the job."

"Are ya serious then?"

"Absolutely."

"I've lost my mind, Ma'am, but I'll do it."

"That's wonderful!" she beamed, impulsively bouncing up to kiss him on the cheek. James reddened.

"Sure, and that beats a stob in the eye with a sharp stick," he grinned.

"Just one more thing," she said, fighting back her own embarrassment. "When we're alone, stop calling me Ma'am."

"Ah, sure, me darlin' Lucille," he chuckled in deep brogue. "What would ye be havin' me call ya then?"

At four o'clock that afternoon Lucin sat across the kitchen table from James as he talked on the phone.

"Brian, me darlin', it's not a big job, just an underground leak beside a house. A few cobbles removed, a little dirt dug out, a cap put on, a couple of your lads will have it done long before lunch. I understand ya got commitments, but a big corporate job like that won't even miss a tiny backhoe and two men ... plus, *plus*, Laddie-Buck, you'd be doin' James Mathew O'Doud himself a good turn. Wouldn't that make your old Daddy proud? I *know* he's dead, ya dummy, I helped carry his box! That don't mean he's not up there lookin' down on ye, waitin' ta see if you'll be doin' the right thing, ya know? Your father's eyes are on ye, Brian, me fair, as sure as our Lord hung bleedin' on the hill at Calvary. How can ye say no to me, a man that's been like an uncle to ye your whole life, when himself is peerin' at ye like a hawk from behind them pearly gates? It's a fine son ye are, sweet Brian, as true and good as a man can be! Aye, that's good. Sure, and I'll be here meself, waitin' to direct the diggin' at the proper place. Fine. Regards to your saintly Mother and your sister Carmen. Bye."

Lucin was smiling at him and shaking her head. "I don't know which was worse," she said, "the accent or the blarney."

"If you're lookin' for a handle on an Irish Catholic, always grab for the guilt. Help will be here at seven in the mornin'."

THREE

Visions come
As if in slumber.
More than dreams,
Faint in
Wakeful remembrance.

LUCIN ATE A LIGHT DINNER and went upstairs early, excited about the guesthouse project. James, not one to procrastinate, already had contacted a remodeling contractor to come by the next afternoon to look over the structure and offer advice about its condition. At her desk, Lucin spent the next two hours doodling on graph paper, sketching out what she remembered of the building, moving walls, expanding areas, playing with what it was and what it might become. She had been involved in projects with several decorators over the years, but never with something as sweeping as actual construction. In some respects, her enthusiasm frightened her, but it was pleasant fright, like the stomach tingle that comes from traveling too fast over a hilly country road.

At around eight she set the thermostat to ninety-four degrees and filled the tub. Slightly wary, she left all the bathroom lights on high, grabbed three or four home-and-garden type magazines and eased into the soothing water. Deliberately concentrating on the magazine, Lucin slowly began to relax as she realized there were no unusual sensations, no sleepiness, no darkening surroundings or receding walls. An hour and a half later, after finding nothing in the magazines that inspired her, she left both them and the tub, slipped into a skiing coverall and boots, and went outside to look at the guesthouse.

Even with a completely clear sky, the temperature remained several degrees above freezing, and Lucin was quite comfortable as she walked across the lawn, past the garage, and toward the stand of trees. A nearly full moon brightened the occasional residual patch of snow, and the swishing friction of the ski-suit added a rhythmic counterpoint to the subtle thud of her boot heels in the grass. She carried with her a flashlight and a folded garbage bag. The light to investigate the interior of the building, the bag to collect anything she might want to take back to the house.

There was little wind. With every second or third step she walked through the moon-whitened vapor of her breath. Lucin smiled. Relaxed from her bath and nude under her coverall, she moved through a nearly perfect night. As she cleared the elms, she saw the water.

The cobbled area beside the old servant's quarters was covered in a pool. About twenty feet across and roughly circular in shape, water had seeped up through the earth, filling the slight depression as the dense stones pushed their way down into the sodden dirt. In the light of day it would have been seen for what it was, little more than an overgrown mud puddle, but at night, especially *this* night, under the crystal sky and the immense moon, the puddle was a miracle. Its luminescent surface shimmered slightly, moonshadow from crisp winter elm branches traced their leaf-less webs upon the ground, and moonlight became dancing silver, almost too bright for the night. Lucin's breath caught in her throat, and she took a half step to keep her balance. Nearly mesmerized, she dropped the garbage bag to the ground and sat upon it cross-legged, watching the water.

The rippling interplay of light and dark performed for her. Motes of moonlight, fallen from limitless height, flickered and frolicked above deceptive depths, and all was reflected in her eyes. The darkness pulled back from expanding luminescence as the refracted slivers of silver filled her vision, her mind, her being. A sigh came from within and without her as she released the here and now. With the freedom of that release, the water lifted her, and the moon carried her away.

In an hour, a day, a year, a century, it left her as it had come, now kneeling and watching the gentle flicker of water on a moonlight night, sitting on her heels by a pond. Moving her eyes from the water, she saw the delicate bridge extending to the tiny island in the middle of the pool, the sentinel stones holding the bridge in place, the sleeping hyacinth and pine, the exquisite cherry and dwarf plum trees, the care-fully raked path, the artful bamboo fencing, the elegant tea house across the pond, all made larger and more distant by darkness and mysterious moonglow. The plank-ing on which she sat trembled from footfalls, and she turned to see the *Mama-san* striding in her direction, an oil lamp in her hand. Dressed in a night kimono of plain white cotton, her hair held from total disarray by pins, the woman smiled down at her.

"Child, what are you doing? Why are you not in the sleeping chamber? You are not dressed for such a cool night, and you should have been asleep three sticks ago!"

"*Gomen nasai*, so sorry, *Mama-san*. I only came out to watch the moon-water for a while. It is very beautiful, *neh*?"

"Yes, it is and so are you, too beautiful to become old and wrinkled at age eight. I would have to give you to the *eta* if you were old and wrinkled. They could teach you to skin cats. Would you like to learn to skin cats?"

"*Iye*, no, *Mama-san*. I am too pretty to learn anything from the *eta*," smiled the child. "I will grow to be lovely and learn from you."

"And what will you learn from me?"

"I will learn to make music and sing and dance and tell stories. And I will learn the honorable art of pillowing and how to make men happy in their Peerless Parts with my Vermilion Chamber."

The older woman laughed. "Yes, you shall, Child. That is why I paid your father such an outrageous sum for you. You will learn all those things and much more. But if you are to learn, you must first be obedient, *neh*?"

"*Hai, Mama-san*. I must be obedient."

"And why must you be obedient?"

"It is my duty, *Mama-san*."

"*Hai*! Duty is everything, Child. Your duty to me, a wife's duty to her husband, a husband's duty to his lord, the lord's duty to the emperor. All life is duty, is it not?"

"All of life is duty, *Mama-san*."

"Then will you stop coming out here and sitting all night? It makes you too sleepy to do your chores."

"I will try, *Mama-san*, but it is so lovely here."

"I do not usually bargain with my property, Child, but you are exceptional and show such promise, I will bargain with you. Will you strike a bargain with me?"

"*Hai, Mama-san, dozo*. Please."

"Very well," the old woman smiled indulgently, "here is my bargain. Since you love to sit in the garden and watch the moon on the water, I will allow you to do so one night each week, and I will sit with you and teach you to drink tea from an empty cup. Is that fair?"

"Yes! Oh, very yes!" beamed the child.

"Good! Then we have struck our bargain. From this moment you and I begin again. For you to become a courtesan of the first rank, which is the reason I brought you here, you can no longer be who you once were. Only the most beautiful lilies bloom on the pond at night. From this night forward you will be called Moon Blossom. Is that agreeable with you?"

"*Arigato goziemashita, Mama-san*! Thank you, thank you! I am in your debt!"

"A debt that will reward me handsomely, after you learn about singing, dancing, the art of pillowing, Beauteous Barbs, and Golden Gullies, *neh*?"

"*Hai*! *Arigato, Mama-sama*!"

"And eventually, Moon Blossom, it is I who will be in your debt."

"*Wakarimasen, Mama-san*. I don't understand."

"You will, Child. You will," said the old woman. She stood and bowed formally to the young girl. "*Yokoso oide kudasareta*, Moon Blossom. Welcome to my house."

The child stood and returned the formal bow. "*Domo arigato, Mama-san*. Thank you."

"*Ichi ban*, Blossom-san. Very good. Now, enjoy your time in the garden for no more than another stick, then do your duty and go to bed, or I shall call the *eta* to come take you away." The woman stalked off into the night, muttering about ungrateful children.

Moon Blossom returned her gaze to the moonlight on the water, full of joy to have begun her new life of learning all about singing, dancing, pillowing, Beauteous Barbs, and Golden Gullies. Eventually the flickering motes rose from the water to engulfed her and lift her up. When she again returned to herself, she was sitting cross-legged, looking at a large mud puddle lightly coated with ice, shivering from the cold, with legs that felt like wood. Carefully Lucin eased her numb limbs out in front of her and wiggled her bottom on the garbage bag. Groaning with pain, she attempted to rub some circulation back into her knees and calves while even more cold crept up through the seat of her ski-suit. After a time, she creaked to her feet and stood rubbing her backside.

"Golden Gully, my ice-covered ass!" she muttered to the night. "Frozen gully is more like it!"

Slightly embarrassed at her vocabulary and laughing at her choice of words, she limped off in the dark, through the trees and toward the house. By the time she reached her room, most of what had occurred by the puddle had retreated from her conscious mind. A hot shower steamed warmth back into her bottom and legs, and she crawled into bed, barely awake. The next morning she opened her eyes to again find herself sleeping nude, with a pillow high between her thighs and thoughts of Peerless Parts and Vermilion Chambers, Beauteous Barbs and Golden Gullies dancing in her head.

"What?" she asked aloud, groggy and confused, as she levered herself up on one arm. Her weight shifted on the pillow and a ricochet of pleasure flashed between her legs.

"Oh!" she said, and fell back to her side, opening her thighs and pulling the pillow even higher. Another flash. "Uuuh." Sleep tugged at her, but so did the pillow. Only semi-aware of her actions, she reached behind her with one hand to hold it firmly against her bottom, while she held a corner of it in front of her and pulled upward, unconsciously finding a rhythm of movement between her and the silk-covered goose down. Not fully awake and not completely asleep, freed momentarily of inhibitions, deliciously female and delightfully independent, with shadowy thoughts of barbs and gullies manifesting in her semi-conscious mind, she slid on the slick silk, seeking only sensation. Grunting, as she pulled upward on the pillow-case, her right hand grazed her breast, and she sought its rapidly hardening peak.

"Jesus," she murmured, moistening her lips, and then again, "*Jesus!*" as she jerked into total wakefulness. Puritan embarrassment slapped through her, and she tore herself away from both the pillow and the moment, flopping to her back and trembling. Independent of her will, her hands sought more pleasure, and she rebuffed them, lurching from the bed and striding toward her dressing room, uncertain of her feet, uncertain in her mind. Running her fingers through her hair to free some tangles and keep her hands busy, she grabbed the first jeans she saw, a rather snug pair of Levis, and forced them up over her hips without underwear. She dropped a heavy cable-knit sweater over her head, stuck her sockless feet into the Gucci loafers, quickly tied her hair back, and stumbled down the stairs and into the kitchen. Stephanie was unloading the dishwasher. James sat at the table, coffee cup in hand.

"Good morning," Lucin blurted.

"Good morning, Ma'am," said Stephanie. "If you don't need me right now, Miz Montgomery, I'm going to do some laundry."

"That's fine, Stephanie."

"Yes, Ma'am," the young woman replied and went down the basement stairs.

Lucin leaned on the cabinet with one hand and poured coffee with the other, sloshing some on the counter. She nearly dropped the container of cream lifting it from the fridge and finally settled heavily into a chair across from James, crossed her legs, and began to bob her foot rather violently up and down, her arms folded across her chest. He looked at her and grinned.

"Top of the morning, Lucille," he said.

"Hello, James," she replied, unsuccessfully attempting to control her foot.

"Are ya alright, then?"

"Of course I'm alright. Why wouldn't I be alright?"

"I don't know, Ma'am."

"Well, I am. What makes you think I'm not alright?"

"Experience."

"Experience?"

"Yes, Ma'am," he twinkled. "In my experience there are three main reasons a woman pump-handles her foot and leg like that." Lucin instantly forced herself to stop. "Especially if she has her arms crossed up real tight like you do." She willfully lowered her arms, glad for the thickness of the heavy sweater. "She's either very angry, or very worried, or …"

"Or?" asked Lucin, sipping coffee as casually as she could.

"Or," James continued, "it's something of a much more personal and private nature, Ma'am."

"I asked you to stop calling me Ma'am."

"Irritation is another symptom, too," he chuckled. "The pump's started up again."

Lucin looked down to see her leg bouncing of its own accord. She thrust her feet flat on the floor. James stood up.

"I'm goin' out ta look over what the boys are doin' with their backhoe," said James, lifting his coat from the chair back and heading for the door. He stopped and looked at Lucin.

"Lucille, me Darlin'," he said, unable to contain his grin, "they recommend cold showers for problems such as these, but I've never found them to be an effective treatment, myself."

Her mouth open, she watched him leave before she could think of anything to say.

Lucin sat in the kitchen, feeling nearly as empty as it was, nothing inside her but hard surfaces, tile, and glass.

What was going on? The lost time in the tub, the lost time sitting out in the middle of the yard in the middle of the night … sleeping in the nude and aroused! Straddling her pillow like some … like some … could she talk to Jolee about this? No, that would be too embarrassing. Not that Jolee wouldn't understand. From the way the woman talked, she probably walked around wet most of the time any way. God! Where were these thoughts coming from? And James! He knew! From the minute she walked into the kitchen, he knew! In his way, he even told her he knew. He thought it was amusing! His eyes were laughing at her. Hmmm. Maybe knowing she was aroused excited him. He *was* a comfortably attractive man, a little over-weight, nearing sixty, but *very* male … Jesus! What was she doing? Sitting in the kitchen, thinking about James, her foot bobbing away with a mind of its own, thighs clamped together, that persistent little tingle growing between her legs, and a lump growing deep in her throat. Stop it. *Just stop it!* Get out of these tight jeans, get into some *underwear*, for God's sake, and get busy doing something!

Maybe she *could* talk to James.

The end result was the elimination of the entire cobblestone patio, down to about twenty inches below ground level, with the middle one-third of the area dug out to nearly forty inches deep. A trench led from that to the east side of the garage to allow the installation of a new waterline from the shut-off valve one of the workmen had found inside the structure. The original dig had consisted of only the deepest part, but James was a very persuasive man. The cobblestones were piled between the excavation and the tree line, the majority of the dirt on the north side of the hole.

"Well, there you are, Mr. O'Doud," said the backhoe operator. "All loaded up. We'll be goin' now."

"Sure, and it's a grand job you boys did, especially workin' through your lunch hour and all. I'm sure the Missus will be more than grateful and reward ya in kind."

"You have our names."

"Aye, Lad. Never fear, I'll be in touch with ya." He stood and watched the truck and backhoe rumble off down the road.

"All that digging for one broken waterline?"

He turned to see Lucin standing behind him, wearing a dark blue Polartec bodysuit and a black leather car coat. Her hair was down, and she'd applied make-up. She seemed to be holding herself a little distant.

"Only if ya want to get rid of all the cobbles and get the site ready for a new patio or party area. I thought perhaps it would make some options available to ya. Give you some choices."

"That's very thoughtful of you, James."

"That it is. It seemed to me you could use a little thoughtfulness."

Instantly her eyes filled with tears. "I need *something*, maybe just to talk."

"I've got a man inside the place now, pokin' around to see how bad it is. As soon as he's done, I'm all ears if ya need 'em and all yours if ya need me." At that instant a short, redheaded, middle-aged man walked out of the building.

"Jimmy me boy," he shouted. "I just got a call they need me over at the office. I'll have it on paper for ya tomorrow. It's a handyman's delight, no doubt about that, but I think we can save the old girl." He grinned. "Drop by after lunch, and I'll give ya the good and the bad news."

"Michael, old lad, 'tis sweet and fair ya are! I'll be castin' me eyes on your lovely face tomorrow." The man chuckled and began walking off the property to the street on the back side.

James looked at Lucin and found she was grinning at him. "It's me heritage," he admitted sheepishly. "You get a couple of us old lads together, and we talk like bloomin' idiots. It's almost two, have ya had lunch?"

"No."

"Me neither. Why don't we go to Clancy's, grab a corned beef sandwich and a corner table, drink a black and tan or two, and see what we can do to help you feel better?"

"That sounds wonderful," Lucin smiled.

"Ah, and sure it is, Lucille me darlin'. It's one of the most wonderful things in the world."

Clancy's was nearly empty after the lunch rush, except for a few die-hards with their feet welded to the brass rail. James led Lucin to a booth at the rear of the upper level. He lit a candle to push the gloom back a bit and create an area of intimacy. A blond, slightly heavy-set waitress slugged up the five stairs to their location. Her forty-year-old face lit up and became quite pretty when she spied who was sitting in such an out of the way location.

"Jimmy! It's fine to see ya! I thought maybe the sheriff finally caught up with ya." She put her hand on his shoulder, and he rubbed her back briefly in greeting.

"Connie, me sweetheart. Lovely as ever."

Connie looked at Lucin with appraising eyes and an open smile. "Who's this, then?"

"Constance, I'd like to present me niece, Lucille. Lucille, this is the light of me life, Constance."

Connie's smile became a grin. "I didn't know Jimmy had a niece named Lucille," she said.

Lucin smiled. "Neither did I," she said. "James and I are friends. We needed a place to talk."

"He's good at that. As of now, this section is closed. What can I bring ya?"

FOUR

What was, calls me
Over unreal distance.
I am there
But for the hedges
Of my mind.

LUCIN LOOKED AT THE MENU while James made small talk with the waitress, but couldn't find exactly what she wanted. "Could I just get a Caesar salad, no chicken, and a glass of white wine?"

Constance smiled at her indulgently, and James snorted. "Where do ya think ya are, Lucille?" he chuckled. "This isn't the Grand Street Café ya know. Connie, me fair, bring us three corned-beef on rye sandwiches, a side of those beautiful potato wedges, and two pints of Guinness, if ya will."

"Sure," she replied, backing toward the steps, "and a double helpin' of privacy, too."

"A corned-beef sandwich and beer?" Lucin asked, slightly incredulous.

"Beer?! *Beer*?! Sweet Mary, how can ya call the nectar of the gods beer? I didn't say beer, I said *Guinness*! Lord, I'm dinin' with a heathen!"

Lucin grinned. "Alright, alright, when in Rome ... I'll drink some bee ... uh, Guinness, but a corned-beef sandwich is a little much for me."

"Don't forget the pickle and the potatoes."

"No potatoes."

"Look at ya, you're all skin and bones. I've seen the way you eat, pickin' at that rabbit food. I hear ya upstairs, clankin' away on those machines of yours, climbin' to nowhere, walkin' to no place. How tall are ya?"

"What?"

"How tall are ya?"

"Five-seven."

"What do ya weigh, then?"

"James!"

"C'mon, 'fess up. What kinda poundage are ya packin'?"

"One hundred and six."

"I got memories that weigh more than that!"

"Stop it," she grinned.

"The shadow of me *ass* weighs more than that!"

"Stop it!" she laughed.

"I'll bet ya have to brace yourself before ya pull the drain plug on the tub!"

"*James!*" she giggled, "Now quit!"

"Ya need to switch some of your concern from life to livin', young lady, and no truer words were ever spoken by the Saints."

Thirty minutes later, Lucin pushed her plate away. "That was wonderful," she said, looking at the third of her sandwich she couldn't finish.

"Ya eat like a sparrow," complained James, "but ya did try."

"Well, *you* made up for it. Two sandwiches, all the potatoes and, what's that, your third b ... Guinness?"

"Aye," he replied, draining his glass. "Drink up, and we'll have another."

Steeling herself, Lucin took the last of hers in three swallows. "It really *is* good," she admitted. "I've never had it before."

Constance arrived, set down two more pints, picked up the dishes, winked at James, and vanished. Lucin took a sip.

"Now look at that," said James. "Ya don't *sip* Guinness, ya drink it! Tilt it back, Lucille. Two full swallows at a time. It'll get easier as ya go."

She did, wiped the foam from her lip, and smiled. "It *really* is good," she said.

"There's hope for ya, me Darlin'," James said and drained half his pint. "Drink up, and then we'll talk."

She looked owlishly at her fourth pint as Connie chuckled and departed with an empty glass. James smiled at her.

"Are you plying me with liquor?" Lucin asked.

"Yes, I am."

She thought a moment. "Are you trying to get me drunk?"

"No, I'm not."

"Then why all the beer ... *Guinness!* Why all the Guinness?"

"I'm tryin' to get you honest."

She peered at the table for a while, put her chin in her hand, leaned toward him a few inches, and smiled. "Jimmy, me boy," she said, "I am all screwed up."

"Aye, ya are," he laughed, "but not as screwed up as ya were when we walked in this place. Talk to me, Lucille. Ya cannot embarrass me, ya cannot shock me, and ya cannot run me off. Now talk."

"I think I might be losing my mind," she confessed.

"If ya were, ya wouldn't think so. What's goin' on?"

"I think I'm having fugue states."

"And what would those be?"

"Uh, going away. Mentally going away. Losing time."

"Losing time?!"

"The first time was the other day when you picked me up after my nail appointment at that shop next door."

"*Wa.*"

"What?"

"*Wa.* That's the name of the store. It's Japanese. It means peace, tranquility, harmony, balance. Things like that."

"Really?"

"Aye."

"How do you know that?"

"I spent some time in Japan when I was in the Navy."

"*Wa.* That's nice."

"Anyway ..." urged James.

"Anyway, while I was in there I stopped by this little pool with water trickling down a rock, and it was so peaceful, and it sounded so nice, and I just looked at it, and then this man came over and said I'd been standing there for, like, twenty minutes, and was I okay, and he was so strange! He seemed to be amused by me, and I thought he touched me but he was too far away, and then you came, and I went out to the car, and you wondered what was wrong with me, too."

"You watched the water for twenty minutes?"

"That's what he said. It felt like a minute or two to me."

"And he touched you?"

"I thought he did. It felt as if he put his hand on the small of my back and ran it up to my neck, but when I turned, he wasn't even close to me. He was just standing there, smiling."

"Are you frightened of him?"

"Not exactly," she said, taking a long swallow of her Guiness. "I felt like he knew me or something."

"Does he?"

"No. And, it seemed as if I knew him, or remembered him, or, God. It's just so strange! He didn't look familiar, he *felt* familiar."

"But the two of you hadn't met."

"No. I'd never seen him before. He's oriental. His name's Tami. He introduced himself." She shifted her attention to the partially empty glass in her right hand. "This is really *good*," she said.

"That it is," he smiled. "They've got lots of it here. We won't run out."

Lucin carefully focused her attention on him. "So then we came home, and Harrison couldn't stay for lunch and flew away and then later I got into the tub, and I flew away."

"You flew away?"

"Yep," she said, taking another long pull from the glass. "I lit some candles and turned the tub up to a hundred and my tummy got real warm, and the room went away, and then it was five hours later, and I hadn't been asleep, and I got out of the tub and got my robe and ... oh!"

James waited for a moment. "Oh?" he asked.

She drained her glass and examined it from a range of about twelve inches. "It's empty," she stated. As if by legerdemain, Constance appeared with a fresh brew.

"Thank you, Connie. I find Guinness quite tasty." She switched her attention to James. "This is really good," she whispered.

James grinned. "Oh?" he asked again.

"Jimmy, me Darlin'," she said, "after the 'oh,' it gets kinda personal. What the hell." She leaned forward and lowered her voice. "I became aroused."

"No!" he laughed.

"Yes. And then I went to bed and stayed aroused and when I woke up, I was sleeping with no clothes on, and I *never* sleep with no clothes on, and I had made friends with my pillow, and I had never made friends with my pillow before."

"Made friends with your pillow?" he asked, knowing the answer but enjoying himself.

"Yep," she said, her nose buried in the glass. "When I woke up, my pillow was between my legs." She paused and scanned the area for a moment. "James," she whispered, "I liked it. A lot."

"Nothing wrong with that."

"Yes, there is! It's not *nice*."

"Ah. That sounds like your mother talkin'."

"So then I came downstairs without make-up or anything and my hair tied back, and you said I looked less frig ... uh, *rigid* and fixed me breakfast and were kind to me. You are a nice person, Jimmy-James. Did you know that? Didja know you were a nice person?"

"Sure," he smiled.

"Well, you are. I like you, James."

"Thank you."

"You're welcome. Then *last* night, last night was *really* weird. I went upstairs and looked at some house plans and stuff and took a bath, and the room didn't go away but then, but *then*, I put on my ski suit and came outside to look at the guest house, only I never made it to the guest house 'cause there was a pool, and I sat down to look at it, and then I went really far away, and I was looking at this other pool, only it wasn't me looking at that pool, it was a little girl, only it *was* me, see? It was *me*, only it was from a really long time ago, I think."

James was intrigued. "Then what happened?"

"Could I have another one of these?" she asked, holding up the half-full glass of Guinness and attempting to focus on his face.

"That one'll be about all, I expect."

"Okay."

"Then what happened?"

"I don't remember a lot, but this woman who was kinda like my aunt who owned me gave me a new name, and I told her I wanted to learn all about singing and dancing and barbs and golden gullies. Then I was back in the yard, and my ass was frozen, uh, my bottom was cold, and I came back to the house and took a shower and went to bed, and when I woke up this morning I was naked again, and I made *close* friends, really close friends, buddies almost, with my pillow, and I jumped out of bed and ran downstairs, and you thought I was funny and told me a cold shower wouldn't help and left. You knew I was in a, state, didn't you, Jimmy ... James ... Jimmy. Didn't you, *James*?"

"I'm not blind, and I'm not stupid."

She looked at him for a long moment. He returned her gaze.

"I wondered something in the kitchen, James. Can I ask you?"

"Saints, preserve us. Sure, go ahead."

"When you knew I was in a state, did that make you in a state too, James?"

"Finish your beer. It's time to leave."

"You didn't answer my question."

"Finish your beer."

"You didn't answer my question, Jimmy," she grinned, looking at him through big eyes over the rim of her glass.

"Ask it again when you're sober, and I'll answer it then."

"You just did," she beamed, looking very satisfied with herself. "Thank you, James. I am very complicated, uh, complimented."

"C'mon, me darlin' Lucille," he chuckled, "and I'll walk ya to the car."

She lolled against the seat on the way home.

"James?"

"Hmm?"

"Am I drunk?"

"Nope. You're just lit."

"I haven't been drunk since college. My roommate, Sarah, and I got this bottle of Sloe Gin–"

"Sweet, Jesus! How could ya be pourin' that in your face?"

"And drank the whole thing, then put a bottle of Ivory in Memorial Fountain. You shoulda seen the bubbles! I never told Harrison. He would have thought it childish."

"You knew Harrison when you were in college?"

"I'd known him and his family for years. We started dating when I was a junior. Got married when I was a senior."

"I bet that broke some hearts."

"What?"

"Your other boyfriends."

"Didn't have any."

"No?"

"No, not really. Not even in high school. My mother didn't approve."

"Your mother didn't approve of dating?"

"My mother didn't approve of dating or boys. She didn't really approve of anything."

"How'd she feel about sex?"

"My mother didn't approve of *anything*, James."

"What about your Dad?"

"Daddy died when I was nine."

"Sure, and why wouldn't he?"

"What?"

"That's a shame. I'm sorry."

"Thank you."

"Did your mother remarry?"

"Oh, no."

"So your dad died when your mother was young, she didn't remarry, didn't approve of dating or boys or sex, you didn't date until you were in college, had one boyfriend you'd known for years, and married him. That about right?"

"Uh-huh. Are you sure I'm not drunk?"

"You'll be fine after a nap."

"I will? Will I?"

"You'll be sober anyway."

"Thanks for talking with me, James."

"My pleasure. It's a start."

"A start?"

"We'll talk some more."

"Will there be more Guinness too?"

"If that's what it takes," he chuckled.

"What's wrong with me, James?"

"I don't think there's a thing wrong with ya in the world, Lucille. I just think that there are some things that aren't right with ya. How old are ya?"

"I'm thirty-one."

"Well, look at that now. You're still a baby! You've got your whole life ahead of ya, ya just need to learn how to live it more on your terms. There's nothing here ya can't handle, me sweetheart and fair."

"But what about the visions and things?"

"Sometime I'll tell ya about my granny. She was fey, ya know."

"Fey?"

"Sure. We're home. Let's go inside, you take a nice nap, and if I'm around when ya wake up, we'll have a little chat. If not, we'll talk tomorrow."

He helped her inside and to the stairway. She paused on the second step and looked at him. "Thank you, James."

"Sure."

"You were, weren't you?"

"What?"

"In a state."

"A small one," he grinned. "Like Rhode Island."

She smiled. "I knew it," she said, and began to climb the stairs.

James put the Jag in the garage, climbed into his old Chevy, and headed back for Clancy's. When he walked in the door, the night shift had already begun to gather. Shouts from various corners greeted his arrival, and he took a seat at the bar. Kelley automatically placed one in front of him without being asked. Before his second swallow, Constance materialized beside him.

"I always thought the angel of mercy to be a smaller and more delicate thing than you are, Jimbo," she said. "Takin' in waifs now, are we?"

"I woulda been back sooner," he teased, "but I had to tuck the poor child in bed for her afternoon nap. Good and faithful and true, I am, ya know." He slipped his arm around Connie's waist. "Jealousy is a hateful green-eyed demon, Constance, me fair, and it ill becomes ya. Would ya begrudge a man comin' to the aid of his employer, now?"

"That's your boss?"

"That's right."

"Many a man would envy ya such a situation," she grinned.

"And many a lesser man would be takin' advantage of it, too," he said.

Connie placed her hand on his cheek. "They're all lesser men, James."

"Thank ya, Darlin', and it's a fine judge of character ya are."

"What's the matter with the poor girl?"

"She frightened of life, afraid of her urges, doesn't know a thing about men, feels abandoned by her husband, and now is hopin' she isn't losin' her mind."

"Poor little rich girl."

"Aye."

"And you are gonna help."

"Aye."

"Is it any wonder I love ya, then?"

"Be a fool not to, Constance. What time do ya get off?"

"About thirty minutes after we walk through my door," she twinkled.

James grinned. "What time do ya leave work?" he said.

"Fifteen minutes, or the end of your Guinness, whichever comes first."

"Mind me elbow, Darlin'," said James. "I got some drinkin' to do."

FIVE

Beneath white winter's dust,
The new shoot begins its journey ...
Unaware of coming trials,
Or the kindness
Of the snow.

LUCIN, complete with furry tongue and fuzzy brain, was sitting at the kitchen table eating crackers and Waldorf salad when James entered through the rear door.

"Hello, James," she flushed.

"Mrs. M," he replied, repressing a smile. "May I join ya for a time?"

"Of course," she said, not quite able to meet his gaze. "Some salad?"

"My tapeworm would go 'round the bend. I had lunch with me old friend Michael, the very lad that came to look over the place for ya yesterday. There's good news and bad news," he said pouring some coffee and crossing to the table. "Which would you like first?"

"The bad news," Lucin said, glancing at him, then looking away to focus on her plate.

He placed his cup on the table and remained standing. "The inside of the place is shot. It's all old horsehair plaster and lathe, riddled with mildew and rot. The plumbin' is older'n me, the wiring is brittle and way below code, the sills are rotten, the ceiling is separating from itself, and so on.

"The good news is, the overhead joists, rafters and the floor can probably be saved as well as the main support timbers and headers in the walls. They're all oak. Michael claims you can strip it all out and build around what's solid, or tear it down and start from scratch. The cost will be about the same. Plus, you'll need to be decidin' what ya want to do with that great mudhole where the cobbles were. Anyway ya look at it, he said ya got a mess on your hands. Myself, I'd put it a bit different."

"How would you put it?"

"I'd say it's a fine challenge for a woman of your mettle. Worthy of your will, ya know." In spite of herself, Lucin smiled into the salad. "Are ya goin' to come out and see me today?" James continued, "or are ya going to dive headfirst into whatever that is you're eatin'?"

"I'm embarrassed."

"Sure. I can see that."

"I was awful yesterday."

"Not true. I never go drinkin' with awful women."

"You know what I mean."

"Aye, I do, but you're wrong. You were several things, but awful was not among 'em. You were warm, truthful, vulnerable, funny, sweet, and kind. Awful, you were not."

"James," she whispered, "I told you things I had no business telling you! Personal things, private things!"

"That ya did. I felt quite honored."

"Honored?!"

"Sure. When ya find out someone trusts ya enough to confide in ya, it's a great honor."

"What must you think of me?"

"I think you're a darlin' girl and a lovely woman, that's what I think. A darlin' girl who's carryin' her poor repressed mother around in her hip pocket, who's never asked for what she wants because she's never known what that was, and a lovely woman who's sampled little of life because samplin' isn't 'nice,' and who needs to let some of what's inside outside before she bursts or spends her life unhappy and repressed like the unfortunate who gave her birth."

"I was entirely too forward with you, James."

"James, she says," he grinned, rolling his eyes. "And only yesterday she was callin' me Jimmy."

"That's what I mean! James, I even asked you if you were, uh … excited!"

"*In a state* were the words you used, I believe."

"Oh, God. See? That's what I mean. How could I ask that?"

"You wanted to know," he chuckled. "Nothin' wrong with curiosity."

"It's not that simple!"

"Sure it is. The important things are always simple, me Darlin' and fair. Into the kitchen walks a lovely, attractive, young woman, obviously in a condition of, let's see … hormonal liberation, and I, being not unaware of what such things can mean, responded like a male of the same species, then took the wisest path."

She glared at him, then broke into a smile. "You *ran*," she said.

"I left."

"You *ran*."

"I exited."

"You *ran*."

"Aye, that I did," he chuckled. "Like the hounds of the hot place were on me heels."

"Listen to me," she laughed. "I'm sitting here talking about it! This is *not* me! I'm sorry, James."

"Now that's strange."

"What?"

"Yesterday, when I admitted to ya that I had been in a state, ya didn't look sorry a'tall, a'tall. Ya seemed quite happy about it."

"*James!*"

"The door's right over there, if you're lookin' for someplace to run."

"I was terrible," she muttered.

"No, you weren't, Sweet Lucille," said James, his voice soft and warm. "You were guilty of nothin' more than bein' a female. There's a bit of a tease in all of ya, y'know. And a bit of the harlot, and a bit of the angel, and a bit of the temptress, and a bit of the Holy Mother, and thank God for all those wonderful bits that make each of ya what ya are."

"And what's that?"

"The most wonderful creatures that have ever drawn breath below the heavens. Don't ya know how marvelous you women are? We men don't stand a chance against ya! The strong ones are stronger, the mean ones are meaner, the tough ones are tougher, the smart ones are smarter, the good ones are better, the true ones are truer, and ya spend your lives trying to love us and save us from ourselves, bindin' our wounds, polishin' our egos, raisin' our children, and puttin' up with our bad habits. And for that, ya get to watch us die and spend your last years alone. Maybe that's the payoff. Maybe finally bein' rid of us is your reward."

Tears in her eyes, she stood and faced him, placing her hands on his shoulders. "I want to give you a hug, James ... Jimmy."

"Of course ya do, Sweetheart," he twinkled. "And why wouldn't ya?"

She pulled his head down and kissed his cheek. He engulfed her like a bear. The feel of him, the touch of him, the presence of him, even the smell of him washed over her, and she felt like both a child and a woman in his tender embrace. She clung, drawing from the well, soaking up his strength and kindness, power and gentleness. When he released her, she felt slightly dizzy and adrift, not wanting to let go. Denying herself more, she kept her hands on his forearms and looked up at him.

"Thank you, James," she whispered.

"Aye, Lucille," he smiled, leaning back a bit. "It was my pleasure, rest assured."

She dimpled. "You're not in Rhode Island are you?"

"No," he replied, sitting down, "but I can see it from here."

They talked about other things for awhile, the guest house, contractors, what to do with the hole, reaching no decisions and letting themselves settle back in with one another, finding the proper distance again. After a moment or two of comfortable silence, Lucin looked at him.

"Honestly, James, I don't know what to do with the place."

"Get away from it."

"What?"

"Get out of this house. Go do something you wouldn't think of doing."

"Like what?"

"What did you do back in Pennsylvania during the last days of winter?"

"Pretty much what I do here, plus spend time with my mother, go to the club, things like that."

"How 'bout when you were a girl? What did you do when you were alone?"

She thought for a moment. "From the time I was small until I was a senior in high school, I skated."

"There ya are."

"Ice skating?"

"Why not?"

"I haven't skated in years!"

"How long has it been since you rode a bicycle?"

"I don't know where a rink is."

"The Carriage Club's rink is still open. You're a member."

"I don't have any skates."

"Rent some."

"I'll fall."

"Imagine that. Would you be the first then?"

"No," she grinned.

"Well then, it's settled. Change your clothes and go skate. Have a good time. I'll see ya Monday."

"You're not going to drive me?" she teased.

"Just to hang around and watch yourself fallin' down? Saints preserve us, I'd be too embarrassed!" He waved as he went out the door.

Upstairs, Lucin put on tights under an old pair of maroon ski pants, a dark gray cable-knit sweater over a snug black turtle-necked jersey, and tied her hair back with a black silk scarf. Slipping into a pair of packs, she dropped two different weight pairs of socks, some knit gloves, and her wallet into a small bag and put on a black nylon and fleece windbreaker. Distaining any additional make-up, she trooped downstairs, grabbed the keys to the Jag and headed for the garage. Less than twenty minutes later she had given her keys to a parking attendant and was standing on rubber matting, balancing on the blades of a rental pair of figure skates, stashing her jacket and bag under a bench. The rink was not crowded. Only two or three adults were on the ice, a half-dozen younger people and three or four children completed the compliment of skaters. In the center, a man worked with a small girl, obviously teacher and student. Lucin clumped to the edge of the ice. Oh well, James had been right so far. Stepping through the open gate, she pushed off onto the surface.

Stroking awkwardly around the perimeter of the rink, she felt totally out of her element. The ice, slightly rough, the skates, totally rented, and the fourteen year abyss between when she'd last been on the ice and now, combined to send her struggling around the edge, bent at the waist and not the knees, head in front of her feet, swinging her arms in the lurch of a beginning skater. Completing only one lap, she clutched at the gate, broke a nail through her glove, and scrambled off of the ice as the music stopped and the rink was cleared for the Zamboni. God it was hideous!

As she sat and watched the ice being resurfaced, her embarrassment began to ease away. So what if she hadn't skated in years? So what if her skates were ill-fitting rentals? So what if she fell on her butt? To hell with what these people thought. She didn't know any of them anyway. She had come here to skate and she was going to skate and that was that! She loved skating when she was young and had given it up only because demands of family took up more and more of her time. Well it was *her* time and if she wanted to spend it lurching around in circles like The Mummy on ice, she would! Contemplating the mental image of herself as The Mummy brought a grin, and suddenly she was ready to go back on the ice, wanted to go back on the ice, *needed* to go back on the ice. She re-laced her skates, moved to the rail, and waited for the Zamboni to finish polishing the surface. As she stood, a voice broke through her reverie.

"Excuse me ..."

She turned to see a woman standing beside her. Late thirties, too blond, too much eyeliner, too much lipstick, plumply overweight, and completely overdressed in fox and silk.

"Yes?"

"Aren't you Harrison Montgomery's wife?"

"Yes, I am," Lucin smiled.

"Well, just hi!" gushed the woman. "I'm Shelia Hartrick. Doug and I just live down the street and around the corner from you, the large Tudor with the court-yard? I just saw you with Harrison in the small dining room here one day, but simply couldn't get by to introduce myself!"

Lucin kept smiling. "Hello, Shelia. I'm Lucin."

"Beg pardon?"

"Lucin. I'm Lucin."

"Loo-SIN. My, isn't that just quaint? I don't believe I've ever heard that name before. Is it foreign?"

"I have no idea."

"Well, it's just so nice to meet you, Lucin. I drive by your house several times a week, but simply never have time to stop. Welcome to the neighborhood."

"Thank you, Shelia."

"I'm vice president of the Neighborhood Association. It'd just be awful nice if you or that husband of yours could attend our meetings!"

"I'll be more than happy to speak to him about it," Lucin replied, clinging to her smile.

"You know, I thought I saw you just coming out of Clancy's Bar and Grill down on the edge of the Plaza with an older man the other day."

"You did," said Lucin, "with James. He's my driver. He was kind enough to treat me to a corned-beef sandwich and a Guinness or two."

"Oh! Well, of course, I didn't mean anything. It's very nice to have good relations with the help, I suppose."

"Yes, it is. James is a lovely man and a good friend. I find really good friends hard to come by, don't you, Shelia?"

The Zamboni lumbered off the ice and the skaters returned as Shelia considered her next move. Nodding toward the children on the rink, she spoke.

"So which one is yours?"

"Which child?"

"Yes."

"None. Harrison and I don't have any kids."

"Oh. You're childless. I just though that since you have skates on, you were here with, well ..."

41

"No. I'm here to skate. Do you—?"

"Oh no! Not me. I'd just break every bone in my body! No, I'm here to support my daughter." She pointed proudly out into the center of the ice where a leggy little girl, all knees and elbows, clad in two hundred dollars worth of practice leotard and six hundred dollars worth of skates, performed under the watchful eye of her coach.

"Isn't she just precious? She just passed her pre-juvenile test, you know."

"Really? How old is she?"

"She just turned seven. Kennedy has been skating in group lessons since she was four, but last summer we added one-on-one instruction in a public rink, until this private facility opened for the winter. We also started ballet last year. She's just doing so well. We always knew she would. We put her in the best pre-schools with just the best input and stimulation. She's just got a case full of medals and ribbons in her room."

They watched the youngster for a moment, as she attempted a combination jump. When the maneuver was complete, the coach stopped her and began to offer instruction.

"Well, what was wrong with that?" complained Shelia. "It looked perfectly good to me!"

"It was a Lutz-loop combination," said Lucin, unable to resist. "She's flutzing the Lutz. She's leaving her outside edge and rocking to her inside edge just before she jumps. I wouldn't worry about it if I were you. It's a common mistake. Even good skaters make it."

Sheila quickly turned her attention to the ice. "It's alright, Kennedy!" she shouted. "Keep trying!"

"Kennedy?" asked Lucin.

"Yes," muttered Shelia, almost snapping. "Kennedy Paige Hartrick."

"Well," smiled Lucin. "Isn't that just unusual. Tell her to keep practicing. Almost anything can be accomplished with practice. If you'll excuse me, I really need to get moving before I chill. It's been awfully nice meeting you. Perhaps we'll see each other again." Leaving Shelia standing by the rail, she pushed out onto the ice, and suddenly her stroke was back.

She drifted lazily around the rink with almost no effort, leaning into crossovers, enjoying the feel of her edges biting into the ice. Backwards, she picked up speed, trusting her body's muscle memory, her arms outstretched for balance, her hands artfully poised without conscious thought. Slowing, she slipped easily into figure eights, stretching as she changed edges in the figure, extending her free leg, gliding in the turn. Catching herself smiling she stopped, then began other figures, carefully tracing her own cuts in the ice with intense concentration written on her face as she slowly inscribed the surface with her passage. Forward and backward, inside and outside, on she glided, at last stopping to rest near the center of the rink. She glanced to her left to see Kennedy Paige Hartrick staring at her with big eyes. She grinned at the child and received an answering smile.

"Hello," Lucin said.

"Hello," the girl replied. "I'm a figure skater, too. You're very pretty."

"Thank you," Lucin said, gliding toward the girl. "I was just thinking how pretty you are, too. I met your mommy, and I've been watching you skate. I think you're very good."

"I practice a lot," she said. "Sometimes my mom yells at me."

"Moms do that when they want their daughters to do well. She's very proud of you."

"I know," sighed the child.

"You just keep practicing, Kennedy. Maybe we'll skate together sometime. My name's Lucin."

"Your name's pretty, too. I gotta go." She scooted off across the rink toward her waiting mother.

With center ice to herself, Lucin let it out a bit. Warming up again with a three turn or two and a few sweeping turns into pivots, she eventually worked up to a forward scratch spin, drawing her arms down across her chest, increasing the speed of the spin as fast as she dared. Inspired, she flashed down the ice into a waltz jump, passing effortlessly from forward on the outside edge to backward on the outside edge, in time with the music over the speakers, in sync with the skater she used to be. Exhilarated by the moment, she grinned and coasted down the ice, as several skaters applauded nearly soundlessly in gloves and mittens. She'd have to call Jolee's anytime number about her broken nail when she got home, but it was worth a fistful of broken nails to feel as free and fine as she felt stepping off of the ice.

SIX

How much, I wonder,
Waits for me?
Destiny's secret voice
Calls in faint
Confession.

THE NEXT MORNING Lucin finished her bagel and juice in an empty kitchen. She rinsed the plate and left it in the sink beside the glass and returned the cream cheese to the fridge.

The cream cheese had tasted wonderful. It was not something she usually ate, but James had commented on how thin she was. Perhaps a few added pounds would bring back some of the figure she'd had in college. Not Rubenesque to be sure, but certainly more lush than she'd maintained in recent years. It seemed fairly obvious to her that James and Constance had a certain interest in each other, and Constance was slightly heavy. Maybe that was James' preference, mildly overweight women. That wouldn't happen, but maybe a pound or two might improve her curves. She'd weighed a hundred and five after she got off the treadmill that morning. Perhaps she was a little too thin. She'd gain a few pounds, certainly not over one-fifteen, and see if James noticed. He definitely noticed Connie.

The shop was dark when Lucin arrived, but she could see Jolee's faint form moving around the gloomy interior. She knocked on the glass door and was quickly admitted.

"Mornin', Sweetie!" piped Jolee. "C'mon in. Coffee's about done drippin'."

"Thank you so much for seeing me today," Lucin said. "I'm sorry to bother you on your day off."

"I had to come down and check on the cleaning crew and do some book work anyway. When you got your own business there are no days off. I'm the toughest boss I ever had, but I just gave me a raise last month, so I ain't too bad."

"Still, thank you."

"Honey, you are just givin' me an excuse to sit and gab awhile. I'm the one who should be thankin' you. Black coffee, right?"

"Uh, no. Cream if you have it."

"I have it. Whipping cream. It's my only vice!" Jolee laughed, fussing over the coffeemaker. "I thought you took your coffee black."

"Usually I do, but I've decided to put on a little weight."

"Good idea. You're skin and bones, Sweetie. There's a man behind this, huh?"

"What?"

Carefully and slowly, Jolee enunciated. "There is a male of the species behind this weight gain, isn't there?"

"Of course not!" Lucin blustered.

"Ha! Honey, I don't even have to be holdin' hands with you to know that's bull-shit. If that lie had been any bigger, it woulda left tracks on my blouse! Are you tel-lin' me the truth? Mind if I smoke?"

"Uh, yes ... no, yes!" Lucin stammered. "*No*, I don't mind if you smoke and *yes*, I am telling you the truth!"

Jolee grinned. "No, you're not. *Yes*, you *do* mind if I smoke ... and *no*, you are *not* telling me the truth. Give it up, Kiddo. This is Jolee you're talkin' to. And relax. I don't smoke, at least not very much."

Blushing, Lucin recovered some of her composure. "You are ruthless," she smiled.

"Yep. Give. Who is he?"

"It's not like that!"

"What's it like?"

"He's my friend."

"Friends are nice," Jolee grinned.

"He's my driver, James. He's also going to oversee the re-construction of my guesthouse for me. He is a kind and decent man who has treated me very well, and I feel affection for him."

"What's he look like?"

"He reminds me of Robert Mitchum a little. He's about fifty-five or sixty, six-two, over two hundred pounds, Irish, and he makes me feel safe."

"And he said he thought you were too skinny."

"Thin. He said thin."

"So now you're gonna gain weight."

"A little."

"Uh-huh."

"My God!" blurted Lucin. "Am I that transparent?"

"Human, Sweetie. It's called human. So, you gonna take a run at him?"

"What!"

"Hey," Jolee grinned, "experienced men can be wonderful. They may not have testosterone dripping out of both ears, but they sure as hell know what it is they're doin!"

"Jolee!"

"Go for it. Probably be the best you ever had. Hell, send him over here. I could use a little re-construction!"

"*Jolee!*" Lucin shrieked, laughing.

"Take it easy, Honey," Jolee giggled, "I'm just havin' a good time."

"He got me drunk."

"What?"

Slowly, over the next two hours, the torn nail was repaired and the story came out. Lucin told her everything, from the time lost by Tami's pool to the adventures with her pillow, to Rhode Island and all the connecting events. It poured from her in sweet release. Jolee listened carefully, joked little, and commented only when necessary to keep the flow going. At the end of the conversation, Lucin was nearly exhausted.

"Lunch," said Jolee.

"Lunch?"

"Lunch! You buy and drive, and the repair job is on the house. C'mon," Jolee continued, standing up. "Grab your coat. Don't think about anything, don't analyze anything, just get your stuff and let's go to the Classic Cup. You need food. We can't have you wasting away. Jimmy, that Irish devil, is waiting in the wings!"

Lucin looked up from her salmon salad and grimaced. "Honestly, Jolee, I am *not* after James!"

"You're not, huh?"

"*No.* He's old enough to be my father. I am not after anything."

"Sure you are. You're after love and concern and romance and safety. You're after that light men get in their eyes and that light women get in *their* eyes. You're after that feeling that comes when somebody gives a damn about you, and shows you they do. You're after response and appreciation and validation and reaction. What the hell is wrong with that? We all *want* those things, we all *need* those things, we all *look* for those things. James gives those to you! It's only natural that you're attracted to him. Hell, I never met the man and *I'm* attracted to him. None of that means that you have to drag him off into the giggle grass! From what you've said, he's gonna give you that stuff whether you play hide the salami or not. Enjoy it! You can damn sure bet that he does."

Lucin stared out the window for a moment. "So it doesn't mean anything."

"Sure it means something. It means a hell of a lot! Just 'cause it probably *is* harmless, doesn't mean it has to *feel* harmless. If it gets your blood going a little, have fun. It's play. It's fantasy. It never has to be any more than that." Jolee paused and leered at Lucin. "But it could be," she growled.

Taking a sip of dessert coffee, Jolee readied herself for Lucin's indignant blush. "So, how often do you masturbate?" she asked.

"*Jolee!*" Lucin choked, jerking in her chair.

"Lighten up, Honey," Jolee grinned. "There's just us girls here. Hell, a couple of my best friends have batteries! Take it easy. I don't even want you to answer that, I was just going for the shock factor."

"Well, it worked," Lucin replied, glancing around to see if anyone overheard.

"How's your fantasy life?"

"My what?"

"Your fantasy life."

"My fantasy life?"

"Yeah. What do you fantasize about?"

"I, uh … I guess I don't. I mean, I daydream, sure, but I don't really fantasize."

"Why not?"

"Well, it's not real life, is it?"

"You probably don't even read romance novels, do ya?" Jolee grinned.

"I read fiction now and then."

"But not romance."

"No."

"So you drift off in Tommy's shop by the pond for twenty minutes, come back to find a very attractive man smiling at you, and then feel guilty. You go away in the tub for hours, get all warm and gooey, and then feel guilty. You sit outside in the dark, go off to China or Japan or someplace, and then feel guilty. You wake up in the morning humping your pillow, launch yourself out of bed, and then feel guilty. You spend time with James, who is a *man*—by the way, react to him like you're a woman—and then feel guilty. Honey, you are damn near living a fantasy! You ever drop the useless guilt and open up, there won't be enough vitamin E in town to keep up with you," Jolee laughed. "You need to get over it, let James pat your butt, and be a girl!"

"I just don't think that's me."

"Right now it isn't. Lean over here. I wanna say something to you."

Lucin leaned across the table close to Jolee's very serious face. "What?' she asked.

"*Fuck*," said Jolee.

Lucin colored and immediately pulled back. Jolee grinned.

"Girlfriend, you have *got* to loosen up a little bit! C'mon, pay the check and take me back to the shop. I need to get some work done and go home and take a nap. Jerry's coming over for dinner tonight, and he is very athletic."

Lucin's head spun on the drive back to the shop. Jolee was so honest, so open, so frank in her opinions about men and women, romance and sex. It was kind of refreshing and a little scary. How many people were like that? Did everybody just talk about it? Surely not. Lucin had never really been comfortable in groups, had never really had close friends and intimate conversation with many people. Even in college, she had been so bound by duty to her mother and her family that her life had never truly been her own. There were rules for behavior in her family's circles, standards of conduct, even limits in conversation. It was the same in Harrison's family. When they had married during her senior year of college, her personal environment had not changed very much. He was seven years her senior, already established as a junior partner at Revere and Lodge and had the same generational background to a large degree as she did; married life was a transition to a life not much different than she had known.

Trained thoroughly for such things and used to the responsibility, she was the perfect hostess at obligatory dinner parties, supervised the staff well, knew the pedigrees of all the "right" people, dressed correctly, made excellent dinner conversation, contributed to the proper causes, made phone calls for the correct charities, stayed in contact with the right sorority, shopped in the acceptable stores, dressed in the acceptable way, went to the acceptable stylist, drove the acceptable car, behaved in the acceptable manner, and lived the acceptable life. Now, in Kansas City, it seemed that everywhere she turned, unacceptable situations and events were all around her! Jolee's conversation was *totally* unacceptable, as was Lucin's behavior, even her *thoughts* with and about James, her dreams, her visions—her *pillow!*

She could just turn her back on it all. She could stop this whole thing before it went any farther — reduce her contact with James to a bare minimum, find a new manicurist, volunteer at a hospital, contact the local chapter of her sorority, get her life back to normal! As soon as the Revere and Lodge office was firmly established, she would naturally fall into the position of being the senior partner's wife with all of its attendant duties. Her time would be spent in the manner for which she had been groomed all her life: supporting her husband's career, furthering his position, guiding his social commitments and prerogatives, and being the woman behind the man. She had literally been born into the position, almost as surely as if she were royalty, and, in a way, she was. The problem, as she was beginning to realize, was very basic. Being royalty simply wasn't much fun.

But there was so much more to life than only fun, at least much more to *her* life. Jolee was Jolee, a free spirit, a woman without the responsibilities and demands that Lucin had lived with all her days. Her family and families like hers were responsible for thousands and thousands of people, providing work and paychecks and benefits and hospitals and programs. This type of responsibility was totally foreign to people like Jolee and James. They could not understand, they could not appreciate, they could not *imagine* what she had been prepared for.

Her mother would call Jolee and James "the salt of the earth," but if she were truly honest with herself, Lucin knew that "salt of the earth" is not what her mother meant. Her mother meant "the little people" — those beneath her station, the masses supporting families like hers and maintaining their wealth and position, all those making their way of life—and the responsibilities that came with their way of life—possible. What was more important — her duty to her heritage or her duty to herself?

As if she were reading Lucin's thoughts, Jolee spoke up.

"You're being awfully quiet, Sweetie. You know, you don't have to give up what you have to get what you want. The key is balance. Nobody can have it all."

Lucin pulled into the shop's parking area to see a white Chevy van parked in front of the store next door. As she stopped her Jag, Tamiko Asaruka stepped out from behind the van, carrying a box.

"Oo!" exclaimed Jolee, "it's Tommy. Let's see what he's up to!" She opened the door and stood up. "Thank goodness I got here in time," she teased. "I just love to see a good lookin' man work. Hiya, Tommy!"

"*Ah, konnichi wa*, Jolee-*sama!*" he grinned. "I too am glad you have arrived. You can help me unpack my new merchandise and be the first to spend all your money!"

A bit self-consciously, Lucin stepped from the driver's side and looked at him over the top of the vehicle. Tamiko saw her and gave a slight bow.

"Lucin-*san*, I am honored that you are here. It is my pleasure to see you again. Please, both of you, I have just returned from Japan and have some things with me to unpack. Come inside, come inside. Tell me what you think."

"C'mon, Honey," grinned Jolee, walking toward the store. "Have some fun!"

Lucin, thinking better of it, followed Jolee through the door. When she crossed the threshold, she again felt Tami's hand on the small of her back, and the heat rushed up her spine to her neck. He stood ten feet away and smiled at her. The smile was intimate without being forward, casual without being flippant, intense without being intimidating. Carefully she returned it. He opened his mouth and whispered to her, and the sound seemed to come from just inches away.

"Uncertainty moves as errant wind across the fields," he said. "Although its purpose seems lost in random flight, the wind arrives at fate's destination in spite of the doubtful path." He smiled again. "You are safe here."

"I know it," she said. And she did.

For the next hour Tami, Lucin, and Jolee unpacked boxes of wonderful jade carvings, delicate fans, some raw silk kimonos that Jolee found *fascinating,* rolls of straw mats, small rice-paper-screens, elegant lantern-light-fixtures, and some exquisite stoneware with marvelous glazing. Looking up from a particularly lovely tea set, Lucin noticed Jolee was gone.

"She left about ten minutes ago," Tami said. "You were occupied."

"I know it's foolish," Lucin confessed, "but some of these things really seem to call to me. They feel so … familiar. Silly, isn't it?"

"Not at all. What we are ties us to what we were. Memory comes not only from the mind but from the spirit." He regarded her with a level gaze, then grinned. "How do you like my inscrutable oriental shtick?"

"Very impressive," she laughed. "Did you mean it?"

"Absolutely," he replied.

"Really?" she enquired, her interest showing.

"Sure. Our past doesn't end with our birth. Within us lives the past of our ancestors in what some people call cellular memory, as well as other times our own spirit has manifested itself. All of these affect us in various ways. Some subtle, some not. The day my pond caught you, for instance."

"So that was from a past life, huh?" she smiled, obviously doubtful.

"Perhaps," he said. "At least, it is what I prefer to believe. It has been proven to my satisfaction many times. Even your own beloved philosopher, Mark Twain, said he found it no more amazing to have lived a thousand times than to have lived just once. Who am I to argue with Mark Twain?" The grin was back.

"Well, your pond certainly did catch me," Lucin admitted. "There's no doubt about that."

"Ah," smiled Tami, carefully lifting a red lacquered box about the size of a cigar humidor from a carton. "There it is."

"What is it?"

"It may eventually be a gift for you, or, maybe not. Time will tell," he answered, placing the box underneath the counter and out of sight.

"What?"

"But I do have a gift for you today," he continued, moving to a magazine and bookrack and removed a notebook-sized paperback. "Although it is not from Japan, in many ways it is very Japanese." He handed the volume to Lucin. It was a coffee table picture book of Japanese gardens.

"Oh my," she exclaimed, leafing through the pages. "This may be exactly what I have been looking for! I have this rundown guesthouse to re-do and a hole in the ground beside it. This is wonderful! Thank you so much, but please, let me pay for it."

"You are going to spend a great deal of money on your project. A portion of that will come to me. The book is a wise investment on my part. It is yours. Take it with you, look through it, return with ideas, and I will assist you, if you like."

"Are there people in this country who build gardens like this?" she asked, barely able to take her eyes from the pictures.

"Those photos are all American gardens. Two of them were done by my uncle, one in Topeka, one here in Kansas City. I'm sure he would consider a project I was involved in. I designed both the gardens he has in the book."

"Let me look at it for a few days and I'll come back. When would be good for you?"

"I'll be here whenever you return. Enjoy the book."

"Thank you very much, Tami," she said, heading for the door.

"By the way," he said, stopping her in the doorway. "Next time I should have a shipment in that will interest you. A couple of dozen raw silk and brocade pillows, about four inches thick, very firm, with a large roll of piping around the entire edge. I believe you might find them quite ... exciting. Please visit me again, Lucin-san," he said, with a small bow. "I will count the moments until you return."

SEVEN

Stirred by ageless murmur,
Restless memory wisps
As autumn smoke
From the valley
Of my heart.

LUCIN TOOK THE LONG WAY HOME, her hands hard on the wheel, valuing control. What was going on? Her second exposure to Tami Asaruka had been even more mysterious and compelling than her first. As if he *knew*, he presented her with the book on Japanese gardens. As if he *knew*, he mentioned the pillows. And the box. The red lacquered box. For the briefest instant Lucin had wanted to touch it, almost *needed* to touch it, not to take possession of it, but to *re-take* possession of it. The feeling was fleeting, but there. Like a flash of lightening on a distant horizon, gone in an instant, but clinging to her retina for a moment before fading away.

The morning with Jolee had been fun. Lucin was used to the politics of family and social life. Jolee's honesty and sometimes startling candor were refreshing. She had made good sense with many of the things she'd said. In spite of the immense social gulf between them, Lucin certainly felt more challenged and stimulated with Jolee than she ever would in the company of someone like Shelia Hartrick. The two women were as different as night and day, and Shelia was much more of Lucin's world. For most of her life, Lucin had moved in circles populated by Shelia Hartricks. Women who focused on form rather than function. Women who valued appearance more than substance. Women who had no real lives of their own. Women whose challenge was to find enough to do with their time, to present their husbands in the proper light, to live vicariously through their children, and not to drink that fourth martini at Saturday's dinner party or the second glass of gin on a boring Tuesday afternoon.

It was there waiting for her, too. The cage of boredom, the clutch of complacency. James knew it, saw it plainly and, in his way, warned her. Jolee raged against it in her way, trying to draw Lucin out and be her friend. And why not? There were any number of reasons Lucin could never be close to people like Jolee and James and, no matter how she examined those reasons, they were *wrong*. James and Jolee *were* the salt of the earth, people to be enjoyed without condition or expectation, people it made her happy just to be around, people who cared about her, not because of her money or position, but because they saw something in her that she also saw in them.

And then there was Tami. What did he see? What did he know? Just the thought of those questions caused a tiny shiver to race up Lucin's spine: always in black, always seemingly relaxed and at ease, always exuding a quiet warmth she could feel from halfway across the room. How could he touch her from that distance? How could he whisper in her ear from so far away? And when he told Lucin that she was safe, she believed him absolutely. She had never met a man who displayed such interest in her and yet, the interest was not only *not* alarming, it was nearly comforting. It certainly was not fueled by the heat of sexual curiosity, she knew how to recognize *that*. It had its sexual side, she could feel it, but it seemed to be more sexual *concern* than sexual challenge. With Lucin's newly erratic libido, she knew she must be very careful not to send Tami the wrong signals. Right. As if that were possible. He had probably never misinterpreted a signal in his life.

Then there was this whole thing about memory coming from the mind and the spirit. Obviously, Tami was referring to reincarnation. Lucin had taken a couple of comparative religion courses in college, she understood the concept, but she had been raised an Episcopalian. Not that she had ever been active in the church. Services were attended because they needed to be. It was important to be seen as a religious and moral person. She and Harrison still went from time to time, socially compelled to make the occasional appearance and be seen in the right context.

The truth was, many of the pieces in Tami's shop called to her, felt so familiar to her eyes or in her hands. Oriental decorating and collecting had never interested her until she had walked into his store. Now she was on the way home with a book on Japanese gardens and almost couldn't wait to look through it and decide on what she was going to do with the guesthouse and grounds. The book! For the first time since she and Harrison had been together, Lucin had accepted a gift from another man. A man she found oddly attractive. A man that Harrison didn't know existed. A man who had that lovely strange box — a Pandorian enigma that possibly was also for her.

She wrapped her mind around the box for a moment and felt a stirring of heat just below and behind her navel, a centered warmth that quickly became a familiar sphere, pushing its delicate tendrils downward in liquid exploration. The need was there, and then the rush. Sitting at a stoplight, Lucin clamped her legs together and clutched at the wheel, as sweet anticipation rippled through her low belly and released between her thighs. She pushed her head back against the rest, straining with the joy of it, her mouth opening in soundless expectation, tears at the corners of her eyes, nipples startlingly erect against the fabric of her bra. "Aaaahhhunnh!"

The horn sounding just behind her car punctured her reverie and Lucin jumped, jerkily accelerating through the intersection and weakly steering to the curb. Where did that come from? She trembled behind the wheel, thrusting in the seat, unable to move her legs apart as the residual ripples fluttered through her body. The orgasm curve flattened out and, as the quivering left the back of her knees, and as the arches of her feet relaxed, she glanced guiltily around as if fearful of being observed.

"Oh, my!" Lucin said aloud, as the last twitches chased the butterflies from the pit of her stomach. Warm scratching defeated the itch between her legs and dampness soothed the heat. "Oh, my," she said again, her shoulders falling and low back relaxing into the seat. No warning. No preparation. Just *there*. So sudden and out of *nowhere*! Her body had responded independently of conscious thought or desire. Nothing like that had ever happened to her before in her life! Wheew!

A nice hot bath. That's what she needed, a nice hot bath and her new book. She pulled away from the curb to continue her drive home, her left hand cradled ever so comfortably deep in her lap.

When Lucin walked through the side door and into the kitchen, she found Stephanie putting some cut greenery into the trash compacter.

"Stephanie! It's Sunday. Don't you have anything better to do than fuss around here?"

"Hi, Miz Montgomery. I found some lovely flowers and just dropped by with them. There's a bouquet in the dining room and one on the landing by your bedroom. Roses down here and lilies upstairs. I'm fixing my boyfriend dinner tonight, and I saw the flowers while I was out shopping."

"It's very kind of you to think of me in such a way. Thank you."

"You're welcome, Ma'am."

"Stephanie?"

"Yes, Ma'am?"

"When we're alone, why don't you call me Lucin? It's just us girls here, after all."

"Uh ... if you'll call me Steph. Okay?"

"Okay, Steph," Lucin grinned. "Now go away. Fix dinner for your guy and enjoy the evening."

"Yes, Ma'am," she said, grabbing her coat and walking to the door. "I'll see you tomorrow ... Lucin."

Lucin poured herself a cup of coffee, added whole cream, sat down at the kitchen table, and opened the book. Twenty minutes later she poured out her untasted coffee, clutched the wonderful volume under her arm and headed upstairs.

In the bedroom, Lucin dropped her clothes into the hamper, slightly embarrassed but smiling as she noticed the damp panties, and slipped into her short robe, wishing it was silk instead of terrycloth. Barefoot, she padded into the bath and began to fill the tub, setting the thermostat to one hundred degrees. She removed a few votive candles from the cabinet, lit three or four, turned up the rheostat for the spotlight over the tub, and then, on a whim, stepped out into the hall and collected the bouquet of lilies from the landing. Putting the vase on the edge of the tub surround beside the book, she hung up her robe and slipped into the swirling water.

Nearly an hour later, candles burning low and tired of holding the heavy book, she placed it back on the surround and sank to her earlobes. She turned down the overhead light and luxuriated in the heat and near darkness. Languidly, she plucked a lily from the vase and held it, caressing the gentle bloom with the tips of her fingers, enjoying the definite female shape of it in the dim light, moving it close to her face and inhaling the serene aroma. The water enveloped her, the scent surrounded her. With a sigh, Lucin closed her eyes and let it happen.

"Ah, Child … are you enjoying your bath?"

"Oh yes, *Mama-san*," the young girl smiled, opening her eyes. "The water is so relaxing and the lilies so fragrant. The bath is beautiful."

"*Anata wa yoku nemutta ka?*" she smiled. "Did you sleep well?"

"Oh, very yes, *Mama-san. Domo.*"

"It is time to leave your slumbers. You have only a short time left to remain in the bath. Soon I will send in *Onna* to pluck you from the water and dress you. To-night it is our honor to entertain Goroda-*sama*. You will assist."

"I will? Oh, thank you, *Mama-san! So-desu? Arigato goziemashita!*"

"Yes, it is the truth. You are welcome, Child. You have worked very hard and you have earned this opportunity."

"Will I sing for Goroda-*sama*?"

"No, Child, you will not sing."

"Will I dance then?"

"No, Child, you will not sing nor will you dance," smiled the *Mama-san*.

The girl pondered this information for a moment, then her eyes widened and she stood up in the bath. "Oh, *Mama-san*," she exclaimed, her eyes wide and shining. "Am I then to be given the honor of pillowing with the illustrious Goroda-*sama*?"

Mama-san whooped with laughter, then covered her mouth and regained a little composure. "Moon-Blossom, you are wonderful!" she laughed, "but no, you will not pillow with Goroda-*sama*. Goroda-*sama* will pillow with Kitten, who is of the first rank, and with a boy I recently purchased."

"But, *Mama-san*," protested the girl, "I have been here for a long time. I have studied, I have worked, I have learned. I am ready!"

"Your Open Lotus has yet to bloom, Child. There is not even a hedge around your Heavenly Pavilion! You are still too young! What would you do with Goroda-*sama's* Torrid Turtle? He would pierce you like a chopstick through a butterfly. Would you have me lose all the money and time I have invested in you and your training?"

"Oh, no, *Mama-san*," the girl replied, her eyes downcast.

"Very well," the woman replied, controlling her smile. "Tonight you will bring the fish and rice that Kitten will serve as the *Gei-sha* entertain. You will then wait to bring Kitten any additional food that Goroda-*sama* might require. That is all that shall be required of you. Your lessons are going very well and you have made me proud. Perhaps next season, or the season after, you will sing or dance for our clients. Later, and only later, will you pillow."

"But, *Mama-san*," she replied, still with humble expression and downcast eyes, "I have seen the red boxes with their *harigata, konomi-shinju*, and *himitsu-kawa*, I have talked with the ladies, and I dream of Beauteous Barbs and Steaming Shafts."

"In your dreams is where they will stay for now, Moon Blossom, for in dreams is where they feel most turgid and taste most sweet. Do not be in such a hurry to grow up. Your Jade Gate will open soon enough, and it will open from your own hand

and not some Ponderous Pestle! Steaming Shafts and Beauteous Barbs must wait for awhile."

"Yes, *Mama-san.*"

"Good. Finish your bath, my precious flower. *Onna* will lay out your *tabi*, under-skirts, kimono and *obi* for you. Get dressed, let her arrange your hair, and come to see me. We will talk and eat a little soup before you carry food."

"Thank you, *Mama-san*, for the opportunity to be of service to your house."

"*Do itashimashite*, Sweet Child," she replied, walking to the door. "You are welcome. Think nothing of it."

Moon Blossom smiled and eased back down in the water. Closing her eyes, she allowed her thoughts to drift. Her eleven-year-old mind reeled at how fortunate she was to live here with the beautiful ladies and Mama-san, to learn all she was learning, to be able to someday pillow with skill and art, and to eventually make enough *koban* to buy her contract from *Mama-san* and be truly free. But first there would be tremendous Torrid Turtles and honeyed Heavenly Pavilions and bulging Beauteous Barbs and gifted Golden Gullies and straining Steaming Shafts and jubilant Jade Gates and the joys within the red boxes and so much more that the ladies knew all about and that she was just beginning to learn. Life was so exciting, was it not? She wanted their cries of joy to be hers. She wanted to giggle and laugh and tease with them. She wanted so much to be a part of everything that it was very difficult to be patient. Perhaps tonight she would linger close to the *shoji* screen to hear what she could hear when Kitten pillowed with Goroda-*sama*. Perhaps tomorrow, she could even talk with Kitten a little, if Kitten would speak with her about such things. After all, Kitten was a lady of the house and fully grown. She was nearly fifteen. Thinking about such things almost always made Moon Blossom restless. Sometimes such thoughts even brought a glow to her tummy. She liked the glow.

Lucin's nearly closed eyelids distorted the flame from the one remaining candle into tendrils of golden light that splayed out in the darkness of the bathroom. She lay deeply submerged in the tub, the lily floating on the water near her face. Her lower lip was caught in her teeth and she was partially turned on her right side, her knees drawn up and slightly apart. The middle two fingers of her right hand caressed her mound in rapid, repetitive strokes, the middle two fingers of her left hand probed to the third knuckles in languid penetration. Her mouth was slightly open and a continuous low growl slithered from between her lips. Short rapid thrusts controlled her pelvis without conscious will. The sphere glowed in her low belly, pushing waves of heat that ricocheted between her legs, punctuating her rhythm. The brass ring hung there in the dark and she lunged for it, the growl becoming a panting moan, the thrusts becoming grinds, the caresses becoming clutches, urgent and nearly frantic. More than sweet release, this was vital, demanding, clawing, primal! A hot, seething, *necessity* of an orgasm charged through her reptile brain and ripped through her body.

Legs now straight and trembling, shoulders rigid and shaking, sphincter tight and quivering, breath hissing from between clenched teeth, head lashing from left to right, she fought with it, raged with it, grappled with it, wrung it out and immersed herself in it. Fluid with fingernails, it washed over her. Liquid with fangs, it gnawed on her. With sweaty hands, it clutched at her, grasped at her, tore her open and plunged into her, filling her up to overflowing. Spurting seething jets of raw remembrance, it pulled her head back by the hair, spread her wide, and had its way with her, snorting in her ears, the pounding of its heart shaking the room, the slap of its thighs splashing water from the tub.

Panting, she lay on her back, only her face above the water. Spasms rippled through her body, shooting up and down from where she held herself. Contractions of relief swept through her and her body jerked and trembled from them, totally beyond her control, completely past her *need* to control. Over a nearly endless amount of time, it slowed to trembling surges and she rolled to her side, again drawing her knees up, quivering with each fresh ignition of ragged pleasure, caressing herself with each new spark of sweet pain. Her stomach fluttered, her nipples throbbed, her bones ached, and she lay in the water occasionally twitching from the relief of it.

Eventually she sat up, weakly clutching at the sides of the tub, opened the drain, and struggled into a standing position, stepping out onto the mat with knees that nearly failed to obey her. Wrapping a towel around her glistening body, she blotted herself dry as she staggered stiffly to the bed. Even though it was barely dark, she eased between the sheets, pulled a pillow tightly up inside her thighs and lay back with a groan, another ripple pulsating through her belly and out between her legs. Exhausted, she flipped covers up over her body, adjusted the pillow again, sighed, and let go. She was nearly asleep when the voice came.

"Clouds and rain," it said.

"Wha?" she muttered, fighting sleep, raising to one elbow. Nothing. She lay back down and began to drift off.

"The clouds and rain," came the voice. "Never are we closer to the gods, Moon Blossom. Never are we more in the embrace of the spirits."

"*Gomen nasai, Mama-san,*" murmured Lucin, not quite awake or asleep. "So sorry, but I'm very tired. Perhaps we can talk later."

"Indeed we shall, Child. Sleep well, Little One."

Nearly three miles away, Tamiko Asaruka, sitting at his evening meal, smiled.

EIGHT

Fate colors
My passion.
Memory lights
My way.
What was is yet to be.

LUCIN AWAKENED, firmly clasped about her pillow. She lay quietly for a time, running over in her mind the events of the prior day and evening. Delicious shudders accompanied her memory and she smiled languidly at the recollections. Nothing like yesterday had ever happened before! First while she was driving, and then the wonder of the tub. It had been, far and away, the most intense physical and emotional experience of her life! *Nothing* compared to it. She could still feel the residual effects, the "itch" thing, the delicate wisps of heat below her navel caressing her insides. She slid the pillow from between her legs and the silken rasp of it against her mound caught her breath in her throat and sent quivering ripples between her thighs. She had to get up before it started all over again. Smiling at her embarrassment, Lucin slid across the sheets on her bottom, loving the feel of the slide, and stood beside the bed.

Nude, an unusual condition for her, she walked into the bath and looked around as if expecting to see the room changed. All was surprisingly normal. The only indication of the events of the night before was a badly wilted lily lying on the bottom of the tub. Using only two fingers, she picked it up and dropped it in the trash. On the way to the shower she inspected herself in the mirror. It was not something she regularly did and required a bit of courage. Turning sideways and rising to her toes, she looked at her body. James was right. She should gain a few pounds and look more like a girl. The weight would fit well. Lucin's breasts were firm and taut. Her butt didn't sag. Ten pounds would fill out her bust and make her look more womanly. In college she'd heard a frat rat comment on her "nice ass". She was considerably lighter now than then. Even one-twenty might not be out of the question.

Lucin didn't dally in the shower. Just the act of washing herself brought color to her cheeks and threatened to re-light the flame. She resisted the urge to linger, quickly soaped and rinsed, washed her sticky hair, then nearly bolted from the cubicle. She sat on a towel on the toilet while using the hair dryer, brushed her teeth, decided against any make-up, and walked into the dressing room. There she donned a pair of loose fitting peasant's pants in a pale gray cotton-silk blend, a maroon raw silk long-sleeved t-shirt, and a pair of tennis shoes. Book in hand, she replaced the lilies on the landing and was halfway down the stairs before she realized she'd put on no undergarments at all. She turned to go back up, then stopped. It was her house. It was her body. She had on *clothes*. She was *covered!* Why be such a prude? Besides, she felt good not to be restricted and bound up. By the time she reached the bottom of the stairs, she could feel her nipples straining against the silk. Slightly flushed and smiling, she walked into the kitchen. James was sitting over a coffee cup at the table. He looked at her casually, then quickly inspected her again, and raised an eyebrow.

"Well now," he twinkled, rising to his feet. "Top of the mornin' to ya, Lucille. Take a seat and I'll pour ya a cup."

"Good morning, James," she nearly stammered, feeling her ears get warm. "Thank you, with cream, please," she continued, dropping into a chair, releasing the book, and quickly folding her arms.

"Cream, ya say," he teased. "Be careful now. Cream'll put on a pound or two." He opened the fridge and poured some Half and Half into her cup, then placed it in a saucer, added a spoon and set it before her, reaching over her shoulder to put the saucer on the table. Lucin shifted slightly in her seat.

"Thank you," she said, crossing her leg, then placing it back on the floor before she started to bounce her foot. James sat at the end of he table and grinned at her.

Lucin looked at him. "What?" she asked.

"Ah, me Darlin' and fair," James chuckled. "Don't be takin' this the wrong way now, for you're a lovely girl and a real pleasure to me eyes, but ya got the look about ya this mornin' like you're not over last night yet."

"What's that supposed to mean?" she blurted, refolding her arms and crossing her legs.

"Well, if you'll pardon me for bein' blunt, ya look like ya fell off the train halfway home from Rhode Island, y'know."

"*James!*" she shrieked, and began to laugh. Then it was all right. She fell back in the chair letting her arms dangle by her sides, legs sprawled out in front of her and let it all go. After a moment, she clutched at her stomach and rocked forward, placing an arm on the table for balance. "Oh, James!" she choked, regaining some control.

James took a sip of coffee and continued to grin at her. She looked at him.

"Jimmy, me boy," she said, "if the truth be known, I spent the whole night in Rhode Island and I missed the train completely. I've been hitchhiking for the past two hours."

"Well, fear not, Lucille," he said, patting her on the wrist. "Your ride's here. Would ya like to stop for lunch and a Guinness on the way home?"

"I can't think of anything I'd like better," she smiled. "It will give us a chance to talk about some things, including the guesthouse. I've got a couple of ideas I'd like to go over with you." She looked around the kitchen as if seeing it for the first time. "Where's Stephanie?"

"Ah. She phoned about thirty minutes before you came down, saying she'd be a little late and she hoped you'd understand."

Lucin smiled. "I do," she said.

"Also, your manicurist, Jolee I believe, phoned to cancel your appointment for Wednesday. She has to go out of town. She said she had a cancellation at ten-thirty this mornin'. If you'd care to have that slot, just stop by."

"You talked with Jolee?"

"That I did, and introduced myself. She seems like a fine manicurist." His eyes crinkled.

Unable to resist, Lucin continued. "She does men, you know."

"That's the impression she left me with," he grinned expectantly.

"Their *nails*, James. She does their *nails*!" Lucin laughed, coloring a bit.

"Aye, and what did ya think I meant?" he asked, his eyes wide and innocent.

"I know exactly what you meant, James O'Doud!"

"Sure ya do, but ya wouldn't have joked about it a week ago, now would ya?"

Lucin looked at him for a moment. "You're right. A week ago I wouldn't have joked about it. I probably wouldn't have known there was anything to joke about."

"There's a name for that, y'know."

"Really? What?"

James winked at her. "Progress," he said. "If ya want that appointment with the darlin' Jolee, why don't I drop ya off, then I'll pick ya up and we'll got to Clancy's for a pint or two and somethin' to put some weight on your bones."

"That sounds wonderful."

"Fine. I'll get the car while you go upstairs and finish dressing, or at least change that top. I don't think my heart can stand much more of this."

"James!" she giggled.

He paused at the door. "And don't forget what your dear old mother told ya. In case we get in a wreck, make sure ya put on underwear. *Clean* underwear."

It was a beautiful day. Wispy clouds, nearly sixty degrees, light breeze from the south. Lucin glowed. James noticed.

"Sure, and you're lookin' fine today Lucille," he said, as they motored up Ward Parkway.

"Thank you, James. I feel wonderful."

"Aye. A visit to Rhode Island can do that for ya."

"Yes it can," she blushed. "James … Jimmy, I must tell you something. I want you to know how safe you make me feel."

"Well," he smiled, "that's nice then, isn't it?"

"Yes it is. I appreciate it. Your warmth and humor and concern make me feel very special."

"It's special ya are, Lucille, me Darlin'. I'm too old to waste my love on mere mortals."

She hesitated a moment, then plunged ahead. "I love you too, Jimmy," she smiled, touching his arm.

"Sure ya do," he grinned. "You're no fool."

When they pulled up in front of *Nails!* James got out and opened Lucin's door. Jolee stepped outside the shop.

"Glad you could make it, Sweetie," she said.

"So am I," answered Lucin. "Jolee, this is my friend James. James, this is Jolee."

Jolee advanced on him and held out her hand. "It's very nice to meet you, James."

"Well, now," smiled James, taking her hand in both of his, allowing his eyes to slide easily over her, "then think how fine it must be for me. Beautiful sunshine, spring's warmth, and now such a lovely lady with her hand in mine. I am truly blessed, Jolee. Thank you for bringin' me such pleasure."

She looked at him for a moment, leaving her hand where it was, then began to chuckle. "Lucin said you were Irish," she dimpled.

"Aye, I cannot escape it."

"So, how's that work for you?"

"You'd be a better judge of that than I," James grinned, lightly caressing her fingers. "What do you think?"

"So far, so good," Jolee smiled, slowly drawing her hand from between his. "So far, *very* good."

A chuckle rumbled from James' throat. "It's nice to meet a woman of such easy honesty and fine taste. I'll be on me way now and return in about an hour." He stepped back to the car and got inside. "You're a rare one, Jolee, and fine too. I appreciate ya. Sure, and I hope to spend some time in your company again." The Jag rumbled and pulled away.

"Oh, my," said Jolee, watching the car leave and lightly fanning herself with one hand. "I could use some coffee. How 'bout you, Honey?"

"Uh ... yes, please," answered Lucin, following her inside the shop. "With cream."

Sitting down with the coffees, Jolee looked at Lucin. "Does James treat *you* like that?"

"Oh, no. No. Not at all like that," she replied, still a little stunned.

"Good thing, huh?" grinned Jolee.

"James is a wonderful man. I think highly of him."

"Good thing, huh?" Jolee persisted.

"God, yes! If he treated me like that, I don't know what might happen."

"Sure you do, Honey. You know *exactly* what might happen! That is a *very* charming man. Woof! I bet a girl would have no doubt he'd been there."

"Jolee!" laughed Lucin.

"I don't know how you stand it. I'd either have to avoid him, or take some very serious action."

"Jolee, he's old enough to be our father!"

"Boy, could my heart belong to Daddy," Jolee said wistfully, playing it to the hilt. "I wonder if he'd consider adoption? He could read me a story, tuck me in, spank me if I was bad ..."

"You are *awful!*" giggled Lucin.

"Loosen up, Sweetie," Jolee laughed, "and don't tell me you've never thought about it. I know better."

"Well, I've never thought about it like *that!*"

Jolee leered at her. "Well, maybe you should," she growled.

"Maybe I should," Lucin smiled.

Jolee peered at her rather critically for a moment. "You've got a nice shine on today," she observed. "What's new?"

"Oh, God. You won't believe what happened yesterday after I left here!"

"Sure I will," Jolee grinned. "Let's get you soaking, we'll fix those other nine monsters and you can tell me all about it."

"Wow," Jolee said, doing the final light buff. Lucin looked at her. "Wow," she said again. "In the car on the way home, right outta the blue!"

"Yep."

"And then in the tub."

"Like nothing before in my whole life!"

"Sweetie, that was like nothing before in *my* whole life either."

"It was amazing, Jolee. Just awesome."

"I want one."

"What?"

"I want one," teased Jolee. "I want one of those for my very own! I've been chasing an orgasm like that for over half my life, and you get it! The rookie hits a grand slam! It isn't fair!"

"It doesn't seem very fair, does it?" Lucin giggled.

"No. Loan me James. It's the least you could do."

"I'll ask him."

"Thank you. You know, Tommy's involved in all this somehow. All this started after you spaced out in his shop."

"That's something else," Lucin replied. "After you abandoned me there …"

Her phone rang.

"Hello?"

"Hey, Luce."

"Harrison!"

"That's me."

"Where are you, Darling?"

"Omaha. On the way home. I couldn't get a direct flight. I'll be in around four or so."

"Oh, Sweetheart, that's wonderful. You sound tired. Are you alright?"

"Sure, Luce. Just really beat."

"I'll have Stephanie prepare a nice dinner and then you can get some rest."

"Thanks, Luce. Two meetings tomorrow afternoon, a day or two in Kaycee, then back to Philly I'm afraid, but things are moving fast now. Looks like this whole thing might be settled by early winter and all this travel will slow way down."

"That would be nice."

"You bet. I love you, Lucin. I'll see you late this afternoon."

"I love you too. Want me to pick you up?"

"That's okay. I got a limo reserved. I'll see you at the house, Baby. 'Bye."

"Goodbye, Harrison."

"Hubby coming home?" asked Jolee.

"Yes, late this afternoon."

"Don't hurt him."

"What?"

Jolee grinned.

"Oh, stop," laughed Lucin.

The shop door swung open and James stepped inside. "Well now, Jolee," he said, "have you sharpened her talons then?"

Instantly, Jolee corrected her posture and dropped her voice half an octave. "Like razors, James. Sharp is my specialty."

"You'll have no trouble convincin' me of that," he smiled. "I have no doubt you can be a dangerous woman." He turned to Lucin. "No need to hitchhike, Ms. Montgomery. Your chariot awaits."

"Thank you, James," she smiled. "I'll be right out."

"Yes, Ma'am," he replied, and went outside.

Taking Lucin's credit card, Jolee smiled. "Visions in the night, parties in the tub, and now hubby's coming home. Things could get real interesting, girlfriend."

"Oh, God. I have to relax with all this."

"You can do it, Sweetie. Go for it. I'll see you next week."

"Thanks, Jolee. I appreciate you listening to me."

"Honey," grinned Jolee, "I wouldn't miss it for the world."

James and Lucin beat the lunch rush to Clancy's and went to a table on the upper level. Lucin phoned Stephanie about supper, told James about Harrison, studied the menu, ordered Shepard's Pie from a smiling Constance, and announced she was working under a two-pint limit. James ordered the same and advised Constance he'd see her about four-thirty. The Guinness arrived, they both took a drink, and Lucin looked at James.

"Japanese," she said.

"Why would ya be sayin' that to me now?"

"That's how I want to do the guesthouse. I've found someone to design an oriental garden where the yard is all dug up and someone to build it. I want the house to reflect the garden."

"It's true. The Japanese have some lovely gardens."

"I also want to use the frame from the original house, but I want to open up that really trashy bedroom to the outside as a covered porch and connect it to a deck that will overlook the garden and pond."

"Tomorrow I'll call me old pal Michael and discuss with him who best might be qualified to design the changes to the structure in light of how the garden is created. I assume the garden is the focal point for the house."

"That it is, Jimmy me boy," Lucin grinned.

"And what are you smilin' at," he asked, taking another drink.

"At you, you rogue."

"Rogue is it? And what did I do to deserve that?"

"You charmed Jolee right out of her socks!"

"Ha! You're assumin' it's her socks that interest me, Lucille."

"James!" she laughed.

"Nobody charms that darlin' girl out of anything she isn't completely willin' to be charmed out of. Make no mistake about that."

"Oh, I think she's willing enough. God! James, listen to me! What am I saying?"

"The truth, the way I see it," he laughed. "I don't know if Jolee and I make such a fine idea. She's awful young."

"Well, that's nice of you, James. Most men wouldn't let that stop them."

"Don't misunderstand my motives, Darlin'. She's got too many good years left yet for me to be ruinin' her for every other man on the planet," he twinkled. "It just wouldn't be fair to the dear child."

As Lucin struggled to keep beer from coming out her nose, Connie arrived with the food. They ate in silence for a while.

"Back to your garden," said James. "I think it's a fine idea. Something like that can be a true work of art, good for the eyes and the soul."

"That's what I think," Lucin agreed.

"It would even be easy enough to build some sort of wood or bamboo fence between the stand of trees and the garage for privacy."

"James, that's a wonderful thought. With something like that to block the view, the garden could be it's own little world."

"Aye, that's the idea," he said. "You've spent your whole life livin' in other people's worlds, me Sweetheart and fair. Perhaps now it's time you had one of your own."

NINE

Hopeful expectation
Unfulfilled,
Becomes sad acceptance ...
A spreading stain
Upon my heart.

JAMES DROPPED LUCIN OFF at around two o'clock, then drove to the garage to park the Jag. Stephanie was working in the kitchen.

"Hi, Steph!"

"Hello Ms. Mont ... uh, Lucin. I'm sorry I was late this morning. I overslept," she said, blushing a little.

"Was it worth it?"

"Oh yes," she smiled.

"Then that's fine. I need you to work a little late this evening, if you can."

"Sure, I'll be glad to."

"Well, then it all evens out. What's for dinner?"

"When you called and said comfort food, I went to the butcher and got a beautiful beef loin roast. I thought I'd put some cloves of garlic in it, brown it, rub it with sesame oil, roll it in a little cracked pepper and sea salt, add some small Yukon Gold potatoes and carrot chunks, a stalk of celery and stick it in the oven. Medium or medium rare?"

"Medium rare will be fine."

"I'll make a gravy with the stock for the potatoes and carrots."

"God, Steph, that sounds wonderful."

"Baked apples for desert?"

"Perfect. Forget a salad or appetizer. Harrison will be very tired. Lots of protein and carbohydrates. He'll sleep like a log. He needs it."

"Yes, Ma'am. I'll get the roast ready for the oven about four-thirty, dinner around six?"

"Fine."

"I'll straighten things up right away."

"Take it easy, the house is alright. Just pick up a bit and change the bed linen upstairs."

James walked through the door and headed for the coffee pot.

"Bring your coffee into the dining room, James," said Lucin, picking up the book and heading that way. "I have some stuff to show you."

They spent the next thirty minutes looking through the pictures and discussing the transformation of the house and yard.

"You're nervous," James observed.

"What?"

"You are nervous, a condition of heightened uneasiness, anticipation with a touch of fear, things like that." He smiled at her.

"I'm a wreck. My husband's coming home. I shouldn't be like this just because Harrison will be here soon."

"Why not? In his absence you've taken to drink, wild fantasy, wanton behavior, and caused me to enter into a small state. Good God, Lucille," he grinned, "you're nearly a scarlet woman! The poor unsuspecting devil stands almost no chance a'tall, a'tall."

"James!" she laughed.

"Let me rephrase," he continued. "You have begun to take some control of your own life, you have begun to liberate your thoughts, you have begun to feel a different potential within yourself, and you've started to have fun. What's wrong with that?"

"Nothing, I suppose."

"*Nothing, I suppose,*" he mimicked. "Me darlin' girl, 'tis a grand and glorious thing that's upon ya! You should rejoice that it's happenin', not *worry* about it."

"But I'm different than when Harrison went away."

"Aye, ya are. And you'll be different the next time he returns, too. Just try not to overwhelm him or yourself with the difference. Give the poor lad time to adjust. I can't think of a single reason why he won't come to appreciate it."

"You don't know Harrison."

"I know he's in need of a bit of liberation his ownself."

"Harrison is a good and decent man who loves me very much."

"And why wouldn't he? You're a fine woman, a fine woman who's laboring under the weight of an immense shadow."

"An immense shadow?"

"Aye. Like all shadows, it has no substance, but still it represses you and binds you to the earth. Look around, Sweetheart. Your mother is *not* here."

She smiled at him, and took his hand in hers. "You are an extraordinary man, Jimmy O'Doud."

"Aye, that's true enough. Your husband is too, y'know. He just doesn't realize it because he's too busy bein' an overachiever. He has his own shadows to deal with. Go easy on him for a while. When he gets more settled in his business he'll be more receptive in his life. This time isn't about him anyway. It's about you. Take care of yourself now and you can take care of him later."

Lucin leaned forward and kissed him on the cheek. "You always say just the right thing," she smiled.

"Sure and I'm just tellin' ya what ya already know, me Darlin'," he said, standing up. "I'm off. I'm gonna drop by Michael's place on the way to Clancy's and show him this book. Give him an idea what we're about. I'll see ya in the mornin' and we'll talk some more about the new place. Just remember that light defeats shadows. Be *who* ya are, and *what* ya are will shine. Be *what* ya are, and *who* ya are will shine." James looked down at her for a moment, then grinned. "Just don't scare hell out of the poor lad!" He lightly caressed her cheek and headed for the door.

Lucin went upstairs and changed into a dark gray pantsuit and white t-shirt, brushed out her hair, added some make-up, jewelry and a pair of two inch black velvet heels. When she came downstairs, Stephanie was browning the roast in a skillet.

"It looks beautiful, Steph."

"Thank you," smiled the girl. "I'll roll it in the pepper and salt in a minute, and put it in the oven. About an hour and a half, I think."

The side door opened and there, with a small overnight bag and a suitcase, stood Harrison.

"Hello, Luce," he grinned.

The hug was warm, loving, reserved, and typically Harrison. Lucin's attempt to escalate it into an embrace was gently rebuffed as he pulled away a bit. "Good to see you," he said.

"Welcome home," she smiled. "I missed you."

"Your mother sends her best," he replied, releasing her and backing up a step. "She wants to know when you're coming out for a visit."

"I'll call her. You look so tired, Harrison. Are you okay?"

"I'm better than okay," he smiled. "Things are going really well. It's a lot of hard work and hours, but it's coming together." He looked past Lucin. "Good evening, Stephanie."

"Good evening, Mr. Montgomery. Dinner in about an hour and a half. Pot roast."

"Pot roast?" he said, looking at Lucin.

"You sounded so frazzled over the phone that I thought you needed some real comfort food. Pot roast with carrots, potatoes and gravy. Stick to your ribs and help you sleep."

He smiled. "That's very thoughtful, Luce. It'll give me a chance for thirty-six holes to get the added weight off," he chuckled. "Thanks. Pot roast is perfect. I shouldn't need much help sleeping. This will probably induce a coma."

"That was the plan. I love you."

"I love you, too. I'm going upstairs and put this stuff away, take a shower, and get ready for dinner. See ya in a while."

She watched him climb the stairs and resisted the urge to go with him. Harrison did not like to be disturbed when he returned home from a trip. He would carefully put all his things away, each in the proper place, each in the proper space relative to everything else. His dirty clothes would go in the hamper, all else neatly back in the dressing room. He'd spend thirty minutes or more in the shower and another ten carefully wiping down all damp surfaces and cleaning up after himself. He would invest ninety minutes in unpacking, undressing, cleaning up and re-dressing. When he left the area, it would be spotless with no indication he had ever been there. Harrison admired order and routine.

To pass the time, she set the table with the good damask cloth and their best china and crystal. She got down one of the old candelabra and filled it with six of the twenty-four inch tapers she kept under the buffet table. The lilies were still lovely and she carried them down from the landing and placed them on the table. Stephanie was taking the roast out of the oven just as Lucin finished wiping down the silver gravy boat. She heard Harrison enter the dining room, opened a bottle of an Australian Merlot, and carried it into the table. He stood there in wingtips, dark brown slacks, a deep gold turtleneck, and a medium brown Harris tweed jacket. Harrison always wore a jacket to dinner. He smiled at her as she used one of the long matches to light the candles.

"You look great, Luce."

"Thank you, Sir," she dimpled. "It must be the candlelight. You look more rested after your shower. How are you feeling?"

"Tired, hungry, glad to be home, however fleetingly."

"Sit," she said, not quite forcing a smile. "I'll check on Stephanie and dinner."

The dinner was so good that it pulled Lucin back from the edge of a slight depression. Harrison ate more than usual and watched with near amazement as his wife tore into the pot roast as if she had not eaten in two days. She turned down desert, but had more potatoes and carrots as he ate his baked apple. He seemed slightly amused.

"What?" she asked.

"You seem to have developed a real appetite while I've been gone."

"I guess I have," she replied, controlling her answer.

"Well, that was wonderful. Another glass of wine and I am off to bed. I have a luncheon meeting tomorrow with the realty people on the offices in Crown Center and temporary housing for staff and families, and then a two o'clock with Bright Associates on spousal employment re-location and related employee considerations. Things are moving right along, Luce. Even with the Nagata people."

"Nagata people?"

"Nagata Industries of Japan. They're working on putting a plant outside Kansas City. The firm is handling all the paper for them. It's one of the reasons we relocated. It looks like that is coming together. Hope to have it assembled and in place for construction in July or August. Millions per year to the firm. Millions. The supervising senior partner will do very well, also."

"That would be you."

"That would be me. The staff we re-locate and hire at first will probably do nothing but Nagata's business. It's a very big deal."

"Congratulations."

"Premature, but likely. Thank you. And for the excellent dinner and the marvelous company. I'm sorry, Sweetheart, but I just have to go to bed. I'm dead on my feet." He stood and bent to kiss her cheek.

"You go on, Harrison. I'll be up in a couple of hours. I'll try not to wake you. Sleep well."

"You too, Luce. See you in the morning."

When Lucin walked into the bedroom three hours later, Harrison, his pajamas buttoned to the throat, was lying on his back and snoring softly. Gently, she smoothed his rumpled blond hair and pulled the comforter up to cover his chest. In her dressing room she disrobed and got into her pajamas. It seemed odd to be dressing for bed. Sliding between the sheets, she felt so restricted, so confined. She could put up with the pajamas, she supposed—installing a pillow snugly between her thighs—but there were some things she was not going to do without.

She awakened a little after seven, and lay there for a time enjoying sensations and listening to Harrison breathe. When things began to get a little too intense, she sighed and rose. After a brief shower, she slipped into a bra and panties, tapered black velvet slacks, and a dark blue velour top. She added low gray heels and a matching silk scarf, a touch of eye shadow and lipstick, and ambled downstairs.

The kitchen was empty. She ground some fresh beans and started coffee, dropped a bagel into the toaster, got some cream cheese out of the fridge and popped it into the microwave to soften it a bit, put some Half and Half into a cup to allow it to warm up a little and got out a plate for the bread. When the bagel popped up, she slathered on a quarter-inch layer of the cream cheese and carried it to the table. She interrupted the brew cycle to get some very strong coffee and sat, looking out a window toward the guesthouse. Just as she finished the bagel, Lucin heard Harrison begin to move about upstairs. She put the plate in the sink, wiped the crumbs off the counter, and carried a second cup of coffee back to the table to enjoy a few more minutes of solitude and thoughts of the garden. She was two-thirds of the way through the second cup when she heard the side door open and James stepped into the room.

"Top of the mornin' to ya, Lucille," he beamed. "Don't ya look lovely this fine day."

"Ah, Jimmy, me boy, and doesn't it warm me heart ta see ya, me Darlin' and fair." she quipped in retort. "Can I pour ya a cup of coffee then?" They stood smiling at each other across the table.

"You could pour me one," said Harrison, grinning at both of them from the dining room doorway.

"Mr. Montgomery," said James, never missing a beat, "welcome home. I hope you're rested and well after your trip."

"Thank you, uh, 'Jimmy'," Harrison replied, adjusting the belt of his dressing gown and crossing to kiss Lucin on her slightly pink cheek. "I'm quite well and gratified to see you and 'Lucille' getting along so well." His grin grew even wider and left no doubt he meant what he said.

"She's a fine lady," replied James, "and I hold her in high esteem."

"I'll get you some coffee, Harrison," interjected Lucin, nervously striding to the pot as she collected herself. "I have retained James to oversee the reconstruction of the guesthouse and the garden that will go with it."

"Really? You're actually going to attack that pile of rubble?"

"We've already had a contractor stop by, and James has been looking for someone to design the makeover."

"That's wonderful, Luce. The place is an eyesore. It'll be nice if you two can do something with it."

"That's why I'm here," said James. "I have some information."

"Well, I'll leave you to it," said Harrison, "and take my coffee in the den with the morning paper. I need to see what's been going on around Kansas City during my absence. Nice to see you, James. It's good to know you'll be with us for awhile longer."

"Thank you, Sir."

Accepting a cup, he smiled at Lucin. "You two go ahead and take care of business, Luce. I'll see you this afternoon after my second meeting." He kissed her on the cheek again and left the room. She and James looked at each other and a chewy slice of guilt shot between them. As if on cue, they grinned.

"It's true, y'know," whispered James, stepping close to Lucin's side.

"What?" she asked, looking up at him.

"Ah, Darlin', nothing cements a relationship as well as sharin' a delicious little secret or two."

That morning they met with a young construction architect named Cahill Dunn, sent by Michael, and went through the entire house. After nearly three hours of dusty measuring, prodding, poking and pounding, they sat in the kitchen over tea and coffee.

"If you want to stay with a slightly oriental flavor throughout, Miz Montgomery," said Cahill, "I suggest we rip everything out of the interior. Your trusses are oak. We can take out every inside wall and not weaken the basic structure. Then we wall up a nice large bath area, complete with a soaking tub. Every other interior divider can be mobile. The Japanese are famous for their use of space. I'd suggest sliding *shoji* screens. The bedchamber, living area, kitchen, all of it can be either wide open or partitioned off. Very versatile ... and once we rip out the ceiling and expand it upward into a vaulted space to the roofline ... very roomy. A couple of skylights, some hanging plants ... gorgeous!"

"That sounds wonderful," Lucin smiled.

"Outside," Cahill continued, "broad multi-paned windows, vertical cedar or redwood board and batten siding stained a dusky spruce color, darker shutters and trim. It will blend well with the stand of trees between the house and the garage and will not detract from the garden you have planned. It's a great idea you had about opening up the rear corner bedroom. We'll make it into a deck under roof, drop eight inches or so at its perimeter and surround it with an open ell-shaped lower deck that extends twelve or sixteen feet down the side and rear of the house from that corner. You can then wrap your garden area around the deck on two sides of the home, with the covered portion in the middle; very charming and a wonderful place to sit and view the garden. We'll place sliding glass doors on the two walls leading into the house off the deck and add sliding *shoji* screens over the doors. Very warm, very oriental."

Lucin could *see* it. After Cahill and James departed, she walked back to the guesthouse and stood at the rear corner. It was there in her mind's eye. The covered sitting area, the deck, the *shoji* screens leading into her hideaway. She played with it, letting it pull at her, remaining steady in its ebb and flow, allowing images to flit around her like barn swallows. Eyes closed, she smiled at the delicate waterfall, the blooming plum tree, the shimmering pond. The delicate hum of a bee reached her ears; she smelled the rich earth and the slightly acrid odor of a black pine. She had spent so much time in a place like this would be, she had learned so much from a place like this would be that memories of its taste and texture rose about her like a mist and she breathed them in, letting them soak into her skin and rise from her cells.

"So this is it, huh?"

The sound of Harrison's voice slapped at her and she jerked, jolted by its intrusion.

"Oh! Harrison. You startled me. I was a million miles away!"

"I guess so," he grinned. "I saw you standing out here when I drove in. After I rattled around the house for a while, I decided to come out and get you. I swear you haven't moved in thirty minutes. You okay, Luce?"

"Yes," she smiled, covering her irritation. "I'm fine. Just trying to fix things into place."

"What a mess," he observed, looking at the house and the mud hole.

A bit unsettled and resentful of the intrusion, Lucin changed the subject. "How were your meetings?"

"Great," he replied. "Signed the papers with the realty reps on the office space at Crown Center. Finalized the deal with Bright Associates to get our people temporary housing and get started on employment for spouses and dependents. A thousand things could have gone wrong and none of them did. Let's celebrate!"

"Celebrate?"

"Sure. Let's get dressed up. Reservations at eight for dinner at the Savoy. Good food, good wine, good company. Maybe stop by the club for drinks. Let's make a night of it, Luce. What do you say?"

"That's fine, Harrison," she smiled, now completely back from the garden. "Let's do that. Let's make a night of it."

After a shower and very careful application of make-up, Lucin dressed in an off-white teddy with matching garter belt, dark seamed stockings, a black velvet A-line skirt that ended two inches above her knees, an off white silk blouse with long puffy sleeves, and four inch black suede heels with an ankle strap so she wouldn't fall off of them. She added a choker of black velvet ribbon and an onyx stud trimmed with silver in each ear. Looking at herself in the mirror, she was almost embarrassed. This look was a little daring for her, not as conservative as she customarily dressed. It felt good.

Usually these occasional nights out, and the prospect of making love at the end of them, stirred her. Tonight, however, she prepared almost with resignation. It's not that she didn't want to spend time with her husband; she'd loved Harrison for years and still did. He was bright and personable, and he loved her too, she was absolutely sure of that. Contact with Harrison was something she almost always looked forward to with warmth and happy anticipation, but not, she realized, with longing. Not with excitement. Not with butterflies. Not with a glorious itch yearning to be scratched. Reminding herself that it was about her and not about Harrison, she walked downstairs.

He was waiting in the dining room, dressed in a dark blue suit with a gray pin-stripe, a pale blue shirt, and a maroon silk tie with tiny golf tees in the subtle pattern.

He rose when she entered and crossed to her kissing her cheek.

"You look great, Luce. You really do."

She knew it. And what's more, she *liked* it.

Dinner was good. Dinner is always good at the Savoy. The service was excellent, as one would naturally expect it to be. She and Harrison chatted about many things, including the project on the guesthouse. She told him of some of her ideas, mentioned Michael and Cahill, commented on how much help James was, and basically left it at that. She revealed nothing of Tami, nothing of Jolee, nothing of her voyage into the world of Guinness with James, and nothing of the source of her inspiration for a Japanese theme with the garden and house. It occurred to her that she, for the first time in her marriage, had secrets from her husband. She liked that, too.

On the way home, even though they had consumed a bottle of wine and were a bit tipsy, they stopped by the Carriage Club for a drink. The dining room was closed but the bar open, and they took a table near the side door, Harrison facing the windows, Lucin facing the bar. The room was heavily populated with men. Harrison ordered them both martinis as Lucin excused herself and went to the ladies' room. Passing down the length of the bar, she became aware of stares from several of the men sitting there. Ordinarily the looks would have annoyed her, but tonight she felt vaguely flattered, pleased that she was both noticeable and noticed. As she passed the end of the bar, a gentle "my, my, my" wafted behind her, and she couldn't repress a smile. A touch of warmth stirred in her belly as she stepped into the restroom. Looks and stares from strange men had never pleased her, much less caused her to *respond*. But tonight she was responding. She thought about it as she touched up her make-up, darkening the shadow above her eyes a bit, freshening her lipstick.

What was wrong with men liking the way she looked? *She* liked the way she looked. She wasn't "on the prowl." She was just being a girl. She enjoyed the way James looked at her, and now it seemed she enjoyed the way other men looked at her, too. She asked for it, she got it, and it was fun. What the hell. In for a penny, in for a pound. She unbuttoned her blouse another notch and put a little swing in her walk and a little smile on her face, and headed down the length of the bar and back to the table. One man caught her eye and saluted her with a martini glass. Lucin captured the tip of her tongue between her teeth and grinned at him. The "Sweet Jesus" that followed behind her almost made her laugh out loud.

Harrison was most of the way through his drink.

"I ordered us two more," he smiled. "Then we'll go home. Drink up."

Lucin picked up the martini, drained it, and popped the olive into her mouth pulling carefully on the toothpick to release it.

"Suits me," she said, swiveling in her chair until her legs were pointed at the bar. Slowly she uncrossed then re-crossed her legs, allowing her skirt to slide up to mid-thigh, not quite exposing her stocking tops. She bobbed her foot in the four-inch heel a bit and the effect was instantaneous. Several of the men at the bar shifted in their seats and she felt a little nudge below her navel, the nicest little itch and the sweetest little scratch. She *really* liked that.

The drinks came and she moved her legs back under the table, grinning in spite of herself. Harrison noticed.

"Doing okay, Luce?"

"Fine," she said, sipping about half her martini. "Just having fun," she confessed.

"Good," he smiled. "I know places like this aren't exactly your cup of tea. It's nice to see you enjoying yourself."

"Oh, I'm having a wonderful time watching all the people," she said, controlling her grin, swiveling her legs out from under the table and back again.

Lifting the toothpick from her martini and pulling the olive off with her teeth, she could feel another shift along the bar. Lucin almost giggled out loud. A little bit of thigh, a little bit of teeth, a little bit of attitude, and the gallery was in full fantasy mode! She thought about making another trip to the restroom, then discarded the idea. Harrison was oblivious and she wanted to keep it that way. At least for the moment. Thoroughly enjoying being a girl, Lucin swallowed the last of her martini, flashed a grin down the length of the bar, and looked at her husband.

"Take me home, Harrison. Now."

He looked at her, a bit startled, and flushed. "Now?" he asked, reaching for his drink.

"Right now," she said.

Lucin lay in their bed and listened to Harrison washing up in the bathroom. Harrison always washed up after sex. He entered the room buttoning up his pajama top, and slipped into bed.

"That was wonderful, Luce," he said, sliding over and gently kissing her lips. "Just wonderful. I love you, Sweetheart." He moved back to his side of the bed, clicked off his light, and rolled over. Lucin stared up into the darkness.

It wasn't that Harrison was sexually inexperienced, that was not the case. Nor was he pre-occupied or distant. He was fully there, fully attentive, willing to do his best for her. She had never questioned his love or commitment. It was just … something had to be missing. He was the only sexual partner she'd ever had. She'd heard other women talk about … things. She knew that men were different in their technique, size, likes and dislikes, and she'd accepted that in a distant sort of way. Harrison was her husband! She wasn't shopping for another man! True, he was not excessively passionate. Even on those rare times when he indicated he wanted her to take him into her mouth, he remained in control, never really let go. It had always been that way. Back when she was in college and would visit him at his apartment, things were much then as they were now, except the frequency had dropped off as the years passed.

He satisfied her, she guessed. She usually had an orgasm. Even tonight she'd had one. Nothing like the one in the tub of course, but an orgasm. Not even as strong as the one in the car actually, but an orgasm. A nice, tidy, neatly wrapped, little pleasure package, that he worked diligently to give her, doing all the right things in the correct order, dotting his I's and crossing her T's, making sure things turned out well. Tongue A into slit B. Tab C into slot D. Everything in its place and a place for everything. Just like he wiped down the bathroom after showering, just like he cleaned up after sex, just like he buttoned up his pajamas before he came back to bed. Nice, effective, tidy, neat. That was much more than many women had. He loved her, cared about her, was kind and considerate toward her. That was a lot more than some women could ever hope for! She should consider herself fortunate. She did. She really did. Harrison Montgomery was a *good* man. A man who always kept his hands on the handlebars, who never swam too far from shore, who wouldn't cross the double yellow line, who always closed the lid, replaced the cap, and read the directions. Maybe James was right when he said this wasn't about Harrison, it was about her. He warned her not to expect too much, or even want too much from Harrison for a while.

She was changing, that was obvious. Good grief. What was she doing in the bar tonight? Flashing her legs at those men, behaving like some kind of ... some kind of ... woman? That's what James would call it. He'd say she was just being a girl. He'd laugh about it, tell her to enjoy it. She did enjoy it. She enjoyed the way the velvet skirt clung to her bare thighs. She enjoyed the freedom and thrill of not wearing a bra in public. She enjoyed the way she so easily controlled those men. She enjoyed their open admiration. The bounce of a foot in a spike heel, the flash of a stockinged thigh, the swing of a short skirt from an exaggerated stride, such little things, and yet so powerful! She could feel their fantasies around her like cobwebs.

It was a shame James couldn't have been there, he would have loved it. He would have sat back, taken it all in, and actually been proud of her. What if she behaved that way in front of him? What if she teased James? Would he enjoy it? Of course he would. Would she enjoy it, she wondered, rolling to her side and sliding her pillow up between her legs. Oh, my! The spark that shot downward from her belly made her pelvis twitch and sent a ripple up her stomach to her chest. That answered her question. She'd enjoy it alright. She'd already enjoyed it when she sent him to Rhode Island and when her nipples were visible under her t-shirt. It probably wasn't a good idea to tease James though. She'd watched him in action with Jolee. She yawned and snuggled the pillow up a bit tighter. If he turned that Irish charm loose on her things could get out of hand, and James had such nice hands. Closing her eyes, she thought of those hands, sliding under her bottom, lifting her, holding her, preparing her. Smiling, she shifted against the padded silk between her legs. Then she and her pillow drifted away in James' strong and capable hands.

TEN

The night blooming lily
shows petals to the moon.
Gentle color waits patiently
for who comes
after twilight.

THE SUBSEQUENT DAYS were a whirlwind of activity for Lucin. Harrison came and went three more times during the next month. Contractors drove their equipment across the rear lawn, machines groaned and grumbled, trucks arrived and departed, James grinned and griped, and she was at the center of it all. For the first time in years, Lucin was truly busy. So busy, she was even motivated to make herself busier, buying a pair of skates and going to a public rink two or three times a week just for the joy of it. On two occasions she encountered little Kennedy Paige Hartrick and skated with the girl, enjoying her energy, flattered by the child's attention, pleased by the way the seven-year-old felt free to be a little kid in Lucin's company, relieved that on both occasions she was spared contact with Kennedy's mother, Sheila.

She padded into the kitchen one early April morning, wearing her short terry robe and beat-up scruffies, scratching her head through rumpled hair and yawning. James sat at the table.

"Good morning," he said. Lucin gave a start.

"Oh! James. Good morning," she replied, stifling a yawn. "You're early. I didn't expect you yet. I'm a mess!"

"Aye, that ya are," he grinned. "You can't imagine how embarrassed I am for ya, lookin' the way ya do. Should I avert my eyes then?"

"Whatever makes you most comfortable," she smiled, shuffling toward the table.

"In that case, I'll be castin' them upon ya, Lucille, and commentin' that you have become a woman of more substance, and it looks good on ya. Coffee?"

"Please. Black."

"No cream?"

"Black. I *have* become a woman of more substance and the substance has gone as far as it needs to go," she replied, sitting and carefully collecting her robe about her.

"As of this morning I weigh almost a hundred and twenty-five pounds. That is enough."

"The skatin' has been good to ya," James commented. "You've added some muscle."

"It's not all muscle."

"That's true," he chuckled. "Some of it is girl."

"Why, James," she smiled, taking a cup from his hand, "I didn't think you'd noticed."

He sat across the table and looked at her. "Oh, I've noticed, alright. Lucille, me Darlin', surely you've noticed me noticin'."

"I've noticed," she said, her ears getting warm. "I notice you too."

"Do ya now?" he teased.

"You mean a lot to me, James," she replied, slightly exasperated. "Of course I notice you."

His glance grew soft. "Well, now that's flatterin'. Know this, sweet Lucille. If I was a hundred years younger and not in your employ, you would be in a great deal of trouble."

Lucin felt a little ripple in her tummy and flushed a bit. "Is that right?" she asked.

"Aye," James smiled, locking eyes with her. "As right as anything ever could be." They held each other's gaze, and Stephanie entered the kitchen.

"Good morning," she said, shattering the moment. "I hope I'm not interrupting anything."

"Hi, Steph," said Lucin, breaking the eye contact. "You're not interrupting. I was just trying to decide if I should fire James."

"And I was just thinking how much younger I'd feel if I was unemployed," James chuckled. He stood up. "I'm off to the little house. Come down when you can, Miz Montgomery. It's time for you to make a decision or two about what you want to do."

Thirty minutes later, Lucin, hair combed and dressed in snug jeans, a sweatshirt and a light cotton jacket, stepped into the guesthouse. The interior was completely gutted. Where the ceiling used to be were eight by eight rafters on four-foot centers. Above them, the underside of the roof planking showed, climbing to nearly eighteen feet overhead. The horsehair plaster was gone, the walls had been re-studded, and insulation filled the spaces. Instead of a back bedroom there was now a covered deck extending into the house, with nonexistent walls framed to accept two sets of sliding glass doors. Beyond the covered deck and one step down, a second deck, twelve feet deep, extended sixteen feet down the side of the structure and twelve feet across the rear. James stood on the rear deck. Lucin approached him feeling a little shy. He smiled at her.

"Now then," he said. "Don't you look more presentable?"

"So, you're not embarrassed for me any more?"

"I don't think I could ever be embarrassed for you, Lucille," James replied, looking at his feet. He glanced at her briefly, then squinted out over the yard. "I'm feelin' a little embarrassed for myself though, truth be told."

"You, too?" she asked.

"Aye," he grinned, looking at her from the corner of his eye. "Am I still employed?"

"For as long as you want to be."

"Well, I suppose it'd be best for both of us if I kept workin'," he sighed, "although, other options certainly are attractive."

She rubbed his arm. "Aw, Jimmy me Boy," she smiled, "and what would ya be doin' without a job then? Goin' off to Rhode Island?"

"Not Rhode Island," he grinned. "I'd be in a much bigger state than that."

"Texas?"

"Only if you were there with me," James replied, his eyes searching her face. She put her arms around his waist and leaned into him, pressing her cheek against his shoulder.

"I love you, Jimmy O'Doud," she murmured.

He wrapped her up in his strong arms. "And I you, Lucin. If things were different, me Darlin' ..."

"In matters of the pillow, all is private, all is separate from the world," whispered Lucin.

"What?"

"Huh?"

"What?" James asked again, pulling back and looking down at her.

"What's the matter?" she replied, peering up at him.

"What did you just say?"

"I didn't say anything."

"Yes, you did. You said something about pillows and everything is private."

Her head spinning a bit, Lucin stepped away from James, furrowing her brow. "In matters of the pillow, all is private, all is separate from the world," she intoned.

"Where did that come from?" he asked.

"From the garden," she confessed, realizing it was true and panting a little.

"The garden?"

She looked at James and felt a surge of warmth for him. "Uh ... what we do with the house depends on what I do with the garden. I've got to go see Tami. We'll talk more later today, alright James?"

"Are you okay?" he asked, looking at her closely.

"I'm fine," she said, recovering a little strength. "It was just a memory. At least that's what I think it was."

Caught up in her head, Lucin missed her turn off of Ward Parkway and had to backtrack to get to Tami's shop. She parked on the opposite side from *Nails!* so she wouldn't have to contend with Jolee, and went inside *Wa*. Tami broke away from two butterscotch-haired young matrons and addressed her from across the room.

"Lucin-*san*, it is so good to see you. "*Gomen nasai, dozo ga matsu.* So sorry, please wait. I will be with you presently. It is a great pleasure that you have returned to my humble store." The two women looked her up and down, evaluating exactly to whom Tami would be so gracious, then turned away vying for his attention. Lucin began to browse.

At length a reproduction of a painting caught her eye. Dated around 1700 and done in the elegantly simplistic Japanese style, it showed a young girl dressed in a traditional kimono in the near distance, standing beside a low bamboo fence. In the field on the other side of the fence were bare trees and light snow was falling. Standing in the foreground, also in traditional garb, was a full-grown woman with her back to the artist. It was evident that the woman was speaking to the child, perhaps offering her instruction. The girl was listening intently with just a touch of mischief on her delicate face.

Lucin approached the painting almost unaware of her passage down the aisle. She stood before it, face upturned, and regarded it with a gentle smile and sad eyes. For several moments she stood thus, then slowly extended her hand and touched the corner of the simple frame. Tears gathered in her eyes.

"*Mama-san*," she whispered.

"Gone but not forgotten," came the quiet answer, and she turned to see Tamiko Asaruka standing a respectful six feet away, his eyes shining. He bowed deeply and smiled. "The past is separated from the future only by the now. It is in the now we shed tears. You show great respect, Moon Blossom. You bestow honor on her."

Lucin focused on him as best she could and wiped the tears away before they could fall. "What did you call me?"

"I called you Moon Blossom."

The room swam and she extended an arm for balance. Tami took it and guided her to a nearby bench. Lucin sat heavily and stared blankly at the floor for a few moments, then turned to him where he knelt beside her and searched his face. "Who *are* you?" she asked, a slight tremor in her voice.

He grinned and chuckled. "Tamiko Asaruka," he said, "just a lowly Japanese merchant. Who do you think I am?"

"I don't know," she smiled, feeling more in control.

"Ah. Now *that* is progress. The more we believe we know, the less we will be able to learn. A sure path to knowledge is the admission of ignorance."

"More inscrutable oriental stuff, huh?"

"Yeah. Cool, huh?"

"Very," she smiled.

"Don't wanna lay too much of it on you at one time," he said, rising to his feet. "While you were looking at the picture I closed the store. I am at your service, Lucin-*san*. What may I and *Wa* do for you this fine day?"

"I want a garden."

"Of course you do."

"And I'd like you to design it."

"It would be my honor."

"Perhaps you could come to my home and look over the site?"

"This afternoon?"

"Ah ... fine. We'll have coffee."

"I don't drink coffee."

She smiled. "Then allow me to invite you over for tea."

"Tea it is," he laughed.

"What's so funny?"

"*Sumimasen.* I'm sorry, Lucin. In my culture, inviting someone over for tea can mean several things, none of them casual. When a woman invites a man, it means only one thing."

"Oh," she responded, blushing slightly, then collecting herself. "And what would that be?" she asked with just the hint of a smile.

Tami leaned toward her and looked intently into her eyes. His murmured answer seemed to come from just beside her ear. "She wants him to design a garden," he said.

Too jumpy for more than a small salad at lunch, Lucin sent Stephanie out to pick up green tea and a pot and cups of oriental design. She spent the next hour in the shower and putting on make-up, chiding herself for behaving like a schoolgirl. After a thorough browse through her dressing room, she settled on a pair of dark green velvet slacks, a jade green, long sleeved wraparound blouse in lined satin, and jade green flats. God! She was behaving like she was going on a date! This was Tami, coming over to look at the guesthouse and the torn up earth beside it. It was not the damn senior prom! Still, she could not suppress her excitement. There was more here than just a visit from an inscrutable oriental. This, she felt, was truly the start of something, perhaps even the *completion* of something. Emotions whirled around her like leaves in the wind, so fast and furious she could only catch snatches of them as they darted by. She was happy, she was fearful. She was excited, she was apprehensive. She was pleased, she was nervous. She remembered her seventh birthday.

Her mother had a man bring a pony for everyone to ride. Joyful at the prospect, Lucin was almost too paralyzed with fright to sit on the placid animal. When it was over, she felt cheated because her fear had prevented her from really enjoying the experience. Feeling foolish, she hung around downstairs until three o'clock, opening the door herself when she heard Tami slam the door on his van. She watched him walk toward her, dressed in his usual black. There was no wasted movement in his stride at all. He almost seemed to slide across the drive. He noticed her looking at him and smiled.

"Lucin-*san, ikaga desu ka?*" he asked. "How are you?"

"I'm fine, Tami. I'm also glad you could come." She stepped back from the door to allow him room. He moved into the entry hall as if he owned the place.

"I am honored to be invited into your lovely home," he smiled, not really looking around.

"Please come to the dining room," said Lucin, only slightly flustered. "Tea is waiting." She walked a few feet in front of him, and could feel his hand again on the small of her back. Goosebumps traced their way lightly up her spine. She thought she heard him chuckle. Once seated, he became all business, and began to explain to her the intricacies of designing a garden. They had talked about fifteen minutes when Lucin heard James enter the kitchen. She called to him and he made his way to the dining room. Tami stood up. He and James looked at each other as she made introductions. James bristled a bit and rose to his full height, then bowed slightly from the waist, never taking his eyes from Tami.

"*Konnichi wa, Tamiko-san,*" he said. "*Dozo suwaru. Gomen nasai, nihon go ga hanasemasen.*"

78

"*Wakarimasu*, James-san," laughed Tami, returning his bow. "*Yoi Taihenyoi. So desu?*"

"*Hai, honto*," James smiled back. "*Iye, kotaba shirimasen.*"

Lucin looked confused. "What are you two talking about?

"James said hello, asked me to keep my seat, and advised me he did not speak Japanese. I asked him if he were telling me the truth as I thought he did very well. He assures me he *is* telling the truth and does not know many words."

"James," said Lucin, "you never told me you spoke any Japanese."

"I really don't," he replied. "Just enough to find my way back to the ship."

"You honor me, James-san," smiled Tami. "Thank you for your kindness." He turned to face Lucin. "It must be a great comfort," he continued, "to have such a man watching over you. He has the gentleness of a poet and the spirit of a warrior. This man is a loyal friend and an implacable enemy." He turned back to James. "It is my pleasure to meet you, Sir," he continued, offering his hand. "I am pleased to know that Lucin-san is in such concerned and capable care."

James chuckled as they shook hands. "Aye, and 'tis a fine one you are too, Lad. I'm glad to meet you at last."

"And take my measure," said Tami.

"That too, *Tamiko-san*. Make no mistake about it."

"Well?" Tami grinned.

"I expect you'll do. I also expect there is a great deal more to ya than you let on. I know you've had considerable effect on Lucille here, but it seems to be for the best. If I have any doubts on that score I'll come visit with ya privately, y'know."

"My door is always open to you, James-*san*."

"Aye. Ya can count on that, Tommy me boy." They stood looking at each other, both smiling quietly.

"Are you two done?" asked Lucin, glancing back and forth between them.

"That we are, Darlin'," said James, bowing slightly to Tami. "I'll be on my way. I'll see ya in the mornin' and we'll talk about the house." He backed through the doorway and was gone. Tami relaxed off the balls of his feet and sat down.

"What was all that about?" asked Lucin, slightly shaken.

"He loves you," smiled Tami.

"He threatened you."

"He was totally within his right to do so. In his position I would have done exactly the same."

"What?"

"James sees himself as your protector. As such, it is his duty to let me, someone who is outside your home circle but still has influence on you, know that he will stand for no nonsense."

"What you and I do is our business!"

"Of course it is, and James knows that. You're missing the point. He would never interfere with us, but he wanted me to know that if I ever caused you a problem that you felt strongly enough to involve him in, James would be in it until the end."

"Oh. I see," said Lucin, feeling slightly proud of James.

"He is very devoted to you. If someone were to cause you harm, I expect he would deal with them rather harshly. In James, you have a true ally and friend. That should please you. He is a good man." Tami paused and a slow smile overtook his face. "He certainly put me in *my* place."

"That doesn't seem to overly distress you."

"Not overly, no. I have no intention of angering him or you. James and I will do fine. You and I are already doing fine."

"We are?"

"*Hai,* Lucin-*san.* In more ways than you know."

Tami retrieved a sketchpad from his van, and they spent nearly an hour by the house as he made notes and drawings. Lucin described to him what she wanted and he put it into perspective and form. At the end of the session she looked at a rough drawing as they stood on the deck.

"That's wonderful. You really caught what I saw and felt."

"It will take me a couple of days to do the finished draft, then we'll discuss plants and groupings, and decide on exactly how it will go together."

"How do you do this? Do you remember gardens from your childhood in Japan?"

"Sure. So do you."

"So do I what?"

"Remember gardens from your childhood in Japan."

"I've never been to Japan."

Tami touched her cheek. "I didn't say *this* childhood, Moon Blossom."

ELEVEN

Quiet memory waits for me.
Remembrance stirred from shadows
Of another time,
As real as now …
As fleeting as dew on waking grass.

LUCIN WAS NERVOUS. Tami was coming over. During the three days since he had visited her home and done the preliminary drawings of the garden, she'd felt out of balance. Her sleep had been erratic, her days rippled with lethargy and bursts of energy, her emotions alternating from near euphoria to near depression. James had noticed and asked about it, but she had cut him off almost cruelly. He smiled and kept his distance the way men do from women they believe have gone a bit hormonal, biding his time until she returned to normal, treating her with exaggerated concern and care. This afternoon, with the impending arrival of Tami, James had vanished entirely. Sitting in the kitchen musing on James' behavior, Lucin felt a brush of warmth across the small of her back. She opened the side door as Tami stepped up on the landing. In his right hand he carried his sketchpad, in his left was a large, nearly flat rectangle wrapped in heavy brown paper.

"Good afternoon, Lucin," he smiled. "As always, you travel directly from my eyes to my heart."

"Hello, Tami," she blushed. "What a lovely thing to say. Come in."

He moved past her and carefully leaned the large parcel around the corner against the dining room wall.

"What was that?" she asked, as he tucked it out of sight.

"It is your first housewarming gift. Please do me the honor of accepting it as an unworthy attempt to show my esteem."

"Thank you. I am honored by your graciousness." She carefully bowed from the waist. "*Arigato goziemashita, Tamiko-san.*"

"Very good, Lucin-*san*!" he laughed. "Very well said!"

"I've been practicing," she grinned. "Tea?" she added, gesturing to the kitchen table.

"Fruit juice if you have it," he replied. "I have not eaten since breakfast and I could use a little nourishment."

She rummaged in the fridge for a moment. "Orange-pineapple?"

"Wonderful," he said, laying his sketchpad on the table.

"Good. Then we will drink juice and you can show me how beautiful the garden will be."

He looked at her and chuckled. "Lucin, I know these past few days have not been easy for you," he said. "Accepting change is sometimes difficult. Watching your progress is a joy."

"My progress?" she asked, feeling gooseflesh rise on the backs of her arms.

"Of course. In some ways, you are becoming a little Japanese."

Lucin looked at him. His eyes danced. With nothing to say, her only choice was offer him a small bow. It was the Japanese thing to do.

Tami's glass was nearly empty as he watched Lucin intently look over his final sketch. When she turned to him, her face was aglow.

"This is wonderful," she beamed, "really wonderful. Can we do all this? Is there enough space?"

"Certainly. It will not be a walking garden, but a viewing garden. Everything will be downsized. The larger plants and features of the garden will be placed closest to the viewing points, with the smaller foliage and accessories farther away near the rear of the area. This creates the illusion of distance and size. Combine that with wrapping the pool around the corner of the deck with the waterfall at the point farthest away from the house, and it will appear to be much larger than it is. Dwarf maple and plum trees will heighten the illusion and the small Japanese willow beside the waterfall will pull it all together."

"Can we fence it off from view from the house and the neighboring property?"

"A living fence. Bamboo. We will sink large clay chimney tiles twenty-four inches into the earth around the perimeter and plant the bamboo inside the tiles so it won't take over the entire garden. We can probably even get six to seven foot plants, so the garden will appear more finished."

"Tami, it's beautiful."

"I would add one thing," he said, giving her a small bow. "Here at the rear of the house I would extend the deck by the edge of the pond and construct a bath house overlooking the water. It can be enclosed with sliding windows in the winter and opened during warm weather. The tub itself would be for soaking only. Nothing as western as motorized jets or bubbles. Just a simple round tub about six feet across and four feet deep with a built in bench around the perimeter, heated of course, but with subtlety, not splash."

"Perfect."

"It will also leave you with a much more open feeling in your bathroom. Japanese spaces are often very small, so clutter must always be avoided. Simplicity and emptiness make for much better *wa*."

Lucin pointed to what appeared to be a bare spot in the overhead drawing near the edge of the pond on the side of the house. "What goes here?"

"Patience," smiled Tami.

"What?"

"That area is about four feet square. I have shown it covered in washed gravel. It is a place for patience."

"Patience."

"That's correct."

"Alright. When can we get started on the garden?"

"Very good, Lucin," Tami grinned. "Very Japanese. When a question will not or cannot be answered with words, a wise person waits for the answer to be revealed in another manner. Already patience grows in that spot."

Lucin returned his grin. "Perhaps, but not very much. When can we get started on the garden?"

"It has begun. My uncle Eddie is out there by the house as we speak."

"Your uncle Eddie?"

"Well, his name isn't really Eddie, and he's not actually my uncle. Uncle is a term of respect and he has used the name Eddie for years. It's easier to remember and pronounce than his real name. Just call him Eddie. He will not be offended."

Lucin called him Eddie and he called her *Ru-sin-san*. Tiny and bald, Eddie scampered about the piled dirt and hole like a squirrel, pointing at this and that, shouting at Tami in Japanese, stepping off distances, waving his arms, acting out the moods to be portrayed with different plantings in various areas of the garden. Lucin could not tell if he was sixty or eighty but became convinced he was the most alive man she had ever seen. After about fifteen minutes of the display, Eddie walked to Lucin and gave a quick bow.

"Okay," he said. "I do. Very goo'. Garden be all place rest. See with eye, see with heart, see with spirit. *Kami* come heah. You feel bad, come heah, feel betta. Frien' have trouble, bring frien' heah. Trouble reave. You have goo' garden. Much wa. Much peace. Many question come this place. Many ansa come this place. I make for you. Okay?"

"Okay," smiled Lucin.

"Okay," Eddie agreed, snapping off a tiny bow. "Start tomorrow. You talk *Tamiko-san*." He turned and walked off toward the house.

"I guess it's time to go," grinned Tami. "Eddie and his two sons will be back tomorrow and start work on the landscaping. It will all go through me. If he needs anything, I'll tell you. If you have questions, come to me. As far as Eddie's concerned, I am responsible for the garden. I work for you, he works for me. It would be impolite for him to have much direct contact with you. That doesn't mean you can't hang around and watch things progress, it just means that everything relative to design or completion must go through me. I hope that's alright."

"That's fine."

"Good. Try to understand that Eddie is asking the earth to release a portion of itself into his hands. More than just an artist, he is a creator. This garden is, in some ways, a religious commitment to him. He will manifest it through himself in harmony with the spirits of the rocks, trees, plants, water, and soil. Until it is finished, this place will be his life. Even afterward, he or his sons will come here to maintain it on a weekly basis. He will watch it grow and mature as if it were his child and, in many ways, it will be. He knows I understand all this and he is comfortable with me. You are a westerner. He does not understand westerners, nor will he split his concentration from the garden while trying to understand one. That would be an insult to the earth. Eddie will not insult the earth anymore than he would insult his mother. Are you comfortable with that?"

"I guess so."

"Good. It won't take long. He and his boys will be here every day that the weather permits until it is finished. It should only take a few weeks. I'll make a full list of what is needed from the nursery and such. In a day or two, you and I will go spend a lot of your money."

"What about the bath house?"

"Eddie will build it."

"The tub?"

"Eddie will build it. He or his sons will plumb it and wire it too. It will pass inspection and easily surpass code. Now, I must go. He will be impatient to get started. Stay here and enjoy the garden as you see it in your mind. Listen for the water, smell the plants, feel the *wa*. Leave your impressions in the air and the earth. Eddie will use them to help guide his work."

"You're serious, aren't you?" Lucin asked.

"Completely. As the pebble sinks to the bottom of the pool, its path can still be traced upon the surface of the water."

"Ah …" Lucin smiled, "you inscrutable Orientals."

Tami grinned. "Ain't we somethin'?" He turned and headed for the house.

Lucin spent the next hour walking through the house, finally attaining a vision of what she wanted to achieve in the interior, then stood in various places where the garden would grow, allowing herself to relax and be in the moment. From the corners of her eyes she caught glimpses of iris blooming beside water, wisteria hanging above delicate ferns, a moss covered stone lantern, clumps of dense mondo grass, a gnarled juniper, a lotus balanced on its own reflection in a still pool, a planked bridge, a thousand shades of green and gray, black and brown, each separate yet all together.

From deep within her the tension of the past few days released and Lucin stood smiling as the tears came. This was to be *hers*. Her refuge, her sanctuary. A place where she would find peace and comfort, solitude and satisfaction, understanding and awareness. Here, the past would lead her to the future with the present as a bridge to other things, other ways, other times. It would be her own "floating world", a place of magic and memory, meaning and mastery. Here the willow could weep with joy, the lily open with possibility, the water splash with promise, the stones wait with anticipation. A long ago garden scrolled behind Lucin's closed eyelids and she was lifted by remembrance.

Opening her eyes in the late afternoon sun, she saw the hole, the piles of dirt, the clods of earth and grass, and she began to laugh. She was still grinning when she entered the side door to the kitchen and found James sipping a cup of tea as he sat at the table.

"Would ya look at that now," he said. "Herself has a smile on her lovely face. Sure and I've been missing that, I have."

She crossed to stand in front of him, leaned down, and took his face between her hands. "Jimmy me boy," she said, "I've treated ya badly the past few days. Ya didn't deserve it and I'm sorry." She kissed him gently on the mouth, lingering just a bit, allowing her tongue to barely graze the inside edge of his upper lip. Surprised by her actions and slightly dizzy, she pulled away a few inches, a startled look on her face.

"Sweet Jesus," said James, gazing up at her. "If that was a apology for something ya did wrong, allow me to encourage ya to fuck up at least twice a day."

Lucin stood up for balance as James wrapped his arms loosely about her waist. She took a half step forward and looked down at him. His upturned face smiled at her from between her breasts. Casually, as if he'd done it for years, he gently stroked her bottom. "Lucille, me darlin'," he grinned, continuing the fondling, "perhaps this would be a good time for me to pour ya some tea."

He stood up slowly, allowing his rising body to brush hers until he was at full height. Moving his hands to her hips, he rocked her back and forth a bit. "Or perhaps you'd care for something of a more substantial nature," he enquired, now looking down at her.

Unable to resist the delicious momentum of the moment and enjoying the growing need in her body, Lucin put her hands on his biceps and reached up to bite him lightly on the chin. James' body gave a tiny tremble and a low grunt rose in his chest. Leaning back from the shoulders and in from the waist, Lucin looked at him, savoring the intimate contact. "Tea, I think," she whispered.

"Aye," came the hoarse reply. James, his hands still on her hips, pulled her tightly against him briefly, then released her and backed up. "Tea it is, then," he said thickly. "Set yourself."

Weakly, Lucin dropped into a chair and resisted the urge to cross her legs against the tight zipper of her corduroy jeans. Heart pounding, she wiped sweat from her upper lip with her thumb as James fussed overlong at the stove, gathering a cup, dropping in a bag, pouring steaming water. At length he turned around and walked stiffly to the table, quickly settling in a chair of his own. He slid the cup in front of her and grinned. "Now, wasn't that interestin'," he said.

"Very," she blushed and began to giggle.

"What are ya laughin' at, then?" James asked, enjoying the look of her.

"Jolee."

"Jolee?"

"Something she said to me a while back."

"Which was?"

Screwing up her courage, Lucin continued. "She said that if I wanted to feel like a girl, I should just let you pat my butt."

"Trust my judgment, Sweetheart," James chuckled. "I did, and Jolee was right. You felt just like a girl."

Laughing, Lucin flipped her teabag at him. "You know what I mean!"

James picked the bag up off the floor and placed it on the table. "Sure. I know exactly what you meant," he teased. "And let me offer my full cooperation in such matters in the future. Should you require my assistance, I am at your disposal."

"You're too kind."

"Aye," he said sadly. "It's a curse."

"Poor baby." They smiled at each other for a few moments, holding eye contact, enjoying the intimacy. Then James spoke.

"So, about the garden. Is it all settled?"

"I think so. As far as the contractor is concerned, Tami is in charge. Everything will be done through him. I've also decided how I want the interior of the house done. I'll need to talk with the architect so things can get started there, too."

"It seems this might be a good time for me to head off to Florida to do some fishin', if it's alright with you."

"Of course it's alright with me. Expenses paid. You have more than earned some time away. I'll miss you, James. Are you taking Connie with you?"

"Alas, no. Connie is no more."

"What?"

"Aye. Her mother has taken ill in Chicago and her father can't cope all by himself. Constance left two days ago to relocate and be closer to her family."

"James, I'm sorry."

"No point in bein' sorry about life. Things happen."

"You must miss her."

"Sure. She's a fine lass."

"Then this would be a good time for you to get away."

"I suppose," he sighed. "If you find it agreeable, I'll spend tomorrow gathering what I'll need and be on me way."

"That's fine. Whatever you'd like." James rose and wandered toward the door. Lucin trailed along behind him. At the doorway he turned to face her.

"Well then," he said.

She looked up into his face. "I really can trust you, can't I James."

"You can do, be, or say anything, Lucille. With James O'Doud you are absolutely safe."

She stood on her toes to give him a peck on the cheek and James had her, one hand behind her head, the other at the small of her back. Full length against her, he took the breath from her lungs and gave it back, then took it again in a kiss so demanding and urgent, so deep and intimate, that she hung in his arms like a rag. Without will or strength, she gave all she could and took all she could from the vortex that swirled around her. Helpless, she succumbed to it and let it take her, lost in its upward spiral, gone in its timeless caress.

Without a word, James released her against the doorframe and vanished into the growing dark. Weak and dizzy, she slid quietly to the floor, panting as she heard his door slam, trembling as she felt his car leave the drive.

It was ridiculous. She was a married woman! James was old enough to be her father! She was acting like she had no commitment, no responsibility, no obligations, no … morals! This absolutely had to stop, this *thing* with James. Sure he had a profound effect on her. It took her nearly ten minutes to get off the floor. James was a very attractive man, very self-assured and masculine, but she wasn't some cheerleader mooning over a senior, she was a full-grown woman with duties and constraints! Now here she was, sitting alone in the kitchen, reminding herself to be a good girl, all because some big Irishman had rubbed her behind and kissed her.

God! Now she was lying to herself! James didn't start it, *she* did. *She* kissed him while he sat in the chair. *She* licked his lip, *she* initiated the contact. When he escalated the encounter, she could have broken away, she could have stopped the whole thing right there, but she didn't. Only when James deliberately gave her a choice did she back off. Only when he laid the responsibility for the whole thing in her lap, did she actually get a grip on her emotions. With the slightest bit of extra effort, he could have had her on the kitchen table! If he had treated her the way he treated Jolee, she would have climbed him like a rope, husband, home, reputation be damned!

That kiss! That kiss at the door blew out all the stops. His hands on her bottom were wonderful, his body sliding up hers delightful, their bellies against each other marvelous ... but that kiss! It was as if he inhaled a part of her soul. She'd never felt so helpless, so overwhelmed by a man in her life. In that one kiss he drained her of any will but his own. He could have said anything, asked anything, done anything with her at that moment, and she would have celebrated the chance to part of it with him. It wasn't the domination of the female by the male. It was her need to surrender to James. Instead, he left her leaning against a wall for support and even that wasn't enough. She was so far gone in the midst of him and the need for him that she couldn't even stay on her feet. She had never been kissed like that, never knew anyone could be kissed like that! The whole thing was completely past her experience.

Once, at a party when Harrison was a new junior partner at the firm, one of the veterans gave him a piece of advice. In his way, James had told her the very same thing.

"If you wanna run with the big dogs, Kid, you better be willing to do more than just bark."

She had just been run over by one of the big dogs, and she loved it. In spite of all the reasons she should not even consider such a thing, she wanted more of it. And, James was gone.

Lucin was halfway up the stairs on her way to bed, when she remembered the package that Tami had placed in the dining room. Trooping back down, she collected it and struggled its two by three foot bulk into the bedroom. She placed it on the dresser across from the bed and leaned it against the mirror. A pair of cuticle scissors pierced the paper and she carefully pulled the wrapping away. It was the picture, the one with the *Mama-san* and the young girl in the snow that had so captivated her at Tami's shop. She backed up and sat heavily on the bed, staring at it intently. The picture washed over her and she began to cry. At length, she lay back on the bedspread and let go.

"Sweet child, why are you so sad?"

"Oh, *Mama-san*, I have worked so long and practiced so hard, yet sometimes I feel like I will never take my place among the ladies."

"You are an excellent student, Moon Blossom. It is only your age that limits you."

"I do not want to complain, *Mama-san*. I hold you in the highest esteem, and being here with everyone is great joy. I should learn to control my impatience. Please forgive me. *Sumimasen, Mama-san*, I am sorry." The girl had such a pitiful look in her eyes that the old woman began to chuckle.

"*Gomen nasai*, Blossom, so sorry, I am not laughing at you. I laugh at the reason for my visit and why it will bring you both joy and relief."

"*Nan desu ka*? What is it, *Mama-san*?" the girl asked, excitement creeping into her voice.

"*Izumi-san* tells me that your Lotus has begun to bloom. Is that correct?"

"Yes, *Mama-san*. It has bloomed with the new moon for six months now."

"She also tells me that around your Heavenly Pavilion there has grown a hedge. Is this also true?"

"Oh very yes!" exclaimed the girl, becoming excited by the line of questioning.

"That is why I have brought you this," said the woman, reaching into the sleeve of her kimono and withdrawing a wrapping of heavy black silk. She laid it on the mat in front of the girl. "It is yours," she said. "Open it."

With trembling hands, Moon Blossom carefully unwrapped the layers of material until she disclosed the contents. "A *Harigata*!" she exclaimed, her eyes eagerly traveling over the piece of carved ebony. "It's mine?"

"Yes, child. It is yours. Now you have the best part of a man that is even better than the best part of a man, for it will never snore, never complain, never fart, and never grow wilted and soft when you need it most."

"Oh, *Mama-san*! *Arigato goziemashita*! *Domo arigato*!"

"You are very welcome, Blossom. Think nothing of it. It is time for you to have a *Harigata* of your own. It is time for your Jade Gate to be opened."

"And after my Jade Gate is opened, I will learn of the world of pleasure!"

"That is correct," laughed Mama-san, enjoying the young girl's enthusiasm.

"And then I will be ready for Steaming Shafts and Torrid Turtles and Peerless Pestles and Beauteous Barbs!"

"In time, yes, my child."

"I will open my Jade Gate tonight," said the girl, then paused with furrowed brow. "Will it hurt, *Mama-san*, to open my Jade Gate?"

"Possibly. I will send *Izumi-san* to your bedchamber this night to assist you and make sure all goes well. She will spend the next few nights with you and your *Harigata*. You have much to learn. She will help you enjoy acquiring knowledge of how to bring yourself pleasure. When you know how to bring pleasure to yourself, you will be better aware of how to bring pleasure to others. When you know how to accept pleasure from yourself, you will be more willing to accept pleasure from others."

"I promise, I will do my best," said the girl, caressing the carved ebony with both hands.

"I'm sure you will, Moon Blossom," smiled the old woman. "Just remember that the night is for magic, and magic answers only to itself."

"Thank you, *Mama-san*. Thank you very much."

Smiling in her sleep, Lucin Montgomery also offered thanks to the *Mama-san*.

TWELVE

Past and present shadows intertwine
As silk sleeves soaked in darkness.
Does the rose remember
Yesterday's dew?
Do I?

THE NEXT MORNING Lucin slept late, schlepping her way into the kitchen in baggy sweats at nearly nine o'clock to find Stephanie unloading groceries.

"Morning, Steph," she yawned, dropping into a chair.

"Morning, Lucin," Stephanie grinned, giving her the once-over. "Coffee?"

"Desperately."

"In your hair?"

"A cup will be fine," Lucin smiled. "God, I can't wake up. I'm so foggy."

"If James comes in and sees you like that, he's gonna give you a real hard time," Stephanie laughed, pouring coffee and bringing it to the table.

The comment hit Lucin like a blow. "No James today," she said. "He's taken some time off to go fishing."

No James today, tomorrow, the next day, or the next. No teasing, no exaggerated brogue, no wonderful insights, no easy wisdom, no tender hands, no comfortable chest, no ... no James. Oh my. It was as if someone let the air out of her, leaving her deflated and empty. After the fondling and that amazing kiss of yesterday, facing James today would not have been easy and she felt a certain amount of relief that she didn't have to deal with it, but it was infinitely preferable to not having James around at all. What? Stephanie was saying something ...

"I'm sorry, Steph. What did you say?"

"Just that James is a nice man."

"Yes, he is."

"I'll miss him."

"So will I."

"I know."

Conversation ceased. Stephanie began washing counters and appliances as Lucin stared into her coffee, shoulders hunched, lightly hugging herself. She missed James more at this moment than she'd ever missed Harrison. That wasn't right. Neither was the way she'd behaved with James. She led him on, encouraged him. Against all her upbringing, all her training, all her beliefs, all her morality, she had made advances toward another man.

"It's a quarter to ten, Lucin."

"What?"

"It's a quarter to ten," Stephanie repeated. "You have a ten-thirty appointment."

"Oh, shit … uh, shoot! Shit!" stammered Lucin, as she bolted for the stairs.

Thirty-five minutes later, showered, brushed and combed, wearing penny loafers with pennies and without socks, straight-legged stone washed blue jeans, a heavy white broadcloth shirt, and a plum lightweight hooded Gore-Tex shell, she hit the driver's seat of the Jag, turned on the wipers to keep the light mist off the windshield, and tore down the drive. Eddie and two other men were at work beside the guesthouse. She was less than five minutes late when she walked in the front door of *Nails*!

"Hey, Sweetie!" shouted Jolee as she headed for the coffee pot. "Cuppa mud?"

"Thanks, Jolee. Black."

"Comin' up. Have a seat."

Lucin hung up her damp jacket and eased into a chair at the manicure table just as the front door opened and Tami stepped into the room.

"*Konnichi wa*, ladies," he smiled. "I hope you will forgive my rude intrusion this morning."

"I could forgive you of damn near anything, Tommy-son," grinned Jolee. "Want some coffee?"

"Thank you, no, Jolee. I must return to my store in spite of your very kind offer," he smiled at her, his eyes sparkling.

She raised an eyebrow and looked at him speculatively. "Maybe someday I'll make you an offer you can't refuse."

"Can the bamboo refuse the offer of the rain? Can the lotus refuse the offer of the sun?"

Jolee grinned. "Can the bullshit get any deeper in here?"

"Not with the shoes I'm wearing," laughed Tami. "I came in to ask Lucin-*san* to drop by on her way out." He turned to Lucin. "I have a list of plants and materials for you."

"Already?"

"Eddie is impatient."

"Okay. I'll be over when I'm done here."

"Very well," he said, opening the door. "Thank you, ladies. I'll return to my store enriched by your beauty and grace." Tami bowed and was gone.

"God, our kids would be beautiful," said Jolee, sipping her coffee and sitting across from Lucin. "Let's see those claws, Kiddo, and catch up. How ya doin?"

The entire story came out. Lucin told her everything about the encounter with James.

"Wow."

90

"It's getting serious, Jolee."

"Maybe. Probably not."

"What's that supposed to mean?"

"You pushed a button, he pushed a button ..."

"He could have had me, Jolee."

"So what? He coulda had you months ago if he'd wanted to. If James turned it loose on you, you'd fold like a cheap lawn chair, and you know it," Jolee grinned.

"A cheap lawn chair?" Lucin laughed.

"Work with me, for chrissake!" giggled Jolee. "Suppose James had gotten rug burns on his knees and your shoulder blades, what's the big deal?"

"What's the big deal!?"

"Yeah."

"The big deal is I would have made love with a man other than my husband!"

"No, you would have *fucked* a man other than your husband. You and James make love every time you get around one another! You have a whole relationship that is based on the fact that you love each other. Fucking is just mutual masturbation! Making love is something else entirely. You and James make love all the time. It's only natural that you'd wanna play giggle and grab. Christ, I'd jump James in a heartbeat, and I *don't* love him. Who the hell you think you are ... Saint Joan? She was probably a dyke anyway."

"I don't know what to do."

"Fuck him."

"Jolee!"

"Okay, *don't* fuck him. Have fun, don't have fun. That's not what's important."

"What *is* important?"

"Do you wanna run off with James, get a vine covered cottage, and have his babies?"

"No!"

"There ya go! If you wanted to spend the rest of your life with him, then you'd have a problem. Wanting to get down and dirty isn't a problem, it's just natural. You oughta go out with me sometime. We'll hit a couple of bars, eyeball some butts, shake a little ass, turn a few guys down and have a *great* time. I guarantee you will not be groped and you will not fall in love. I also guarantee that you'll be wet enough to slide down a thirty foot banister with no panties on, friction free."

"*Jolee!*" Lucin shrieked.

"Don't tell me you don't like being looked at, I know better."

"Well ..."

"And don't tell me you don't like being in control either."

"Well ...

"Uh-huh.

"I guess what really bothers me is that this morning I realized I'll miss James more than I do Harrison."

"Not true."

"What?"

"Not true. You know Harrison. You've lived with him for years. You've been intimate with him for years. He holds no surprises. He is *probable*. You won't miss

James nearly as much as you miss the James *possibility*. Possible is almost always more fun to fantasize about than probable."

"Hummm."

"Gotcha, Honey."

"I never thought about it like that."

"Whatdaya mean you'll *miss* James? Is he gone?"

"For a week or two. His girlfriend has moved away and he had planned a vacation to go fishing, so he took some time off."

"His girlfriend left?"

"Uh-huh."

"Gee, that's a real shame," Jolee grinned. "Maybe he'll need an understanding and compassionate breast on which to lay his little head."

"Jolee ..."

"A firm embrace to ease his troubled spirit."

"Jolee ..."

"Some silken thighs on which to rub his beard."

"Jolee!" Lucin giggled.

"If you don't wear him out before I get my mitts on him, I might take old James on the ride of his life!"

"Jolee, stop it!" Lucin choked.

"Hang around with me for awhile, Sweetie, and you'll admit one of life's basic truths."

"What?" Lucin laughed.

Jolee looked her very seriously. "Girls just wanna have fun," she said. "And we deserve to."

Lucin found Tami sitting at his counter looking over two full legal pad sheets of list.

"I need all that?" she enquired.

"Probably. Perhaps even more. There are always things forgotten. Wanna go spend money?"

"Now?"

"Sure. Lunch is on me, if you can stand to cater to a Japanese appetite."

"Uh ... I'll try. You mean Sushi or raw fish? Something like that?"

"Even more exotic."

"Like what?" she asked. He smiled at her concern.

"Pizza. I'm Japanese and that's what I'm hungry for."

"Fine with me," she grinned.

"Great. I'll slide into Mazzio's and get us a couple of slices on the way. Your car?"

"Okay. Where we going?"

"Single Tree Nursery, way south. We'll get to ride in our own golf car in the rain. You'll love it."

Thirty minutes later that's exactly what they were doing, pulling out of the parking area at the nursery in a light rain shower, Tami at the wheel of an open golf car.

"Wonder what this baby will do?" he asked, and floored the accelerator. They rocketed down a narrow gravel path at twenty miles an hour, Lucin bouncing helplessly and laughing.

That's how they spent the afternoon. Tami tearing up and down paths, stopping to throw a tree in the cart's tiny bed, then roaring off to the main building to deposit his prize. Back and forth they went. Laceleaf Japanese maple, flowering quince, lily of the valley, seed pine, black pine, dwarf willow, river birch, blue carpet juniper, Irish moss, and more collected in their pile. Tami also ordered washed pea gravel, cypress mulch, and together they chose several large and many smaller stones. Sodden and soaked, they went inside the warm building where Tami picked out the liner, pumps, and filter for the pond, drip irrigation components, and an overhead misting set up.

"We'll install an automatic irrigation grid for the garden so watering by hand will not be necessary. We'll also mount some misting nozzles in the branches of that big oak tree that hangs over the side of the garden, as well as under the rafters over the roofed portion of the deck. The misters in the shady area will help keep the temperature down during hot weather and promote the growth of moss. If it's ninety-five out there this summer, you'll be able to sit out on your decked area with the misters on, and it will feel like it's eighty. I want you to be able to enjoy this garden anytime, regardless of the weather. With the help of the overhead watering and moss spores, we can age your garden five years by August. Trust me."

"I do, you know," smiled Lucin.

Tami turned and looked at her. "Of course you do," he murmured. "You always have, child."

Something moved between them then, as Lucin felt a warm pressure in her chest and got a little light headed. She grasped a display rack of bamboo chimes for support and their wonderful sound echoed throughout the large building.

"That's what we forgot," Tami smiled. "Chimes."

It was after five when they, bedraggled and dirty, headed back into town.

"Find a drive-thru and we'll grab a burger," Tami said. "I'm starving. My treat."

"Speaking of your treat, I never did thank you for the lovely print you gave me."

"It is nothing."

"It's much more than nothing," she insisted. "You know I was drawn to that painting."

"Sure. Did it give you dreams?"

"It gave me dreams," she admitted.

"Good. We won't talk about the dreams because you are driving and I want to make it home in one piece."

"You know so much more that you'll confess, don't you?" she asked.

Tami smiled at her. "There's a Burger King coming up on the left side. Try that."

They got their food and Lucin parked the car so they could eat.

"Don't you?" Lucin asked around a mouthful of fries.

"Don't I what?"

"Don't you know a lot more about what I've been going through these past months than you'll admit."

Tami took a bite of burger and regarded her. "Uh-huh," he said.

"I've known you before, haven't I?"

He chewed for a moment, then swallowed. "Not exactly, but sort of."

"What's that mean?"

He sighed. "It wasn't exactly you and it wasn't exactly me, but we were sort of both in there somewhere with two people who did know each other."

"What?"

"You're gonna love this," he grinned. "There is no simple answer, but the answer is very simple. Even though all things constantly change, everything remains as it was. Our essence, yours and mine, never changes ... yet you and I are always in flux. We never stay the same. That is why when you asked if you had known me I gave you the answer I did. Even though you and I have been in each other's company before, this is the first time we have been together."

"Oh, that's clear," she laughed.

"I know that you have undergone some real changes. You are not the person you were six months ago, nor are you the person you will be six months from now. One of the reasons we have met is to assist in some of the changes. This is also why you know Jolee and James. It is opportunity for growth. Yours, mine, and theirs. Nothing happens by accident. You are green, Lucin, and you should be glad you are."

"I should be glad I'm green?"

"Sure," he grinned. "If you're green, you grow. If you're ripe, you rot."

"Oh, great."

"It is also impossible to grow without assisting others in their growth. It's all intertwined."

"Don't be offended, but this sounds like so much metaphysical clap trap."

"That's because much of the popular side of metaphysics is clap trap. I will tell you this. Things will become clearer soon, but with each answer will come more questions. At the risk of sounding like a sideshow psychic, there is no destination. There is only the journey. What is required from any of us is acceptance. Understanding comes at its own pace."

"Which means that you are not going to tell me anything."

"Pretty much," he grinned.

"Well," she said, starting the car and returning his grin. "If you're not gonna put out, I'll just take you home."

"Don't give up," he laughed. "There's always next time."

"There'll be a next time?"

"Ah, Moon Blossom," he whispered, and she felt warmth grow at the small of her back. "Always there is a next time."

THIRTEEN

How did you vanish so easily
As if into evening fog?
Even spring's rain
Descending from nothing,
Falls on me here.

HARRISON WAS HOME FOR SEVERAL DAYS during the next three weeks. Lucin felt a distance of her creation between them, but could not seem to do anything about it. She tried to be caring and accommodating to him, they even made love twice, but she was not really there. She felt as if she were not really anywhere. Harrison, terribly busy with interviews and arrangements for the new offices, didn't seem to notice. He gave the construction of the house and garden only a passing glance, not even walking to the site to see what was transpiring, and seemed distractedly amused at the importance Lucin attached to the project. It was as if they were orbiting separate spheres, their paths touching briefly with each revolution as both followed a different course. Far from dismayed by the situation, Lucin found herself to actually be relieved. She had invested in Harrison for many years. The call to finally invest in herself was strong, and she was glad to have little distraction.

The house was coming along very well. The ruined bedroom was now the outside deck, walled off with floor to ceiling windows and glass doors, concealed on the inside by sliding *shoji* screens; and the floor had been patched and covered in hardrock maple stained glossy oxblood. The sidewalls were board and batten of rough sawn ash, stained light almond. The few stationary interior walls were covered in pale yellow raw Chinese silk. The ceiling, rising now to fourteen feet, was finished the same as the outside walls, only slightly darker, with the beams and joists matching the floor. The skylights were in place, the kitchen and bath flooring completed in gray and green slate tiles, and *shoji* screens closed off the sleeping area but had yet to be installed throughout the rest of the house. The kitchen appliances and cabinets were still to be fitted, and the bathroom walls, most of the trim, the lighting fixtures and sconces, the window treatments, and the installation of the heating and cooling units remained undone.

The garden was formed, complete with the unlined pond. The water lines were laid and buried, the rockwork for terracing was in place, the bath house and tub finished and waiting, the misting nozzles attached to the large oak and the underside of the deck ceiling, seven foot bamboo from Eddie's own garden had been planted in tiles around two sides of the perimeter, and all the small trees, save the dwarf willow which would hang partially over the pond, had been placed. All that remained was the installation of the liner, the addition of water, ferns, shrubs, flowers, grasses, mulch, gravel, and accent stones for the garden to be complete.

Returning to the kitchen after taking the workers a pitcher of mid-morning raspberry tea, Lucin heard Stephanie answer the phone.

"James! How are you? That sounds like fun. Fine, still the same. No. She went too, oh! Here she is. I didn't hear her come in. Just a minute. Lucin, it's James. He wants to talk to you. I'm on the way to the market. I'll be back in a couple of hours." She handed Lucin the phone as she went out the door.

"James, hello."

"Ah, Lucille, me darlin' and fair, how are ya then?" came the chuckling reply.

"It's good to hear your voice, James."

"Aye and yours too."

"It's been three weeks. I miss you. When are you coming home?"

"I miss you too, Sweetheart. I figure I can live without ya for just another week, and I'm on me way back."

"I don't know if that's acceptable. The original deal was for two weeks. You've already gone over your limit."

"I didn't think you and I had any limits."

"James O'Doud, this house is empty without you in it, but it will be here whenever you decide to come back."

"And where might you be, then?"

"Waiting right here."

"Is that a fact?"

"Aye, Jimmy me boy, that is a fact."

"What if I decide to stop off in Rhode Island on me way?"

She laughed. "You might find me waiting there for you."

"Well, Lucille, if I don't find ya in Rhode Island, maybe I'll find ya in the kitchen."

The side door swung open, and there, cell phone in hand, stood himself, James Mathew O'Doud.

"Sorry James," said Lucin, "I have to go. An Irishman just came through the door." She dropped the phone, took three steps, and leaped.

James plucked her out of the air in a full body hug, her arms around his neck, her feet six inches off the floor. He easily held her there, laughing into her ear as she laughed into his, enjoying the moment and the welcome.

"Aw, Jimmy," she blurted while kissing his cheek, "it's good ta see ya."

"Sure, Lucille," he said, returning the kisses, "and it's a sight ye are yourself."

Resisting the urge to wrap her legs around him, Lucin pulled back and kissed the end of his nose. "Are you going to put me down?"

"Don't spoil the moment. I'm enjoying myself," he replied, shifting his weight so her lower body swung from side to side. "How 'bout you?"

"Of course."

"Well, now that you've admitted it, I'll let ya go," he said, allowing her to slide ever so slowly downward along his body until her feet finally reached the floor.

By the time she stood independent of his support Lucin was in full blush. His arms still around her, James kissed her gently on the lips, then pulled back a quarter of an inch.

"Red looks good on ya, Lucille," he said, releasing her and taking a step backward.

"Coffee?" she croaked, fighting the glow in her belly.

"No," James croaked back.

"Tea?" she said, reaching for his forearms and tightening her knees.

"Not that either."

"There must be something you want," she asked, embarrassed by her words and loving the growing itch.

"Aye, that's true," he replied, his voice thick and low.

Lucin stepped forward so they were nearly touching, feeling her nipples harden and the glow begin to spread. She raised her face, loving the moment. "And what would that be?"

James dropped his right hand and rested the palm across her low belly and upper thigh.

"That," he said, "would be enough." He spun her around and slapped her lightly on the bottom. "I'm goin' down to look at the place, why don't you take a cold shower."

"Me!"

"Aye," James grinned, backing out the door. "It appears to me that ya might be in a state. I'll be back in a bit. That'll give ya time, if you'll pardon the expression, to get a grip on yourself."

Lucin sat at the table and crossed her legs. It was sometime before she realized she was smiling. She hadn't smiled much in the last three weeks.

An hour and a half later they sat together as Lucin worked on half a chicken salad sandwich and James devoured two with chips and iced tea.

"They're doin' a grand job," he said. "Another week or two and the whole project will be done. It's back to the limo service for me."

"Not necessarily," Lucin said. "Harrison would like you to consider working for his firm. They're going to lease a stretched Mercedes and will need a driver to be available on short notice. The job is yours if you want it. You can stay here and they'll give you a beeper or a cell phone. You'd have to be available twelve hours a day six days a week and you'd keep the car with you. You'd make about what you're making now, plus benefits."

"When would the job start?"

"In about a month. They're moving staff and equipment in now. They'll put you on retainer as a contract employee until then."

"And I'd still have to hang around with you?"

"'Fraid so."

James raised an eyebrow. "Could I depend on you behavin' yourself?"

Lucin smiled. "Probably not," she said.

"I'll take it."

"Together again."

"You won't be my employer any more, right?"

Puzzled, she looked at him. "Right. Why?"

"I just realized that I'll have no recourse with a sexual harassment suit," he said.

Lucin winked. "Why don't we fall off that bridge when we get to it," she said.

"Aye, and it's a peach ya are, Lucille. I did miss ya and I do love ya. Now I have to go look for a furnace and air-conditioner for your new digs, then price some counter tops and cabinets for the kitchen and a hood for the hibachi." He stood up and she rose with him. "I'll see ya tomorrow."

"I have an early appointment to get my nails done. Will you be here for lunch?"

"Count on it," he said, examining his fingers. "Whatdaya think? Do I need a manicure?"

"You?"

"If I'm gonna be driving around a lot of those high-priced lawyers and such, I need to look my best."

Lucin's grin got wider. "I'm pretty sure Jolee would make every effort to accommodate your needs," she teased. "Want me to ask her for you?"

"That's a very kind offer, and I know you make it from the heart, but I think my nails will have to do the way they are."

"Just trying to help."

"Sure ya are," he said, opening his arms. "I'll see ya tomorrow."

"I'm glad you're home, Jimmy," she whispered, moving into his embrace and snuggling against his chest.

"Lucille, me darlin'," he murmured, "so am I."

That night after a long hot bath, Lucin got the best night's sleep she'd had in weeks.

After her early appointment with Jolee, Lucin walked down to the guesthouse to look around and found Eddie and his sons placing the liner in the pool. She watched them work for a while, positioning perimeter stones, gradually filling the liner with water, constantly re-arranging rocks as the liner shifted and stretched. After about two hours all appeared to be in order and Eddie moved to the back corner of the excavation behind a built-up pile of earth and stones. All of a sudden, water flowed from between the top stones and splashed down the incline, cascading into the pool below. Eddie returned to the garden and watched the waterfall critically. After a moment, he walked to Lucin.

"*Ru-sin-san*," he said. "Watta not goo'. I make betta. You go way, come back almos' suppatime. Much more goo'. Not see now, okay?"

"Okay, Eddie. I'll come back late this afternoon."

"All betta. No forget come back. All betta." He grinned and bowed.

She returned his bow and walked off toward the house.

Stephanie was vacuuming upstairs and there was a note on the kitchen table saying that cornbread was on the counter and navy bean soup was in the fridge. Lucin was lifting bowls out of the cabinet when James came through the door.

"What's for lunch?" he asked, casually moving up behind her and resting a palm on each shoulder.

"Cornbread and beans," she said, leaning back against him to enjoy the warmth of his heart between her shoulder blades. "Beans are in the fridge."

He kissed her ear and moved to rummage in the refrigerator.

"Get your nails done?"

"Yep," she replied, removing the plastic wrap from the corn bread and putting large and small pieces on plates.

"How was Jolee?"

"She seemed a little distracted today. What makes you ask?"

"Just curious," he said, spooning beans into bowls and putting them in the microwave. "Coffee, tea … me?"

"Milk will be just fine," she said, "for now."

"Hope springs eternal, Lucille," James chuckled, getting out milk and glasses.

They ate in silence for a while, glancing and smiling at each other, glad to be together. "So," Lucin said, "what are you up to today?"

"You and I have to go let you choose which counter tops you want and there's a copper range hood I want to show you, plus the cabinets will arrive today and you need to look at a bathtub or two. When all that's done, I am gonna take a wee nap and clean up."

"A nap?"

"Aye."

"What? Got a heavy date tonight?"

"If you must know," James replied, attempting to look indignant, "it's possible that a young lady and I are going out this evening."

"James!"

"What did ya think? I was gonna spend the rest of me life waitin' for you?"

Lucin poked him on the arm and chanted. "James has a *day-ate*, James has a *day-ate!*"

"Saints preserve us," he grumbled.

"Who is it?"

"Now what makes ya think that's any of your tiny business?"

"C'mon. Who?"

"A lady of my acquaintance."

"A name, James. I want a name."

"You may not always get everything you want, y'know."

Lucin stood up and sat on his lap, entwining her arms around his neck and leaning in toward his ear. "Oh please, Jimmy," she begged, loving being naughty. "Please tell me who it is. Please? Pleeeze?"

"Sweet Jesus," cringed James, "I've got a lunatic on me lap."

Shifting her weight back and forth, Lucin nipped at his earlobe. "Jimmy," she growled, "I'd do almost anything for you if you'd tell me. Almost *anything!* Wouldn't you like me to do almost anything for you, Jimmy?"

"If you'll get off me lap before ya break somethin', ya crazy woman, I'll tell ya!"

"Who?"

"Get up."

"Who?"

"Get up!"

"Who, James?"

"Jolee, for chrissakes!"

Lucin shot to her feet. "Jolee?"

"That's right, Jolee," he muttered, leaning over and gasping a bit, "but there may be no point to it. I believe ya may have damaged the little fella!"

"Where are you going?"

"To the emergency room if I can get to the car," he complained.

"You're alright. I didn't feel anything break," she said.

"Perhaps I'll live," he groused.

Lucin pulled her chair over very close to James and sat down, her knees between his. "Where you taking her?"

"Christ, I don't know. Maybe we'll drop by Clancy's for a bite to eat."

"Clancy's?!"

"And what's wrong with Clancy's? You got a snoot full there if I remember correctly."

"That was therapy. This is a date."

"Aw, geeze."

"Ruth's Chris."

"On Forty-Seventh Street?"

"That's the one. Steak and lobster."

"All ya can eat for two hundred dollars."

"Money is no object, James."

"It isn't?"

"What about flowers?"

"Flowers?"

"Gotta have flowers."

"Maybe I'll take her some when I pick her up," James replied hopelessly.

"Nope."

"Of course not. How foolish of me."

"Don't make her have to hassle with a bouquet when you show up. Send one yellow rose, just one, to her shop this afternoon. On the card put something simple and direct like 'see you at eight' or whatever. Give her chocolates when you arrive. Not a big box, just a nicely wrapped selection of six or eight truffles. Then Tuesday, if things go well tonight, send two dozen roses to her shop. Anything but red or white. Lavender is nice. Again a simple card. 'Wonderful' or something like that."

"Anything else?" James said.

"Take the Jag, drink wine, and buy new underwear."

"Good God!" James said. "Why don't I just stay here and rub your lovely bottom. I'd enjoy myself and things would be a lot less complicated."

"I just want you and Jolee to get off to a good start. Besides, you can rub my bottom anytime."

"Is that right?"

She leaned forward and kissed him lightly on the lips. "Count on it, Jimmy."

Around five Lucin walked back to the garden. The waterfall was gurgling nicely, the willow was leaning over the pool beside the cascade, and all the perimeter stones were in place. Eddie was attaching a small wooden box to the side of the oak tree. He noticed her, grinned, and came trotting over.

"You rike?"

"Eddie, it's beautiful."

"Much betta. Watta more goo'. You sit on deck, watch watta, feel peace. Den mosquito come. Buzz aroun', much bite. Not goo', very pain."

"I never thought about mosquitoes. What can we do?"

"Put fish in watta. *Shubukin*. Eat babies. For mosquito in air, have gif' for you."

He slipped on a pair of leather gloves and groped under the edge of the deck, retrieving a small cloth bag. He reached into the bag and brought out a closed fist. Carefully working with the gloved hand he delicately revealed a small furry fanged face.

"Bat," he said brightly. "Got six of dem. Put in house on tree, they stay heah, eat bug and mosquito when fly at night. Mosquito no bite *Ru-sin-san*. All happy. Goo' garden," he beamed.

"Thank you, Eddie. That is very kind of you."

"Welcome. Very peace. Bat goo' ruck. Okay?"

"Okay," she bowed and headed back to the house. Sitting in the kitchen, she began to laugh. James had Jolee, she had six bats. Finally, order had come to her world.

FOURTEEN

As spring blossoms into summer
Perhaps I too
Will open petals to the sun ...
Nectar waiting
For the sip.

SUNDAY MORNING, Lucin was stuffing banana, pineapple, ice, and peach yogurt into the blender for a smoothie, when James came wandering into the kitchen.

"Add some orange juice and another banana and I'll join ya for a glass, Lucille."

"James," she smiled, "how'd your date go?"

"Just mix your concoction and say good morning, ya great busybody," he muttered, stifling his grin.

"Good morning, Jimmy. How'd you and Jolee get along?"

"I don't hear ya mixing anything," he replied.

Lucin kicked on the blender and retrieved two glasses from the cabinet. After a moment's pause as the machine clattered away, she filled the tumblers, carried them to the table, sat with one knee touching James' thigh, and smiled at him.

"Give," she said.

"Give what?"

"Information. How'd it go?"

"How'd what go?" he asked innocently.

"Your evening with Jolee," she replied patiently. "Have a good time?"

Slowly James drank about half his smoothie, then looked at her. "I'm sorry, what did you ask?"

Moving her knee up and down against James' leg, Lucin smiled. "I asked how your date with Jolee went."

"Oh, Jolee! We went out, y'know."

"Really?"

"Sure. Last night."

"No kidding? How was it?"

"How was what?"

"Your evening with Jolee."

"Oh, that. It was okay."

"Okay, huh?"

"Sure. Just a date. You know."

"Whatja do? Whereja go?"

"We went out, we came back. Nothing special," he continued after chugging the last of his juice.

"Quid pro quo, Jimmy. I've told you a lot of things."

"Aye, ya have. And I appreciated your honesty. But I'm sober."

"James," she said, leaning forward and smiling at him. "I am perfectly capable of sitting on your lap and chewing on your ear until you tell me the whole story. Every sordid detail."

"Lucille, me darlin'," he replied, cupping her chin in his hand, "there is very little on this earth that appeals to me more than your lovely bottom warmin' me lap, y'know. And the thought of your delightful arms wrapped around me dirty neck brings chills to me spine, but alas, I've got to be on me way. I've no time to be playin' pattycake with a nosey young wench like yerself today." He kissed her quickly on the lips and stood up.

"James," she threatened, "if you walk out of this kitchen I will never fix you another smoothie."

"I'm gonna miss 'em, Sweetheart," he confessed, grinning at her. "Just like I'm gonna miss you, but I got to be on me way. Have a fine day."

"I have ways of making you talk!" she shouted through the screen at his retreating back, then giggled as she finished her drink.

Looking out the kitchen window, she noticed Eddie's truck parked down by the little house and saw him fussing in the garden. She got out more fruit and yogurt, mixed up another small pitcher of smoothies, grabbed a glass and headed out the door. She arrived at the garden to see Eddie sprinkling water and spreading dirt all over a large pitted stone lantern placed in a bed of ferns near the base of the oak tree. The little man came walking over as she filled the glass.

"*Domo*," said Eddie, smiling at her. "Goo' morning *Ru-sin-san*."

"You're welcome," she replied. "Good morning. What are you doing?"

"Make dirt stick to rantern. Put moss spore on dirt, keep wet in shade with spray up in tree. Pretty soon all moss grow on rantern top. Fern grow on groun'. All in shade unda tree. All dark, all green. Rook old. Put dirt up side of tree. Moss grow up trunk. Rook goo'. Okay?"

"Okay," she smiled.

"Today put fern unda fron' edge deck, both side. Tube bring watta. Fern grow all along board two feet up, aroun' all deck an' bathhouse. You take bath en' of week. Tub goo'. No drip. Very hot. Goo' for *wa*. Okay *wa*?"

"Yes, I understand *wa*."

He looked at her seriously for a moment, weighing something in his mind, then spoke.

"How ma' you Japanee?"

"What?"

"You Japanee. How ma'? Granfadda? Granmodda?"

"Me?" she asked, surprised. "How much am I Japanese?"

"*Hai*. You Japanee in you blut. Fam'ry blut Japanee, yes?"

"Uh … oh, blood! No, no, I have no Japanese blood in my family."

He peered at her. "No? No blut?"

"No."

He looked at her intently, then shrugged. "Okay. Thank for drink. Back to work now, okay?"

"Okay. Just leave the glass and pitcher on the lawn. I'll get them later."

"Okay, reave grass on groun'," he replied, moving back to the lantern.

Lucin walked back to the main house, amused and complimented that Eddie thought she might be part Japanese.

She skated for a couple of hours that afternoon, encountering Kennedy Paige Hartrick and enjoying her company on the ice, flattered at how the young girl attempted to emulate her strokes. After she got home, she worked out lightly for a while, took a long hot bath, wrapped a towel around her head, slipped into her short terry robe and scuffies, and padded downstairs to paw through the fridge. She was sitting at the table, munching an apple and cheddar cheese, when James walked in behind her.

"Mother of God, but you're lovely when you get all dressed up," he teased.

"I want some answers from you, O'Doud," she threatened, not turning around.

"Do ya now? As me dear mother used ta say, 'be careful what ya want, the devil may give it to ya.'"

"If the devil is in this kitchen," Lucin smiled, slowly turning around, "he's behind me. James! Look at you!"

Leaning against the counter, wearing a dark blue double-breasted suit with a gray pinstripe, a brilliantly white silk shirt, and a dark maroon tie, James grinned at her.

"Aye. 'Tis a fine sight that I am. Can ya control yourself then?"

"I don't know," she chuckled, putting her hand over her heart. "I feel I may swoon. You look very nice. *Very* nice."

"From one fashion plate to another," he said, eyeballing her ratty robe and scuffies, "I consider that to be quite a compliment."

"Well, you look great, Jimmy. You really do. Nice suit."

"I had to get somethin' to cover up all me new underwear," he smiled.

"You have new underwear?"

"Aye. Just as you advised me."

"Ooh! Lemme see."

"Now, now, now. Let's not be lettin' your libido get away from ya, Lucille. Maybe I better get out of here while you still have some control of yourself."

"Another date with Jolee?"

"And just what business would that be of yours?"

"Another date with Jolee?"

"Read any good books lately?"

"Another date with Jolee?"

"Holy Mother, there's no stoppin' ya! Here I get all dressed up just to sweep ya off your feet, and you accuse me of seein' another woman."

"All this is for me?" Lucin asked, wide-eyed and open mouthed.

"Aye, but I'm not sure you can take it. Maybe I better leave and let you settle down a bit. Wouldn't want you to get in a state."

"Specially if you transported me across a state line. There're laws against that kind of thing."

"There's laws against all kinds of things you make me think of, Lucille. Have a pleasant evening."

"Take the Jag. Jolee likes the Jag."

"Thanks, but I'll take the Chevy," he replied, rubbing her on the shoulder as he walked by. Stopping by the door, he turned around. "Goodnight, Sweetheart."

"Have fun, James," she said, as he stepped out the door.

Lucin hung around downstairs for a while, then turned in early with a book on oriental design. She was asleep by ten.

Rested and up early the following morning, Lucin made coffee and was well into her second cup when she heard James' car in the drive. She carried her cup to the window seat and watched him quietly open the door and slink two steps into the kitchen, tie askew and carrying his suit jacket.

"Busted," she said. James flinched at the sound of her voice.

"Sweet Jesus," he moaned, not bothering to turn around.

"And just where have you been, young man? I've been waiting up all night. You didn't call, nothing. You could at least be responsible enough to pick up a phone. I'm sorry. You're grounded!"

"Are ya havin' a good time, then?" James asked.

"Great. This is so much fun, it was worth waiting up all night."

"Ya know you can go to the hot place for lyin'."

"Fresh coffee in the pot, big boy. You strong enough to pour your own cup?" She moved back to the table and put her cup and saucer down, then advanced on James, slipping her arms around his neck. "Good morning, Jimmy," she said. "You can rub my bottom if you like."

He draped his arms around her low back and gently patted her upper butt a couple of times. "Sweet Lucille, it's a grand sight ya are," he grinned, giving her a tender hug and a kiss on top of her head.

"That's all you got left, huh?" she teased.

"God, you are relentless," he laughed.

"Never mind. I have my sources," she said, walking to the telephone and dialing. She waited for some time, then spoke.

"Good morning, Sunshine, it's Lucin. Lucin! Get up, get dressed, get out, and meet me for breakfast. I don't care, get up! Get up, get up, get up. What? You bet I am, a big one. Crawl out, splash some water on your face and whatever else that needs it, and meet me at Mama's for breakfast. My treat. Mama's. Across from D'Bronx on Westport Road. So was your mother. Thirty minutes. Don't be late or I'll come looking for you. Okay, Sweetie. See ya soon. Don't forget to put clothes on. I love you too, Jolee. Get your ass outta bed. Bye." She turned and beamed at James.

"You are a vile, twisted, nasty woman, Lucille," he grimaced.

"Can't talk right now, Jimmy me boy. I have to get ready for breakfast."

When she came back downstairs after changing clothes, James still sat at the table, now hunched over a cup of coffee. He looked at her balefully.

"Have a good morning, James," she said, stopping beside him. "I'm off to breakfast." She leaned down and kissed his cheek.

"Evil," he moaned, not looking up. "Evil woman."

She licked his earlobe, giggled, and headed out the door.

Mama's was not overly busy. Lucin seated herself in a booth near the rear facing the door and ordered coffee. Sitting alone at a corner table just inside the entrance, she noticed a man scribbling diligently on a sketchpad. About fifty, he wore his graying hair in a razor cut with two or three earrings in each ear. He had a dark cultivated tan, light blue eyes and wore hiking shoes, stone washed blue jeans with a pressed crease, a lime green polo shirt with a tangerine collar, several rings, and a Rolex that cost as much as a double-wide mobile home. Lucin's coffee arrived as Jolee walked through the door. She scanned the room with slightly bloodshot eyes, spotted Lucin, pulled on a bra strap, and walked to the booth.

"God," said Jolee, as she flopped into the seat. "What makes you think I need company to suffer. I was doing fine by myself."

"Beautiful Monday morning, your shop is closed, I thought you might be lonely. I didn't want you to feel nobody cared about you."

Jolee smiled. "Jesus, you're a terrible liar. Seen James?"

"I was in the kitchen when he came slithering in. I startled him. Looks like you pretty much wore him out."

"Him? Him! How the hell do you think I got in this condition?"

"I'm all ears."

"Now we get to the truth! You just invited me here to get the scoop on me and James."

"Exactly. Talk."

Jolee pulled Lucin's coffee to her side of the table and took a sip. "That," she said, "is one sweet man. He's kind, he's considerate, he's caring, he's ..."

"Friendly, brave, helpful, courteous, reverent ..."

"All right, all right. You ever heard that line about old guys taking all night to do what they used to do all night?"

"I have now," laughed Lucin.

"Well, he takes all night, alright. That boy left tracks all over the place! Christ! He didn't take me anyplace I'd never been before, but we sure visited a lot of seldom seen locations. It's a damn shame for you that you and he never did the wild thing, Sweetie. James spoiled me like a baby. Wow!"

"Wow?"

"Wow. James is an artist. It was marvelous, he was marvelous. We're taking the night off tonight. Time for him to overdose on vitamin E, time for me to treat a severe case of beard burn." She grinned at Lucin. "I am a *very* happy woman. I also like him a whole bunch. It doesn't get much better than this. Tomorrow night, I'm fixing him dinner."

"Wow."

"You betcha, Honey."

"So, you and James are an item?"

"I hope so. We are as far as I'm concerned. We'll see what happens after the sweat dries." Jolee smiled and stared thoughtfully at the tabletop for a moment, then looked up. "He makes me laugh, Lucin, and he touches my face." Tears glistened in her eyes. "It's always the goddammed little things, ya know?"

"James is a wonderful man."

The waiter showed up with another cup of coffee, appeared confused for a moment, and placed it in front of Lucin. They ordered, and Jolee lit a cigarette.

"I didn't know you smoked," Lucin said.

"Five or six a day. Bother you?"

"No. It's fine."

"So what's new with you, Sweetie."

"The house and garden are nearly finished," she replied, looking over Jolee's shoulder at the man in the corner for the fourth or fifth time. "Harrison is out of town a lot, I'm skating about three days a week, and Tami is still crawling around in the back of my head. You know, same old stuff."

"What's so interesting behind me?"

"I'm just looking at that guy at the corner table. He's drawing or something."

Jolee looked over her shoulder, then grinned at Lucin. "That's George. I do his nails." She swiveled back around. "George. George!" she shouted. He looked up. "Come join us, Honey."

"Jolee, you sexy thing, come join *me!*" George shouted, flashing perfectly capped teeth. "More room and our own private corner. Bring that attractive young woman with you, too, Darling! I'd love to be seen with her. Hell, I'd love to *be* her!" He stood up, laughing and clapped his hands. "Hurry girls, come sit with me. It will make my morning!"

Jolee beamed at Lucin. "Grab your coffee, girlfriend. You are gonna love George."

They moved toward the table as George adjusted chairs and made room.

"My God, Jolee," he blurted, gaping at her. "Hard night? Cucumber slices wouldn't touch those peeps! I hope it was worth it. You look like you'll be sore for a week! Kiss, kiss, Love!" He leaned forward and kissed her on both cheeks as she laughed, then turned to Lucin.

"Dear me, aren't you lovely? Peggy Fleming at thirty with a touch of Audrey Hepburn and a dash of Elizabeth Hurley. I am George, my dear. Just George." He took her hand and kissed it.

"Hello, George," Lucin smiled. "I'm Lucin Montgomery."

"Lucin," he mused. "Loo-SIN. Love that last syllable. So sit, sit, sit, and tell me how you possibly came to know this red-haired devil named Jolee."

"She does my nails."

"Mine too! Isn't she wonderful? Rembrandt with a file and orange stick. Just soaking for her is pure pleasure. Imagine how much fun soaking *with* her would be! Oh, pardon me, I am such a serpent," he laughed, and fanned himself. "And you, Lucin," he gushed, "why am I not dressing you? We are worthy of each other, Darling."

"George is a designer," Jolee interjected, noting the confusion on Lucin's face.

"Oh," Lucin replied. "I noticed you sketching while I waited for Jolee."

"Just killing time while slumming," George laughed. "Truth be told, I am not just a designer. I am a costumer. The debutants in Mission Hills feed my body, the local theatre companies feed my spirit, but you, Lovely Lucin, would feed my soul! With you as my canvas, art could be the only outcome. God, I spend so much of my time dealing with petulant, flat-chested, bony teenagers, or their frustrated, saggy-bottomed mommies, that you would be an exercise in ecstasy! Say you'll be mine." He giggled and handed her a card. "Save me from the debs and the droops, Lucin. Let George dress you!"

Laughing, Lucin accepted his card. "Actually," she said, "this could work out very well. I've been feeling a need to add some oriental influence to my wardrobe."

"Japanese, Chinese, Mandarin?"

"Japanese, I think. Silks and cottons."

"Daywear, evening wear?"

"Evening and night wear. And this may seem strange, but perhaps some costumes for skating, too. I'm a figure skater. The skating costumes could be anything. Not only oriental."

"Oh my," said George, "I'm seeing some things now. Stand up, Dear, and turn slowly around."

Rather self-consciously Lucin rose and did as she was asked, then took her seat.

"Now, be honest," beamed George, "for the skating, what are we selling here? Sex or grace?"

Lucin colored a bit. "Sex," she admitted.

"Darling, with you, that is an easy sell. You must call me. We'll get together and let our imaginations run amok!" He glanced at his Rolex. "Shit! Must dash," he exclaimed, leaping to his feet and throwing a ten on the table. "Jolee, you wanton hussy, always a pleasure. Get some rest and some aloe, you hound! Lucin, we are going to be *so* good together. Ta, ladies. George loves you both!" He tore out the door.

"What was *that?*" Lucin laughed.

"That," grinned Jolee, "was a flaming queen who is one of the best designers on the planet. He is one of the sweetest and most talented people I know, and he wants to work for you. Lucin, George has a waiting list of people who want his services. People book designs from him two years in advance of an event, and he actually asked you to come over to his studio."

"Is that okay? I mean, do I have anything to worry about?"

"Only if he breaks a nail," Jolee laughed. "George gets really bitchy if he breaks a nail."

FIFTEEN

What once was I
That led me here?
Ancient ivory calls,
And I am reminded
Of myself.

AFTER JOLEE LEFT to go home for a nap, Lucin sat in Mama's and mused on her encounter with George. He had compared her to Peggy Fleming! Not to mention Audrey Hepburn and Elizabeth Hurley. God! And Eddie thought she might have Japanese in her background. These were not comparisons anyone would had made just a few months past. She *was* changing. Look how intimately she teased James, how she behaved in the Carriage Club bar, how she laughed with Jolee. Some of her recent liberation must show on the outside also. From what Jolee said, the offer George had made was unheard of. Here in the restaurant, dressed in jeans, a light cotton sweater and old running shoes, she'd noticed several men openly looking at her. And, because it was Westport, a couple of women, too.

Then there were the house and garden, probably the most visible outward manifestations of her inward changes. Radically different than anything she would have conceived a few months before, she seemed to grow with them, and it all came back to the first time she walked into Tami's shop. He was at the nexus of all this, all these changes within and without her. Almost beyond her will, the Jag headed for his place. And Lucin, as she was becoming more and more willing to do, went along for the ride.

"Lucin!" Tami said. "By God, howdy!"

"By God, howdy?"

"Just a little change of pace." Tommy chuckled and took both her hands in his. "How are you?"

"I'm fine, Tami," she said, feeling warmth rush up her arms to her shoulders and the room get a little cottony. "I have come to spend money."

"Please," he twinkled, bowing deeply, "allow me to welcome you to my humble shop."

For the next two hours she wandered around his store, gathering purchases. A tea set, a sake set, some lovely silk pillows with heavy embroidery and thick piping along the edges, four pieces of artwork including one of three courtesans playing in the bath, a couple of lovely screens, some candleholders, and several other pieces. Tami left her totally alone unless she had a question, but every time she decided on an item she would feel that familiar warmth in the small of her back and find his eyes on her. She realized she was being guided. She didn't mind. At length, he approached her.

"What else today?" he asked.

"I need a bed, a futon."

"Traditional Japanese?"

"Yes."

"Wrong, Gringo," he grinned.

"Wrong?"

"A Japanese futon is relatively thin so it is easy to roll up and store. It is also made of many layers of cotton. Cotton compresses. Very hard and uncomfortable for western bones. Go to any futon shop and get one with a good core of foam rubber or something comparable. Do not put it on a frame. Put it on the floor on the *tatami* mats I will sell you and keep it double covered with the fine cotton sheets and mattress pads I will also sell you. Changing a zippered cover on a queen size futon can kill a strong man."

She picked out several sheet sets and a couple of pads, and walked to where Tami was figuring up her bill. She paid by credit card and accepted her receipt.

"I can have these things delivered tomorrow," Tami said, "if that's okay."

"Sure, my bedroom is finished and it can all go in there."

"Great. How's the garden?"

"Beautiful. It's really coming along. Do you know what Eddie asked me?"

"What?"

"He asked if I had any Japanese blood in my family."

"Really."

"Yes. He seemed so sincere."

"Eddie is a perceptive man."

"I was very complimented ... what?"

Tami looked at her for a moment, then sighed.

"What's the matter?" she asked.

"Nothing is the matter," he explained. "I have been waiting for what should be the obvious right time for what I am about to do. There has been no obvious right time, but I feel it ill advised to wait any longer." He grinned. "Don't look so serious, Lucin-*san*. You will leave here alive. Everything is fine. I have a gift for you."

"Another one?"

"Yes," he smiled. "Another one. This one is personal."

"Personal?"

"Intensely so," he chuckled, unlocking a wooden cabinet and rummaging around inside for a moment. "Ah, here it is."

110

Lucin watched him place a box, beautifully finished in red lacquer, on top of the counter. It measured about eighteen by twelve inches by four inches deep and was held closed by a brass clasp.

"Oh," she said, feeling the air thicken about her. "The box."

"Indeed," he said. "The box."

Lucin felt a tingle race up the backs of her arms and a flutter tickle the pit of her stomach. With a slightly dry mouth she continued. "What's in it?"

"Ah," replied Tami. "That is the question. You may take it home and look for yourself, or you may open it now, and I will explain the contents. It is your choice to make."

Lucin looked at him uncertainly. "Sounds ominous."

Tami grinned. "Ominous is the incorrect term. I'm afraid I have made more of this than I should. It really is not an overly serious event. In this box are some things I wish you to have for a variety of reasons, not the least of which is whimsy. There is absolutely nothing to be concerned about, there is no reason whatsoever to be afraid. Essentially, the box contains nothing more earth shaking than toys."

Lucin swallowed, feeling warmth radiate from the box. "Show me."

"Are you sure?"

"Yes."

"Very well. Then, for the moment, let us assume the roles of instructor and student. I am the teacher, you are the acolyte. Agreed?"

"Yes."

"Lighten up, Lucin. This will be fun. Open the box."

With slightly shaky fingers, Lucin freed the clasp, and lifted the top of the case. Inside, the contents were covered by a heavy black silk cloth.

"Before we go any farther," Tami said, "I will tell you that the items within this container are very old. Exactly how old, I do not know, but surely hundreds of years. They are also, for the most part, ivory. An attempt to assess the value of these items would be foolish, for the value must be assigned by the one who possesses them. We may assume, however, that they are *very* rare. Lift the cloth."

Controlling her anticipation, Lucin grasped the front corners in her fingers, slowly lifted the cover and placed it over the inside of the open lid. There, carefully contained in sunken chambers, gleamed the yellowish-white of highly polished, very old ivory. She looked at the contents for a moment, then blushed and giggled, putting her hand over her mouth.

"Dildos?" she asked, feeling her pulse rate rise.

"More or less," Tami said. "They are called *Harigata*. The large one is the *Katana*, the medium-sized one the *Wagasashi*, the smallest one the *Tanto*. These are also the names of the three Samurai blades. Notice the intricate carving and high relief on the *Katana*, as well as the slightly protruding structure on the top of the shaft at the base," he continued, lifting the first *Harigata* from its recessed silken nest. "It is designed to provide maximum stimulation through both size and texture for a woman of experience and confidence."

"I would think so," said Lucin, her eyes wide as she examined the nine-inch piece of beautifully carved ivory Tami held in his hand.

111

"As you can see," Tami continued, replacing the *Katana* and lifting out the *Wagasashi*, "this *Harigata* is not so large or so deeply carved for heavy texture. It is for the woman of more modest experience and needs."

"I can see that," said Lucin, grinning in spite of herself and her deep heartbeat.

Carefully, Tami replaced the *Wagasashi* and removed the smallest instrument. "This," he said, "is the *Tanto*. Notice that it is less in shaft circumference than the other two, and is smooth in texture. It is for the young woman of no or limited experience, or for use in what would be termed the back passage."

"The back passage?" blurted Lucin, a bit shocked.

"Yes. It is designed for both women and men to use by itself, or in conjunction with the other *Harigata*."

Feeling heat rush to her face to join the glowing egg growing in her low belly, Lucin swallowed. "Of course," she said.

"Next to the *Harigata* in these chambers," said Tami, directing her attention to the center of the box, "are the *Konomi-shinju*, also called pleasure pearls. There are four strands of various sizes of ivory beads, spaced out by knots along very strong silk cords. These are also inserted up the back passage of both men and women and withdrawn either slowly or in a rush at the moment of clouds and rain. Do you understand clouds and rain, Lucin?"

"Orgasm?"

"Indeed. The withdrawal of the pleasure pearls at the correct moment heightens the sensation considerably."

"I'll bet it does," she blushed again, feeling her sphincter tighten and giggling in spite of her best intentions.

"Next to the *Konomi-shinju* we have the *Himitsu-kawa,* or 'secret skin'. These are ivory rings that are placed either just behind the head or at the base of a man's Peerless Pestle. They are designed, by either texture or location, to bring heightened pleasure to the lady through increased stimulation and tactile response, or to prolong the man's ability to keep his Steaming Shaft, uh ... steaming, as it were."

"One would hope for the best," said Lucin, very seriously. Tami broke up. He gathered himself after a moment and looked at her.

"This box was used by courtesans in Japan for many years. I was fortunate to acquire it. It is now yours with my compliments."

"Why me?" she asked, carefully covering up contents and closing the box.

"Ah," he said. "That is not simple to answer. Let's just say because that's the way it should be."

"But surely you could market it for a lot of money."

"I suppose I could, but it came to me as a gift. It is only fitting that I pass it on."

"This is all part of what has been going on with me, isn't it?"

"Yes."

"And you're still not going to tell me what that is, are you?"

"No," he admitted.

"Well, I thank you for the wonderful gift," she said, shifting her weight in response to the growing itch, "although I am not exactly sure what I am going to do with it."

Tami smiled and bowed slightly. "Oh, Lucin-Blossom," he said. "I am sure you will think of something."

SIXTEEN

With patience,
The parched earth
Is rewarded by the rain.
The rose
Opens to the returning sun.

ON THE WAY HOME, Lucin—the glowing sphere very much intact in her low belly—stopped by a store in Westport called Futon Warehouse and spent time browsing to dissipate some of the tension of riding with the box next to her on the front seat. Eventually she purchased an oriental style linen cabinet and a queen size futon, with delivery promised for the following morning. When she returned to the Jag, she transferred the lacquered case to the trunk for the balance of the drive, a little embarrassed by her stimulated reaction to the ancient ivory implements. Still disturbed, she left the box in the rear of the car and entered the kitchen. James was sitting at the table.

"Top of the afternoon to ya, Lucille," he grinned, observing her with obvious pleasure.

"And to you, James," she flushed, moving on slightly weak knees and transferring her attention to the coffeepot so she wouldn't have to look at him.

"Are ya alright, then?" he asked, swiveling his chair to see her better. She could feel his eyes like warm breath.

"I'm just fine," she said, rattling the cup and saucer, pressing her pelvis against the lip of the counter. "No date tonight?"

"Nope. You're stuck with me, Darlin'. I was just thinkin' of walkin' down to look at the garden, but I'll linger awhile and have a cup with ya," he said, rising to his feet and approaching where she stood, "if you're buyin'."

Still not looking at him, she carefully finished pouring her coffee and shakily poured his, their arms touching in the process. Lucin felt the contact nearly as electricity and almost jerked in response. "It's on me," she said, replacing the pot.

"Sure, and it's a fine lass ya are," James kidded, patting her lightly between the shoulder blades.

She leaned into him, touching as much of her left side against his right side as possible. James moved his arm down to lightly encircle her waist and she pressed harder, a faint sigh escaping her lips. Slipping her left arm around his back, she rotated slightly to move the body contact to the front of her thigh and pressed her breast into James' rib cage.

"Oh, God," she whispered, increasing the pressure, "what am I doing?"

"Just fine, I'd say," murmured James. He tightened his arm around her. Instantly, her breathing became erratic.

Trembling with the contact and keeping her head down from embarrassment, Lucin felt a lump arise deep in her throat. Gently, James took her free breast in his hand and her breath turned hot, rushing from her nose in tiny snorts. Without will or thought, her hand found him through his slacks and, as he grew to fill it, she pressed her palm against him, feeling his heat through the thin material. She turned farther, thrusting herself against him, rotating her thighs apart to accept his leg, using the heel of her hand against his hardness, loving the sound of his gasp.

She answered with a gasp of her own as James moved his arm downward from her waist and grasped her bottom, his hand deeply under her, nearly between her legs from the rear, lifting her up onto his slightly angled thigh. She clung to it with her own, the itch and scratch growing between her legs as he slid her up and down against him, the golden heat of anticipation firing in surging pulses from her low belly.

Her grip of her hand on him became her only focus outside herself, and she clutched at James, squeezing as hard as she could, her head thrown back, mouth open, breath ragged, her feet completely free of the floor, as he slid her up and down, forward and back. The murmur between her legs became a growl, her breathing a series of explosive moans. She clamped her thighs and rode with the rhythm of James' hand, tears collecting under her closed eyelids, completely lost in the power of him, the pace of him, the feel of him against her hand and between her legs. God! She was *right there*. Right on the edge, right at the brink. His lips against her ear, James whispered one word.

"*Now.*"

The growl became a roar and the scratch chased the itch up from between her legs, through her center and into the back of her throat. The golden heat in her belly erupted into spurts of white lava, synchronous with her pulse, her breath, her grinding thrusts. James seized the rhythm in his deeply intimate grasp and augmented it with heavy pressure between the cheeks of her bottom, urging her, helping her over the top. Squeaks and hisses came from her open mouth, her head lashed with her body's beat, her ankles locked, her thighs tightened, and over she went, careening down that long tunnel, in the clutches of a sweat-soaked and salty-sweet slippery surrender to sensation and satisfaction that left her limp and quivering against him, clinging to his shoulders as he supported her, burying her face in his chest, afraid to look at him from the embarrassment of it all. They stood thus for a few moments, she occasionally twitching from release.

"Let me go," she murmured into his shirt.

"Nope."

"James, let me go."

"Not a chance."

"James, I said let me go!"

"Aw, Darlin', I know you're self-conscious right now," he said tenderly. "You never, not for any reason, have to be embarrassed with me."

"I'm terrible," she mumbled, still refusing to look at him.

"You're wonderful," he chuckled, dropping his hands down past her butt and grasping the top of each thigh, then lifting her until her legs spread around his waist. He walked to a chair and sat, leaving her straddling his lap. "We are going to sit in this intimate position until one of several things happens."

"Like what?" she asked, smiling in spite of herself.

"You decide to sit in a chair and behave, you get so excited by me pressin' between your lovely thighs that ya swoon, or I get so excited pressin' between your lovely thighs that I swoon. The one thing that will not happen, is you runnin' away." He lifted her face with a finger under her chin and kissed her gently on the lips.

"I love you, James," she said.

"No reason not to," he grinned.

Twenty minutes later they sat side by side in two chairs. Lucin finger combed the damp hair at the back of her neck and glanced at James. He smiled at her and sipped his coffee.

"Just answer me one question," he said, putting his cup back in the saucer.

"What?" she replied, still having difficulty looking him in the eye.

His face became very serious. "Was it good for you?" he asked.

Startled, she looked at him for a moment, then began to laugh. He joined her, and she leaned against him and let go, shaking with her mirth. After a moment, wiping tears from her eyes, she pulled away and turned to him.

"Didn't you notice?" she asked.

"Aye," he said, "I noticed."

"Good for me, frustrating for you. That's not very fair is it?" she asked, only slightly teasing.

"That's the way things are sometimes," he shrugged, still smiling.

"I'm sorry, James. I don't know what came over me."

"I know what came over me, Darlin'," he said. "You did. I take that as a true compliment, y'know."

She looked away. "I don't know what to say James. I behaved terribly. I'm ashamed of myself."

"Who do ya think you're talkin' to?"

She looked at him. "What?"

"Who do ya think you're dealin' with? I'm not some besotted thirty-five year old refugee from a golf course tryin' to rub his John Thomas up against your ass in a crowded elevator! This is me, Lucin, James Mathew O'Doud. You're not entitled to suffer shame on my account, or *our* account. I love ya, right down to the ground. '*I behaved terribly, James. I'm ashamed of meself, James*,'" he taunted. "By the black-hearted balls of Judas, don't ye understand, Lass? You can paint your naked body bright purple and walk down Main Street with a chimpanzee on your head while ya sing

115

Christmas Carols, and I'm still gonna feel about ya just the way I do right this very moment!"

Tears leapt to her eyes and she took his face in her hands, kissing his forehead, nose, and lips. "Aw, Jimmy," she smiled, "it's a fine lad ya are."

"Aye, that's true enough," he smiled, and returned her kiss, lingering a little. She responded with more pressure and touched his lips lightly with her tongue. Things escalated for a moment, then James leaned away a bit.

"Where would ya think this is goin' then?" he asked, his voice low and throaty.

"Oh, James," she flushed. "I'm sorry. I don't know why I'm behaving like this!"

"You're behavior doesn't concern me a bit," he replied. "Your motives are what concern me."

"My motives?"

"Aye. Ya have no father in your life, haven't had since you were very young. Ya have almost no husband in your life and haven't had for sometime. As near as I can tell, you have been without much in the way of demonstrations of love and concern from males most of your years. Combine all that with the changes that are thunderin' through ya, and set a handsome lad like meself, who loves ya and cares about ya, right down in the middle of it all, and things get quite warm."

"That's your analysis, huh?"

"Understand, I'm not complainin'. I think ya are a fine, lovely, bright, attractive woman. I don't take ya lightly. As a matter of fact, Lucille, me darlin', there is nothin' I would rather do than go upstairs with ya right now and spend the rest of this fine day and night in your intimate company."

"But?"

"But I'd want ya to be very sure of your motives. Believe me, I would love to take advantage of ya, but I don't want to be takin' advantage of the situation, y'know."

Lucin stared at the table for a moment. At length she looked at James. "You are something else, Jimmy."

"Aye," he smiled. "That I am."

"Well," she sighed, standing up. James rose to his feet beside her. "I'm going upstairs and lie down for awhile. Would you like to come with me?"

He grinned. "Sure, and I'd love to accompany ya upstairs, too."

Realizing what she'd said, Lucin laughed. "What if I think this over and become sure of my motives?"

"I think that would be lovely for both of us."

"What about Harrison and Jolee?" she asked, backing toward the stairway.

"In matters of the pillow," James replied, using her own words, "all is private, all is separate from the world."

Lucin napped restlessly for a couple of hours, then returned downstairs where Stephanie had prepared sautéed Chinese vegetables and Basmati rice. She ate listlessly, sluggish in both her body and mind. As she assisted in clearing the table, the phone rang. She waved Steph off and picked up the handset.

"Hello?" The reply came in an impatient whisky alto.

"Well, I thought maybe you died. You don't call, you don't write!"

116

"Mother," Lucin replied, quiet resignation creeping into her voice. "How nice to hear from you."

"Humph. Are you well, Lucin?"

"Yes, Mother, I'm quite well," she replied, participating in the obligatory dialogue. "And you?"

"Oh, I still have this problem with my knee. Doctor Spense gave me one of those horrible injections again last week, and it seems a bit better, but those pills do so little for the pain."

"The Darvon?"

"I don't know what they are. I just know they don't help very much. Then, of course, my back bothers me so. Doctor Jamison gives me pills for that. They don't work either and they upset my stomach, so I drink that awful liquid he prescribed."

"I'm sorry, Mother."

"Just be glad you're young, Lucin. You have no idea what's it's like to be my age and to have gone through everything I have. No idea at all."

"I'm sure I don't."

"That's another thing you can be thankful for."

Lucin pictured her mother, sitting on the white damask couch in the library, wearing off-white satin lounging pajamas and fifty thousands dollars worth of everyday jewelry, her heavily treated dark brown hair carefully sprayed into immobility, her secret third glass of sherry on the end table.

"Harrison was by for a few minutes at lunch today."

"Was he? Well, that's nice."

"I wonder if you know how fortunate you are to have a husband of his caliber, Lucin. I may never forgive him for moving you clear out there in that cowtown in which you now reside, but, that aside, he is a man of certain accomplishment and station, you know."

"Yes, Mother. I know. Harrison is a good man."

"I don't know how good any of them are, but he certainly is equal, professionally or socially, to anyone in someplace like Kansas City. How do you stand it there?"

"Actually, I'm beginning to like it."

"Really."

"Yes. I'm making friends, I've started skating again, I'm working on a ..."

"Skating?!"

"Yes. Ice-skating. I go two or three times a week."

"You haven't skated since high school!"

"Actually, I haven't skated since day before yesterday. I'm considering taking lessons again."

"Well, I certainly hope you're not wearing any of those vulgar costumes and displaying yourself in public!"

"No, Mother," Lucin replied, biting her lip to keep from adding "not yet".

"Well, that's something at least. Harrison said you're re-doing some small bungalow on the property?"

"That's correct."

"It's something to do, I suppose. Have you contacted your sorority?"

"No."

"The Junior League?"

"No."

"Lucin, how do you ever expect to maintain your station without the correct social contacts? It's beyond me how you can just muddle about in that strange town with all those, uh … people, and not at least *try* to retain some of the benefits of your social position! Your family has worked long and hard to accomplish what we have. Why would you ignore all those obvious advantages?"

"Mother, I am not ignoring anything. I'm simply trying to develop my own life."

"Your own what?"

"Life, Mother."

"Your own life? Why, you have your own life, a perfectly lovely life! At least you did before you moved out to the frontier. You knew the right people, you attended the right events, belonged to the right clubs. Have you even joined a country club?"

"Yes, we have. It's certainly not up to your standards, but it is the very best dreary old Kansas City has to offer."

"Well, at least that's something. I do worry about you so."

"Of course you do, Mother," Lucin replied, growing weary of the conversation.

"Are you taking care of yourself? Do you work out?"

"Yes, I do."

"Well, you can never be too thin, Lucin."

"I suspect Karen Carpenter would take exception to that."

"Who, Dear?"

"Is there a reason you called, Mother?"

"Actually, there is. Your great grandmother."

"Grandma Iona?"

"My mother's mother. She always showed a great interest in you. I was so relieved she died when you were quite young. I always worried she would be a bad influence on you. She was a very strange woman, Lucin, with a totally unacceptable level of independence from the family."

"I don't even remember her. The only way I know her is from the picture on the piano."

"Thank goodness for small blessings."

"What about her? What about Grandma Iona?"

"Well, it seems she has a package for you. An envelope, actually."

"What?" Lucin asked, a shiver running up her spine.

"I had to have some work done on the foundation of the house. The basement wall had cracked in what used to be, years ago, the coal room. It's the area we just used for storing junk down there."

"I remember."

"Well, I came across this old trunk full of musty things that used to belong to your great grandmother when the old woman lived in this house. Just trash, really. Some rotted old shawls, worthless jewelry, old letters, some of her mother's things, and this large envelope addressed to, of all possible people, you."

"Me?"

"I know. It's the strangest thing. I can't imagine what's in it. It's very heavy linen paper, bound in cord and sealed with wax. It's addressed to you with instructions that it was to be given to you when you reached your majority."

"A little late."

"God knows what that strange old woman had to say to you. She never did fit with the family, rarely went to church. What your great grandfather ever saw in her is beyond me."

"I'm sure it is, Mother. What did you do with the letter?"

"I sent it on to you, via Federal Express, yesterday. They guaranteed me that you'd receive it tomorrow."

"Thank you."

"I just can't imagine what's in it. She did have an uncommon interest in you, I must say. When you were a baby, I'd find her in the nursery just watching you sleep. She'd shoo the nurse away, pull up a chair, and look at you for hours. It made me so nervous I added staff so you wouldn't be left alone. I told your father, rest his troubled soul, about it, but he seemed unconcerned."

"Well, I guess I'll know when it arrives."

"Whatever it is, Lucin, just remember that Iona was never really one of us. She was a member of the family, but she never gave herself to it the way your Grandmother and I did, never sacrificed the way we have."

"I'm sure she didn't, Mother."

"Of course not. Well, I must ring off. Good luck with your little project on the bungalow. Perhaps you'll finally get some good from that design class you took in college."

"I hope so."

"Just don't use anything tacky when you decorate. Do they have any good furnishing stores out there?"

"Yes, Mother," she replied, "even a Sears."

"A Sears!"

"Just kidding, Mom."

"Well, I should hope so! Now you contact the local chapter of your sorority, Lucin, and start associating with the right people. Come see me. You know how much I must miss you, Dear."

"I will, Mother. 'Bye."

"Goodbye, Lucin."

Lucin put the phone on the table and slumped back in her chair. God! What an ordeal! She felt exhausted. Interesting about the letter from Grandma Iona, though. Sort of a message from beyond the grave. A chill crept up the back of her arms. It was delicious.

SEVENTEEN

Unknown spirit reaches across the years.
Written understanding of what
Remains in shadow.
I wait for the coming
Of the light.

AFTER HER MORNING SHOWER had cleared some of the cobwebs from her head, Lucin dressed in lightweight nylon jogging pants, her grubbiest pair of tennis-runners, and a moth-eaten old rugby shirt. She pulled her hair back into a sloppy ponytail, applied a little lipstick, and trooped downstairs wearing rimless glasses, her contacts left behind. James stood peering at the coffee pot as it dripped its last drops. Catching sight of her, he grinned.

"Sure, and I wish you let me know when you're gonna dress for breakfast," he teased, "I'd have worn a tie."

She looked at him.

"You can't make yourself unattractive to me," James continued, twinkling at her. "Say good morning."

"Good morning, James," she said, rather stiffly.

"That won't do, y'know," he replied, opening his arms. "I've got to have a hug."

Cautiously, she moved into him and he enfolded her. Her face against his neck, she smelled the faint aroma of Old Spice, felt his breath on her forehead, his chest against her chin, his arms about her back. The strength of him, the solidness of him called to her, and suddenly everything was alright. The timidity was gone. The shyness, the embarrassment, the nervousness at seeing him after the events of the past afternoon all washed away and there was only them, only now. Smiling, she snuggled.

"Aye," he said, "that's better."

"Yes, it is," she agreed, squeezing him about the waist.

James chuckled. "Pour ya some coffee?" he asked.

"Yes."

"Make ya some eggs?"

"Yes."

"Pat your butt?"

"Yes. Please."

Reaching down he briefly rubbed her bottom, then released her. "Go sit," he smiled.

She flopped into a chair as he poured coffee. "That wasn't just a pat, you know," she said.

"It wasn't?"

"No. That was a fondle."

"Ya think so, do ya?" he asked, putting a cup down in front of her.

"Aye, Jimmy, me boy," she grinned. "That's what I'm thinkin'."

"I must be losin' me touch," he answered, putting a small skillet on the stove. "I was goin' for a full-blown grope."

"Better luck next time."

"Next time?"

"Make that anytime."

"Ah, Lucille," he grinned. "'Tis a fine lass ya are."

Her eyes smiled over the rim of the cup.

She was carrying her plate to the sink when Stephanie entered with a bag of groceries. "Morning, Miz Montgomery," she smiled. "There's a van coming up the driveway."

Lucin directed the young man driving Tami's truck back to the street and around to the side of the property to get closer to the guesthouse. As she and James walked to meet him, a larger truck arrived with the kitchen cabinets and countertops and pulled across the grass to near the front of the small house. James greeted the two men in that vehicle while Lucin showed the first driver where the things from Tami were to go. As she stepped back outside, another van arrived, this one from the futon shop.

"Good grief," said Lucin. "It's a circus."

James glanced over her shoulder to the street. "Aye," he said. "Send in the clowns."

Lucin followed his line of sight to see Sheila Hartrick, her blond hair stiff in the breeze, her overweight frame squeezed into tapered green velvet slacks and a pink silk blouse, depart a black Mercedes SUV and begin to flounce her way across the yard, struggling to keep her pink three-inch heels from stabbing into the earth.

James began to chuckle. "Sweet, Jesus," he muttered and drifted away toward the house.

"Lucin!" Sheila warbled. "Hello! Hello, Lucin!"

"Good morning, Sheila," Lucin smiled, as the woman huffed to a stop beside her.

"I was just driving by and saw all this activity. I just had to stop!" gushed Shelia, slowly sinking as her heels disappeared into the turf and her toes turned up.

"Everything seems to be arriving at once," said Lucin, scanning the delivery vehicles and Eddie's truck. "Things aren't usually quite this hectic."

121

"Why, that's a little lake!" exclaimed Sheila, watching Eddie fuss around the pond. "Isn't that just the cutest thing? Is that man Oriental?"

"Japanese," answered Lucin. "He's creating the garden for me."

"A Japanese garden. That's just exciting, isn't it? I think it's just wonderful what you're doing to this old place. Once all these trucks and workmen leave, the neighborhood will look quite nice."

"Thank you."

"Now what's that over there?" Sheila asked, pointing to the bamboo and trying to get back onto her toes. "Is that a hedge? You know, we have a height limit on hedges in this area."

"That's bamboo," Lucin smiled. "Is there a height limit on bamboo?"

"Well I just don't know," Sheila replied. "I don't think we have any bamboo in the neighborhood."

"Well, you be sure and let me know if there is. We'll be more than happy to comply with any rules from the neighborhood association."

"Speaking of that," pounced Sheila, "we have our quarterly cocktail party coming up in a couple of weeks. It would be just lovely if you and Harrison could attend."

"That would be nice, but I never know if Harrison will be in town. He's traveling so much right now, I don't know from one week to the next where he'll be."

"Well, you could just come without him, couldn't you? It's just a friendly get together. This one's at our home, very informal, a way to stay in touch with everybody. Not business, just a social thing. Why don't I just slip the information in the mail to you?"

"Fine, Sheila, thank you very much."

"Why, look! Are those marble counter tops those men are carrying inside?"

"Granite, I believe."

"Excuse me, Miz Mongomery, Ma'am," said James, walking up from behind Sheila and stifling a grin.

"Yes, James?"

"Pardon me for interrupting, but the cabinet maker needs to see you, Ma'am, and you have that appointment with the architect in about thirty minutes."

"Very well, James," Lucin said. "Thank you. You're dismissed."

"Yes, Ma'am," James replied, nearly clicking his heels. "Thank you, Ma'am."

"Isn't good help just so hard to find?" commented Sheila, watching James walk away toward the house.

"James is very good," smiled Lucin. "Well, I'm sorry, but you will have to excuse me, Sheila. Busy, busy."

"I just completely understand, Hon," Sheila gushed. "You know that daughter of mine just talks about you all the time. Lucin this, Lucin that. It's just so cute!"

"She's a wonderful child. I enjoy her company at the rink. She's going to be a fine skater."

"Why, thank you! You just go on with your business, and I'll drop that note in the mail to you," Sheila said, turning to leave. "'Bye now!"

Grinning, Lucin watched Sheila wobble back across the yard toward her SUV. She noticed James lurking by the side of the garage enjoying the spectacle and blew him a kiss.

By noon the deliveries were complete and the workmen had left for lunch. When Lucin entered the kitchen, Stephanie handed her a large FedEx envelope. "It came while you were down at the little house," she explained. As Lucin took it, her hand began to tremble.

"I'll be in the dining room, Steph," she said. "Would you be kind enough to bring me a brandy, please?"

"Yes, Ma'am."

"A large one."

"Yes, Ma'am."

The package contained no note from her mother, only a yellowed envelope in heavy paper. Lucin removed the gold-wire cord from around it, then pulled the strands out of the thick wax that sealed the flap closed. Inside were two sheets of dense linen paper covered in a precise hand and a smaller envelope, also sealed with wax. She took a sip of brandy, adjusted her glasses, and began to read.

My Dearest Lucin,

I know what a shock this may be for you, and I beg your forgiveness. Please do not be nervous or apprehensive, for this missive contains no message of dreadful import or fearful portent. Since you are reading this letter, I am dead, most probably long dead. Understand that as I write this, you are a small child learning to walk and talk and function as a human being. Sometimes I sit and watch you sleeping in your crib, for at such time I can quiet my mind and allow it free rein to see both your promise and your possibilities. I have great love for you and am absolutely sure that you have grown into a woman of exceptional beauty and stature, both without yourself and within your Self. I do not know at what condition or age you will receive this letter, if at all, but I trust divine providence that it will come to you when and as it should. Now, on to business.

My granddaughter, your mother, is a fool. Her only measure of worth is the circles in which she moves and the things she can acquire. She is a selfish, self-centered, shallow person who is little more than a waste of oxygen, but she has done one truly marvelous thing. She has given birth to you. As I write this, I pray you have been delivered from her coldness, her calculating personality, her loveless grasp. She is much like her mother, my daughter. Both of these women have willingly chosen form over function, imagined obligation over realized enjoyment, and appearance over acceptance. They have little use for me, I have less use for them. You, however, are cast of different clay. I can feel it in your tiny heart and hear it in your delicate breath.

I do not concern myself with the men who are your forbearers, for true awareness and power, while it may reside in men, does not flow through them. That is reserved for women. Do not misunderstand me. Unlike your rigid mother and brittle grandmother, I have great use for the male of the species, admire many of their characteristics, appreciate many of their attributes, and have enjoyed the company of more than my share of them in my long life. Now that I am old and dying, it seems a shame to have run out of time when there are so many of them left. I leave men, save one, out of this missive simply because women are the only infallible way to trace lineage. A child can have any number of likely fathers, but only one mother.

The year was 1853, Lucin, when Admiral Perry undertook a "great and noble" mission. He was sent to sea for the purpose of, by diplomacy or force, opening up the islands of Nippon for trade. The Japanese, heavy traders at one time with the Spanish, Portuguese and others, had pursued a course of isolationism from the western world. It was Perry's task to change that. Change it, he did.

123

On that first mission with him, went a young businessman from Boston named Cornelius Biork-lundt. Called a "black Swede" because of his unusual dark hair and ruddy complexion, Cornelius became fascinated by the Japanese and their lovely land. He did not return to America for nearly six years, but stayed in the islands and developed trading outlets through his father's business. As best he could, he learned the language and customs of the Japanese people, and lived in a manner much as they.

Cornelius became enamored of, and involved with, a courtesan of the first rank in the city of Yedo. Presently, as sometimes happens, this young woman became pregnant. To be Japanese and heavy with the child of a barbarian was a huge disgrace. To protect her life and the life of the un-born baby, Cornelius purchased her contract and they fled to Osaka. There he hid the woman from prying eyes and continued his business dealings. Sometime later, a girl-child was delivered from this courtesan. Two days after the birth, she, in a fit of mortification and disgrace, plunged a knife into her own throat and bled to death, leaving Cornelius Biorklundt alone with the tiny infant. For several more years he stayed in the islands, hiring wet nurses for the child and caretakers to see to her needs. The girl did not appear excessively Japanese and, thanks to her father's dark visage and black hair, resembled him a great deal. When she was four years old, Cornelius, now quite success-ful in his business efforts, left Japan and returned to the east coast of America, settling in Philadel-phia instead of Boston, to avoid prying eyes and personal history.

The girl, who spoke perfect English, was placed into home tutorage, then private school, and be-came a dusky beauty, educated and secure in society. That young woman was my grandmother, your great, great, great grandmother. In spite of the distress and shame with which this circumstance has been viewed by our family over the years, in spite of how fools like your mother and grandmother have not even allowed themselves to whisper the facts, in spite of the racist and caste-ridden attitude of the east coast white gentry, I will not see you denied the truth. In your veins, my dear child, as in mine, runs the blood of the Japanese. I consider this fact to be somewhat of an honor, as I am con-vinced you will also. I find the thought that I am descended from such an ancient and enduring culture quite comforting. I also find the knowledge that one of my ancestors was trained in the art of giving and receiving pleasure to be quite liberating.

In the enclosed smaller envelope you will find a pendant. It belonged to that courtesan who killed herself from shame, the woman who is the mother of us all. My mother gave it to me, I pass it on to you. It is my wish that this revelation brings you answers and knowledge that you will find comforting. It is my belief that knowing what we are can have a profound effect on whom we be-come. Because of your mother's and grandmother's fearful denial, the pendant and you are all that remain of her. I have not the slightest doubt that you will cherish it.

In closing, Dear Lucin, I leave you with this. I am objective in my assessments of my daughter, your grandmother, and my granddaughter, your mother. By the time this missive reaches you, I fear what sort of disaster your mother may have become. While I make no excuse for her self-centered behavior, she is, willing or not, a victim in her own way. Compassion is not approval. Understand-ing is not endorsement. Go your own way. Answer to yourself first.

Cultivate your life, Child. It is the finest garden you can grow.

With love,
Grandmother Iona

Lucin read the letter through twice, the second time pushing back tears of relief and joy. Hands shaking, she opened the small envelope and removed from it an ivory pendant about the size of a silver dollar on a jade green silken cord. The pendant was a perfect circle with a carving in the center stretching from the top to the bottom of the piece, the background cut completely away, so the figured appeared to be poised inside a ring of ivory. It was a crane standing on one foot, the same as the one in the window of Tami's store. Wrapping the cord about one hand, she clutched it to her heart and let the tears come.

Noticing her as he entered the kitchen, James crossed into the dining room and sat quietly beside her. Presently she realized she was not alone and turned to him, her face wet, her eyes red and puffy. He smiled, retrieved some tissues from the sideboard, and dabbed at her tears.

"Here," he said, handing her one. "Blow."

She did, then chuckled through her tears. "Thank you."

"Sure. And what are ya readin' that has brought ya to this pitiful state," James asked, stroking her cheek.

"It's a letter from my great grandmother she wrote to me when I was only about two years old. I just got it."

"Well, you know how slow the mail can be," he grinned, moving his comforting hand to the back of her neck.

"Aw, James," she laughed, and the tears started again. She leaned forward into his shoulder and let them come.

At length he lifted her face and kissed her on both eyelids. "That's enough now, Darlin' Lucille. There's no point in makin' yourself sick. C'mon, get a grip."

Wiping her face, she slid the letter to him. "Read that," she said, "while I compose myself."

While James was reading, Stephanie brought her another brandy and one for James. When he finished, James drained his in one gulp and looked at Lucin.

"Well?" she said.

"That Iona was a fine lass I'd bet," he grinned.

"James, I'm Japanese!"

"Aye, that ya are, Sweetheart. Partly anyway. Ya didn't know?"

"Not 'til today. It explains so much."

"It's got to be a bit of a shock. Drink your brandy. Himself doesn't know either, then."

"Harrison?"

"Right."

"No. He has no idea."

"Are ya gonna tell him?"

"I don't know. Maybe sometime. Hug me."

"If I must." They embraced for a moment, Lucin clinging to his solidity and strength until she abruptly pulled away and looked at him.

"James, I'm part Japanese."

"That's true," he said.

"My great, great, great grandmother was a courtesan of the first rank!"

"Aye," he said. "The best of the best."

She thought for a moment and seemed to reach a decision. "I have to sleep in the small house tonight. Will you help me put my room together?"

125

They spent the next two hours assembling Lucin's bedchamber, hanging some prints, putting down the *tatami* mats, positioning screens, setting out candles, making up the futon, scattering pillows, loading the linen cabinet, then broke for an early supper of poached salmon salad. After the meal James looked at her.

"That letter has shaken ya up, huh?" he asked.

"In some ways it's a revelation."

"Aye, the truth can do that."

She carried their dishes to the counter then approached James from behind his chair and, wrapping her arms around his neck, kissed his cheek. She stood up and left her arms on his shoulders. He leaned his head back against her chest and she lightly cradled it there between her breasts, her hands casually resting palms down on his chest. It was comfortable for both of them and they stayed that way, silent for several minutes.

"James?" she said.

"Hmmm?"

"Would you go down and fill the bath for me at the garden house while I shower and grab a few things?"

"Sure. Just back away slowly so me head doesn't fall off."

She squeezed his neck lightly between her breasts and chuckled. "Wouldn't want that." She kissed him again and went for the stairs.

James sighed and walked down to the garden, up onto the deck and out to the small bathhouse. The tub had its own water supply. He removed the cover and turned the tap on full force, activating the heater and the ozone purification system, enjoying the construction craftsmanship of the tub and structure. He'd just shut the water off and stepped out onto the deck when Lucin came walking barefoot around the corner of the house, wearing her short terry robe with a small canvas carry-all in one hand and the red lacquered box in the other. James moved to the sliding glass door and opened it for her, then slid the *shoji* screen aside so she could enter. Bending her knees, she placed the bag on the floor next to the wall, the box beside the futon, then stood and turned to face him.

"Thank you," she smiled.

"Ah, sure," he replied, slowly looking her up and down. Her smile spread into a grin. "Lucin, me darlin'," James continued, "in light of recent developments, you should be wearin' a kimono."

"I'm working on that," she said. "How's the tub?"

"See for yourself. It's warmin' up right now. I wasn't sure what you wanted so I set the thermostat at a hundred." She brushed past him, close enough for the lightest contact, and entered the bathhouse. He came in behind her and lit an oil lamp suspended from the ceiling on a chain. The gathering gloom retreated a bit in the warm light.

"Perfect, James. It's just perfect," she said. "Oh! I forgot fire. Would you light a couple of candles for me in the house? It's going to get dark in another hour or so."

"Fill my tub, light my candles," he bitched, walking back to the bedroom. Inside he fussed a bit with new wicks, lit three, and set his disposable lighter on the top of the linen cabinet. "Call it a house warming gift," he said. "Ya got your bath, you got your fire, and you got your new futon. I'd say you're all set."

"Thank you, James," she said, stepping close to him, "for everything."

"Sure," he replied, slipping his arms around her lower back and leaning over to kiss her cheek. She returned the embrace, her arms reaching high around his neck, and they stood for a moment enjoying each other. James leaned back a little and looked at her, then grinned, slipped both hands under the rear of the short robe to cradle her bare bottom, squeezed, lifted, and kissed her deeply, holding nothing back.

The room tilted a bit, and Lucin was panting slightly when he finally released her to slowly slide the six inches to the floor.

"That box," he said. "If ya ever need assistance with any of its contents, don't hesitate to ask."

"The box?" she replied.

"Aye," he said, catching her face and kissing her again, very hard and quickly. "I spent time in Japan, y'know." He trailed the back of his hand casually upward between her legs and was gone, out the door on the way back to the house.

Lucin leaned against the doorframe and smiled.

EIGHTEEN

Sleeping heart stirs,
Disturbed by fresh awareness.
Waken heart.
My new blood
Awaits.

WALKING DIRECTLY from the garden house to the garage, James got in his old Chevy and headed for Jolee's, swinging by her shop on the way to see if she might be working late. A phone call would have been simpler, but he needed the diversion of driving and some time alone to shake off what he was beginning to regard as the "Lucin effect." *Nails!* was dark, but beside it the lights in Tami's store burned brightly and the front door was propped halfway open by a squat Buddha crouching on the sidewalk. On impulse, James pulled into the parking lot. He walked through the door to see Tami crouching beside a pond, feeding fish.

"Ah, Mister O'Doud!" he smiled, dusting the fish flakes off his palms and offering a hand to James, "welcome to my humble shop. I am honored that you would stop in."

"Good evening, Tami-*san*," James replied, bowing slightly. "The honor is mine." He took Tami's hand. Dry, firm, crackling with energy.

They looked at each other for a moment, measuring, testing, the broad axe and the rapier, the grizzly and the leopard. Finally, James grinned. Tami inclined his head and the tension broke. Understanding flickered between them and they both relaxed. James chuckled with the release and Tami eased down off the balls of his feet.

"Well, Laddie-buck," James said, looking around the room, "this is quite a place you have here."

"Thank you. Pretty standard Japanese import stuff for the most part, but I do get the occasional collectors things in."

"Like red boxes?" asked James.

"How *is* Lucin?" Tami said.

"She was fine when I left." replied James. "Getting ready to spend her first night in the garden house. I filled the bath for her."

128

"Good," said Tami. "It's time."

"Yes it is." They smiled at each other.

"I meant what I said the day we met, you know," Tami continued. "She is very fortunate to have a man such as you in her company. If a plant grows too rapidly without support, it can be easily damaged. Her love for you and yours for her is such support. You encourage her growth and give her strength and a place of safety."

"And you," James countered, "have provided the fertilizer."

Tami grinned and bowed. "Is that a nice way of saying bullshit?"

"What's the difference if it works?" James laughed.

"A difference that makes no difference, *is* no difference," chuckled Tami. "Either way, she needed stimulation and opportunity. You, I, even Jolee have all come together in this place and time to offer her some of what she needs and to receive some of what we need. It is no accident that all of us are where we are."

"Sort of a cosmic thing, huh?"

"Sort of. Do you discount that, James?"

"Not me. I'm not such a fool as to believe that just because I don't understand something, it isn't happening. If God didn't work in mysterious ways, people wouldn't say that God works in mysterious ways. I know there's a connection between you and Lucin and that you have had a very profound effect on her. I know that she has come a long way these past few months and that might never have happened if she had remained where she used to live, in the middle of life long influences. I know that to do what she has done, she also needed her husband to be absent from her life and heavily occupied elsewhere when he is in her company. I know that all of these things, and more I am not aware of, had to come together in just the right way at just the right time. Trying to figure out what's going on is a waste. A fish doesn't need to understand the ocean to swim. He just needs to know that he's a fish."

"The only difference between the path and he who walks it is time," intoned Tami.

James grinned. "Now, what the hell does that mean?"

"I don't have any idea," Tami confessed. "I just like the sound of it." They laughed with and at each other for a moment, and Tami continued.

"So, James, how may I be of service to you?"

"I'm looking for a house warming gift for the lady in question. I thought you might have a nice tea set."

"I have several, but Lucin already purchased one."

"No, I mean the type used in a formal tea ceremony. The kind with the bamboo whisk and ladle."

"Ah! The *cha-no-yu*."

"That's it. I couldn't remember the name."

"The whisk, the ladle, the spoon, the handleless porcelain cup, the narrow deep bowl for hot water, the white cotton cloth, the box for the green tea powder, the earthenware caddy to carry it all, and the small cast-iron kettle."

"Right."

"The kettles are in the back corner. Why don't you pick one out while I go in the rear and get the rest." Tami excused himself and proceeded into the storeroom.

Alone in the storage area, Tami opened a massive, black-lacquered, cherry cabinet and lifted down a wooden crate. Removing the cover from the crate and pushing the packing material aside, he lifted out a fired-clay container slightly larger than a Dutch oven. Taking off the top, he checked the contents to make sure everything was in place and added a small plastic bag of finely powered green tea to the delicate bamboo box designed to contain it. He removed the eighteen-hundred dollar price tag and carried the box out to the front of the store for James' inspection. James approved.

"How much?" he asked.

"Let's see," pondered Tami. "The cast iron pot is thirty-nine ninety-five, tax on the whole thing, uh ... call it three-fifty."

"Three-fifty?"

"Three-hundred-fifty dollars," Tami repeated.

"Ah, you're a darlin' lad, and I adore the dirt on your lovely shoes, but who do ya think you're dealin' with?"

"What?"

"Don't be tryin' ta play me, ya daft inscrutable oriental," protested James. "Three-fifty wouldn't buy that cup, much less the bowl and all the implements!"

"Three-fifty is the price," Tami said. "Take it or leave it."

"Say no more," James replied, holding up his hand. "Me darlin' mother was a Scot. I know a deal when I see one." Removing his wallet, he counted the money out on the counter. "At these prices you're goin' to go broke, y'know."

"This shop was never designed to make a profit. I consider it more of a public service," Tami said.

"And a way for you to get your hooks into poor unsuspecting young matrons."

"And smart-assed Irishmen," Tami said.

"Well, that ya have, Lad. That ya have."

"Sure, and it's all part of me darlin' cosmic plan, y'know," grinned Tami.

After James left, Lucin opened her bag and withdrew the envelope from Grandmother Iona to read the letter again. Finishing it, she shook the pendant out of the smaller envelope and a delicate piece of parchment she had not noticed before fluttered to the futon on which she sat. She picked it up and examined the writing it contained.

My Dearest Lucin,

I have, in my quiet moments of introspection watching you in your crib, come to view you with a certain, for want of a better word, understanding. You and I both came to this earth by virtue of what the Japanese call The Willow World. Without it, we would not exist. Because of it, we can do anything. I see you now as a night blooming lily, fragile, lovely, waiting to be discovered and enjoyed. First, you must discover and enjoy yourself. Above all else, this will ease your path. Above all else, this will offer you choices.

I would leave you with this thought. There are only two things in this world that are without limit: femininity, and the ways in which it may be exploited. Both of these limitless blessings live within you.

Use them well, Child. Use yourself well.
Iona

Lucin felt as if she had been hugged. Placing the pendant about her neck, she held it over her heart and smiled, tears lightly tracing their way down her face. This voice from her past brought her such joy as she anticipated her future. For the first time in her life she felt a continuity, a flow, the support of a foundation that she never realized existed, and yet, there it was. From the pen of a long dead woman, from the womb of an even longer dead woman, sprang her future, unknown, hazy, unrealized, but hers. *Hers.* Not Harrison's, not her mother's, not anyone's but hers. And it had already begun. Her head and heart were both changing, both different from what they were only a short time ago. She was Japanese. Even Eddie had seen it. Surely, Tami knew. And now she sat in her garden house on a futon listening to the gentle movement of water over rocks, smelling the aroma of turned earth and pine. Slowly she rose and retrieved a bottle of Merlot from her bag. Pouring a glass, she walked out onto her deck and to the bathhouse. It was time to go home for a while.

The *Mama-san* looked down at the smiling young woman as she sat on her futon. "Well, Blossom-*san*, do you like your new room?"

"Oh, very yes, Mama-*san*," she excitedly replied. "It is so beautiful, and I have it all to myself. It will be much nicer than living with the other girls. I love them all, but it will be good to be private, yes?"

"Yes it will. How long have you been with me now, Blossom?"

"Since I was seven, Honored Mother."

"And how old are you now?"

"I am almost fourteen."

"You have done very well, my child. You sing beautifully, you dance gracefully, you tell entertaining stories. I am very proud of you."

"Thank you, Mama-*san*."

"And you have become a woman. I observed you in your bath earlier this evening. You are quite lovely. I assume the pathway into your Heavenly Pavilion is open and unrestricted?"

"Oh, yes!" Moon Blossom replied, feeling excitement grow in her heart and warmth bloom in her belly.

"I also assume that you regularly employ your *Harigata* for pleasure."

"Except when my Jade Gate blossoms, every day!"

"*Ichi-ban.* Very good. In the closet where your futon is placed in the daytime, there is a box. Your box."

"My box? A red box?!"

"*Hai!* A red box."

"Oh, Mama-*san*! This is very much! *Arigato goziemashita! Domo. Domo!*"

"*Do itashimashite*, Blossom-*san*. Think nothing of it."

131

"*Gomen nasai*, so sorry, but does it contain all the *harigata*?"

The old woman smiled. "All three of them, plus pleasure pearls and secret skins."

"Just like the ladies have?"

"Just like the ladies have."

"But, Mama-*san*, I am not familiar with the pleasure pearls and secret skins."

"That's alright. Do not concern yourself. *Izumi-san* will return to spend some nights with you to make sure you are acquainted with both their uses and sensations."

"*Izumi-san* is very kind to me, and patient," smiled the young woman.

"She will instruct you, Blossom-*san*. Your time is here and soon your day will come. You will take your place among the ladies of my house."

Tears ran down Blossom's cheeks. "Oh, Mama-*san*, you have been so tolerant of my lack of ability and impatience. For all these years, you have been more than a mother to me. I promise I will bring honor to your house. I promise that I will make you proud."

"I have no doubt of that," the old woman smiled, bending to kiss Blossom on the head. "Why don't you retrieve your box. *Izumi-san* will be here soon." She turned and left the room.

Scooting across the futon, Blossom removed the red-lacquered box from her closet and placed it before her as she sat on her heels. With trembling fingers, she opened the lid and lifted back the black velvet cover.

Morning sunlight stung her eyes and she stretched luxuriously. The sound of gardening reached her. She placed a *harigata* back in the box, wrapped her night robe about her nude body, and raised up onto her knees, peering out the open window.

"*Konnichi wa*, Eddie-*san*," she shouted.

"*Konnichi wa*, Ru-sin-*san*. *Anata wa yoku nemutta ka?* Did you sleep well?"

"*Hai, okagasama de genki desu.* Yes, very well, thank you. *Nanigoto da?* What's going on?"

Eddie grinned. "*Kowa jozuni shabereru yoni natta na!*" he shouted. "You are beginning to speak Japanese very well."

"*Gomen nasai,*" she replied, "*nihon go ga habase-masen.* So sorry, I don't speak Japanese."

"So sorry," countered Eddie, "but you speak it to me now."

"What?" Lucin blurted, staring at him, reality whirling around her confused head.

"*Hai,*" he answered. "Very yes, Ru-sin-*san*. You much speak Japanee. You speak me, I speak you. Very yes. You Japanee goo'."

She sank to the futon and leaned against the wall as the room tilted. Jesus! Where was she?

Sleep reached for her, and she struggled against it, gradually bringing the garden house into focus and reaching for reality. What had happened? She remembered her conversation with Eddie, recalling what they said, but Eddie claimed it was not English, and that she had spoken Japanese to him, and he to her. Motivating herself to at least some movement, she was making up the futon when she heard James' voice from outside.

132

"Are you decent, Darlin'?"

"James! Good morning," she called, quickly putting the box back in the cabinet and gathering the short terry robe about her. "Decent enough for you," she continued, sitting on her heels in the middle of the futon and fluffing her hair. "Come in."

James walked around the deck and entered awkwardly through the sliding glass door, carrying an insulated pot of coffee, a container of cream and two cups on a tray.

"It's the O'Doud door to door coffee supply company, Ma'am," he said. "We aim to please." He toed off his shoes and moved to the bed. She reached up and took the tray from his hands.

"James, you are wonderful," Lucin said. "I'm glad you brought two cups. Sit with me."

"Sure, but not like that," he said, walking to the head of the futon and leaning against the wall as he sat cross-legged. "These old bones feel a lot better when they're leaning back against something."

Lucin swiveled on her butt to face him, pulling on the skirt of her robe to maintain a semblance of propriety. She blushed and moved the tray between them.

James grinned at her. "Sure and you're among friends, Lucille. Don't put all that away on my account."

"I was right," she said. "You really are a rogue."

"Truth be told," he leered, "you bring it out in me."

"Do I really, Jimmy?"

"Aye. That and more."

She rocked forward onto her knees, then onto her hands, and kissed him on both cheeks. "That's the best I can do," she said. "I haven't brushed my teeth."

"I can wait," he said.

Lucin grinned. "Alright," she said. "I'll go brush my teeth and things, you pour the coffee."

James watched her get primly to her feet and walk away, the robe dropping just to mid-thigh. "Jimmy me boy," he murmured, "what the hell do ya think you're doin?"

He heard water running as he put coffee and cream in both the cups, and set them and the tray beside the bed, then went outside and retrieved the gift he'd purchased from Tami. As he came back in and sat down, the toilet flushed. Lucin returned to the futon and sat on her heels facing him, slightly to his left. Her knees didn't quite touch his thigh.

"Now that is lovely, that is," he said.

"What?"

"Ah, there's somethin' of a promise in the look of a woman's knees, bent like that under a short skirt. It's a grand sight."

She leaned forward and kissed him quietly on the lips. "So are you, Jimmy."

"Thank ya, Lass. Ya feed my eyes, ya feed my heart, and now ya feed my ego. There's not much more a man could want."

"There isn't?" she teased, leaning back.

His eyes roamed over her. She didn't blush. "Well ..." he said, and let it trail off on the air for a moment. "Maybe some coffee."

Lucin giggled and handed him a cup, then noticed the fired clay container he'd placed on the other side of the futon. "What's that?"

"Ah, yes. That is a bit of a house warmin' present I got for ya."

"That's sweet of you. Pass it over."

"I don't think I can reach it."

"You just want to watch me crawl over there and get it."

"Aye," he said, "that's me plan."

She made a face at him and did just that with as much dignity as possible. Moving the container up on the bed beside her, she lifted off the top.

"Oh, my."

"It's for the *cha-no-yu*," James said, "the formal Japanese tea ceremony."

"James, it is truly lovely." She picked up the single cup. "This is very old."

"I expect so. Tami had it at his store."

"You got this from Tami?"

"Aye. Fine lad. There's a cast iron kettle that goes with it, but I couldn't manage this, the kettle, and the coffee tray for the walk down here."

"This is beautiful, James, it really is. Thank you so much for such an excellent gift. It will remain here in this house. Perhaps some time you'll come and I will serve you tea."

"Uh … Lucille, maybe you don't understand the true nature of the tea ceremony."

"Of course I do. Perfectly. Perhaps some evening I will serve you tea in my garden house, Jimmy-*san*."

"Now that would be an honor in so many ways. Maybe we will drink tea from the same cup one night."

She placed her hand over his heart. "The night is for magic, and magic answers only to itself," she said, bowing to him. "It is a perfect gift that is made more perfect by the nature of the giver."

James looked at her as if transfixed. "Sweet Lord," he whispered. "Ya are Japanese. I don't know how I missed it." The moment hung there between them for a time. It slipped away as she took a sip of coffee.

"I had a conversation in Japanese with Eddie this morning a little before you came down," Lucin said.

"In Japanese?"

"Yes. I don't speak Japanese."

"But you did this morning."

"Uh-huh. I was dreaming I was Japanese, woke up, looked out the window at Eddie, and we had a conversation. It was very strange."

"I can see how it might be."

"Then I got real bleary and almost went back to sleep. Then you showed up with the coffee."

"And now it's gone. You don't speak Japanese anymore."

"Nope. Strange, huh?"

"Aw, sure. Lucille, me darlin', things have been strange for quite a while, and I wouldn't be surprised if they didn't get worse, or better, dependin' how ya look at it.

Maybe ya just better go along for the ride. It's got to be takin' ya someplace. Ya sure as hell aren't where ya were!"

"That's certainly true," she said. "Here I am, sitting on a bed with a perfectly wonderful man who, as soon as he finished his coffee, is going to rub my bottom while I kiss his whole face. He is then going to leave, whether I want him to or not, because his heart is pure. And I am going to get dressed, go up to the house, and call a man named George about a kimono."

"Is that right?" asked James.

"That's right," Lucin answered, her smile spreading into a grin as a familiar tingle fluttered in her low belly.

"But what if I want another cup?"

"Too late," she said, rocking forward on her lovely knees.

NINETEEN

I see myself
As through swirling mist.
Shifting patterns
Of what
May come.

"OF COURSE I remember you, Dear!" trilled George, as Lucin held the phone away from her ear. "Peggy Fleming, Audrey Hepburn, Elizabeth Hurley and such a Lu-SIN-full name! Oh, you lovely thing, how can George possibly be of service to you, and how is that tawdry sweetheart Jolee that I love so much?"

Nearly overwhelmed, Lucin laughed. "Jolee is fine and as sweet as ever, and I need some clothes."

"My prayers are answered," George gushed. "Come see me, come see me, come *see* me! Wear whatever you like and bring a pair of three or four inch heels and a body stocking. If you don't have a body stocking, I'm sure I have one or two around here that will do. Don't wear any makeup at all, I want your natural color. We'll look at you, we'll have lunch so I can be seen with you, then we'll let our imaginations just frolic! Ha, ha! Did I say lick? I am so naughty. Sometimes I can hardly stand myself!"

After a moment to recover, Lucin giggled. "Where and when, George?"

"Here and now, you luscious creature! I'll drop everything else, as if everything else weren't dropping all by itself, and give you my undivided attention. I'm over here in Westwood." He gave her the address and directions, and she repeated them back to him. "Exactly!" George bubbled. "Now come over. I'm going to sit right beside the door and wait! Blue skies today, Darling. Hurry, hurry!" He hung up.

George's studio was off the tiny Westwood business area in a low building facing a secondary street. Lucin got out of the Jag carrying a small bag and walked to the front door. A postcard-sized sign was displayed below the doorbell that read "George." Before she could ring, the door crashed open and there he was, barefoot in a powder blue muumuu that reached nearly to the floor.

"God!" George grinned. "It wasn't a dream. You're actually here!" Grabbing her by the shoulders, he kissed Lucin on both cheeks and nearly dragged her inside.

The room was large and low with several skylights. About half of its eighty-foot length was carpeted in short industrial gray, the balance in a very light hardwood. The carpeted area contained several tables stacked with fabric samples and bolts, sketchpads, photographs and such. Chairs were scattered about the forty-foot width and used coffee cups perched on several small tables. The hardwood portion was nearly pristine. Banks of track lights projected from the ceiling, and one corner was mirrored from floor to ceiling on two walls, ten feet out from their juncture. A carpeted platform about eighteen inches high and three feet square sat near the corner. Above it were several additional spotlights and two heat lamps. Nearby was one high-backed desk chair on rubber wheels. The neutral gray walls were festooned with sketches of George's work, many in the carpeted end of the room done in watercolor. Off the far side were draped sliding glass doors. There were no windows. As Lucin surveyed the room, George locked and draped the front door. Light classical music wafted gently through the space.

"I have bottled water, I have fruit juice, I have coffee and I have wine," said George, moving toward a cabinet and apartment fridge in the back corner of the carpeted portion. "Anything?"

"No thank you. Not right now," Lucin said, studying some of the watercolors. "George, these designs are wonderful!"

"Thank you, Darling, but this isn't about me. This is about you. Nervous?"

"A little," she confessed.

"Well, that's normal," he replied, walking to the far corner and turning on the heat lamps above the dais. "All you have to do is release yourself to the intimacy of the moment, understand that you are in no danger from George, secure from prying eyes, and appreciated more than you know. What's in the satchel?"

"A body stocking, a change of underwear, and a pair of heels."

"Leave it there. Speaking of underwear," he continued, pursing his lips and peering at her from sixty feet away, "what kind are you wearing under those jeans?"

"Uh, cotton bikini briefs," Lucin replied, slightly embarrassed.

"Through those sliding glass doors you will find a bathroom-dressing area on your right. In that room is a cabinet with some thong panties in the top drawer. They are all freshly clean. Remove your clothing, all of it, put on a pair of those panties that fit, one of the robes you'll find hanging on the back of the door, and return. Get your embarrassment out of your system, Darling. It will only get in our way."

Lucin looked at him.

"Go, go go," George said, waving impatiently at her. "And relax," he grinned. "I am not some sort of amateur gynecologist! Scoot."

Wondering exactly what she'd gotten herself into, Lucin did as she was told. She found the thong underwear slightly annoying, having never worn any before. There were three robes, all silk. She chose the shortest one and smiled as she slipped it on. The room was cool and her nipples rose against the fabric. Oh, well. Naked under the thin silk except for the strange panties, barefoot, goose-bumped, erect-nippled, and self-conscious, she walked back into the room. George was sitting in the chair by the platform holding a large sketchpad.

"Marvelous," he said. "Come stand over here on the dais where it's warm."

He studied her as she walked down the long room, the way someone might observe a racehorse. "Stop," he said, as she neared his position. "Now turn around and walk away from me." She did. "Very nice," he said. "Put on your heels and return to me Darling, I can't stand being this far away from you!" Grinning, Lucin did as he requested.

"You move very well in heels," George said. "Most women fight them. You, on the other hand, surrender to them. You allow them to change your gait and the way you present yourself. I know they're evil and nasty, but you move in them as if they were fun and happy. Good for you. Take them off."

Lucin stood by the edge of the platform and kicked off her shoes, enjoying the warmth of the heat lamps.

"Now, up," George said.

For the next few moments he studied her as she turned and twisted at his direction. From time to time he would sketch frantically, peer at her, then sketch again. Finally, he stopped, and began tapping the pencil on his teeth.

"Drop the robe and kick it to the floor, he said.

Lucin had been anticipating this moment since she went into the dressing room, unsure as to exactly what she would do. Almost to her surprise, she did exactly as he asked. Nude, except for the thong, she stood erect and relaxed with one foot forward, and she smiled at him.

"Enchanting," George said. "Absolutely enchanting. You are truly lovely, Lucin. My God, what a canvas for my art!" He rolled the chair around the hardwood floor. As she held her pose, he sketched madly from various angles. "If you find this too intense or embarrassing, Sweetie, try closing your eyes. I think you'll find that helps."

"No," Lucin replied, shaking out her hair a bit, "I'm fine."

"You certainly are," George crowed. "One thousand fine, just like pure gold."

The sketching continued for several minutes, George whizzing around the floor, asking Lucin to turn and adjust her stance a bit, becoming more and more animated as he realized she was comfortable. He stopped after flipping yet another sheet on the pad.

"Now," he said, "If you'd be more comfortable, please put on the body stocking. I'm going to ask for some movement and some posing. I don't want you to feel ill at ease."

"What's best for your work?" she countered.

"Best for me is nude, of course, but as I said before, this isn't about me, Darling, it is about you."

"Nonsense," Lucin replied. "This is a collaboration. It is equally about both of us." Much more calmly than she would have expected if she'd thought about it, Lucin slipped out of the thong and dropped it to the floor. She smiled at him. "Nude it is, George. I hate body stockings and you need to be comfortable, too. Now, what do you want?"

"I want to just die!" he laughed. "Just die! I will never be happier than I am at this moment, there is no point in going on! Jesus, you are such a prize! I absolutely live for women like you, and there are no women like you! Where can I possibly go from here? The mortician will never get the smile off my face. Call 9-1-1! But before you do that, turn to your left and arch your back. I must sketch."

For the next hour, that is exactly what he did. Barefoot and in heels, Lucin posed for George in almost every stance possible, sitting in a chair, reclining on the floor, even in skating poses, enjoying the glimpses she caught of herself in the mirrors. Finally, George threw his hands in the air.

"Christ, I can't take anymore! Ah! You get some clothes on, you gorgeous thing, and I'll get some clothes on. We'll go slumming at Mama's, eat lunch, and tell each other how wonderful we are! Then we'll come back here and finish up. Tits and ass, Doll. Tits and ass! Never before in my entire life have I so wished I were a *lesbian*!"

Lucin slipped back into her jeans and shirt, omitting both panties and bra, and drove George, now more conservatively attired, to Mama's. She was amazed at her level of hunger. While George ate a dinner salad, she consumed one of Mama's immense grilled cheese sandwiches with tomato and bacon, an order of fries, and a Coke.

"God," she munched. "I can't believe how hungry I am!"

"What you just did," said George, " and did beautifully I might add, takes a lot out of you if you aren't used to it. Posing—especially nude, for the first time, and in front of one who is basically a stranger—is very demanding physically and emotionally. You were magnificent! Truly magnificent. You are an absolute work of art, Lucin, and I treasure you. Now, tell me. What are we looking for in the way of wardrobe?"

"Well, I'd like a couple of robes in silk, kimono style, one short, one long. I'd also like what the Japanese call sleeping or night kimonos in cotton, two or three of them. I want to bring a Japanese influence into some evening and party wear too, but I have nothing at all in mind. I'd like one formal full dress kimono, and possibly two or three costumes for skating."

"Ah, yes," said George. "We spoke briefly of that. I asked if you wanted to sell sex or grace. You said sex."

"Yes, I did," she smiled.

"Wrong, my bountifully breasted beauty! Sex is too commonly sold, and you are so wonderfully uncommon we must take a different approach. With you, you beautifully bottomed thing, we sell possibilities."

"Possibilities?" she laughed.

"Indeed. You sell sizzle, Sweetie, not the steak. Steak is just a piece of meat. Sizzle has possibilities."

"Okay, possibilities."

"Exotic dancers are not exotic, Lucin, they are erotic. Eroticism is absolutely pendulous with possibilities. They don't need to see those gorgeous nipples of yours, they just need to hope they will. They don't need to actually view that scandalous ass, just think they might, or pray they could. They don't need to touch those terrific tits, they just need to think of how wonderful it would be if they did. When we decide to flaunt, Dear Girl, we will flaunt with such style we will knock them on

139

their ass! When we decide to suggest, they will slip in their own drool. And we will do it all with possibilities. Round and firm, erect and proud, sleek and smooth, slick and warm … possibilities! Tell me, are you wet?"

"What?!" blurted Lucin, jolted from the reverie she'd acquired listening to George.

"Don't answer, Sweetie. It's none of my business. The point is, it's a possibility. We will purvey possibilities. Pulsating, passionate, panting, perfumed, perspiring, pliant, pressurized, pink and purple, paradisiacal *possibilities!*" he roared.

"Perfect," Lucin giggled.

"A glimpse of a knee, a sliver of a thigh, the outside of a breast, the small of a back, the slope of a shoulder. And if we decide to get more serious, we will never quite show them what they thought they saw. We will sell them the possibility, Sweet Lucin. We will sell them your sizzle, and sizzle you shall. Ready for more?"

"More?"

"Back to the studio, out of those togs, onto the platform, and under some silk and such. I want to direct a fan at you and do some draping, and see how things respond to the wind. I am going to blow your skirt up, you delightful creature, time and time again. Then I shall visit ice-covered establishments and view women, not nearly as lovely as you, as they slide around the surface. And do you know what I ask in return for this extreme dedication?"

"What?" Lucin grinned.

"Money, you naive child. Lots of your money."

"Then you shall have it," she laughed.

"My God, it *is* true!" George hooted. "You *are* the perfect woman! Lunch is on me, you wasp-waisted minx! It's the least I can do."

Driving home late that afternoon, Lucin was surprised at how tired she was. After lunch, George had her back on the pedestal for nearly two more hours, hanging material over her posed body and aiming fans at her, muttering, laughing, changing angles and cloth. And the measurements! Lucin had been measured for clothing on many occasions, but never as thoroughly as by George. Spine to shoulder, neck to shoulder, shoulder to elbow, elbow to wrist, neck size, neck length, bicep size, forearm size, on and on it went to the tips of her toes, nothing short of a blueprint of her body. She even talked him into a peek at the sketches he'd done of her and was surprised to find a collection of lines and angles, curves and intersections that resembled her not at all, yet suggested a female body with great depth and movement. At about five o'clock he hugged her at the door, gushing with enthusiasm, and kissed her on her way. When Lucin hit the front seat of the Jag, she felt as if she weighed a thousand pounds.

Wanting nothing more from life than food and a hot bath, Lucin entered the kitchen to find Stephanie making coffee. Before Lucin could speak, Stephanie cocked her head toward the dining room. There, sitting at the table, glass in hand, bottle of scotch at his elbow, sat Harrison.

"Darling," said Lucin, nearly running to him, "you're here!"

He looked at her with almost no expression on his face. She stopped short. "What a surprise!"

"Obviously," he said, his voice flat and emotionless.

"Sweetheart, what's the matter," she asked, confused by his manner.

Slowly, Harrison drained his glass and poured another couple of fingers. "Almost every Goddammed thing I can think of," he muttered. "Where have you been all afternoon?"

"With a designer to get some new clothes. Harrison, what's going on?"

"New clothes. Jesus," he complained, his voice flat and brittle. "It would have been nice if you'd been here when I got home. I don't get home very often."

Lucin bristled. "It would have been *nice*," she snapped, "if you'd let me know you were coming. Perhaps I could have arranged some balloons and a pony!"

Startled, he looked at her. She returned his stare with one of her own, not backing down an inch. They battled silently for a moment, then Harrison spoke.

"Really? Balloons and a pony?" he asked.

"Yes."

"What kind of pony?" he continued.

"A palomino, with a little black saddle," she glared, trying not to smile.

"Well. That's different. Next time I'll call." They held eyes for a few seconds. "Jesus, Luce," he whispered, "I'm sorry. It's good to see you. Really good."

He stood up and she walked into his arms.

TWENTY

Desire moves within
Awakening from new dreams.
What I have eludes me.
What I want
I cannot have.

AN HOUR LATER, Lucin was still in the dark about Harrison's unusual attitude. After their initial confrontation and embrace, he had withdrawn into the library for a time, then gone upstairs, avoiding communication or even contact. Stephanie was putting hot garlic bread and salad on the table when he came down, freshly showered and shaved, bottle and glass of scotch still in hand. The level in the bottle was down by forty percent. He finished the glass, placed it and the bottle on the sideboard, and sat down across from Lucin, slightly tipsy and very troubled. She looked at him.

"Sweetheart, what's wrong?"

"Dammed Japanese, that's what's wrong."

She waited silently, knowing he'd continue. He stared at the table for a moment.

"For nearly two years I've been working on this Nagata thing. One of the most successful medical technology companies in the world. Expanded into major foreign markets, likely to develop the first dependable artificial heart. Got a dialysis machine on the drawing board no bigger than a cigar box. Diagnostic optics about the size of a pencil lead. World-class stuff. Wanna build a facility in the central United States they say, wanna physical presence in the country that would obviously be the biggest consumer of their equipment. Kansas City is the logical choice," he said, shaking his head and barely looking up from the tabletop.

"Christ, Lucin! I've been dancing with these people like Fred Astaire! Fox-trotting with the Japanese to keep them happy and interested, waltzing with these fucking Kansas Citians over development rights and taxes and sewers and all the other crap that goes with trying to bring two thousand jobs into this stagnant economy, and doing these dummies a favor! I have busted my butt with the Mayor and city councilpersons and members of the worst school board in the country, kissing ass, shaking hands, schmoosing these idiots, bringing in the offices of a major law firm, waiting for one of these shitkickers to screw the whole thing up, and they didn't. They didn't! It all fell into place. I got three floors of Crown Center real estate just waiting for thirty of our guys from back east. I got headhunters beating the bushes for the best legal talent in the Midwest, I got employment agencies lining up support staff. I got all these balls in the air, and it's working! The firm stands to make a fortune. I stand to make a fortune. And now this!" He was halfway between anger and despair.

"What?" Lucin asked.

"Kiritsubo died. He fucking died! Fifty-one years old, looked forty, great shape, and three days ago he keeled over during dinner and fucking died! Kiritsubo was the driving force behind the expansion of the Nagata company into this country. He masterminded the whole thing, put his weight and power behind it. Now, it could all go to hell in a handcart!"

"Can you do anything?"

"Wait. I can wait. With the firm extended by millions on this project, with people waiting to go to work here, I can wait! Kiritsubo came to power when his predecessor, Serata Onoshi, retired. Onoshi's parents died at Nagasaki during the atomic bomb attack. He didn't want anything to do with Americans. Fought expansion to this country. When Onoshi retired, Kiritsubo seized the opportunity and began overtures. That was four years ago. Now Kiritsubo is dead and that fucking Onoshi has come out of retirement and is back in power in the business group that controls the Nagata company. Jesus, what a disaster!"

"Can you talk to the man? Will he listen to anyone?"

"Sure," Harrison smiled ruefully. "He'll talk, he'll meet, he'll be quite sociable, and then go right ahead and queer the whole deal. He *likes* it, Luce. He fucking likes fucking with Americans! This could ruin me. This could set me back fifteen years. I started this whole thing on our side. If it goes south, the firm is gonna have to have some sorta scapegoat. Me. Christ, those fucking Japs!"

"I'm really sorry, Harrison. Maybe it's not as bad as it seems. Maybe everything will work out just fine. You look awfully tired. Have some salad. Stephanie's fixed a lovely veal lasagna. Why don't you eat and try to get some rest?"

Looking past her, he snorted. "And everything will be better in the morning, right?"

"Not necessarily, but *you* might. I worry about you."

Harrison looked at her and sighed. "You don't get it, do you? You don't understand what a disaster this is. You don't understand what that sonofabitch Onoshi can do to this project, to the firm, to *me*! You build your *little* garden and decorate your *little* house and live in your *little* world. I don't have that level of luxury, Luce. I've got to function out there in shark infested waters. Shark infested *Japanese* waters! It's *my* ass on the line, Luce! It's *my* name on a two-and-a-half-million dollar mortgage, it's *my* reputation clinging by its fingernails! *My* hopes, *my* dreams, *my* life!"

Lucin started to recoil from the verbal assault, then felt steel grow in her belly and power rise in her spine. Of course Harrison was upset and not thinking clearly. Of course he was distraught and afraid, anyone would be. She looked steadily at him as he stared at her until he was forced to turn from her gaze. Very quietly, she spoke.

"The Japanese have a saying, Harrison. 'Do not attempt to fix the blame. Instead fix the problem'."

"Oh, Jesus!"

"They also believe that a person's fate is a person's fate. Life is but illusion."

"You know," he snarled, "the last fucking thing I need right now is some sort of rice-propelled pontification. Least of all from you!"

Feeling very solid and balanced, Lucin rose, smiled at him, and turned away into the kitchen. Stephanie had disappeared. On the counter were two plates and a pan of lasagna. She gathered silverware and spooned some lasagna onto a plate. As she picked it up, Harrison, flushed and tentative, entered the kitchen.

"What are you doing?"

"Good night, Harrison," she said, moving toward the door.

"Where are you going?"

"Down to my little house, by my little garden, to spend the night in my little world. If you wish to insult me further, you'll have to wait until tomorrow."

Lucin ate standing up at her new kitchen counter. The cabinets were all installed, the unusually wide copper hood mounted over the hole where the stove would go and a portion of the counter top beside it. Gaps showed where the dishwasher and refrigerator would be placed and the sink had been set, although its hardware had yet to be mounted. The bathroom walls were finished in light beige tile and pale green trim that looked wonderful with the slate floor. The absence of a tub made the area very spacious. The sink, shower, toilet, and bidet were all in place, water lines connected to the toilet and sink, although the water heater was not yet wired up.

Things were coming along nicely. The garden was lovely in the late evening, a rainbow forming over the pond as the misting units in the tree kicked in, dropping the air temperature ten degrees or so, changing the ambience of the area dramatically, pushing Kansas City a thousand miles away. She stood on the side deck and soaked it in, finding it impossible to stay angry or hurt. It was as if the incident with Harrison happened to another person. She observed it in her memory as a viewer, not a participant.

Harrison had shouted at her for the first time since she had known him. He had treated her as if she were not involved with what made him who he was, as if she were just another acquisition in his life. He had as much as said that she was unable to understand the "real" world, that it was beyond her. That she should just stay in her room and play with her dolls. The dammed thing about it, she realized ruefully, was that he was right. She had never been an equal partner, never knew she could be. All her life she had been trained to be in the right place, do the right thing, say the right words, serve the right wine, know the right people. She had been taught to assume, not a role of support, but a supporting role. Harrison had never seen her in any other light. Neither had she.

True, he had been overly harsh and insulting to her. In light of the fact that his behavior was completely out of character and that he was under terrible stress, she could overlook the hurt as some sort of trauma induced temporary insanity. It was not Harrison's way to behave in such a manner and she had little difficulty dismissing the incident. The fact that a good deal of his hateful criticism was true, gave her pause for thought. More power was coming into her life. She knew that. If it was not feasible for her to maintain a position of equality in Harrison's life, she could certainly take charge of her own. She glanced toward the garage to see James walking around the bamboo in the dim light, paper sack in one hand, two folding chairs in the other. She could just make out his grin. Flipping the switch that activated the low wattage path lights spaced throughout the nearly finished garden, she moved to meet him at the edge of the deck and take the chairs from his hand.

"Ah, me darlin' Lucille," he said. "If you'd rather be alone, I'll turn around and leave ya to your thoughts."

"James, it's good to see you," she smiled. "Sure, and when wouldn't you be the best company a girl could have?"

"Fine, then. You've talked me into stayin', but unfold me one of those chairs. I'm too dammed old to crouch on me haunches like some God forsaken heathen, y'know."

She opened both the chairs and set them closely side by side on the upper deck area in front of her sliding glass doors, as James pulled two tall Styrofoam cups from the sack and filled each with a cold can of Guinness. He handed one to her as they sat, knees touching, and raised his in a toast.

"To men," he said, "and their closed minds and open mouths. 'Tis a fine bunch of lovely lads we are."

Lucin met his toast, then took two deep swallows and wiped the foam from her upper lip with the back of her hand. James grinned at her.

"You heard," she stated.

"Aye. Every word."

She took two more swallows. "Have I ever told you how much I like Guinness?" she asked.

"As I recall," James answered, "ya mentioned that to me once when you were in a drunken stupor and hormonally overwrought."

"Hormonally overwrought!?"

"Aye. I believe the medical term is horny."

"James!" she laughed, and took three more swallows, then peered into the depths of the cup. "It's almost gone," she complained. "Is there more?"

"Sure. I've five more here."

"I think I'll have the next one in the tub," Lucin said, draining her drink.

"Do ya have a way to keep these cold?" James inquired.

"Nope," she said, standing and walking to the door. "We better drink 'em fast."

She was inside for only a moment or two, then walked out on the deck in her short terry robe, a towel over her shoulder, and headed for the bathhouse.

"Give me thirty seconds and bring your chair," she said.

When James entered the bathhouse, Lucin was neck deep in steaming water, almost invisible in the gloom.

"Light the lantern, pour me another one, and sit with me, James."

"Lord knows I love strong women," James chuckled as he ignited the wick. The darkness receded to the walls and the small room was filled with a gentle glow and dancing shadows. He filled her cup and handed it to her, sat beside the tub in his chair, and took another swallow of his Guinness.

145

Lucin tipped back her head and consumed half her drink in several long swallows. She smiled at James, wet hairs clinging to her neck, her face shining with moisture in the lantern light, and licked the foam from her lips. Moving in the cedar tub so she was across from James, she spread both arms along the rim and sighed, the still water reaching to the hollow of her throat. The lamp's dim golden glow transformed her skin into shadowy copper just beneath the surface of the lightly rippling water.

"Sweet Jesus," muttered James.

"Beg pardon?" Lucin asked, raising her eyebrows and looking at him quizzically.

"You heard me."

"I'm sorry, James," she said, tucking her legs under and changing position until her body was behind her and her chin was on the edge of the tub just a few inches from where he sat. "Now I'll be able to hear you better. What did you say?"

"I said drink your Guinness," he laughed.

She raised herself up the side of the tub until her nipples were just below the edge, tilted her head back, and drained the glass as rivulets of water trickled down her shoulders and chest. Finishing, she ignored the foam on her lip, extended her arm over the side of the tub, and thrust her cup at him.

"Please, James," she whispered, "I want more."

"God, you're a mess!" he chuckled, reaching into the sack for another can.

"A mess you helped make," she countered, grinning at him.

"Aye," he replied, pouring the cup full, "that I did. You got Guinness all over yourself. Lick your lip."

"You do it."

"What?"

"You do it. You lick my lip," she said, rising partway out of the water. James leaned over in his chair and, with great deliberation, licked the foam from her upper lip and handed her the fresh cup. She put it quickly to her mouth, restored the foamy mustache, and grinned at him. "More?"

Again he removed the bubbles. Again she restored them. Again he removed them.

"What a wonderful way to drink," she sighed, sliding back into the water and taking a long pull on the cup.

Swallowing the lump in his throat with the last of his brew, James opened up another for himself. "That'd be number three for you," he said, as Lucin attacked her drink again.

"I'm almost ready for number four," she said.

"Four pints of Guinness in about fifteen minutes oughta pretty much have you howlin' at the moon, Lucille."

"God, I hope so," she laughed and swallowed the rest of her drink. She blinked and looked at him from the center of the tub. "I'll take it easier with the fourth one, Jimmy," she said holding out the cup and rising to her knees. The water lapped at the bottom curve of her breasts. James looked at her.

"Well, are you gonna pour it or not?" she asked.

"I haven't decided," he replied, still gazing at her.

"Doan make me come over there," she threatened.

Unable to resist, James laughed at her. Raising a semi-insulted eyebrow, Lucin stood up and stepped to the edge of the tub. The water stopped just above mid-thigh. Grinning, James handed her a can. She clumsily popped the top and poured the liquid into her Styrofoam cup, then handed the can back to James and drank about half the Guinness in three long swallows. Weaving a bit, she stepped backwards to the middle of the tub and stood there in the lantern light, nipples erect, her skin covered in light goose bumps. She looked at James as he looked at her.

"You like?" she asked, turning slowly around, extending her arms and spilling a little of her drink into the water.

"Not bad," James grinned, enjoying himself and her.

"Thank you," she said, blinking at him. "Wait ... not bad?"

"I like," admitted James.

"So does George. George drew me and sketched me and undressed me and dressed me and draped me and measured me and I put on high heels for him and laid on the floor for him and his heat lamps kept me warm 'cause I was naked. We had lunch, too."

"George?"

"He's expensive but he's sure worth it," Lucin confided, and finished the last of her glass.

"George?" James bristled.

"That's his name. Doan wear it out," she giggled, stepping to the edge of the tub and thrusting her cup at James.

"Just who the hell is George?" he demanded.

"Doan worry, Jimmy," she soothed, leaning forward and bracing an elbow on his shoulder. "George is a gay man."

"What!?"

"James is a ga ... George is a gay man, Jimmy," she said, slipping a dripping arm around his neck, her wet breast against his bicep. "He's a designer. He's going to do some clothes for me. He had to look at me and measure me and stuff. George is a homosensual male. Can I have some more Guinness?"

"No."

"Okay."

"Homosensual, huh?" James grinned.

"Yep," she replied, tightening her arm around his neck and leaning into him, dropping the empty cup and placing her free hand on his thigh. "Not like you, Jimmy. Not like you at all."

"That would be because I'm a heterosensual male," he chuckled, slipping his arm around her back.

"Rub my bottom, Jimmy."

"It's all wet."

"So am I," she giggled. "Rub it anyway."

James slipped his hand down under her butt and casually lifted her out of the tub, standing her on the floor in front of him.

"Ooh," she said, and wrapped her arms around his neck, clumsily pressing her nude body against his. James held her with one arm and retrieved her robe from a towel hook with the other, draping it across her shoulders.

"Put this on," he said stepping away from her and dodging her questing hand. She slipped her arms into the robe and tied it. The air seemed to leave her and she slumped against him, swaying. He scooped her up and carried her to the bedroom.

Once inside, he removed her robe and awkwardly dried her as she hung onto him and tried to murmur sweet nothings in his ear. When he got her reasonably dry, James eased her down onto the futon, attempting to untangle her arms from about his neck.

"Come to bed with me, Jimmy," she whispered, pulling at him as he kneeled beside her in the gentle wrestling match.

"Ah, Darlin', as much as I'd like to, tonight is not the night."

"Please, James. Stay with me. I need you." He eased loose and covered her with the comforter.

"Aye, Lass, ya do. And I need you, but not like this and not right now."

"I love you, Jimmy," she murmured, already beginning to settle into the covers.

"Of course ya do, and I love you," he replied, smiling down at her in the moonlight from the window. He tucked the covers around her and walked back out to the bathhouse.

James gathered up the empty cans, blew out the lantern, and stepped back to the bedroom. In the dim light he could see her sleeping form and hear her snoring softly. Thinking himself the lesser of two kinds of fool, he turned away from Lucin and began his slow walk back to the house.

TWENTY-ONE

Does the world change
As I change?
To fear trust
Or to trust fear.
Always, choices.

LUCIN GROGGILY APPROACHED WAKEFULNESS with a pounding head and a furry tongue. Her eyes scrunched in a losing battle against the sunrise streaming in the window, she pulled the comforter over her head and moaned. God. Too much Guinness, much too fast. And James! She'd done it again, thrown herself at him. Mental images scrolled sluggishly across the inside of her eyelids: standing naked in the bath, turning around and displaying herself, dripping water in the lantern light. Well, truth be told, that was *fun*. The expression on James' face as he looked at her was delightful. She liked it. No, more than that — she *loved* it. Not quite awake, she smiled.

Easing her throbbing head back on the pillow, Lucin kept her eyes closed and watched James watch her. The way he was torn between embarrassment and interest, trying to stay cool as he got hot. How he tried to hide the effect she had on him. Smiling, her headache at bay, she pulled one of her new pillows firmly between her legs, wishing the red box wasn't so far away in the cabinet. It was true, she admitted to herself as she moved languidly against the pillow's heavy piping. She liked being watched. She liked the way George watched her as he sketched, appreciating her form and shape with the eyes of an artist and creator. She liked the way James watched her, appreciating her form and shape with the eyes of a male animal. She enjoyed the change in his breathing as she stood and turned in the tub, knowing that as the heat grew in her it grew also in him, that as she got wet, he got hard, feeling his need to scratch her itch. And when he reached under her, the palm of his hand cupping both her bottom and her pubis, and lifted her out of the water, she almost went over the edge. Remembering how it felt, imagining the pulse of his breath near her ear, the weight of him partially suspended above her, the feel of his ribs against the inside of her thighs, the pace of him, the rhythm of him, the *thrust* of him, she pulled the pillow nearly viciously against herself, clenching her teeth with need. Instantly, the warm glow became a flash of wildfire, the itch and scratch battling up from between her legs, expanding through her belly to her low back, soaring up her spine into her throat, making her snort through her nostrils as it flowed down her chest, deeply through her stomach, back into her belly and then settled in a glorious return between her legs.

It was over in just seconds, but the satisfaction lingered with intense resonance, making her quiver against the pillow, her pelvis thrusting in random convulsions beyond her control. She let it happen and shook with it, thrust with it, vibrated with it, the tiniest of squeals skipping through her sinuses, a delicate growl rattling in her throat. She took a deep breath through her nose and smelled him, smelled James as if he were right there. A lump rose in her throat and she could taste him, a combination of the lips and tongue she knew and the manhood that pushed her to where she was. Jesus! She actually had his flavor in her nostrils and his scent in her mouth, the two sensations swirling around each other in her nasal passages, high behind her soft palate, flowing downward toward the warm lump in her throat. Breathing around it, swallowing around it, she grasped a corner of the comforter between her teeth and was pushed over the edge again. This time the itch came from her esophagus and trachea, the scratch climbing up into her head and plunging down into her stomach. The smell and taste of him rattled through her belly and she lay nearly motionless, her low back quivering with the electricity of it, eyes locked shut, diaphragm frozen in place, teeth set in the blanket. When it left, she crumpled into the futon, boneless, without will, without want, a sponge soaked with the taste, the smell, the memory, and the fantasy of James.

An hour later, the light reached for her again and this time she came fully awake. The headache wasn't as bad, but her tongue was worse. She untangled herself from the pillow and sprawled on her back, an arm thrown over her eyes in protest of the morning. Nature shouted and she rolled to the edge of the futon, grabbed her robe, and scurried erratically to the bathroom. Sitting on the toilet, she drew the terrycloth across her shoulders and squinted at the room through slit eyelids, she dragged her fingers through her hair in an effort to get at least some of it pointed in the same direction. At the sink she brushed her teeth and her tongue, leaning over carefully to control the drumming in her temples. She splashed water on her face and dried it with a towel as she eased into an upright position. Collecting her clothes from the night before, she struggled into them, bracing herself against the wall and whispering a litany of Guinness regret. Finally receiving the benefits of circulation and movement, she found her balance mostly restored and clumped out onto the covered deck, grinning ruefully and scratching her head as she yawned. Harrison sat before her, dozing in a lawn chair. In his lap, slipped from his fingers, was a single yellow rose. He was shivering slightly in his sleep, and her heart went out to him. She darted back inside and retrieved her robe. Kneeling, she draped it over his back and kissed his cheek. He jerked to wakefulness and peered at her, slightly confused.

"Good morning, Sweetheart," she smiled.

"I'm an idiot," he growled, attempting to sit up, grab the fallen rose and clear his throat at the same time. "I treated you terribly, Luce," he continued, thrusting the rose at her. "Please forgive me. I love you."

"How long have you been sitting out here, Idiot?"

"Since just after dawn," he replied, stifling a yawn. "I have no idea what time it is now. I wanted to be sure and be here when you woke up." He twisted in the chair, seeking circulation, and noticed the robe on his shoulders. "Thanks for the robe. I got pretty cold."

"It's very gallant of you to go to all this trouble," she smiled. "I think you've suffered enough. Apology accepted, incident forgotten." She kissed him lightly on the lips and stood up. He creaked to his feet and put his arms around her. She could feel him shiver as they stood in the early morning sun.

"You're trembling."

"I guess I am," he admitted.

"We'll fix that," she grinned. "Go to the bath house, take off your clothes and get into the tub. I'll go to the house and be back with coffee, a towel, and something dry for you to put on."

"You're wonderful, Luce," he smiled.

"So are you," she said, "you just don't know it. Go get in the bath. We'll get you warm, we'll get you dry, and I'll show you my little world." She kissed him again, then pushed him toward the rear deck, and headed off across the lawn to the house.

"This is really beautiful," Harrison said, as they stood on the side deck and watched Eddie scurry around the garden, spreading cypress mulch and raking it smooth. Behind them, workmen were sliding the refrigerator into place and connecting water lines in the kitchen. James was supervising the unloading of the air-conditioning condenser at the front of the house.

"It won't be long," Lucin said. "Just a couple more days and things'll be finished."

"Are you going to hire a decorator?"

"No. Actually I'm going to do very little decorating. Minimal furnishings, very simple, very plain."

"Very Japanese."

"Very Japanese."

Grinning ruefully, Harrison continued. "It seems I'm surrounded by Japanese."

"More than you know."

"What's that mean?" he asked.

"Oh, nothing," she smiled, slipping her arm around his waist. "Just the house, the garden, your business. Poor Harrison, everywhere you turn, there it is."

"Luce, I want to tell you again how sorry I am for blowing up at you like that. Regardless of my emotional state, it was inappropriate for me to shout at you and belittle your part in our life."

She squeezed his rib cage. "Just don't let it happen again, Buster."

He returned her squeeze. "Are you gaining weight?"

"A little. The skating makes me hungry, so I eat. I'm staying solid though." Grinning inside, she couldn't help herself. "James says it makes me look more like a girl."

"Well, he would know. With me gone so much, he's certainly seen more of you lately than I have," Harrison commented.

"James doesn't miss much," she replied, turning away so Harrison wouldn't notice the flush she felt rising in her face. "Let's go look at the kitchen and the new fridge."

They spent the next few minutes watching the kitchen range being installed, then Harrison excused himself to go down to the Crown Center office. After he left, James materialized in the living area. He smiled at Lucin.

"So, have the two of you made up then?"

"More or less," she answered.

"Someplace between how hurtful you think he was, and how hurtful he thinks he was, is the truth. Just remember that understanding and testosterone rarely mix well. I'm not askin' ya to cut the lad any slack, just don't give his words more weight than they deserve. That's not good for either of ya."

Lucin looked at him for a moment. "How'd you get so smart?" she asked.

"I was married to a remarkable woman for twenty-nine years. Ya can't spend that much time in the company of an Irish-Scot female and hang on to many illusions."

"You really loved her, didn't you, James."

"Aye. Right down to the ground. Still do."

"What would she think about us?"

"We'd bring out the Scot in her. 'Aw, would ye be lookin' at yerself, ye great git! What a fine rogue ye are then, Jimmy, auld lad!'" he mimicked. "She'd throw back her head and laugh at my foolishness, consortin' with a girl like you."

Lucin grinned. "Is that what we're doing? Consorting?"

"What would you call it, then?" he twinkled.

She paused for a moment and looked up at him with shining eyes. "James Mathew O'Doud," she said, "I'd call it making love."

"Aye, Lass," he murmured, touching her gently on the chin. "That's what I'd call it too, although it's a far cry from the customary definition."

"It is, isn't it?"

"It's like what we have is independent of the rest of our lives, as if you and I are separate from everything else."

"Pleasure is an orb," she intoned. "All that exists is within, all without is not real."

"And that would be more of your Japanese self shinin' through, I suppose."

"I suppose," she chuckled.

"Well, it was evident in several ways last night, with ya floppin' about in yer lovely bath, your velvet self glowin' in the light of the lamp, a Guinness mustache gracin' your luscious lip," he teased.

"James, I am putting you on notice to withhold Guinness from me when I start to get stupid," she blushed.

"I'll do that," he agreed, "as soon as ya get stupid."

"You shouldn't let me get that drunk."

"Me!?"

"Yes, you."

"So, I'm responsible for your self-control then?"

"Of course," she smiled.

"Uh-huh. Now hear this. You gettin' that drunk was what saved us from committin' a terrible indiscretion."

"So that's your plan!" she pounced. "Get me as drunk as possible as soon as possible, so you don't have to take me seriously."

"Nope. Me plan is to let ya drink as much as ya want until ya get to the point where I don't take *myself* seriously."

"Next time …"

"Next time?"

"Next time, you can carry me to bed after two glasses."

"I can, can I?"

"Sure," she beamed.

"Now what makes ya think there will be a next time?"

"Oh, there will be, Jimmy."

"Now, that could be dangerous, y'know."

"I find that I like being dangerous with you," she replied, and grinned at him with her lower lip between her teeth.

"Sweet Mary. I'm beginning ta think ya just like being dangerous."

"Guinness tonight?" she teased.

"And what about your husband?"

"He's flying back to Philly late today. I'll be all by myself," she pouted. "Guinness tonight?"

"Alas, Darlin' Lucille, not tonight. Tonight I am otherwise engaged."

"Jolee?"

"As if it was any of your business, yes, Jolee."

"Good," she smiled. "You need to get out more, James. I don't think it's totally safe for you around here."

"I'm beginning to agree with ya," he grinned.

Lucin spent the afternoon shopping for furnishings. She chose four futon chairs and two low tables for the living area and a couple of hanging lights with round paper globes for between the kitchen and dining space. The dining table was pale birch, square and plain, with four low-backed chairs. She furnished her dressing area with two tall chifferobes in black lacquer and a matching four-drawer chest. For the kitchen, she purchased a toaster, a small microwave, a coffee press, a blender, and a medium-sized charcoal hibachi that would sit on a slab of marble next to the stove and under the hood. To cook, she chose two deep sauté pans, a large skillet with straight sides, one medium saucepan, a counter-top convection oven, and a rice and fish steamer. Her china was plain in low-gloss white, her flatware simple in brushed stainless steel. With delivery promised in two days, she drove home in the late afternoon. As she pulled in the drive, Lucin noticed Sheila Hartrick motor by, stop, and reverse to the house, backing erratically up the street, bouncing over the curb twice before finally pulling in behind the Jag. Kennedy bounced out of the passenger side and ran toward her.

"Lucin!" she shouted.

"Kaypee! Girlfriend!" Lucin laughed, returning a brief hug the child launched at her.

"I'm just so glad I caught you," huffed Sheila, trying not to fall off her yellow heels as she flapped up the drive. "Kennedy Paige, don't just run up and clutch at people! It's not nice!"

"It wasn't a clutch, Mom. It was a hug. Lucin and me always hug each other!"

"Lucin and *I*, Dear."

"I'm sorry, Sheila," Lucin explained. "I guess I started it. I hugged first. I hope you don't mind."

"Mind?" Sheila flushed. "Uh ... no, of course I don't *mind* ... it's just that I don't think Kennedy should go around grabbing people she doesn't know very well."

"But Lucin and me are *buds*, Mom!" piped the child.

"Lucin and *I*, Kennedy."

"We skate together all the time!"

"Forgive me, Mrs. Hartrick," said Lucin, taking a respectful step backwards. "Perhaps I have been too forward. It was not my wish to make you uncomfortable. Kennedy is, of course, your child. Your wishes must come first. It was not my intent to commit an indiscretion or to create disharmony between you and your daughter. So sorry."

Sheila looked confused for a moment, then collected herself. "No, no ... it's *fine*. I just didn't realize you and Kennedy were such good friends ... such *skating buddies*."

"Thank you," said Lucin. "It is my honor to be regarded well by such a wonderful child. You are very understanding."

"Well ..." Sheila went on, gathering herself, "the reason I stopped is the upcoming neighborhood association get together. It's a week from this Sunday at our place at four PM in the afternoon and it is going to just be such fun! We're having a patio party. We'll have drinks and finger foods and a small band and just everybody is going to be there and we just so hope you and Harrison, especially since you are new to the neighborhood and all, can attend."

"As I told you before, I'm not sure if Harrison will be in town."

"Now, that just doesn't make any difference at all! You are more than welcome to come without an escort. It's not a meeting or business or any kind of official gathering. Everybody drinks and eats and dances and just has a ball! We socialize and gab and just spend time together. Sometimes these things don't break up for just hours! Between the full bar and the music, they just go on and on. And it's very informal. Everybody dresses to be comfortable. It would just be wonderful if all your neighbors could finally meet you! I have your invitation right here," she said handing Lucin a pink envelope that smelled like a sandalwood factory. "I just so hope you and Harrison can come, and if not Harrison, then you can just come all by yourself!"

Resisting the urge to gush *"Can I? All by myself?"* at the woman, Lucin smiled. "I'd love to, Sheila. If Harrison is in town, we'll be there. If he is not available, I'll be there."

"Now that's just wonderful!" Shelia giggled. "Well, we'll just see you then, then won't we?"

"Yes, you will," Lucin smiled, as the woman wobbled back to her SUV. Kennedy beat her there, scrambled into the passenger seat and hung out the window.

"'Bye, Girlfriend!" she shouted, while her mother started the car.

"Later, Kaypee!" Lucin waved, as Sheila backed down the driveway. She only drove on the lawn once.

Stephanie had prepared lovely butterflied almond trout with a watercress salad and orange slices in honey for dessert. Lucin ate with her in the kitchen and enjoyed every bite. After dinner, she grabbed a split of merlot, went upstairs, and spent the evening in bed with James Patterson. A dreamless night followed. She awakened only once, the scent of James faint in her nostrils.

TWENTY-TWO

The promise of the night
Is seldom revealed
In the expectation of the day.
Darkness, sweet darkness ...
I wait.

BY THE WEEKEND the house was finished. After Saturday morning breakfast, Lucin walked through it, sliding the shoji screens, changing the configuration of the rooms. The two small, dark apartments had been transformed into a spacious, airy, uncluttered living space with the only three solid interior walls those that surrounded the bathroom. Linen storage had been built into the bath, but there were no other closets, no hallways, no doors except to the outside. It was pristine space, light in color and attitude. Here and there rice mats were positioned on the hardwood floor, and there were areas near the outside entrances for footwear. Shoes were not allowed inside. The bath was spacious enough that the glass block shower had no curtain or closure, just a ninety-degree entrance to contain the splash. The bathroom also had a ninety-degree configuration, eliminating the need for a door. Facing the living area, against the outside of the rear bathroom wall, Lucin had placed a wooden three-drawer Japanese chest, lacquered to a deep black-cherry finish. It needed something of focus, a piece to add that single splash of color to the room. Off she went to see Tami.

"Lucin-san!" he nearly shouted as she walked through the door. "Welcome! I feel as if I have not seen you for weeks. How are you? How is your house?" He approached her quickly, nearly gliding across the floor and took both her hands in his.

"Hello, Tami," she smiled, feeling the warmth of his gentle, yet almost urgent grip slide softly up her arms. Oh. This was different. The delicate hairs on her forearms rose with the quiet heat.

"How may I be of service to you?" he asked, releasing her hands and bowing slightly, obviously glad to see her. "Is your house finished?"

"Almost. The construction is done, the furniture is in place, the prints are hung, but it needs something."

"Color?"

She smiled. Of course he'd know. "Yes, color."

"Come with me," he grinned, and walked to the rear of the store.

Tami led Lucin into the storage area where he lifted a small cedar trunk onto a table. Opening the trunk, he pushed the packing aside to reveal a vase. It was about twenty inches tall and six-sided, an elongated ginger jar shape, but open at the neck. The base and throat were edged in gold. The vase itself was blue. Enraptured, Lucin gazed at it for several seconds before she realized she was holding her breath.

"Oh, my," she murmured. Tami chuckled.

A brilliant royal blue at the top, the color whispered its way down the faceted porcelain sides growing darker with every inch. By the middle of the vessel, it had reached a transparent cobalt, rich and mysterious. The evolving hue led the eye downward to the base — fired in such a depth of midnight blue as to be virtually black, but obviously not black, a blue of such heavy richness that black would not have been dark enough to reveal its depth. The finish seemed deeper than the vessel could contain, spider-webbed in the tiniest cracks imaginable, perfect imperfections induced by the firing of the amazing glaze. To Lucin, the vase appeared as if it would glow in total darkness, such was the power of its spirit.

"Unbelievable," she stated, almost feeling the color on her skin.

"Yes," Tami agreed.

"I want it."

"Of course. It has been waiting here for you since before you came into my shop."

She tore her eyes from it and looked at Tami. "I don't understand."

"Yes, you do," he replied, closing the cedar case and securing the clasp. "Above all others, you understand perfectly." He regarded her with such intensity that his gaze was as heat upon the skin of her face. Her knees began to tremble and she resisted reaching for him to maintain balance. He smiled and backed away a step. Warmth hummed in her low back and strength radiated from it. She swayed briefly, then took it in, allowing his power to infuse her and still the trembling.

"Don't you want to know how much?" Tami smiled.

"I don't care how much."

"My cost plus ten percent."

"Sold," she said, straightening her posture and returning his smile.

He picked up the box and walked out into the shop. "Ah, if only all my customers were as easy as you," he laughed.

At the counter he took her card. "Eddie tells me the garden will be finished today."

"I don't know," she replied. "He was still puttering around when I left."

"He also tells me you speak Japanese."

She laughed. "He told me that too, but I can't swear to it. I was asleep at the time. At least I think I was."

"Sometimes the passage between realities must manifest itself as something we are familiar with and can accept. The feeling of sleep or trance is very common. Know this, Lucin." He paused and stared at her intently. "The sleeper must awaken."

157

His words drifted in the air like cobwebs, their tiny tendrils settling about her head and shoulders. She felt the room close in a bit, the air become dense and thick. She wanted Tami to touch her, hold her, reassure her, but he did not. Instead, he watched. The light began to dim and she could feel her eyelids flutter and her balance slipping away.

"No. No!" said Tami. "Not here, Lucin. Not now, Lucin. No. Come back. Focus! Take my hand and come back."

She clutched at his offered hand and clung to it. With an almost audible rush, the walls receded, the air thinned, the cobwebs melted and she returned, feeling her feet firmly on the floor, seeing Tami clearly with her eyes.

"What was that?" she gasped.

"An indulgence," he replied, smiling slightly.

"What did I indulge in?"

"You didn't," Tami admitted. "I did. I apologize."

"What?" she asked, obviously confused.

"We will discuss it another time. When you return home, you will find that Eddie is finished with your garden."

"He gave me bats."

"He drove you what?" Tami grinned.

"He *gave* me bats," Lucin repeated, smiling.

"To keep the mosquitoes under control no doubt. Very pain."

"That's right," she chuckled. "Very pain."

"I, too, have a garden warming gift. Tomorrow morning I leave for Japan. I will be gone for at least three weeks, probably more. Perhaps I might bring it by late afternoon today?"

"Another gift?"

"Actually this one is as much for the garden as it is for you. The earth gives us so many things. It is only fitting that we should gift it in return from time to time. After dinner, around six-thirty?"

"I would be honored."

"Good. I will see you then." He extended her credit card and the slip. Lucin signed it and placed her copy in the pocket of her blouse. She reached for the wooden case, then stopped.

"One more thing," she said. She pulled the silk cord from under her collar and withdrew the ivory pendant, handing it to him. "It belonged to my great grandmother's grandmother."

Tami studied it for a moment, then placed the pendant between his palms in the attitude of Christian prayer. Slowly a smile came over his face. "Now you know," he said.

"Now I know," she answered, taking it back from him, and picking up the box. "This evening at six-thirty," she continued. "I'm looking forward to it."

"As am I, Lucin-Blossom," smiled Tami, bowing her on her way. "As am I."

When Lucin reached home, she carried the cedar chest directly to the garden house and placed the vase on the black cherry table. The effect was instantaneous. The entire room pulled together around that magnificent blue. Nothing competed, nothing challenged. There was not one complimentary color in the entire area. The vase did not require it, infusing the space with whispers of itself. It dominated and supported, it took and it gave. Both nexus and matrix, it did not shout for attention but rewarded it with murmurs of royal and indigo, cobalt and midnight. It was perfect, Lucin thought as she moved it slightly off center on the table, leaving perfection in the hands of the gods.

When she stepped out on the rear deck, Eddie noticed her and trotted over.

"Ru-sin-*san*," he smiled. "Garden ready to start. I finish."

She looked out over his work. "Eddie, it is beautiful. A masterpiece."

"It pretty okay," he grinned. "Rovely garden, rovely lady. All balance. My honor do this place. Very yes."

"I can't thank you enough."

"Rock thank Eddie, tree thank Eddie, dirt thank Eddie. Eddie thank you." He bowed deeply from the waist and looked at her thoughtfully for a moment. "I ask befo', now ask again," he said. "You Japanee, yes? Got Japanee blut, yes?"

"Yes," she replied, feeling tears gather on her lower lids. "I just found out."

His grin was huge. "Eddie know," he beamed. "You wait. Right back." He trotted off toward his truck.

In just a moment he returned carrying a crockery bottle glazed in soft gray. He handed it to her. "Sake," he said. "Eddie make. You put in hot watta, sit heah on deck in night, pour in cup, drink four five time, six seven time, rook at garden. *Kami* come, spirit come, time stop. Honor garden, honor self. Make much happy, maybe much silly. Goo' time. Enjoy, okay?"

"Okay," she agreed, wiping a tear from her cheek.

"Bring fren', no bring fren', same-same. All okay. Okay?"

"Okay," she replied.

"I come one week, two week, rake, prune, take care plant an' watta. Make shoo all grow. Keep garden goo'."

"That's fine, Eddie."

"Okay," he bowed, and began to gather up his tools.

Lucin watched him go, then went inside and put the sake in the fridge. She fussed around the house for an hour or so, washing down counter tops, wiping down the furniture, battling the excess dust that always seems to accompany new construction. Flitting from task to task, she realized she was nervous. Tami was coming. Exactly what that meant she didn't know. She did know, however, that butterflies the size of tennis racquets were twanging about in her stomach. She checked her watch. Almost noon. Time for lunch. Lunch would settle her down and quiet the butterflies. She was over halfway to the house before she realized she still clutched the rag she'd been using to dust.

James greeted her as she bustled into the kitchen.

"Lucille, me darlin'," he said, "are the hounds on your lovely heels? Ya look like you're runnin' from somethin'."

"Tami's coming over!"

"Lord, no!" James blurted, jumping to his feet. "You take the children to the root cellar, I'll load the rifles!"

159

"What?"

"If it looks like we're not goin' ta make it, I'll shoot ya meself before I let him get his filthy yellow hands on ya!"

"James, what are you talking about?!"

"I promise I'll see ya dead before I'll let ya fall into his heathen clutches," James replied, standing tall with his hand over his heart.

Lucin stared at him for a moment, then sank into a chair shaking with laughter. "God," she giggled, "am I that bad?"

"You were rollin' your eyes like a loose horse! For a minute I thought I was goin' ta have ta slap ya so ya wouldn't swallow your tongue!" he grinned. "Did ya mention somethin' about Tami comin' over?" he asked, settling into a chair beside her. "I wasn't payin' much attention."

"You are wonderful," Lucin replied, rising to stand next to him, leaning her low belly against his shoulder, and wrapping her arms loosely around his neck. "Rub my bottom."

"How 'bout if I just grope your arse?"

"That'll do, I suppose."

Chuckling, James patted her butt and stood up. "Tuna salad and chips. Stephanie is out runnin' errands. It'll be my pleasure to serve ya. Set yourself," he continued, opening the fridge, "and tell me why Tami comin' over has got ya so upset."

"Huh," she said after a moment. "I don't know. Even though I have spent very little time with him, Tami has had a huge influence on my life. He's dropping by to bring me a garden-warming gift. I guess I feel like I'm on trial or something. As if he's coming over to make sure I did everything right. Sort of a Japanese final exam."

"What happens if ya fail?"

"Well ... nothing, I guess. But I don't want Tami to be disappointed in me."

"That'd stop the earth from turning," James smiled, setting half a sandwich and a small bowl of chips in front of her.

"You're right. That's not it," she replied, taking a bite out of the sandwich.

"What is?"

"I doan dough."

"Don't talk with your mouth full, ya heathen."

Lucin swallowed. "I don't know," she grinned.

"Sure ya do."

"I do?"

"Yep. All the time you've known Tami, he's been able to rattle you at will. He knows stuff about ya he has no way of knowin'. He touches ya from across the room, he whispers in your shell-like ear from ten feet away, and, truth be told, he blows your dress up. But all this time, the lad has never taken a run at ya. Never patted your sweet backside, never gotten out of line, never showed any sexual inclination toward ya a'tall. That's tough for a woman to handle, especially a woman who's in the process of figurin' out just how female she really is. Why, if ya didn't have me to bounce off of, ya might have stripped that poor boy to the bone by now."

"James!" she laughed.

"What I'm sayin' is this. Up to now your contact with Tami has been governed by rules. It's been, one way or another, business. Now he's comin' by on a social

160

mission. He's droppin' in just to see you and bring you a gift. Not to show you anything, not to draw a design, not to get information relative to work, just to see you. No rules. Now, I'm not sayin' he's stoppin' by to drag you off into the heather for a little slap and tickle, but the point is, you don't know. And that, me fine female friend, has got your panties in a bunch."

She shook a potato chip at him. "Sometimes you piss me off, Jimmy."

"All part of me charm, Darlin'," he grinned.

"So, will you be around this evening?"

"Oh, no. You're not draggin' O'Doud inta this. The delightful Jolee and I will be spending the late afternoon and evenin' together. You are on your own, Lucille. But I do have a bit of advice for ya."

"What?"

"About thirty minutes before the dear boy is due to arrive, drink four pints of Guinness. It's my experience that'll put a stop to almost anything."

The last third of her sandwich hit him between the shoulder blades as he skipped out the door.

A thirty-minute search through her dressing room produced a pair of black peasant pants with elastic cuffs in lightweight silk and an old royal blue robe with butterfly sleeves in lined satin that she never wore because it was too short. Hmmm. Fairly oriental. A black camisole would keep the robe decent and her black pair of Chinese slippers would complete the effect. Hearing Stephanie come in, she put the clothing on her dressing rack and went downstairs in time to help the girl through the door with her second load of groceries.

"Hi, Lucin," she smiled, blowing a strand of hair away from her face. "Hot out there."

"I haven't been out since late morning."

"It must be eighty-five or more by now. The forecast said low nineties by late afternoon. Great day for me to buy charcoal, huh?"

"Charcoal?"

"I picked up some fillets. Thought you might like steak and veggies over the grill tonight."

"Oh, Steph, that sounds wonderful, but just a salad with croutons for me. I've got to be down at the other house by about five-thirty or six. The man that designed the garden is coming over. I'll fend for myself and James can too. When you get things put away, take off if you like."

"Really?"

"Sure."

"Thanks! Westport, here I come," she grinned. "Where do you want me to put the charcoal?"

"Just leave it on the back porch. I want to take some down to the little house."

Lucin spent the next two hours getting the garden house in pristine condition, carefully cleaning and straightening, making everything as neat and Tami-worthy as possible. She moved two large pillows onto the covered deck at the best possible place to view both arms of the garden. Near them went the hibachi, carefully filled with charcoal, lighting sticks in place. A half-filled eight-quart pot sat atop the grate, the large bottle of sake given to her by Eddie crouched in the water, waiting for heat. Beside the hibachi on a low table was her sake set. By three, everything was as prepared as it could be. She spent thirty minutes looking at the garden to relax, but couldn't shake the jitters of anticipation. Finally, she just gave up and walked to the house.

A long shower settled her down a bit and she padded into the kitchen and fixed a salad she couldn't eat, finally munching down half a bagel slathered with peanut butter and a small glass of milk. Back upstairs, she fussed over her makeup longer than usual, accentuating the slope of her eyes and her cheekbones, attempting to be both obvious and subtle. Her hair, uncut for some time and longer than usual, she pulled into a loose ponytail, allowing the sides to settle on the tops of her ears. Black cotton bikini panties went under the peasant pants, the black camisole under the too short robe. Braless, with no jewelry except the ivory pendant, she buttoned on the Chinese slippers and looked at herself in the mirror. God. She really did look Japanese. Downstairs, she popped an Altoid into her mouth and two more into the pocket of the robe, then walked to the garden house.

By the time her walk was finished, she was covered in a light sheen of perspiration. The misters were on and the garden was at least ten degrees cooler than the outside air. The deck was very comfortable, the view lovely. She kneeled on a pillow and attempted to collect herself. Failing that, she lit the charcoal to heat the Sake, went inside to wash her hands, and began to wait.

Eventually Eddie's truck pulled up, manned by his sons, and they began to remove a large stone from the rear and maneuver it into a wheelbarrow. Just as they started to push it toward the garden, a black Lexus rolled up the drive to the garage. Wearing floppy, black canvas pants, an oversize white silk shirt with the tail reaching nearly to his knees, Tami, his hair loose to his shoulders, exited the car and began walking toward the garden house. When Lucin stepped out onto the deck, he saw her and grinned. Jesus. She could feel him from fifty feet away.

TWENTY-THREE

If substance causes shadows,
Then cannot shadows cause substance?
Is he who smiles in the night
Less real than
He who laughs in the day?

"LOOK AT YOU," Tami said, stepping up onto the deck. "Your heritage is showing, Lucin-san, and showing very nicely I might add."

"Thank you," she dimpled, doing a quick turn and laughing. "You look a little different too. I've never seen you when you weren't all dressed in black with your hair in a ponytail."

"Ah, yes," he smiled. "I find that a great many of the people who buy from my store expect me to have a slight accent and look like something from a Jackie Chan movie. I am not so stupid as to not oblige them."

"Tami the stereotype," she giggled.

"That would be me. Would you excuse me for a moment while I direct Eddie's sons?"

"Of course. What are they doing?"

"Delivering your gift."

For the next few minutes, Tami and the two young men carefully positioned a stone in the small cleared area of the garden that had been prepared for it. After it was gently seated in the earth, some Irish moss and wisteria were planted against it to assist in the illusion that the rock had been in place for some time. When all was finished, Tami said goodbye and the two men left. He returned to the deck and stood beside Lucin.

"There it is," he said. "I brought you a rock."

"Yes, you did. A rock."

"This is no ordinary, run of the mill, garden variety rock, you know."

"It isn't?"

"No. This particular stone has been in my family for many generations. My great, great, great, great, grandfather used this very stone as a doorstop for his outhouse. It

163

has great sentimental value to our family. Not as much as the outhouse, of course, but a shitload."

"I'm very gratified," Lucin said, biting her lip.

"Are you?"

"No," she laughed. "I'd rather have the outhouse."

"How 'bout the truth?" he grinned.

"I'm not sure."

"Eddie found this stone at a landscape dealer several years ago. I noticed it in his backyard and swiped it. I've hidden it from him for about three years. He'll remember it when he sees it. If he feels it has come to the right place, he'll never say a word about the theft. I don't expect to hear from him."

"So, what you're saying is, you've made me an accessory after the fact, and given me a hot rock."

"Yeah," he chuckled. "That about sums it up."

"It's lovely."

"We'll look at it later. Show me your place."

The tour didn't take very long. Tami and Lucin went through the house in just a few moments. She showed him the bathhouse and he regarded the garden from several different angles for a while, then retreated to the deck and sat cross-legged on one of the pillows. Lucin sat on her heels next to him as the misting system kicked on again, the setting sun turning the droplets to molten gold.

"Now that's pretty," Tami smiled. "Lucin, this is really lovely. The house is elegant in its simplicity, the garden turned out really well, this covered deck area is perfect. It's very nice here. Good *wa*."

"Thank you," she said, filling a flask from the bottle warmed over the hibachi. "Sake?"

"Of course. What better way to honor the change of the day."

For the next hour or so, they made small talk and drank. Lucin relaxed and loosened up. Tami was the ideal guest, bright, witty, fun, and she could feel his presence beside her as if a heat lamp were shining on her skin. After they finished the fourth flask, she felt her attention drifting toward the stone. She looked at it where it sat dimly visible in the glow of a walk light. Moonshine flickered on the surface of the pond behind it and a gentle breeze rustled the bamboo hedge. The temperature had fallen, the air nearly cool, as a bat careened low over the water in erratic flight and a frog peeped in the darkness.

The stone rose above the earth to about the height of a fire hydrant, almost two feet across at the base. Forming a right-angle triangle from her perspective, it was dark gray in color, with a few narrow, nearly white vertical striations. The surface was almost mica-like in the way it reflected tiny refractions of light. Even the faint glow from the walk light caused muted twinkles to gently flash on its side. They finished the fifth flask while she peered at it. Tami broke the comfortable silence.

"I would be pleased if you allowed me to name your stone."

"Stones have names?"

"Some do."

"Of course. I would be honored."

"Thank you," he said, and stared at the rock for several minutes. At length, never taking his eyes from the stone, he smiled. "I will call it 'The Waiting Courtesan'," he stated.

"'The Waiting Courtesan?'"

"Uh-huh."

"Why?"

"Regard the stone, Blossom-*san*, and perhaps you will know."

She stared at the rock, and its glittering surface claimed her, leaving her sitting on the deck with Tami and pulling her miles and years and lifetimes away.

"Blossom-*san*, what are you doing?" the old woman asked, looking down at her where she sat by the garden.

"Forgive me, *Mama-san*, I am trying to watch the stones grow, but I cannot concentrate."

"Are you nervous, Child?"

"Very yes."

"Why?"

"I am afraid he will think I am ugly."

"But you are not ugly. You are extraordinarily pretty."

"I am afraid he will not like my body."

"Nonsense. Your body is exquisite."

"I am afraid I am not ready for him."

"When you were nine years old you thought you were ready for Pendulous Pestles and Peerless Parts by the armload," Mama-*san* complained. "Now that you *are* ready, you fear you are not. What am I going to do with you child?"

"Please don't be angry with me, Mama-*san*."

"Stand up!" the old woman ordered. Blossom got to her feet. "Don't look at me," Mama-*san* spat. "After all I've done for you, all I taught you, all I've invested in you, and you sit and whine about your tiny fears like a little child. Turn around and keep your eyes on your feet, you ungrateful wretch!" A maid carrying a kimono materialized beside the woman.

"Untie your *obi* and drop your night kimono to the ground."

"Mama-*san*! Please don't beat me."

"Do as you are told!"

Trembling, the young woman untied the sash and let her kimono fall to the earth. She stood, slightly hunched, looking at her feet in the pale moonlight.

"Perhaps what you are about to receive will change your mind," the old woman snarled, and lovingly draped the new kimono over Blossom's shoulders.

Trimmed on the collar and hem in gold piping, it was of raw Chinese silk in an extraordinary blue. Light royal blue shoulders graduated to cobalt at the waist, then became darker as the material traveled downward until, at the bottom, it was a deep midnight, blacker than black, with the depth of the nighttime sky. The girl took a moment to realize what had happened.

"Oh, Mama-*san*! Look how beautiful it is!"

"Look how beautiful you are, my child."

"But this is very much!"

"So are you, Blossom," she answered, watching the girl adjust the kimono around her nude body. "Tell me, how old are you now?"

"I will be fifteen when the blossoms fall from the cherry trees."

"You are familiar with the contents of the red box?"

"Oh yes, Mama-*san*."

"The pleasure pearls and secret skins, too?"

"Very yes!"

"You have been doing your exercises?"

"Every day many times, Mama-*san*."

"Your muscles are strong?"

"Oh yes. Izumi-*san* says she has never had a student with such a powerful Jade Gate or supple Heavenly Pavilion."

"Good," nodded the old woman. "Then you are ready."

"If you say so, Mama-*san*."

"I say so. Put away your fears. Goto-*san* is a wise and gentle man. He has done this many times for me. It is his duty to bring you pleasure, and allow you the pleasure of bringing him pleasure. Izumi-*san* will bring you some sake. Drink it, sit, and watch the stones. Compose yourself. Goto-*san* will come for you after a time and tomorrow you will laugh at your foolishness and be anxious for him to come to you again."

"Very well, Mama-*san*," said Moon-Blossom, and watched the old woman walk away.

Feeling very happy in her beautiful new night kimono, she quieted herself and regarded a stone. In a few moments the night claimed her and, for a time, she was freely outside herself.

She would never, for the rest of her life, be able to remember that night clearly. His hand on her shoulder brought her to her feet, his palm on the small of her back directed her into the bedchamber where he laid her gently down on the futon and removed her clothing. No words passed between them, but the unspoken language of the pillow flowed freely, as did his hands, his fingers, his lips, and his tongue. It was as if there were many of him, and she trembled under the magic of his tender assault. He tickled, he touched, he traced, he tweaked. He left no square inch of her unattended. Infinitely patient, never demanding, endlessly he brought her pleasure. For an eternity he led her, directed her, guided her to that exact place where he wanted her to go. And when she was arrived, when she was on the edge of the abyss, when she *wanted*, when she *needed*, only then did he enter her.

This was no *harigata*, no soulless length of rigid ivory, this was a *man*. A throbbing, pulsing, blood-filled living thing that reached up inside her again and again, shattering her illusions, overflowing her fantasies, inundating her hopes, washing away her fears, making her grunt and squirm with heated participation. Using the classic "six shallow, five deep" thrusts he transformed her into his instrument and played her like a master. Biting his shoulder to restrict her screams, she clung to him hand and heel, elbow and knee until, at precisely the correct instant, he cast her over the edge.

166

The fall was delirious, joyful, aching, and poignant. She tumbled through it, writhed through it, soared through it, careened through it, chasing her very soul down the long burning cascade and, when she landed, he was there to catch her, hold her, caress her, collect and rebuild her. She huddled against him as if in shelter from the storm, shaking and trembling with the passage of the experience, crying and laughing, clutching and releasing. Drenched in sweat, she slid away a bit and looked at him. He then spoke the only words that would be said that night.

"That was for you. Next is for me. Then comes for us."

She smiled and kissed his chest.

Lucin awoke to dim sunlight from an overcast sky. Her mouth and throat were dry and her lips felt swollen and tender. Raising up from the futon on one elbow, her back twinged with a dull ache and her limbs felt heavy. She eased back down and took stock of herself. Her breasts felt ponderous, her nipples sore. Between her legs she seemed thick and swollen. The *harigata* box was near the bedside and empty, its contents scattered about the futon and floor. What had happened? Where was Tami? Had she … had they? She could not discover his scent in the bed linen, but her nose and sinuses were not functioning any better than the rest of her. She could see no trace of him in the room, but everything had been so real and yet foggy, so vivid and yet shadowed. God! She didn't know. Did it make a difference? Did it? She didn't know that either. Curling into a ball, she pulled a pillow between her tender thighs and gave herself over to sleep. Perhaps the truth lay in dreams.

It was nearly eleven when she woke again, her bladder screaming at her. Quickly she used the bathroom, then crawled back between the covers and tried to think. The events of the night were even more clouded in her mind. She recalled the kimono of the vision colored so much like the vase. She remembered the practiced hands upon her, hands the like of which she had never known. She had fleeting remembrance of what he had done to her, what she had done to him, and what they had done for each other, but who was he? For that matter, who was *she*? She struggled with the reality and fantasy of it all, her head swimming with foggy snatches of the night before. The rumpled covers and scattered implements were no proof of anything. She was well acquainted with the box and its comforts. Answers eluded her, truth eluded her. Mama-*san's* voiced reached her.

"Be quiet within yourself, my child. A woman with a man in the night is without import. Do not trouble yourself. Do not carry the pillow with you into the day."

The words brought her no peace. Restless and upset, she lingered in bed, afraid to rise. Afraid it had all been a dream. Afraid she would shatter the illusion, if it was illusion. Afraid of what else may have been shattered if it was not.

TWENTY-FOUR

My secrets of the night
Are withheld even from me.
Light follows darkness.
As a gift from a child,
Joy follows sorrow.

LUCIN SPENT THE ENTIRE DAY in the garden house, sleeping, waking, tossing, turning, trying to deal with the tangle in her mind, attempting to avoid thinking about anything, afraid to leave her sanctuary and re-enter the world, unsure of what was real. Weak and shaken, depressed and conflicted, she could find no comfort in the garden, no peace within herself, no safety within the walls. Red-eyed and pale, she walked to the main house at dusk. James was sitting in the kitchen. He looked at her as she came through the door.

"What do you need?" he asked.

"I don't know." Her reply was dull and without spirit.

"What would you like?" James continued.

"I don't know." She couldn't meet his eyes.

"What do you want?"

"I don't ... I don't know," she whispered. Leaning on the counter with her back to him, she began to tremble. By the time James reached her, she was crying soft urgent sobs, her fists clenched, nails biting into her palms.

James led her to a kitchen chair, ripped a couple of paper towels off the roll, filled a glass halfway with water, and returned to her side. Sitting, he placed an arm around her shoulders. She shrugged it off.

"Don't."

Smiling, he replaced his arm.

"Don't!" she spat through her tears, twisting away.

Undaunted, he again put his arm around her.

"Goddammit, James!" she cried, straining against him, "leave me alone!"

Ignoring her protests, he turned his chair so he could put both arms around her.

168

"So," he said, "are ya such a bad person that ya aren't worthy of comfort from someone that loves ya?"

She continued to struggle, he continued to hold. She could not prevail against his strength. Relentless, James gently enfolded her against him. The point of no return arrived and she collapsed against his chest amid racking sobs. James stroked her hair and whispered nonsense in her ear as Lucin stepped off into the void, letting it happen, giving it up.

Twenty minutes later he carried her upstairs, removed all her clothes save her panties and camisole, and put her to bed. Returning to the kitchen, James heated some milk in the microwave, added too much Swiss Miss, and took a mug of hot chocolate and two sugar cookies back upstairs. Entering the bedroom, he found Lucin in agitated light sleep. Shaking his head, he moved a chair bedside, placed a hand on her hip and sat there, lightly touching her as he ate the cookies and drank the Swiss Miss. Under his hand she quieted and began to rest. He stood to leave, then bent down and kissed her cheek. In her sleep, Lucin spoke.

"James," she murmured.

"Aye," he smiled, gathering up the empty mug. "You're welcome."

The next morning, Lucin, wearing baggy cotton pants and an oversize tee shirt walked stiffly into the kitchen to find James busily fussing over the stove.

"Top of the mornin' to ya, Lucille, me darlin'," he beamed over his shoulder. "Set yourself. I sent Stephanie away for a while. Scrambled eggs, thick-cut bacon and peach pancakes commin' up. Get your own coffee. I can't neglect me duties right now to get it for ya. You're looking lovely today, by the way."

Almost dumbfounded, she stared at him.

"Say 'good morning, James,'" he grinned at her.

"Good morning," she mumbled.

"Now come over here and kiss my freshly shaved cheek, pour yourself a cup of coffee and drop it on the floor."

Stifling a small smile, she walked to James, kissed him lightly on the neck, and moved to the coffee pot. "Thanks for yesterday," she said.

"No thanks necessary. Anytime I get to carry you to bed and remove your clothes is reward enough for me."

"It seems like every time I make a fool of myself," Lucin flushed, moving to the table, "you're there to keep me under control or pick up the pieces."

"Aye," he teased. "Not since Christ carried the cross has there been such a heavy burden." Loading a plate with pancakes, eggs and bacon, he placed it in front of her.

"I'm sorry, James," Lucin said, staring bleakly at the food, "I appreciate all your work but ..."

"Eat."

"But," she continued, "I'm just not hungry."

"Eat," he repeated, delivering a small pitcher of heated maple syrup.

"I can't."

"Ya can, ya *will*. Eat it or wear it, but you're not leavin' this table without it."

"James ..."

"Don't 'James' me, Lucille. I don't know what's got ya in this funk you're in, but you're not in any condition to give me trouble. I'm bigger than you are, I'm stronger than you are, and, right now, I love you more than you do. This is comfort food made with the O'Doud lovin' touch. When you eat it you will feel better. When you eat it, I will feel better. Eat."

Lucin burped her way to a halt with nothing left on the plate but half a pancake and looked across the table at James. "God," she said.

"More coffee?" he smiled.

"Please. James, that was wonderful."

"Aye. Feelin' better?"

"Yes, thank you. A lot."

"Me mother always said that where the head goes the stomach will follow. If there's somethin' wrong with the head, feed the stomach and the head will usually get better. How's your head?"

"Confused. Very confused. I may have done a bad thing."

"May?"

"Uh-huh."

"It may have been bad, or you may have done it?"

"Yes."

"Well, that's clear as mud then, isn't it?"

Slowly the story began. The stone, the sake, the vision, the morning after. It started haltingly then poured from Lucin in a rush of words and a spattering of fresh tears, but without the relentless despair of the day before. When she finished, Lucin looked at him, her lower lip lightly between her teeth, and waited.

James poured himself another cup of coffee and kissed Lucin on the top of her head as he returned to his seat. He stared at the table for a moment, then looked at her.

"Question," he said. "You and I have come right up against it a time or three ourselves. Does that cause you any guilt?"

Lucin looked out the window briefly then turned to him. "No."

"Hmmm. Suppose then, that you'd dragged me off into your bed chamber and had your lovely way with me. Do ya think you'd have felt guilt about that?"

"No," she stated.

"In that case," he said, "what are your plans for the rest of the morning?"

She reached across the table, took his hand, and smiled.

"Look at that," he grinned. "We turned that frown upside down." They sat quietly for a time, and James continued. "Why do ya suppose that what you *might* have done with Tami causes ya so much grief, and what ya *would* have done with me doesn't?"

"What you and I have is different."

"Isn't that the truth, then," he grinned.

"You know what I mean. It's like you and I are separate from everything else. I love you, James."

"So love makes it alright to cheat on your husband."

"No. But it would be alright for me to be with you. I know that sounds like a contradiction, but it isn't. What you and I do is not related to my relationship with Harrison. Do you understand at all?"

"Aye, I'm afraid I do. It would have no effect on me and Jolee either. You and I are separate, without consequence or complication."

"Yes! That's it."

"But that's not it with Tami."

"Oh, no. Tami is very important in my life. He has done a great deal with me and for me and I feel very indebted to him. I also find him very attractive and unsettling. But, if I slept with him ..."

"Did you?"

"God, James ... I don't know!"

"Well, try this on. If you did sleep with him, was it really you? Might it have been this young Blossom just using you as a ... vehicle?"

Lucin's eyebrows shot up. "I hadn't thought of that!"

"Would that excuse it?"

"I don't know, James. I don't know *anything*."

"You could go ask Tami."

"I would if he were here. He's in Japan. He'll be there for weeks."

"So what are ya gonna do?"

"Oh, God. Maybe I'll go visit my mother for a week or two, spend time with the family, see some old girlfriends, stay away from men."

"Men aren't the problem."

"I know it."

"Besides, you'd be sick of your mother in minutes. You're way past that now, Lucille."

"I know that, too," she sighed. "Maybe it's this whole Japanese thing. Maybe I've gotten too involved, gone too far too fast."

"Or not far enough fast enough."

"You're a big help," she smiled. "Don't you know that you're supposed to wave your Irish wand and make all this go away?"

"I had an uncle that was out one night wavin' his Irish wand, and they put him in jail."

"James!" she laughed.

"You just think about my uncle and his Irish wand," he grinned. "I'll be right back." Lucin watched him head for the utility room and return carrying her skating bag. He dumped it on the table in front of her.

"I know this," said James. "I can't have ya mopin' around here like a little lost lamb for the next six months. Go upstairs, take a nice long shower, dress appropriately, and go skate. Do something physical and don't wallow in guilt or self-pity. Guilt is a waste of time and self-pity is a waste of energy. What happened night before last is not important. What you do with it is important."

Lucin looked at him for a few seconds, then stood up and put her arms around his neck. "I think I'll take a shower and go skate," she said.

"Why didn't I think of that," he replied, resting his palms on her waist.

"Want to come wash my back?"

"And everything else, too," he grinned.

"Thank you, James," she whispered, and kissed his chin.

"Aw, sure," he said, releasing her so she could walk away. "Try not to fall on your lovely bottom."

She stopped at the foot of the stairs and shook her butt. "If I do, will you massage it for me?" she asked.

"Get thee to the shower, ya foul temptress," grinned James.

Laughing, Lucin climbed the stairs out of sight. His grin slowing to a smile, James whistled softly as he put the cups and dishes in the sink.

Depression nagged at the corners of her mind through the shower and the drive to the rink. By the time she parked the Jag and was walking toward the building, she almost wished she hadn't come. It would have been much easier to have stayed in her bedroom and curled up with a book, but she also knew that James was probably right. Shifting her bag from hand to shoulder, she turned the corner to the ice rink entrance. Kennedy Paige Hartrick stood by the door, tears in her eyes.

"Kaypee, sweetie," said Lucin, crossing to the child, "what's wrong?"

Kennedy's eyes brightened and her face flooded with relief. "Lucin! Can I stay with you? It's Tanya's day off. I don't wanna be home in that big house all by myself. It's scary!"

"Where's your Mom?" Lucin asked, squatting down in front of the girl.

"Mom was supposed to be here to pick me up, but she ran over something in her car and the police came and her car won't go and I'm here all by myself! Can I stay with you?"

"I'd love it if you stayed with me," Lucin smiled.

"Yay!" Kennedy grinned. "I'll call my mom and tell her everything's okay," she bubbled, fishing around in her bag looking for her phone. "Could you give me a ride home when you're done skating?"

"You bet. Ask your mom what time she'll get home and I'll be the Kaypee delivery man."

"Delivery lady," grinned Kaypee, clutching her cell phone.

"How 'bout delivery girl?"

"Naw. I'm a girl. You're a lady." The child punched in a few numbers and walked away to speak with her mother.

Lucin watched Kaypee's conversation. She spoke very little and spent most of the time grimacing as she listened to the other side of the conversation. At length, she dropped the phone back in her bag and walked to Lucin.

"Everything okay?"

"Yes. Mom'll be home in a couple of hours. I'm supposed to not ask too many questions, not get in your way, not ask for anything to eat, and not hug you too much."

"Is that right?"

"Yep."

"Well, gimme a hug, and let's go get some ice cream."

"Aren't you gonna skate?"

"Naw. I gotta take care of this mean little kid."

172

Kaypee's face overflowed with a grin and she bounced into Lucin's arms.

"I'm also supposed to tell my coach what's going on," said the child, post hug, and ran off into the building.

Lucin tagged along and found Kaypee talking with a trim man in his mid-thirties while he watched a chubby teen-age girl wobble around on the ice. As Lucin approached, he smiled at her.

"Hi," she said, presenting her hand. "I'm Lucin Montgomery. I'm in charge of this little monster for the next few hours."

"Bryan Delcour," he smiled, removing a glove to shake hands. "I've seen you skate. Very nice."

She returned his smile. "For a beginner."

"You're no beginner. You must have skated a lot when you were a kid. Nobody does school figures to warm up anymore."

"I took lessons for years. Actually, I've been thinking about taking them again. Do you instruct adults?"

"When their egos can stand it," he grinned. "You interested in competing or just showing off."

"Showing off while I stay in shape."

"Great," he said, handing her a card. "I've got to get back to Darlene. Give me a call or we'll talk the next time we're both here."

"Nice to meet you, Bryan," Lucin smiled.

"You too," he replied, then turned to Kaypee. "Take good care of her, Kennedy. She's a prospective student," he said, and skated away in that effortless manner that only comes with thousands of hours on the ice.

Kennedy looked up at her as they walked to the car. "You gonna take lessons?"

"Maybe."

"But you're a grownup!"

"So?"

"Grownups don't take lessons."

"Sure they do."

"But you already know how to skate."

"Suppose I want to skate better?"

"You already skate really good. I like to watch you."

"Thank you. That's a very nice compliment. Even the best skaters in the world take lessons all the time. If they didn't, they wouldn't be the best."

"Mom wants me to be the best. Am I gonna have to take lessons my whole life?"

"Naw," smiled Lucin. "You can quit when you're ninety."

Kennedy looked at her thoughtfully. "You're teasing, aren't you?"

"Yep."

"Okay. I like it."

Thirty minutes later as they sat in a Baskin Robbins, Kennedy wiped whipped cream off her chin and looked at Lucin. "Can I see your little house?" she asked.

"You want to?"

"Uh-huh. I don't like big houses. They make noises. Our house is creepy sometimes."

"I know what you mean."

"If I had a house, it'd be just big enough for me and maybe a friend to come visit, and nobody could come inside without my permission. I'd have, like, my bed and two chairs and a refrigerator, that's all."

"No bathroom?"

The child rolled her eyes. "A course I'd have a *bathroom*. Everybody's got to have a bathroom."

"And just a refrigerator."

"Yup."

"Nothing else?"

"Maybe a toaster."

"Keep the jelly in the fridge?"

"Uh-huh."

"How 'bout the peanut butter? Can't keep it in the fridge."

"Ya keep it in the cabinet."

"Oh! So now you got a cabinet."

"Yep."

"How 'bout the knife to spread the peanut butter and jelly? Gotta have a drawer for the knife. Gotta have a counter too or there's no place to put the toaster. Like milk?"

"It goes in the refrigerator," pounced Kaypee.

"What about the glass?"

"Oh."

"Gotta have another cabinet. Glasses and peanut butter don't go in the same cabinet. Gonna need a sink to wash the knife and glass. What if a friend comes over? Now ya gotta have two of everything."

"Wow."

"Gets kinda complicated," Lucin grinned.

"I still just want a little house."

"Well, let's go look at my little house and see if you like it."

"Okay," said Kaypee, slurping her straw to get that last morsel of chocolate from the bottom of the glass.

"We'll go in through my bedroom," Lucin said, as she led Kennedy along the deck overlooking the garden.

"This is pretty!" exclaimed Kaypee, stopping to view the pond.

"We'll sit out here after you see the house," smiled Lucin, sliding back the screen so they could enter the building. Kennedy stopped and stared at the futon.

"That's your bed?"

"Uh-huh."

"It's on the floor!"

"That's right."

"Beds don't go on the floor. Beds go up on those bed things."

"Not this kind of bed. This kind of bed is supposed to go on the floor."

"Neat!"

They wandered through the house and headed back to the deck. Lucin was nearly outside before she realized Kennedy was no longer with her. Moving back into the living room, she saw the child standing before the blue vase, staring at it. She watched the unmoving girl for several minutes until she noticed Kennedy's eyelids begin to flutter. Quickly, Lucin moved to put an arm around her. The child gave a start, then looked at her.

"Okay?"

"Uh-huh," Kennedy replied, blinking rapidly.

"Where were you?"

"I was walking in the mountains on this little road, and everything was all green and nice and there were lotsa streams we had to cross, then these men came marching toward us and they were all bald on top and wore dresses that were kinda like bathrobes, and had these big swords, and we had to move over and stand real still and bow when they passed. There was this big long line of 'em then there were these guys in just, like, their underwear carrying this big box on poles and there was this other guy sitting in this box and when they carried him by, we all had to kneel and put our foreheads on the edge of the road, and then I woke up."

"Were you scared?"

"Nope. Can we go look at the garden now?"

"Sure," Lucin smiled. "Where do you think that dream came from?"

"The vase told it to me. Are there fish in that little lake outside?"

"Yep."

"Can I see 'em?"

"Uh-huh."

"Cool."

On the way to the car after sitting by the garden for an hour or so, Kennedy looked at Lucin. "I wish you were my mom," she stated.

"Sorry, Kiddo. You already got a mom."

"I know."

"You already got a mom who loves you and wants lotsa good stuff for you."

"I know," Kaypee sighed.

"Tell ya what. Let's form a club. The club of the secret sisters. I'll be your secret big sister, and you can be my secret little sister. I've always wanted a little sister and never had one. Would you be my secret little sister?"

Kennedy shined. "Really?"

"Really."

"Sure!"

"Okay," smiled Lucin. "From this moment forward I pronounce Kennedy Paige Hartrick and Lucin Montgomery to be secret sisters."

Kaypee climbed her.

TWENTY-FIVE

Darkness lifts.
Gray dawn reveals
Truth outside my window.
Smiling at my fear, I chill.
Darkness will come again.

LUCIN FINISHED applying her make-up and peered into the mirror. Sighing, she began to remove it. Things had been like this all week. It seemed no matter what she did, it never turned out right. She was restless and felt as if her skin didn't fit. She was hungry but nothing tasted good. She was bored, but didn't want to do anything. She was tired, but hardly slept. Lethargic, she jangled with nervous energy. She hadn't spent more than three hours in the garden house. Even James wasn't much help. The only time she'd been comfortable all week was the couple of hours she'd spent with Kennedy. Since that morning, she hadn't even gone skating.

Harrison phoned on Wednesday evening. Sounding depressed, he told Lucin he'd be on the coast for another few days then off to Japan for a week or two. He wasn't sure how long he'd be out of the country. Things at Crown Center were on hold. The Nagata account was in danger of slipping away. His reputation was at stake. Things just didn't look good. Not once did he ask her how she was. She wouldn't have known what to tell him if he had.

Putting a bright red sundress back in the closet, Lucin rummaged through the racks for a few moments, finally settling on a lined cotton dress in subdued gray-blue. The neckline was modest, the sleeves capped, the hemline just below the knee. She put on cork-soled sandals with a one-inch heel, tied her hair back loosely with a dark blue scarf, applied a small amount of lipstick, and trudged downstairs.

God! She did not want to go to this party. Sheila Hartrick was a buffoon, Lucin had little interest in who her neighbors were, less interest in meeting them, and no interest at all in making polite conversation with a herd of strangers. Wishing she had never told Sheila she'd attend, she left the house and began the quarter mile walk to the Hartrick residence.

176

A faux Tudor, the house sat back from the road at the end of a cobbled drive. A brick wall was constructed across the front of the structure, gated into a courtyard between the main house and the six-car garage. The area was parked full of cars and she heard music coming from the rear. As she rounded the corner, a pool came in view. There was a small combo playing on the far side of the water. On the near side, tables were filled with munchies and liquor bottles manned by white-coated servers, chairs were scattered about, women gossiped in the shade of a large awning assembled over the bar area, and men swung invisible golf clubs in the shadow cast by the rear of the house near the shallow end of the pool. Everybody was drinking and, judging by the volume of laughter and conversation, the booze was doing its job. Lucin stood and watched for a moment unnoticed, then Kennedy, wearing a wet bathing suit and a damp towel, bounced out of the pool house behind the musicians and spotted her.

"*You're here!*" she waved, and came running around the pool, the sound of her bare feet slapping the concrete audible above the noise of the crowd.

Smiling, Lucin walked to intercept the child. "Kaypee! You're all wet!"

Kennedy slid to a halt and grasped Lucin's hand in both of hers. "Mom said she didn't think you'd come, but I knew you would 'cause you said you would. I can't stay out here 'cause Mom says it's a big people party, so I hid in the pool house until I could say hi to you," she grinned. "See ya!"

Off she went, skipping toward the rear of the house. Lucin watched her go, then turned to find Sheila Hartrick advancing on her. Dressed in a red blouse, yellow satin pants, red shoes, and a broad straw hat with a wide red ribbon, Shelia looked ready for Macy's Parade. Clutching her hat with one hand and a Long Island Iced Tea with the other, she swayed across the cobbles on three-inch heels. Lucin stifled a grin.

"Well, I'm just so glad you came!" gushed Sheila. "You just get yourself a drink now, and I'll introduce you around. Everybody's here, all your neighbors. Kennedy Paige was just so afraid you wouldn't be here, but I told her not to worry. I want to thank you for bringing her home the other day."

"It was no trouble. We had a good time. I hope everything is all right."

"Well, just fine!" Sheila replied, leading Lucin toward the group of women. "I get my car back Tuesday or Wednesday. That shopping cart got up underneath it and tore something loose. Thank goodness that woman and her little boy weren't hurt."

"That is fortunate," Lucin said, biting her lip against the vision of Sheila and her SUV careening out of control through a grocery store parking lot.

"Arleen! *Arleen!*" shouted Shelia, waddling toward a tall, silver-haired woman in her late fifties who turned and looked at her with steel gray eyes. Her gaze shifted to Lucin and she smiled. Panting a bit, Sheila continued.

"Arleen Creighton, this is Lucin Montgomery. Lucin, this is Arleen. I'm just going to leave you with her while I conduct my hostess duties. Arleen just knows everybody!" She turned and lurched away.

Arleen took a sip of her martini. "Not true," she stated, sidling toward the bar. "I don't know the Pope. What are you drinking, Dear?"

"Perhaps a tonic water," smiled Lucin.

"Good idea. Stay sober so you can leave early. The alternative is to get shit-faced so you can stand to stay late. Either way you're not really here."

Lucin laughed. "Ms. Creighton," she said, "all of a sudden I'm glad I came."

"Call me Arleen," was the reply. "We'll put some gin in the next one and you'll tell me all your secrets."

"You first," grinned Lucin.

"My dear, I am the Grand Dame of this august assemblage. I have been here longer than anyone else in this insular little group. I have more money than all of them and less to prove than any of them. I come to these little get-togethers for the entertainment value and to let the supplicants kiss my ring. Ellis, my husband, passed away nearly ten years ago and left me with more money than I can possibly use. He was an unimaginative man who may have been dead for a year or more before I noticed, but we did love each other after a fashion. I stay in his house because I really do miss him, and I stay in rustic old Kansas City because I despise Beaver Creek. You?"

"I am here because my husband is opening a branch of his law firm in Kansas City. I am at this party to get Sheila off my back and to see her daughter, Kennedy Paige."

"Kennedy Paige," said Arlene. "Isn't that awful?"

"Horrible."

"You're the one who has recently done the reconstruction on the guest house on the old Thorson place."

"That's me."

"The one whose husband is out of town so much."

"Uh-huh."

"The one with that interesting houseman-chauffer."

"James O'Doud."

"So, Lucin Montgomery," Arlene smiled, accepting a fresh martini, "let's get right to it. Tell me something so I can spread the word and quiet all the curiosity."

"What?"

"Are you screwing him?"

"*What*?

"James. Are you screwing him?"

Unable to do anything else, Lucin laughed.

"Not that I give a damn," Arleen went on, scanning the crowd from her nearly six foot height. "Sheila seems to think you are and has offered that opinion for public consumption. I'm always on the lookout for the opportunity to tell Sheila that she is full of shit. I enjoy watching her grovel. So, are you?"

"As a matter of fact, I am not screwing James. He is currently involved with my manicurist, Jolee."

"From *Nails!*?"

"Yes."

"Wonderful! Good for Jolee! The next time I am in, I will tease her about it. I hope you aren't offended by my directness. I do not participate in gossip. I prefer to know the truth, so I ask."

"No offense taken, Arleen. I appreciate your candor."

"I thought you might," she smiled. "Directness is in short supply these days. If you were screwing James, it would hardly be a scandal. Many of the houses in this neighborhood have paths worn to virtual trenches from back door to back door. If you choose to remain until the bitter end this evening, at least half of the men here will attempt to pat your ass. Hell, some of them will even attempt to pat mine. Not that I mind, you understand, but I find that as I get older I become more selective."

"Is it that bad?"

"Bad is a relative term, Lucin," Arlene smiled. "Even dressed down as you are, you put the rest of these heifers to shame. Already you have attracted the attention of the male contingent." She raised an eyebrow and nodded in the direction of the men's group. Lucin followed her gaze and found several of the husbands openly appraising her.

"God," laughed Lucin, "I feel like I'm a window display."

"Make no mistake, Dear. You are. If you were wearing a bright red sundress and three-inch heels, they'd be drooling in the pool. Fun, isn't it?"

"It certainly could be, I suppose."

"I find there is little that is more entertaining than a man with his nose pressed up against the glass," chuckled Arlene. "Oh, good!" she continued, watching their hostess, now slightly sweat stained, wobble her way through the throng. "Here comes more light relief. Sheila, oh, Sheila!" Hat askew and glass empty, the woman lurched to a halt next to Lucin.

"Yes, Arleen?" she smiled.

"I have questioned Lucin at some length," Arleen smiled down at her. "Once again, it has been determined that you are full of shit."

Jerking as if she'd received a blow, Sheila muttered something about running out of ice, and staggered off into the crowd.

"Jesus, Arleen, that was *cold!*" Lucin giggled.

"But short-lived. She won't remember it tomorrow. Perhaps I should remind her at a later date."

"Perhaps you should."

"Well," smiled Arlene, "before all the women begin to cluster around to meet you, let's get me a fresh martini, you some gin to go with your tonic, then we'll walk over into that gaggle of knuckle dragging testosterone and I'll introduce you to all the boys. Can you handle that?"

Lucin laughed. "I think it would be good for me."

"Perhaps," agreed Arlene. "I *know* it would be good for *me*."

During the next three hours Lucin met about fifty people whose names she would not remember, got fondled several times, turned down two invitations for a late night drink, several to test out a new hot tub, and one offer to walk her home. After the initial introductions she stayed mostly apart from the festivities, preferring to allow curious wives or horny husbands to come to her. She declined the offers to dance with the men as well as the offers to sit with the women. Arleen drifted by several times with comments and encouragement, and at dusk Lucin excused herself to walk home. She entered the kitchen to find James eating a small bowl of ice cream.

179

"Fresh back from the ball," he grinned. "Got both of your slippers?"

"Barely," she smiled.

"Have a good time?"

"In some ways. Your name came up."

"My name?"

"It seems you and I are the subject of considerable speculation, Jimmy, me boy."

"And would there be any accuracy to these vicious rumors?"

"Some," she smiled.

"That's encouragin' then, isn't it? Can I ply ya with some ice cream?"

"Thanks anyway," she said, moving to stand beside where he sat. "I'm going upstairs, take a long bath, and go to bed. But," she continued, turning around, "ya can pat me bottom if ya have a mind to."

"Sure," James agreed. "If it'll help ya feel better."

Lucin accepted several pats, then turned, and kissed him on the top of his head. "Sweet James," she said, "'tis a joy to feel the touch of a familiar hand."

"Aye, it is, Lucille," he grinned. "And the same for a familiar bottom too, ya know."

TWENTY-SIX

Past aside,
The present calls
With obligations to myself.
Debts owed
That only I can pay.

LUCIN SLEPT LATE on Sunday and lazed around for the entire afternoon, still feeling somewhat tentative and confused over the night of Tami's visit. Because of meeting Arleen at Sheila's party and James' steadfastness, she was emotionally much more stable. James was right. In spite of the nagging curiosity and lurking guilt, the truth was, if she had gone to bed with Tami, there was little she could do about it now. If she hadn't, all of her anguish was for less than nothing. Either way, what was done, was done. She sat by the garden until well after dark Sunday evening, took a long soak, drank some sake, and spent a dreamless night. She was eating a dry bagel, drinking a can of V-8, and contemplating a trip to the ice rink, when her cell phone went off just after nine Monday morning.

"Good morning, Darling! Did you spend a Lu-SIN-full night?"

"George?"

"In the flesh, such as it is, Sweetie. Run a brush through your hair and across your teeth, throw on minimal clothing, and meet me at my manse. I will show you some togs and listen to you tell me how truly wonderful I am!"

"You have some things?"

"I dally not, Dearest. You are my priority, my inspiration, my muse! Come to George's just as fast as your gorgeous bosoms can bounce here!"

Lucin removed the dead phone from her ear and chuckled her way to the bathroom to brush her hair.

George, wearing cranberry linen slacks and an orange silk pullover threw open the door before she could ring and beamed at her.

"Darling, you've come!" He gushed, glancing at her yellow tank top, white walking shorts and flat sandals.

181

"Hello, George," she laughed, accepting an embrace and kisses to each cheek.

"God! You look wonderful. The only thing that stops you from being absolutely spectacular is me, and I've stopped stopping you!" He grinned at her and rolled his eyes. "So, how *are* you?"

"I'm fine, George," she smiled, feeling slightly overwhelmed. "I didn't expect to hear from you quite so soon."

"Well, I put a couple of saggy-bottoms and a fledgling anorexic on hold and went right to work," he grinned, backing away so she could enter. "Coffee? Tea? Wild sex? Disregard the last of those three choices, Darling. I just got caught up in the moment!"

"Tea is fine," Lucin smiled, taking a stool at the small counter area.

"I have a cinnamon-tangerine Oolong that is *very* exciting," George replied, brushing her cheek with his hand as he wafted by. "Subtle, but wanton. Serene, but wicked. I find when I hold it on my tongue, it reminds me of you. Do you mind?"

"Not at all," Lucin laughed. Unable to resist his momentum, she continued. "I'm flattered by any connection with your tongue, George."

"My God!" he crowed, whirling to face her. "Inappropriate conversation! My favorite! Look at you. You're blushing!"

"I am not," Lucin giggled, lowering her head.

"You are too! Is this precious, or what? Never again will you be able to drink tea without thinking of George's tongue!"

"George!"

"Don't 'George!' me, you repressed minx!" he pounced. "You're almost squirming on your stool. God! Isn't this *wonderful?*"

"*Stop it!*" she laughed.

"In thirty seconds you'll be dripping wet, and all because of *me*. How glorious!"

Leaving Lucin to collect herself, George added loose tea to a small pot, poured in boiling water, and put it aside to steep. He set out two cups and saucers, placed paper napkins on the counter, took her right hand in both of his and looked at her.

"Fun, huh, Sweetheart?" he asked, and kissed the back of her hand.

"Yes, it was," Lucin smiled, tears of laughter shining in her eyes. George rubbed one off her cheek with his thumb and held it up for her inspection.

"See!" he beamed. "I told you you'd be wet."

"I have two of the most wonderful people that sew for me," George commented, rolling a rack from the corner to where Lucin sat, as she finished her second cup of tea. "He does the machine work, she does the hand work and the cutting. Together, they are remarkable." He removed a cover draped over the rack and began sliding garments on hangers toward her.

Two sleeping kimonos were first, one in light gray silk, the other of delicate eggshell cotton. Next came a kimono-cut short lounging robe in pale green raw silk, with a nearly invisible pattern of Bonsai trees, one value lighter in color, worked into the fabric. That was followed by another kimono-cut lounging robe, ankle length, in dark brown silk with a repeated pattern of interlocking circles in black. It was fully lined with cream-colored satin, and had extended stylized sleeves that hung nearly to the floor.

Going over the garments, Lucin was amazed. "This workmanship is wonderful. The stitching, the pleats, the lining. I've never seen anything like it!"

"And they will fit beautifully," smiled George. "They will enhance what is already there, my dear. A truly lovely woman of exceptional presence and carriage."

"Thank you, George," she blushed.

"Now," he said, rubbing his hands lightly together. "I don't have the traditional full kimono conceptualized yet, nor the evening attire, but look at this." Down the rack, he slid a skating dress.

In cobalt blue, the silk was diaphanous. Done as a kimono that stopped at the very top of her thighs, the dress had an open plunging neckline with a wide shawl collar to the waist. Beneath the neckline, as if for modesty, was a second collar in sky blue done as an under-kimono. The effect was carried through what appeared to be an under-skirt, the panty, and repeated in the squared sleeves that dangled a foot below her arms. The dress was complimented in an abbreviated black obi cinching the waist, hiding the darts that gathered the material above the swell of her hips.

"George, this is beautiful."

"When that skirt lifts above your exquisite bottom, Darling, heads *will* turn. Your hair up, a little work with makeup to bring out the almond in your eyes, a light base to pale your skin a bit, and the effect will be exquisite. It will carry you, and you will support it. Theatre at its finest!"

"You have done a wonderful job!"

"We're not finished."

"We're not?"

"I have one more. Call it an exercise in whimsy. It is another skating dress. Indulge me. Even though you don't like body stockings, go into the dressing area, put on the one you find there and return."

The body stocking was sleeveless and went from the base of her throat to the bottom of her feet, matching her skin tone almost exactly. Unlike similar garments however, this one had slightly stiffened and padded bra cups built in. Instead of a flattening effect, it supported her, pushing her up and in, adding cleavage. Studded in rhinestones, the neckline was a necklace. Next to the body stocking hung tights. In medium taupe, they were slightly shiny and gave the impression of having a full-length seam up the rear of each leg terminating in what appeared to be high-sided black bikini panties. After struggling and straightening for some time, at last Lucin made her way back to George. Watching her walk toward him, he smiled.

"Perfect," he said, holding up a jacket. "Now this."

Done in the style of a double-breasted 1930's suit, the jacket was dark brown with a light brown pinstripe. The four-button sleeves had built-in French cuffs showing a perfect half-inch of eggshell white. The shoulders were slightly padded for a squared off look. None of the six buttons on the jacket functioned. The overlapping lapels were secured in place with a continuous band of Velcro allowing the daring neckline to remain daring without revealing anything more than Lucin's augmented cleavage. The hem of the jacket stopped a fraction of an inch below her butt, allowing flashes of high thigh or bikini panty whenever she moved. The center vent opened nicely to reveal glimpses of her bottom. Sewn from a dull finished, textured, lightly-lined rayon, the jacket looked like a wool blend, but moved as if it were silk. The waist, slightly tapered, accentuated her figure and added length to her legs.

"George," Lucin said, grinning into a full-length mirror, "this looks positively sinful!"

"Now we'll make it look dangerous," George replied, producing a dark brown snap-brim fedora with a small red feather in the band. "Gangsterism on ice, Sweetie," he glowed as she settled the hat rakishly over one eye. She posed, one arm and one leg akimbo and stuck her tongue out at him.

"Now that," beamed George, "is an offer that not even Vito Corleone could refuse. Like it?"

"I love it!" Lucin blurted, mugging at herself in the mirror.

"From your neck to your feet, you are completely covered, completely concealed," George said, "and yet, you appear to be hazardously unclad! We are selling the sizzle, Darling, and you do sizzle. You must come by one day with your skates. I have dark brown covers for them and I want to immortalize you on film for my wall of fame. Nothing garish, Lucin, just a three by five foot poster surrounded by flashing lights!"

"I'll pose for you anytime," she said, giving him a hug. "I couldn't be more pleased." She looked in the mirror for another moment, feeling the gentle warmth begin to glow in her belly. "I am going to do it," she stated.

"Do what?"

"Take skating lessons."

"You must let me see you skate! You can flaunt and flow, and I can immerse myself in fantasy. Then, when all eyes are on you, you can come give me a hug, and I can feel all of that glorious envy!"

An hour later, the back seat of the Jag festooned with garment bags, Lucin arrived at the rink. Standing in the lobby, she saw Bryan Delcour talking with a young woman. When the conversation ended, she approached.

"Hello."

"Hi. Oh, hi! Lucin isn't it?"

"I'm surprised you remembered my name, Mr. Delcour," she smiled.

"Hard to forget. Kennedy talks about you all the time. And it's Bryan."

"Okay, Bryan. When do we start?"

"Lessons?"

"Yep."

"Are you sure you want to do this? Most of my students are under four feet tall," he grinned. "It's a brutal world for adults."

"I'm sure," she smiled.

"Why me?"

"Kaypee likes you."

"Kaypee?"

"Kennedy Paige."

"She seems to be instrumental in all this."

"She's a great kid. We have a secret sister club. We're the only members."

184

"That's good. Kennedy can use the support. Her mother is more results oriented than support oriented. The kid works hard. You're a source of inspiration for her, you know. She wants to skate as well as you do."

"She needs to skate better than that," Lucin confessed.

"She will if she wants to. The biggest difference between the bottom ninety percent and the top ten percent is one hundred percent effort. She has the talent. The dedication is what's necessary. If she can develop that, she could be good."

"I never did take it that seriously when I was young," Lucin said. "I skated because I was fairly adept at it and had fun."

Bryan scratched his head. "It goes a lot deeper for the top talent. It's a need, a compulsion, a force that's all but irresistible. An instructor can't teach it, create it, or develop it. It is either there or it isn't. The best somebody like me can do is try to keep up with it. Competition is fierce, egos are immense. Sometimes it's gratifying, sometimes it's rewarding, sometimes it isn't pretty, but it is always intense."

"You sound like you've been there."

"I was nationally ranked in my late teens, but when the competition includes people like Brian Boitano and Scott Hamilton, you've got to be better than I was. I went pro and skated with the Ice Capades for several years. When that folded, it gave me the impetus to do what I'd been wanting to do for a while, get off the road and teach. Working in a traveling show like the Capades is hugely demanding both physically and emotionally. I was worn out. I took about a year off; then started as a private instructor. I've never regretted taking on my students," he smiled. "I have occasionally regretted taking on some of their parents."

"I promise my mom won't interfere," chuckled Lucin.

"Good. We'll start tomorrow."

"Tomorrow?"

"Yeah. My little guys usually do at least two fifteen minute lessons a week. Let's start you at one thirty-minute session. Sound okay?"

"Sure."

"How's ten-fifteen Tuesday mornings?"

"Fine."

"Great. I have Kennedy at ten on Tuesday and Friday. You can follow her on Tuesday. She'll be inspired to practice harder if Lucin is skating."

"So now I'm motivation, is that it?"

"You bet. I'll use anything I can find to keep these kids going. For Kennedy, that's you."

"I'm honored," Lucin smiled.

Bryan looked at her seriously. "Why skating? Why now?"

"You don't mince words, do you?"

"Nope. Why?"

"More reasons than I'm aware of, I suspect," Lucin admitted. "Part of it is that I skated when I was young. It's a tie to my childhood, a time when I had more fun than I'm having now. Part of it is that I have too much time on my hands and I need to exercise discipline. Part of it is that I need something of my very own that is independent from my regular life. Part is a need for accomplishment. To do something and get better at it."

"Wow," Bryan grinned. "That's a lot more complicated than 'my mom wants me to'. If I recall correctly, you don't want to compete."

"No, just show off," Lucin laughed.

"Well, you look good on the ice. With some work, you could look great. You'd have most of the skaters around here stopping to watch. Anybody ever mention you look a little like Peggy Fleming?"

"Yes, but not on the ice."

"We'll work on that. Tomorrow morning, ten-fifteen, right after your little sister."

Lucin was unloading garment bags from the rear of her car when James walked out of the house.

"Sweet Mother, Lucille, did ya leave anything for the rest of us?"

"James, hi! Just what I need, a big strong man," she said, batting her eyes at him.

"Uh-huh," he replied, skeptically, gathering up the six bags while Lucin collected the hatbox. "Upstairs?"

"For now," she replied, holding the door open for him.

He handed her the bags, one at a time, as she hung them in the dressing room, and began removing the clothes.

"This is some of the stuff George is doing for me," Lucin said. "Pretty, huh?"

"Aye," agreed James, his eyes twinkling as he looked at the short green robe. "Are ya gonna model this for me, then?"

"Maybe sometime," she grinned.

"Aw, sure. Teasin' me now, are ya?"

"As a matter of fact, there is something I'll model for you," she answered picking up the hatbox. She opened it and placed the snap-brim on her head, tilted to one side and pulled down low over her eyes. "What do you think?" she asked striking an exaggerated pose.

"Now which kimono does that go with, the one from the Japanese Mafia?"

"It's for skating," she smiled, lifting the double-breasted jacket out of the last bag and holding it up in front of her. "It goes with this."

"My goodness," James commented, "I've got a bit of a lump in me throat. And what else accompanies the ensemble?"

"At the rink, or just between friends?" she grinned.

"Just between friends, of course," came the hoarse reply.

"How 'bout brown suede heels and a pint of Guinness?" asked Lucin, catching the tip of her tongue between her teeth.

"Sweet Jesus," James muttered. "That I'd dearly love to see."

Feeling the warmth build and having a wonderful time, Lucin took the next logical step. "Are ya goin' ta be around this evenin' then, Jimmy me boy?"

"Alas, no. This evenin' I'm otherwise engaged."

"Ah, well," she teased, "your loss, then."

"Aye," agreed James, backing out of the door. "Joe Cocker said it best, y'know."

"What'd Joe Cocker say?"

"You can leave your hat on," James replied, and headed down the stairs.

TWENTY-SEVEN

What can be done to ease my heart?
What I have
Slips away.
What I want
Remains unseen.

OVER THE NEXT THREE WEEKS, Lucin became immersed in skating. Bryan was an excellent instructor, patient and demanding, understanding and committed. Kaypee was overjoyed to have Lucin with her on Tuesday mornings and soon wheedled her way into a Lucin carpool to and from the rink. Watching all the youngsters on the ice and reveling in her association with Kennedy, Lucin's thoughts began to drift toward children. Kaypee, in the direct honesty of her age, brought it to a head during a ride home after lessons.

"Why don't you have any kids? They'd be lucky to have you for a mom."

"You know, Girlfriend, I've been wondering that myself."

"I could play with them and even baby-sit when I get older," Kaypee stated. "You should have some."

"Some?" Lucin grinned at her. "How many, ya think?"

"Four or five," Kennedy replied, thoughtfully.

"That many?"

"They could skate, too. Bryan'd give 'em lessons."

"You've got this all worked out, huh?" Lucin laughed.

"I've been thinking about it."

"So have I, Kaypartner."

"So?"

"So, what?"

"So when ya gonna have a baby?"

"I don't know," Lucin grinned.

"Could you have one this summer?"

"No, that might not be possible."

"Well, you should have one real soon," Kaypee stated.

187

"Don't you think I should talk it over with their daddy?"

"You could surprise him."

"That'd be a pretty big surprise."

Kennedy was silent for a moment staring out her side window. "Sometimes my mom asks me what we talk about."

"She does?"

"Uh-huh."

"What do you tell her?"

"Nothing. I just tell her we don't talk about anything."

Lucin chose her words carefully. "Your mom cares a lot about you. I think she wants to know what's going on in your life. It's okay to tell her, if you want to."

"Nope."

"Why not?"

"She's not in our club."

Stifling a smile, Lucin continued. "You tell stuff to lots of people that aren't in our club."

"Not about us."

"What do you and your mom talk about?"

"She mostly just asks questions or tells me what to do."

"That's all?"

"She's on the phone a lot. Mom's pretty busy I guess."

"She loves you, Kaypee."

"If I had a little girl I'd be really nice to her," Kennedy observed.

"You would, huh?"

"Yep. I'd treat her like you treat me."

Unbidden and unexpected, tears leapt to Lucin's eyes. She blinked them back and battled the lump in her throat as Kennedy stared at the dashboard. The driveway arrived and Lucin pulled up beside the Hartrick courtyard. Feeling a need to expand contact with the child, Lucin spoke.

"I'm gonna go practice tomorrow afternoon around two. If you want to come along, ask your mom. If it's okay with her, give me a call and we'll go together."

Kennedy turned to face Lucin. "Will I be as pretty as you are when I grow up?"

Feeling something release inside her, Lucin swallowed. "Of course you will, Sweetheart. You're beautiful now."

"I love you," Kaypee stated and bounced out the door. Lucin watched the child's colt-legs carry her toward the house, the skate bag slapping against her thighs, and let her tears come.

Lucin arrived home to find Stephanie preparing fried chicken salad for lunch.

"Lucin, Mr. Montgomery called from Los Angeles. He'll be in around eight tonight. I'll be glad to work late."

Lucin's head spun. Still attempting to recover from the conversation with Kennedy, this new information knocked her off balance. She'd talked with an extremely frustrated and conflicted Harrison a few days before, when he'd phoned from Japan. Angry and depressed, it was clear to her that he believed the whole deal with Nagata Industries was falling apart. She felt terrible for him but also slighted, because he showed very little interest in how things were going for her. His conflict with the Japanese was very difficult. Harrison was not an insensitive person, but the stress of the situation had caused him to pull inward, centering almost exclusively on himself and his problems. Even though she understood, it still hurt. Thoughts careening through her head, she realized Stephanie was speaking.

"… if that's alright with you."

"I'm sorry, Steph. I was out in left field. What did you say?"

Stephanie smiled. "I was wondering if lamb chops and rice with peppers and squash were okay for dinner?"

"Fine. Just fine."

"I'll get started on the house, change the bed linen and all that stuff right after lunch."

"What? Oh, sure. I'm going down to the garden for a while. I'll have my salad later," Lucin said, her eyes far away.

Through the rest of the day, Lucin immersed herself in feelings, attempting to go with what she felt instead of what she thought. Tami, Kaypee, James, children, babies, herself, skating …. Unsettled and somewhat confused, she examined her relationship with Harrison. Since the beginning, it had been a trade off she'd willingly made. Excitement for solidity, spontaneity for dependability, passion for permanence. Harrison had always been a known factor in her life, but the last two or three occasions she'd spent time with him, he had been emotional and erratic, unsure of himself and his place in his world. Her training told her to fall back and give him the quiet support of the "woman behind the man." Lucin was willing to do that, if the support extended both ways. She was not, however, willing to lose her life in his anymore. Her taste of independence had created an appetite for more, a need for expression, a desire to be a partner and not just a support system for somebody else. Harrison had become an uncertain commodity. She would do her best for him, as long as it was also best for her, but she would no longer place her wants and needs in the shadow of his. Dressed in lightweight almond cotton slacks, a short-sleeved white silk blouse and beige flats, she waited for her husband to come home.

It was nearly nine when the taxi arrived at the house. Harrison entered the kitchen with two bags and dropped them to the floor. He looked haggard, smaller than the last time Lucin had seen him. Circles under his eyes were emphasized by a pallid complexion and his shoulders seemed to sag. Lucin stepped into a hug. He felt delicate to her, nearly frail.

"Hey, Luce," he murmured.

"Oh, Sweetie. You look so tired."

"Just a world-class case of jet lag and an overdose of Japan. I'll be fine."

She kissed both his cheeks. "Have you eaten?"

"Only on the plane. I'm not hungry, just beat. I barely know what day it is. It's selfish, but I just want to go upstairs, take a shower, and go to bed. I hope you don't mind."

"Of course not," she smiled. "You go on up. I'll come tuck you in a little later."

189

He kissed her gently on the lips. "You're terrific, Luce. I really am glad to be home. It has been a miserable trip." He turned, leaving his bags on the floor and started for the stairs.

A few minutes later, Lucin went upstairs and found Harrison in his underwear, sprawled corner to corner across the bed. She covered him with a lightweight blanket and turned out the light. Back in the kitchen she thanked Stephanie for the extra effort and gave her the next morning off. Taking a Guinness out of the fridge, she walked across the lawn toward the garden house.

At nine the next morning, Harrison entered the kitchen to find Lucin, wearing her long kimono-robe, sitting at the table.

"Good morning, Sweetheart," she smiled, rising for a hug. "Rest well?"

"Best night's sleep I've had in two weeks," Harrison answered, kissing her on the cheek and glancing at the robe. "New?"

"Uh-huh."

"Japanese?"

"Sort of. I had it made."

"God," he grinned ruefully, scratching his head, "I'm surrounded."

"I gave Stephanie the morning off. What can I fix you?"

"Just coffee," he replied, dropping heavily into a chair. "I'll grab an early lunch when I go down to the office."

"So the trip didn't go so well, huh?" Lucin asked, pouring him a cup.

"Christ, I don't know," came the weary answer. "It's another world over there. Everything is small. We stayed in a western-style hotel so it wasn't so bad, but space is at such a premium, you wouldn't believe it. Pedestrians are shoulder-to-shoulder, restaurant tables are almost on top of one another. There's this place in the airport where you can rent a sleeping chamber for the night. Not a room, but a chamber. This tube sunk into a wall. You slide into the damn thing feet first onto a mattress like the morgue or something. There are ladders on the wall so people can get to the top bunks. It's like old-fashioned iron lungs. People everywhere!"

"Pretty bad, huh?"

"Don't get me wrong. The Nagata staffers went out of their way to make us comfortable. American-style food was available, we had real toilets and showers, all that kind of stuff, but, as I said, it's another world. We only dealt with Onoshi's people. Those who had been aligned with Kiritsubo before his death weren't allowed near us. We had at least one meeting each day and yet nothing was ever decided. Nothing! All that time we went in circles. Everybody was polite, all smiles and good wishes, wanting everything to work out, and lying through their teeth. I have never been involved in anything like it! You couldn't get a straight answer out of one of those idiots if you had a gun on him!"

"Maybe you didn't deal with anybody who was empowered to make a decision."

"That's the thing. We only saw Onoshi once. Almost two weeks, and the sono-fabitch only saw fit to visit us one time for lunch! He ate raw eel and raw octopus, and never said a word. God! I damn near gagged."

"What did you have," Lucin asked, stifling a grin.

190

"Steak. Kobe beef. Best part of the whole trip. The rest of it was just a waste of time and energy."

"Maybe not."

"Oh, yeah?"

"Maybe. The Japanese look at business differently than we do. It's a chess match, war if you like. Stalling you on this trip, making you wait, producing no progress, all that is just tactics, sparring, testing the strength of the opponent, keeping the enemy off balance."

"I am not their Goddammed enemy!" Harrison blurted. "I'm trying to help those paranoid assholes!"

"Are you Japanese?"

"What?"

"Are you Japanese?"

"That's a stupid question, Luce!" he flared.

"Indulge me," she responded quietly. "Please answer."

He glared at her. "No, I am *not* Japanese."

"Then you *are* the opponent. You *are* the enemy. You are not from the land of the gods. You do not serve the system. You are not familiar with the code of Bushido. To them you are a barbarian. You can never be anything else. They are afraid of you. Even if you partner with them in business, even if you believe you have their trust, that will *never* change."

"Afraid of me?"

"Yes."

"Why the hell are they afraid of me? I'm trying to help their company!"

"You are a westerner. You are not descended from the gods. You create. The Japanese are great refiners, but not creators. Throughout history they have used other cultures and civilizations to further their own growth and technology. From the time of the ancient Chinese when they improved the manufacture of steel, to the time they nearly sank the American automobile market, to micro technology, the Japanese specialize in taking something that already exists and making it better. This requires great diligence and secrecy. They keep their knowledge and intent behind the hedge of their teeth. They smile, they bow, they agree, and then they do what they want. The truth is a tool, not an absolute. They are afraid of you because you are direct, because you represent industrial might and technology, and because you destroyed Hiroshima and Nagasaki."

"What! The atomic bomb? Christ, Lucin, that was over fifty years ago!"

"No time at all when your civilization is thousands of years old. No excuse at all when the son is compelled to answer for the sins of the father."

"Oh, Christ!"

"Harrison, you must realize that you do not and cannot understand these people. You are not equipped to. The cultural gulf is too wide and they have no desire to be understood."

He looked at her for a moment. "I just spent nearly two weeks getting the runaround every fucking day from those three-faced bastards," he snarled. "My career is slipping away, my life is slipping away, and it sure as hell does me a lot of good to come home and have you defend them!"

"Defend them?"

"You heard me! What makes you such an expert on Japan anyway?"

"I don't claim to be an expert, Harrison."

"You're dressed up like some kind of Geisha-girl, spouting Japanese rhetoric! What am I supposed to think?"

Lucin slid her chair back and stood up. "Please excuse me," she said with quiet control. "Of course it was not my intention to insult you or cause you to anger. You are my husband. I would never align myself with those who oppose you. My only thought was to help you understand the nature of your enemy. I can see I have failed. Please accept my humble apology for creating disharmony and for my feeble attempt at communication. So sorry."

He stared at her, open mouthed, as she turned and left the room.

When Lucin entered the kitchen again, she found Harrison gone and James eating a tuna sandwich.

"Trouble in paradise?" he smiled.

"You heard?"

"Sure."

Passing behind where he sat, Lucin hesitated a moment to place a hand on each of his shoulders and rest her chin on the top of his head. "Only a lot," she replied, sadly. "Sometimes I feel that Harrison doesn't think I know anything."

"Aye. It's hard for him."

"Him?"

"Sure. You're outgrowing the pigeonhole he's had you in all these years. He doesn't know what to do with that. It scares him. He's already frightened about this Japanese business, now here you come dumping rationality and wisdom on his frustration and fear, and he trots 'round the bend. Typical male reaction. He can't go out and bite a wildebeest, so he snaps at you."

She smiled and kissed his ear. "So now I'm a substitute for wildebeest?"

"Yep," he grinned. "Lucille of the Jungle. Bet you'd look great in a leopard-skin loincloth."

"Something off the shoulder, short skirt, slit up one side?" she teased.

"The mind reels," he chuckled, reaching behind him to pat her on the calf. "Can I build you a sandwich? It would mean a lot to an old man like me to satisfy at least one of your appetites."

Laughing, she sat beside him. "Half of one. I'm going skating in a little while. You satisfy a lot of my appetites, James, even when you're defending my husband."

"Not defending," he said, opening the fridge, "explaining. The abyss between men and women is wide and deep. Fragile is the bridge that spans it."

"Fragile is the bridge that spans it?" she grinned.

"Aye," he chuckled. "The best thing you can do with the dear lad is just be patient. That doesn't mean you have to accept anything you don't want to. It doesn't mean you can't go your own way when you need to. It doesn't mean you can't take his head off if he needs it. He still sees you as the same woman he knew when the two of you first got together. Variations from that threaten him. Ya see, there's a built in problem when men and women get together. Relationships start off with the woman hoping the man *will* change and the man hoping the woman *won't*. False expectations right from the start."

"James, you're amazing."

"And I make a mean sandwich," he replied, placing a plate before her. "You need to take care of yourself, me darlin' and fair, and give this thing between you and Himself the room it needs to grow. If that means going at it tooth and claw, or withdrawing almost totally, then that's what you should do. If you want it to work out, that is. There's always an *if*. Life is choices, Sweetheart. Just choices."

"O'Doud Philosophy 101."

"400 level instruction available upon request," he leered. "You bring the Guinness."

She smiled. "Guinness and I have a bad record. Will you stop me at two?"

James kissed her gently on the cheek. "Aye," he whispered. "If you'll start me at one."

A little before two, Lucin pulled up beside the Hartrick courtyard, expecting to see Kaypee skip out to the Jag, swinging her skate bag. Instead, she watched the child walk slowly to the car, head down, the bag bumping her legs. Kennedy opened the door, dropped the satchel on the floor, flopped into the seat, and stared at the dashboard. Lucin rolled slowly down the drive and back to the street, watching the girl from the corner of her eye. After a couple of blocks, she spoke.

"Kaypee, what's wrong?"

The child chewed her lip for a moment and a tear coursed down her cheek. "My mom's sending me away," she said, still staring straight ahead.

"What? Where?"

"She's making me go to a skating camp with a new teacher a long way away, until school starts. I don't wanna go, Lucin! Bryan's my teacher. I don't wanna new teacher, and I don't wanna leave you!" She wiggled out of her seat belt, pressed up against Lucin's side, and began to cry.

Willing away her own tears, Lucin put her arm around the girl and continued the drive in silence, feeling Kaypee's occasional shudder as she held her special sister close.

TWENTY-EIGHT

The lotus opens,
Petals spreading,
Freely showing her colors.
Is less demanded of me
Than of the flower?

LUCIN COULDN'T LACE her skates. She sat on a bench staring at the floor and thought about losing Kaypee. Kennedy moved listlessly about the ice, occasionally wiping her eyes with her sleeve. Bryan Delcour thumped over on the rubber flooring and sat down.

"You here, Lucin?" he asked.

"Barely," she replied, looking numbly at him. "Kaypee talk to you?"

"Yeah. She gave me a note from her mother explaining the situation."

"And?"

"And, the kid is going off to Tulsa the day after tomorrow for a month of intensive training."

"A month?"

"She'll get back just before school starts."

"How do you feel about that?"

Bryan paused for a moment while he considered his reply. "Well, it'll make or break her. She'll come back either sick to death of the whole thing or as dedicated as a child her age can be. She's gonna get a lot of ice time, a lot of instruction, a lot of frustration, and a fair amount of trauma. It will be totally different than what she's been used to. Personally, if she were my child, I wouldn't send her into that kind of intensive atmosphere yet."

"Are you familiar with the program?"

"A little. Guy named Michael Case runs it. Pretty fair skater in his day. Put this skating school together a few years ago. He uses higher-level students as assistant instructors and cranks through a lot of kids. For the young children they provide twenty-four hour a day care and supervision. Makes a ton of money."

"What do you think of it?"

"I think he makes a ton of money," Bryan grinned. Lucin smiled in spite of herself. "It's Mrs. Hartrick's choice," he continued. "It'll impress the other status conscious parents at the next garden party. It'll also get Kennedy out of your clutches for awhile."

"I'd thought of that," Lucin agreed.

"Is this conversation off the record?" Bryan asked.

"Absolutely."

"Sheila Hartrick is a small, narrow, frightened woman who wouldn't know a toe pick from a tipi. She doesn't spend one out of ten ice-hours with her child, and when she does show up, it's a social event timed to coincide with attendance of those she considers to be the most desirable parents. The best thing I've seen happen to Kennedy since I've known the child is you. That's just one of the reasons Sheila can't stand you."

"Just one, huh?"

"Also you're attractive, you can skate, and you don't give a damn about money or position. And, of course, Kennedy adores you. With Sheila, everything is a play for power. She'll even use Kennedy to push people around."

"So she sends her away."

"Yep. More to deny you access to the child than to deny the child access to you."

"And it's my fault."

"Don't be stupid. It's Sheila's fault. She treats her kid like a show dog. She just wants to be there when the awards come in so she can bask in the success of her child. The only revenge she can get on you for being a nicer person than she is, is to send her daughter where you can't poison the kid's mind. How this affects the child means nothing to her. She just wants to get a lick or two in at you."

"God. I didn't want something like this to happen."

"Take it easy. It probably would have happened anyway. Like I said before, it'll make great conversation that Kennedy is away for intensive training, plus it'll get the kid out of Sheila's badly-colored hair for a while. You may be just the icing on the cake." He glanced across the rink. "Oh, good. Mrs. Reynolds and Tiffany just came in. Great kid. Can't skate, but she's a great kid. Speaking of skating, start thinking about what you want to do for your performance in the February show at the Carriage Club."

Lucin blinked. "The February show?"

"Absolutely."

"Me?"

"Yeah," he grinned. "It's not a competition, but you will be one of the featured performers. Roll it around in your head. Then we'll talk, consider music and costumes, and I'll start on the choreography for your program."

"My program?!"

"Hey, you said you wanted to show off." He grinned at her and moved out onto the ice for Tiffany's lesson.

As Bryan left, Kennedy arrived. "Doncha wanna skate?" she asked.

"No, I don't think so, Sweetie."

"Me neither."

"Well, how 'bout I buy ya a big ol' hamburger, some curly fries, and a shake?"

"Like at McDonald's?"

"Naw. Like at Otto's. Ever been there?"

"Nope."

"It used to be a gas station, Kaypartner. You are in for a treat!"

Forty-five minutes later, Kaypee wiped burger grease off her chin, slurped on what was called the best chocolate malt in Kansas City, and grinned across the table at Lucin. "This is really good. My mom would never bring me here."

"Why not?"

"'Cause nobody she knows comes here. It's cool!"

"I'm glad you like it."

"I'm full."

"That's okay. You ate a lot." Lucin looked at her for a moment. "I'm gonna miss you a bunch for a mean little kid, ya know."

Kennedy's expression darkened. "I'll miss you too," she said.

"I want you to do very well during the next month, Kaypee. I want you to come back a better skater and a better person. I want you to have a great time, a lot of fun, make a herd of new friends, and have a boatload of neat stuff to show me."

"I don't want to go."

"I know you don't, and I don't want to have to wait a whole month to see you again, but this is your mother's decision. So, if I were you, I'd work hard and play hard and meet really good skaters and learn things and have fun."

"I'll try," the girl sighed.

"So, I've been thinking," Lucin went on. "I've been thinking that I can't possibly go a whole month without talking to you. I've been thinking that I want to know what you're doing and how you're doing and what's going on in your life while you're gone. I've been thinking that we need to keep in touch, so I can find out all these things about my favorite sister. I've been thinking that you need a cell phone."

"I got a cell phone."

"But this will be a special cell phone. This will be one you stash in your skating bag and keep with you while you're gone so you can call me anytime you want."

"Really!?"

"Yep. A special secret sisters cell phone for special secret sisters. What do you think?"

"A secret phone?"

"A special secret sisters cell phone," Lucin grinned.

"Could it be pink?"

"Out of the question."

Kaypee hesitated a moment. "Well, what color then?"

Lucin leaned across the table, a serious expression on her face. "The same color as puppy poop."

Kennedy cracked up.

The special secret sisters cell phone turned out to be hot pink, with Lucin's cell and both home numbers programmed into the memory. It was hidden in the bottom of

Kennedy's bag with its charger when Kaypee said goodbye and jumped out of the Jag at the Hartrick courtyard. As Lucin prepared to drive away, Sheila came trotting toward the car. Overly made up, wearing turquoise shorts above plump knees, a bulging yellow tank top, and high-heeled sandals, she huffed to a stop beside Lucin's window.

"Just hi!" she warbled.

"Hello, Sheila," Lucin replied.

"I guess Kennedy told you about her wonderful opportunity."

"She certainly did."

"We're just so pleased. It's an excellent program, very expensive, very difficult to gain entry. We're just positive it will do her a world of good. She'll be away until two days before school starts."

"I think it will do her a world of good, too," smiled Lucin. "A change of scenery, new people to meet and relate to, new ideas, new authority figures. A month is a long time in the life of a child. Plenty of time for her to change and grow. Why, you might not even know her when she gets back."

"Well, it's only a month."

"Yes, but at her age, with all the new experience, it'll be like a semester at college. Good for you, Sheila. It takes a lot of courage to relinquish influence over a child like that."

"We're just sure everything will be fine."

"It probably will," Lucin agreed. "I'm sure there's nothing to be concerned about."

"So are we," Sheila replied, biting her lower lip.

"I think your confidence is terrific, Sheila. I wouldn't worry about a thing. Have you already paid for the school?"

"Uh ... yes."

"Well, then you're committed, aren't you?"

"Uh ..."

"I admire that commitment. Oh, I know a lot of young girls like Kennedy Paige are very impressionable, especially when they're away from home among lots of new influences, but you know your child much better than I. It's a very selfless thing you're doing," Lucin smiled, slipping the car into gear. "Must dash, Dear. Ta!"

Pulling down the drive, watching Sheila frozen in her rear view mirror, Lucin couldn't repress a smile. The smile left when she pulled into her own drive and saw Harrison in the yard swinging a golf club. It was mid-afternoon. He never came home during the afternoon. He waved when she got out of the car.

"Need a caddy?" she shouted.

"I need you!" came the return shout, and he was trotting toward her, the golf club left behind in the grass.

The embrace was tentative and uncertain, but it was an honest embrace. When he pulled away, his eyes were shining with tears.

"I treated you like shit again, Luce. You don't deserve that."

She took his hand and guided him toward the garden. "No, I don't. And you don't deserve whatever it is you're going through that has you so desperately worried." She led him onto the deck. "Sit. I'll be right back." Lucin hit the override to start the misters cooling the area a bit and stepped into the kitchen, returning with two cans of Guinness and two glasses. Harrison was watching the rainbows flashing in the sunlight.

"Guinness?" he asked accepting his can. "You drink Guinness?"

"Don't blame me," she smiled. "Blame James Mathew O'Doud. He brought it into the house. I like it."

"I can't believe you drink beer," Harrison stated.

"Beer? Beer! Saints preserve us," she complained. "This is Guinness, Laddie-buck, nectar of the gods! Sweet Mother, I'm drinkin' with a heathen!"

Harrison stared at her a moment, then began to laugh. "Alright," he said, "who are you this time, and when will Lucin be back?"

"That's part of what has you so upset, isn't it?" Lucin asked.

Harrison sobered and looked at her. "Yes. I guess it is."

"Well, let me answer your question. I'm still Lucin, I'm still your wife, and I still love you, but I'm not sure anymore who Lucin is. I am reasonably sure sometimes who she isn't."

"I'm not sure who she is anymore either," he replied, sadly.

She smiled. "I bet you're not, but that's the way it is. If I can deal with it, so can you. I'm sorry if that sounded cold. It really isn't."

"I, uh … geeze, Lucin. You've gained weight, you live half your life like a you're a Jap, you've started ice skating, you drink beer, uh, Guinness, and some of the stuff that comes out of your mouth is like nothing I've ever heard from you before! Christ, Sweetheart, what's the matter with you?"

"A lot less than there used to be."

"See! That's what I'm talking about!"

"Yeah," she grinned. "It's a bitch, isn't it? Drink your Guinness," she encouraged, taking three long swallows. "It's good for you."

"Oh, God."

"Harrison, I know all this is a shock, but have a little faith. I'm still me, I'm just spreading out a little. I'm not going to hold up a liquor store or anything. What are you doing home in the middle of the afternoon, anyway?"

"I'm flying back to the home office tomorrow morning. I thought I'd take a break."

"You need more breaks. If you were around a little more, I wouldn't be such a shock every time you come home."

"Yeah, well, the next time I come home I'll have a shock with me, and I am going to need your help."

"A shock *with* you?"

"I heard from the Nagata people today. Onoshi, the head guy, is coming to Kansas City in about two weeks."

"That makes sense."

"What?"

"It makes sense that he would come here."

"It does, huh?"

"Is he coming to the house?"

"He wants to, yeah."

"Did you invite him?"

"Why should I? He didn't invite me to his house."

"He wouldn't. You do have him worried, though."

"I have *him* worried?"

"You bet," Lucin smiled.

"I don't understand."

"In Japan he treated you badly, made you wait, only saw you once himself, and you put up with it. You didn't protest, you didn't storm out, you just took it. You lost face. Had you raised hell about it you would have lost even more face, but he would have had to placate you in some way, to restore *wa*. Then he would have also lost face and you would have gained face."

"Oh, Jesus. This is ridiculous!"

"Not to them. Pay attention. Now, he's coming to Kansas City, but only for a short time, right?"

"Less than two days."

"Right. You go to him for almost two weeks, he comes to you for less than two days. He gains face, but the whole thing is still even."

"Why?"

"He didn't invite you to his residence. That's sort of an insult. You didn't invite him to your residence. Insult returned, tie score. If you had invited him to come to your home, he probably would have refused and gained face. The point is, you didn't ask him, so he had to ask you. In doing that, he lost face. When you agreed, you gained face."

"Why do these people go through all this crap?"

"It doesn't make any difference. Why is not important."

"Okay. Then why is it so important for Onoshi to come to my home?"

"If you would know where your enemy is going, seek out where he has been."

"What?"

"He believes he will gain insight into your motives and character if he can see a more personal side of you. If he can get inside your house, he will be better able to get inside your head."

"How come you know all this stuff?"

Lucin smiled. "I have a Japanese friend."

"Who?"

"I don't really know her name. I just call her Mama-*san*. It's a term of respect or affection. It has nothing to do with 'Mother'."

"Am I gonna meet this woman?"

"I doubt it. She's very old and doesn't get out much."

Wrapped up in his own problems, Harrison let it go and thought awhile, then looked at her. "Well, since you seem to know everything else," he challenged, "what do I do now?"

"You bring him home with you, but only for an hour or two, and you don't take him to the house. You bring him here, to the garden. Ask him over for drinks. I'll take care of the rest."

"You will?"

"Trust me. Make it late evening, near dusk."

199

He looked at her for a moment, wheels clicking over in his head. "Why not? It can't get anymore screwed up than it is."

Ignoring the insult, Lucin finished her Guinness and retrieved another one. "I've been thinking," she said.

Pulling back from his own preoccupation, Harrison turned his focus to her. "About?" he asked.

"Having a baby."

The words bounced off of him. "I'm sorry. What did you say?"

"I've been thinking about having a baby."

He seemed to diminish in size a bit and peered at her. "A baby?"

"Uh-huh."

"A baby," he stated.

"An infant, a child, a small human being," she replied, slowly and clearly. "You could be the daddy and I could be the mommy. You see, sometimes men and women fall in love and there's this big bird, they call it a stork, and when these two people wish very hard, sometimes this stork brings them a little bundle of joy. I've seen it in books and on pickle jars."

He stared at her blankly as she slugged some Guinness. "You want to have a baby," he said.

"I'm not big on the idea of actually giving birth, if that's what you mean, but I'm certainly willing to if the stork turns out to be a myth."

"You want to have a baby?"

"Actually, I would like for us to have a baby. Lotsa people do, you know. The pitter-patter of little feet, tricycles in the driveway, things like that."

"In the middle of everything else that's going on in my life, you spring this on me?"

"Relax, Harrison," she smiled. "I'm not pregnant, I'm just thinking about it."

"I'm sorry, Luce. This hit me out of the blue. Of course you can have a child if you want to."

"We."

"I mean, I'd never deny you motherhood. There's plenty of room for a nursery and a nanny. It might be really good for you."

"Us."

"This could be an excellent idea," he said, standing up. "Why don't we talk about it some more after this Nagata Industries thing is settled? A baby. You're a good age right now, and you don't want to wait too much longer, I suppose." He leaned over and kissed her on the cheek. "Now might be the appropriate time for you to become a mother." He patted her on the shoulder and turned away, walking toward the house. Lucin watched him go and shook her head.

Jesus.

200

TWENTY-NINE

My pillow
Has become
Covered with dust.
Should I brush it off
For him?

AT DINNER THAT EVENING, Harrison was somewhat distant. He was not avoiding conversation with Lucin, just preoccupied. She willingly gave him his space, still slightly insulted by his lack of understanding about her wanting a child. In truth, she didn't really understand it either. Children had never been a priority in her life. She'd never before wanted a child of her own. She'd never seriously thought about being a mother, much less a mom. She'd never even had a relationship with a child until Kennedy had come along.

Kennedy. God, she adored that kid. During their time together she'd catch occasional glimpses of the world through the eyes of a child. The clear simplicity of right and wrong, the funny little things adults have forgotten how to see, the easy joy of accomplishment, the ability to be in the moment. She was not so foolish as to believe Kaypee was all sweetness and light. She was fully aware that the girl tried hard to be good when they were together. She knew that familiarity bred, if not contempt, at least erratic behavior. But that was part of it all, wasn't it? Raising kids was the most important job in the world and yet nobody needed a license. There was not the simplest of qualifying tests. Parents, even the best intentioned ones, even the brightest ones, even the wisest ones, made mistakes constantly. She would, too. But one mistake she would not make was to abdicate the raising of her baby to someone else. If she had a child, there would be no full-time nanny. There would be no full-time day care. If she had a child, she would raise that child, guide that child, prepare that child to the very best of her ability. Then she would pray she hadn't screwed the kid up for life. To do all that, the child also needed a daddy. A father, while absolutely necessary, was simply not good enough. Harrison might be prepared to be a father, but being a daddy was the farthest thing from his mind. It was certainly true that he had a lot going on in his head, and that she had tossed the baby idea at him with no warning. If he needed time to think about it and get used to it, fine. She could wait. She needed to think about it for a while, too. Rationally, she knew she couldn't have a duplicate of Kaypee. Emotionally, she knew that was what she wanted.

Harrison turned in early and left Lucin to her own devices. She rattled around the house for a while, attempting to quell the thoughts that flapped through her head. Concern over Kaypee, Harrison's failure to recognize his position in possible parenthood, the upcoming visit by the Japanese, her skating program, Sheila Hartrick's manipulations, and a dozen other things circled in her mind like moths in a jar. After an hour or so, she sought respite in familiar surroundings. She prepared some green tea and retired to her bathroom. Lighting several votive candles, she poured sea salt into the tub as it filled, set the thermostat to one hundred, shut off the lights, and eased her stiff body and troubled mind into the steaming water.

Sinking to her chin, she looked at the softly glowing lights through nearly closed lids, watching the flames create stars against the darkness. Sighing with relief, Lucin trailed her hands lightly over her body, feeling the physical and emotional tension begin to seep away. Starting at her toes, she willed her muscles to relax, allowing the tension to dissolve into the soothing water. She let herself grow lighter in weight and substance. Sighing with anticipation, she waited for the walls to disappear, or Mama-*san* to come, or the heat to build in her low belly, calling for the itch and scratch she loved. Whatever, was fine with her. She had earned this escape, this indulgence. Giving herself over to it, she relaxed with expectation.

Nothing.

Oh, she settled down a bit and the water felt good, but the thoughts still battered her brain. No receding walls allowed her to escape to sweet oblivion, no Mama-*san* talked with her in the garden, no open-mouthed shudders of sweet release pummeled her.

Nothing.

After nearly an hour, she left the tub, slipped into her new short green robe, and padded barefoot downstairs. She was surprised to find James in the kitchen with two sugar cookies and a short glass of milk.

"Well, Lucille, me darlin'," said James, rising to his feet, "I didn't know anyone else was about. Would ya be carin' for a cookie or two then?"

Conscious of the fact her robe was short and under it she was nude, Lucin moved carefully to a chair and sat. "Thank you, James. I would. Even though it's late, you're home early. I didn't expect to find you here."

"Aw, well, dear Jolee is a bit under the weather," he chuckled. "She's suffering with the type of feminine ailment that makes her want to weep right after she slips an ice pick between my short ribs because I neglected to smile when she threw a brick at me. I find that such illness can best be served by my absence. If I'm not there, she can't kill me and I'm unable to give her reason to, although reason seems in short supply. She's a grand lass in spite of these occasional bouts of insanity."

"I see," Lucin smiled.

"So do I," he replied, bringing extra cookies and milk to the table. "That's a lovely garment you're almost wearin'. One of the new ones?"

"Yes," she admitted, blushing a bit and adjusting the robe. "I didn't know you were here."

"Good for me," James grinned. "Your hair's wet. Been in the bath?"

"Trying to escape."

"Any luck?"

"No," she answered around a bite of cookie. "Not a bit."

"Where's himself?"

"He went to bed over two hours ago."

"And what's troublin' you?"

"Oh, nothing. Just restless."

"Lucille, you lie to your friends and I'll lie to mine, but let's not be lyin' to each other. What's goin' on behind those beautiful eyes?"

"Really, James, I'm fine. It's just that ..."

The story came pouring out. Lucin talked of the visit from the Japanese just two weeks away, the commitment to skate a program, and Harrison's attitude toward raising a child.

"I think it would be grand if ya had a wee one," James beamed. "Uncle Jimmy. I could spoil the dear thing rotten, drop it back in your arms, and run like hell!"

"You would too, wouldn't you?" Lucin smiled.

"Aye. I'd be a proper uncle. Tell me something, did your mother and father raise you?"

"Not really. I had several nannies and the servants."

"How 'bout your husband?"

"Pretty much the same thing."

"Then what makes ya think he'd expect to do it any other way with his child?"

"Well ..."

"Unless I miss my guess, both of your fathers were not home a lot and left the duties of caring for the children to the mother, who passed those on to someone else most of the time. Correct?"

Lucin stared at the table. "Correct."

"The poor lad doesn't know any better, and why should he? He was reared to believe that the responsibility for the child was always somebody else's. It's up to you to educate him. You're the one who's spent all the time with the young girl you've told me about. You're the one who's seen how her idiot mother behaves. You're the one who thinks your hors are moanin' full blast for a baby of your own. He has not been part of all that. It beats me how women seem to expect men to be drippin' with mother instinct!"

"You don't understand."

"Ah, but I do, Darlin'. I've been there. It's you who don't understand. You can't have the Hartrick child. She does not belong to you. You can't take her from her foolish mother and ya can't make another one just like her. When ya have a child, it will be *yours*. Ya won't be able to show it a good time and then take it home. Ya won't be able to take it skatin' and then drop it off. Ya won't be able to be its friend, you'll have to be its *mother*, and that is a damn sight more difficult than the games you've been playin' with the little lass from up the street!"

"So you think what I'm doing with Kennedy is wrong?"

"I think what you're doin' with Kennedy is wonderful! You're giving her something to shoot for, an example of a woman other than her mother. I think that God was lookin' out for the child when he brought you into her life. In the grand scheme of things, she may be one of the biggest reasons you came to Kansas City, not countin' the joy you've brought into my tired old life, but ya cannot have her and ya cannot make her! You must understand that in your heart as well as your head, or you'll have a baby for the wrong reasons. When you want a child because it will be part of you and your husband, a new person that you can fuss over and worry about, that will make you happy and make you sad, that will frustrate the hell out of ya and bring you joy, that you will love all the time and not like some of the time, that will disappoint ya and make you proud, will still do what it damn well pleases in spite of what you tell it, and will still turn out to be whatever it chooses in spite of what you want ... when you think you're prepared for all that, then have a baby ... and you still won't be ready! About the only mistake you *can* avoid, is havin' a baby for the wrong reasons. That's a decision you make with your head and your heart, together. If ya decide with either one by itself, you're a bleedin' fool."

"Sounds like the voice of experience," Lucin said quietly.

"Aye. It is."

She smiled and placed her hand on his cheek. "Thank you, James. It seems I can always count on you."

"Yes, you can," he replied, turning his head to kiss her hand.

"So with Harrison," she continued, sliding her chair closer to keep a hand on his arm, relishing and needing the physical contact, "I should just back off until this whole thing with Japan is settled."

"If that seems right to you, yes."

"Speaking of this whole thing with Japan, every time I try to talk with him about it, he blows up. I feel like he has no confidence in my judgment at all."

"That's probably because he has so little confidence in his own judgment. You said he's bringing them here?"

"Uh-huh. I think I've convinced him to let me handle their visit to the house."

"Then, if I were you, I'd do whatever I thought was best. Trust your insight. Whatever seems right probably is. He's screwing it up doing it his way, perhaps a change of tactics is needed."

"I think so," she smiled, "and I've got a couple of ideas. I have to visit my designer tomorrow. I need some help from George."

James grinned and glanced at her short robe. "He's already done me a lot of good."

She laughed and stood up. "You like?" Lucin asked, posing and turning around for him.

"Sweet Jesus," James murmured. "You could make a statue sweat."

"I don't care about statues, Jimmy me boy. But I really think I'd enjoy making you sweat."

He extended a hand to her waist and pulled her closer to his chair. She moved willingly and placed a forearm on each of his shoulders. "Lucille, you are hard to resist."

Leaning forward, she kissed him softly on the lips. "Maybe someday you'll stop resisting," she whispered, as she stood up and took a half step backwards, tugging at his hand.

"This has gone as far as it should go," James replied, not allowing her to pull him to his feet. "Especially with himself in the house."

"I have another house," she teased.

"Aye, and I have a room that I'm going to while I can still walk," James grinned, sliding sideways out of his chair to maintain proper distance. "Get away with yourself while I still have me honor."

"Better lock your door, Jimmy. There are things that go bump in the night," she pouted, moving away toward the hall. "Pleasant dreams, Sweetie."

"Sleep well, ya great brazen lass," he chuckled as she began to climb the stairs. "Oh, by the way, Jolee informs me that Tami has returned from Japan. Just thought you might like to know." Lucin didn't answer. She needed to focus her energy on keeping her knees functioning.

Tami was back.

In the bedroom, Harrison, his pajamas buttoned to the neck, was snoring softly. She took off her robe, slipped into a nightgown, and eased quietly into bed beside him.

Sliding a pillow firmly between her legs, she lay staring into the dark. Sleep was a long time coming.

Tami was back.

THIRTY

Alone, with no one to wait for,
The memory of us, unfulfilled,
Laughs in my heart.
Disappointment cannot blossom
In the light of such joy.

LUCIN DIDN'T AWAKEN until nearly ten the next morning. On Harrison's pillow she found a note apologizing for his outburst, telling her he was on the way to the airport, assuring her that he would bring the Japanese businessmen to the garden as she advised, and promising to call in a few days. She jumped out of bed and fairly flew into the shower before she remembered that Tami had returned. Thoughts of Tami would have to wait, she told herself. First came George. Fifteen minutes later, dressed in rolled up medium-brown linen shorts, flat sandals, and braless under a yellow silk t-shirt, she pulled her hair back into a ponytail, slipped on a lined vest in antique gold cotton, and grabbed the phone.

"George here. Speak to me!"

"Hi, George. It's Lucin Montgomery."

"Lucin, Darling!" George gushed. "I just looked in the encyclopedia under perfection, and there was a picture of you! Oh, you wonderful thing, how *are* you and whom do I have to kill to make you happy?"

"I have a fashion emergency," she giggled. "Can I come over?"

"Come over? Come over!? Why, you gorgeous thing, you can *live* here! I'll just spend the rest of my life waiting on you hand and foot, or boob and bottom if you like. How can you even ask such a thing? My casa is yours! Come, come, come! George waits with bated breath and espresso. Pack it all in something sinful and scoot on over. I shall slay your dragon and you can award me your scarf. Ta!"

Thinking that George started her day better than anyone she'd ever known, Lucin flew down the stairs, flashed through the kitchen, and thrashed the Jag to his studio in record time. As usual, George flung the door open before she reached it.

"A vest to hide your nipples and rolled up shorts to display your limbs! An absolute study in contradiction," he piped gleefully, gathering her into his arms and nearly carrying her inside. "Not a word," he continued, closing the door. "Just walk around where I can view your luscious self for a moment or two while I heat the croissants. The espresso is coming down now, half-caff so we won't vibrate apart. Then you may describe the impossible that I shall accomplish for you, because my heart is pure and my love is true!"

Two minutes later the espresso and croissants hit the bar top and George beamed at her. "Give," he said.

Lucin explained what was going on, gave him a brief outline of the situation, and apprised him of the urgent deadline. He casually waved it away. "Darling, I shall do what must be done. What do you have in mind to wear at this meeting? What strikes your fancy?"

"I believe it must be strong. It must show power as well as an understanding of Japan not only as it is, but also as it was. My garden will surprise the man. So must I. It is vital that my appearance affect him, but not offend him. It is important that I get his attention, so he will be interested in me as a person."

"Well," George mused, "we must slap him with a velvet glove. Drink your coffee, Dear, and consume your croissant. As much as I would adore watching you masticate, I must peer into the distance and think. Give me five minutes." He walked to the far end of the room and sat on the floor, staring at the wall.

It took nearly fifteen minutes, but, at length, George returned to the bar carrying a sketchpad. "Lucin, light of my life, my great tawny animal," he smiled, "we are going to knock his fucking oriental socks off."

An hour later, Lucin arrived home to see Eddie puttering around in the garden. She drove the Jag to the garage and walked to the small house.

"Run-sin *san*," he grinned, trotting over, "goo' see you! Garden pretty okay, yes?"

"It's beautiful, Eddie."

"It young. One year, two year, more betta'. Twenty year, very goo'."

"Eddie, I have a favor to ask you."

"Shoo. What want?"

"I want you to teach me to speak Japanese."

He looked at her with raised eyebrows. "Teach Japanee? Take rong time. You speak Japanee. Speak to me in garden."

"I know. I can't explain how that happened. But I can't speak it now."

"Shoo you can. Mine mus' be open. Word come, you get out of way."

"Please, will you help?"

"Help with word, help open mine?"

"Yes. Of course, I'll pay you for your time."

"Ask as friend?"

She smiled. "Of course."

"No insul' Eddie with money," he said, matching her smile. "Why want learn?"

"In two weeks a very powerful man is coming to visit from Japan. It is important that I be able to speak to him with the proper respect. My husband is depending on me."

"Ah. Matta' of honor, yes?"

"Yes."

"Duty, yes?"

"Yes."

"Okay. I help. Every day, ten day, I come heah. We sit. You close eye, open mine, open heart. Eddie teach some word. You rissen, you rememba'. Start now, yes?"

"Yes."

"Goo'. Bow to me, very low, show respect. I teacha', you studen'. Mus' show great respect."

"Thank you, Eddie-*san*," she said, bowing low.

Eddie nodded curtly. "Go sit on deck. Close eye, open inside, wait."

While Lucin sat, Eddie finished his work. Nearly two hours later he squatted next to her and began to speak slowly and distinctly. In some distant place, Mama-*san* smiled. Nearly three miles away, so did Tamiko Asaruka.

Lucin came back as if from a nap, Eddie sitting on his heels beside her.

"Okay?" he asked.

"Yes," she replied, allowing things to swim into focus. "Fine."

"Goo'. Mus' go. Almos' t'ree o'clock. Have work. I be back afta' suppa' tomorrow. Meet heah. You do goo', okay?"

"Thank you, Eddie-san," she replied, rising to her feet. "You do me great honor with your teaching. I am in your debt." She bowed low from the waist and held it for a moment.

Eddie nodded and smiled. "Nighttime, go bed, open head an' heart. Much happen while sleep, okay? No try unnastan'. No try figure out. Accep'. Okay?"

"Okay, Eddie," she smiled.

"Okay," he nodded and turned away, walking to his truck.

Feeling a little disoriented, Lucin sat down for a moment and looked at the garden, waiting to become grounded. As she came to be more centered, she began to analyze what had happened. Almost immediately, pain began in her low forehead. "No try unnastan'," she smiled. "Accep'."

The smell of charcoal welcomed Lucin from a nap on the futon. Stretching slowly and yawning luxuriously, she clamped her thighs securely around the pillow that lay between them and rocked back and forth, realizing that she felt wonderful. She was covered by a light sheen of sweat and, as she threw off the coverlet, her skin became deliciously cool. Her nipples hardened almost immediately and she gently touched them with the tips of her fingernails. Umm.

Reluctantly, Lucin abandoned her play, used the bathroom and quickly showered to freshen up. She slipped into her shorts and t-shirt, dropped her panties into the hamper and walked barefoot to the house. James was outside the kitchen door, putting swordfish steaks on the grill.

"Well," he grumped at her, "I was wonderin' if you were ever gonna get up. It's nearly seven!"

"Spying on me, James?" she asked, standing beside him and peering at the grill.

"Most certainly not," he protested indignantly. "I was window peeping if you must know."

"How was it?"

"Not too bad," he grinned.

"See anything you liked?" she inquired, easing her hip against the outside of his thigh.

"Naw. You were under the covers."

"Sorry I wasn't more cooperative," she teased, casually rubbing him with her hip. "You should have stayed for my shower."

"Now, don't be messin' with me concentration. Grillin' swordfish is a delicate task requirin' total commitment."

"I'm sorry," she chuckled, walking behind him and allowing her hand to graze his butt as she passed by. "Where's Stephanie?"

"She went to her folks' house for dinner. She promised to clean things up when she got back, if I'd fix supper."

"So we're alone then, is that it, Jimmy me boy?"

"Aye."

"All by ourselves with nobody else around?" she asked, gently rubbing the small of his back.

"That we are, ya brazen hussy."

Feeling the slow, warm desire beginning to grow, Lucin couldn't resist indulging it. Pressing her body against James from the rear, she wrapped her arms around his waist.

"So what are we going to have, Jimmy?"

"Swordfish sandwiches on egg bread with me own special sauce," he said, leaning back into her, "and Irish potato salad."

Rocking her pelvis from side to side, Lucin chuckled. "And what do we get for dessert, Jimmy?"

"Sweet Jesus," James complained. "I've gotta turn these steaks!"

"So what do we get for dessert?" Lucin repeated.

"Fresh strawberries and cream, ya great tease!"

"Ooh!" Lucin murmured, attempting to ease her knee between James' legs, "sounds sticky. Am I gonna get all sticky with you, James?"

"For the love of Christ," he protested, waving a spatula behind his head, "If ya make me drop one of these steaks on the ground, you're in more trouble than Judas himself!"

"Now Jimmy, don't be getting' so excited," she cautioned. "We wouldn't want any of that swordfish layin' in the dirt, ya know." Rising to tiptoe, she licked the back of his ear and stepped away. "I'll just go inside and get out plates and stuff, okay? Oh, in your condition, you would be wise not to stand too close to the grill," she advised. "It's hot."

"James," said Lucin, finishing her last bite of potato salad, "you are an amazing man. That was marvelous."

"Aye," he grinned across the kitchen table, "it's a rare one I am."

"So why don't I hire you to be my personal assistant."

"And what would my duties be?" he grinned.

"Oh, drive me around, draw my bath, cook for me, pat my bottom, listen to me bitch, wash my back, solve all my problems, wash my front, make my bed, give me hugs and kisses, feed me bon-bons, tell me you love me, things like that."

"Sounds like a lot of work," he said, carrying the plates to the sink. "How much would it pay?"

"The salary would be directly commensurate with your, uh, performance," Lucin smiled, crossing her legs.

"I don't know," he pondered. "I'm not as young as I used to be."

"Oh, I would never discriminate against you on the basis of age," Lucin insisted, her foot bouncing. "Performance would be the defining factor."

"Would the job include room and board?"

"Food and a place to sleep. Plus a room too, if you wanted one of your own," she grinned.

"How's ten bucks a week sound?" he asked, sitting down at the table.

"When can you start?"

"I don't think startin' would be the problem," James chuckled. "Would you like your dessert now, Lucille?"

"Sit still," she replied, rising to her feet. "I'll get it." She opened the refrigerator door and withdrew a bowl of strawberries.

"Don't forget the cream," James reminded her.

She placed the bowl on the table and sat beside him. "I have a better idea," she smiled, taking a small strawberry from the bowl. She placed it between her teeth and leaned forward. James bit the exposed half off and they chewed with their lips touching.

"Better than cream," he said.

The delicious tingling making her rock in her chair a bit, Lucin placed another berry between her teeth. Just as James reached it, she sucked the strawberry into her mouth. His lips touched hers. "Come and get it," she said. James managed to retrieve half of the fruit and pulled away a bit, laughing. Lucin leaned forward and licked juice from his chin.

"Another one?" she asked.

"And another, and another," he said, and suddenly the berries meant nothing. Their world was reduced to lips and tongues, the hands and palms, touching, exploring, lost totally in each other, the sweetness of the moment more fruitful than anything from tree or vine. Panting into each other's mouths, both were startled by the intensity, the strength of the need that had grown between them. Urgent without being hurried, sweeping without being overwhelming, it lifted them as they lifted each other, confident in its expectation, secure in its anticipation. Everything had come together in this instant. All the time, all the teasing, all the waiting was about to end. It was glorious, and they both reveled in it, giving the need its space, letting the momentum build at its own pace.

Stephanie's car pulled into the drive.

Neither of them would ever remember exactly what happened in the next sixty seconds, except they separated. Thirty minutes later, James was headed to Clancy's for a pint or four, and Lucin was in the kitchen, making small talk with Stephanie.

Unable to sit still, Lucin prowled the house for a while, then walked to visit the garden. Sitting on the deck, she watched the bats wheel and turn as they snatched mosquitoes from the air. The lights of the garden gave it a mysterious look, making it appear larger and deeper than it actually was. She sat, listening to crickets, the on again—off again peep of the small frogs, the occasional splash of a fish in the pond. Feeling disappointment and yet relief at the turn of events, she let the night take her, and once again sat overlooking the other pond. Alone there too, she watched stones grow, and drank tea from an empty cup.

Near dawn she returned, and went inside to her bedchamber. Removing her clothes, she lay down on the futon and remembered his tongue, his taste, and her need of him. "Someday, James," she whispered into the pale darkness as she reached for the red lacquered box.

THIRTY-ONE

Questions never answered
Are still unasked.
Doubt remains
Warm in my heart.
Only my pillow knows the truth.

LUCIN AWOKE LAZILY around nine, smiling as she enjoyed the comfort of the futon and the pillow between her legs. Slowly she stretched, pulling both herself and her body back to reality. Umm. She and James had come so close. She chuckled, recalling it, glancing at the half empty box beside the bed, warmed by the memory of strawberry intimacy. Even though she had availed herself of the pleasures of the red lacquered box at considerable length, the glow remained, and she strained against the pillow for a few moments, luxuriating in her need, teasing herself against the thick roll of piping until the heat reached her throat. Throwing back the covers she lurched into the bath and finally to the shower where the slippery soaping was longer and more intense than usual. The spray and steam seduced her and when it was over, she was slightly embarrassed to find herself spraddle-legged on the shower floor, propped against the glass blocks, shivering with the intensity of the release. Thinking of Harrison, she felt a blush rise in her face as she got to her feet. Wondering what his reaction would be to her wanton behavior, she grinned as she began to towel off.

"That ought to take care of things," she said aloud, as she stepped out into the bathroom.

But it didn't. Walking to the main house with hard nipples, a tight throat, and a renewed desire, she knew it hadn't. A drop of water ran from her hair down her neck, between her breasts, and across her tummy. She shivered and felt her sphincter tighten. "Damn," she whispered.

An empty kitchen greeted her. She poured coffee, opened a small container of peach yogurt and sat, elbows on the table, resting her chin in her palm, staring morosely out the window. The phone rang.

"Are you still alive?"

212

"Oh! Hi Jolee."

"Hi Jolee, my butt. Where the hell have you been? I haven't seen you in weeks!"

Lucin grinned. "You've got James to pick on, you should be nice to me."

"Oh, yeah. I forgot. Hi, Sweetie. It's been a long time. I'd be happy to work on those ragged talons of yours, or are you soaking for someone else now? Should I be jealous?"

"No, you shouldn't be jealous. You know you're the only one. How can I possibly make this up to you?"

"I have a cancellation at eleven. I could do your nails, and you'd be right next door to Tommy-son when it's all over."

Lucin swallowed. "Actually, my nails are a mess and I do need to see Tami."

"I bet you do."

"No, I really do."

"Sure, Sweetie. That's what I said," Jolee teased.

"There are some things I need."

"We all have needs, girlfriend."

"Jolee," Lucin giggled.

"I got some needs he could fill."

"You said eleven?" asked Lucin, trying to get the conversation back on track.

"Yeah. You remember where the shop is? Right next door to Tommy's place."

"I remember," Lucin laughed.

"Okay. See ya at eleven. Take a cold shower." Jolee hung up.

Lucin sipped her coffee and smiled, realizing her legs were crossed and her right foot was bobbing. Vigorously.

Upstairs, she dried her hair and carefully applied minimal make-up, accenting the almond tilt of her eyes. She slipped into a new pair of white silk thong panties and a spaghetti-strap sundress in crisp yellow cotton. High-heeled, cork-soled sandals and a ponytail tied with a yellow scarf were followed by lipstick and a light misting of White Shoulders and she was out the door. When she walked into *Nails!*, Jolee approved.

"That oughta do it," she grinned, eyeballing the short skirt and low neckline.

"This old thing?" Lucin asked. "I just found it in the back of the closet."

"Uh-huh. That's a fuck-me outfit if I ever saw one. Nice make-up. Horny?"

"Jolee!"

"Never mind. I can tell by the way you walk. Sit down, soak, and catch me up. I haven't seen you in a month."

For the next thirty minutes, omitting adventures with James, Lucin told Jolee what had been going on, including the puzzling night by the garden.

"So you don't know if it was Tommy or not?" Jolee asked.

"No."

"Damn! I can't imagine it. I believe you; I just can't imagine it."

"I can't either, but that's the way it happened."

"So what are you going to do?"

"Well, I really do need some things from his shop. I thought I'd go over and see if he mentions anything."

"And if he doesn't?"

"I don't know."

"You could just ask him. You know, something casual. "Hey, Tommy. Did you fuck my brains out the other night?""

"*Jolee!*" Lucin shrieked.

"What?" Jolee grinned. "Too subtle?"

Laughing, Lucin was unable to answer.

"Or," Jolee continued, "you could just walk in, plant a lip-lock on him and grab his crotch. When you're done, if he says, 'You again', you'll know for sure the two of you got together."

"That'd work," Lucin giggled.

"So what *are* you going to do?"

"I guess I'm just going to play it by ear. See how he acts toward me."

"You could play dumb and act like it never happened. Take it for what's it's worth."

"I don't think I can do that."

"Naw," Jolee smiled. "I couldn't either. Wow. This is a new one on me, Sweetie. Just when I thought I'd heard everything … so, ya gonna take a run at him?"

"God, Jolee, I don't know that either."

"You're dressed for it."

"I'm married."

"Yeah, ya are, but it's a strange relationship. Are you smart enough to handle Tommy without beating yourself up about it for the rest of your life?"

"Who knows?"

"Well, it would either push you and Harrison farther apart or bring you closer together. What it would not do is have *no* effect."

Lucin stared at the table for a moment. "Any suggestions?" she asked.

"Can't tell you what to do, Sweetie. I do know that being faithful to yourself is more important than anything else. You've changed a lot since I've known you. You're a much more open and self-assured person than you were when we met. I'd hate to see that growth stop. There's a lot more going on here than just wanting to get laid. You know it and I know it. If it were me, I'd just wing it and see what happens. But that's me. You and I are different people. I *do* know, that if the lovely and talented James O'Doud wasn't keeping my horns trimmed," she grinned, "I'd be on Tommy like a cheap suit."

"Interesting image," Lucin smiled.

"Ain't it just?" Jolee grinned. "I've thought about it a lot."

"I don't know what I'm going to do," Lucin confessed.

"That's probably best. Leaves you more room to maneuver. You're done."

"Already?"

"Yep, finished. You can't hide behind your nails anymore. You don't have to go home, but you can't stay here. Pay me, and get out. I'd go next door, if I were you."

In the seven or eight steps from Jolee's front door to Tami's, Lucin's emotions ran the entire gamut. Joy to fear, happiness to dread, they battered her as gusting wind assaults the willow. In those few paces, Lucin came to feel almost exhausted. She tugged open his door as if seeking shelter, shelter in the eye of the storm.

The front area was empty, but he was there. She could *feel* him. His strength, his caring, his will washed all about her. Lucin stood still in the center of it, moving slightly with the flow, keeping her balance physically and psychically. Blossom flickered at the edge of her consciousness, watching and waiting. Tami's voice wafted from the rear of the store.

"Lucin-*san*, how good of you to come. I have been anticipating your arrival. Just a moment please, and I will be out."

Tami. Oh, God. What was she even doing here? Resisting the simultaneous urges to run to the rear of the shop, and flee out the door, she held her position and waited. Presently he came striding into the showroom, all in black, hair tied into a ponytail. A grin split his face when he saw her, and he moved through the store in an effortless glide. Locking her knees, Lucin took his outstretched hands. The warm chill of him climbed both arms and settled in the back of her neck. She nearly groaned.

"It is so good to see you," Tami smiled, leaning forward to kiss her lightly on the cheek. His breath whispered across the side of her face and neck, warm velvet on her skin. He leaned back and released her hands. The loss of his touch was more than physical, and she inhaled sharply.

"How have you been?" he continued.

"F-fine," Lucin stammered, attempting to breathe around the lump that had sprung to her throat. "Did your trip go well?"

"Marvelously," he said, as if amused by her. "I have some wonderful things that will be arriving soon. I am brewing tea in the storeroom. Would you care for a cup?"

"Yes, please," Lucin replied, searching for something to focus on.

"Excellent. It is a blend of green and black that I sometimes can get from a friend in China."

"Thank you," Lucin said, bowing slightly. "I am honored."

"Your heritage is showing," Tami smiled. "Am I to assume that we are not quite alone?"

Fuzzily, Lucin realized what he had just asked. "I don't believe we are," she said, Blossom coming to mind.

"That's okay," Tami laughed. "There's plenty for everybody."

The tea was exceptional and they drank in silence for a time, as Lucin gathered herself. "I need several sake flasks, a pair of straw-soled sandals, and a pair of those socks with the split between the toes."

"*Tabe*," Tami said.

"Yes, *tabe*. My first of two Japanese lessons for today."

"Two?"

"Some people vital to my husband's business are coming to visit from Japan in a few days. It's important that I make a good impression. Eddie is teaching me Japanese."

"Ah, yes," Tami smiled. "I saw him yesterday. He said he was helping you remember."

"Remember?"

"There is much more to Eddie than meets the eye. He spent many years in a monastery after World War Two."

"World War Two? How old is Eddie?"

"I don't think anyone, least of all him, knows for sure. Close to ninety I would think. If he says he is teaching you to remember, that's exactly what he's doing."

"He claims I spoke Japanese to him one morning before I was completely awake, but I don't really remember how it happened. He comes over every evening for an hour or so. We sit by the garden and he talks to me. I get woozy then kind of come back, normal up, and he goes away."

"You should feel very honored," Tami replied. "Eddie is a great teacher. It is rare that he would take a student for just a few days or one that was not Japanese. Actually, it's more than rare. To my knowledge, it's unheard of."

"You've known him for a long time?"

"He was my master when I was very young. I studied martial arts with him for ten years. Push hands and sword. Eddie is amazing. He can control his body weight, punch something without coming in contact with it, kill with the smallest touch. He is a very unusual man."

"And he builds gardens."

"Yes," Tami smiled. "His creative urge is very strong. How is your garden, anyway?"

"Eddie says in twenty years it will look good," Lucin grinned.

"He'll probably be here to see it," Tami laughed, rising to his feet. "Let's find your sandals and *tabi* and let you select some flasks." He followed her to the front of the store.

The selections were piled on the counter when he disappeared into the back again for a moment. When he returned, he was carrying a large crockery bottle.

"If this meeting is important, you should serve good sake. Take this with you. Eddie makes it."

"He gave me a small bottle as a garden warming present," Lucin said.

"Ah! That's right. I had forgotten. We drank some of his sake the evening before I left for Japan."

"The night you gave me The Waiting Courtesan."

"Has the stone grown?"

"I watch it carefully," she replied, "but I can't tell."

"Don't watch so carefully, just observe," he said, placing her purchases in two plastic bags.

"About that night," she said, and he looked at her with such force she felt weak. "About that night," she continued, willing herself to be strong.

"Yes?"

"This is sort of embarrassing. Some things are unclear to me. May I ask you a question about that evening?" Her heart was pounding so loudly she was sure he could hear it. She clutched at the edge of the counter for balance.

"You may ask, of course," Tami replied, his face becoming impassive.

She looked at him for a moment. "Will you answer?"

"Probably not."

"Why?"

216

"The night is for magic. Magic answers only to itself, Lucin. It does not answer to you, it does not answer to me. Never ask magic for answers. Magic does not like to be insulted."

"But I have to know if it was real!"

"No one knows what is real."

"I have to know."

"No, you don't."

"I do."

"There are times when only the pillow is real. All else is without substance or import. These times are gifts. We accept them, thank the gods, and go on our way. Why, how, if, and the rest of it has no meaning. To such a gift, this reality is nothing. To this reality, such a gift is nothing. The two should not be brought in contact with each other. No good can come of it."

"No good can come of it?!"

"That's correct."

"That's the type of answer you'd give a child!" she flared. "For nearly a month I have wondered exactly what went on. I've worried about it, dreamed about it, agonized about it, fantasized about it, and now you tell me it means nothing?"

"That's correct."

"Well, it may not mean anything to you, *Buster*," she bellowed, "but it means a Goddammed lot to me!"

He stared at her for a moment, and began to laugh. The more he laughed, the more he had to, and soon Tami was rubbing tears out of his eyes. In the face of his hilarity, Lucin calmed down. By the time Tami collected himself, Lucin was smiling. He took her face in his hands and kissed her gently on the lips.

"You are wonderful," he said.

She rested her forehead against his and let their breath mingle. "And you, Asaruka, are in a lot of trouble," she replied, and kissed *him*. She let the heat churning in her belly flow up through her body and out her mouth as she leaned into him, tongue probing, teeth nipping, drawing the air from his lungs and returning it. When she pulled back, Tami looked a little stunned. Lucin released him and gathered her two bags.

"A man with a maid in the night may be without import, you inscrutable heathen asshole, but if that 'maid' is *me*, it's fucking well loaded with *import*! I may never ask you the big question, Tami," she growled, "but if I do, you *will* answer. Count on it." Five seconds later she was out the door.

THIRTY-TWO

My uncertain heart,
Excited,
Fears what may come.
Joy and sorrow
Are the same.

THE NEXT SEVERAL DAYS were more than hectic. Kaypee phoned about every other evening, at first unhappy about being stuck in Oklahoma and away from Lucin, but adjusting to her new surroundings. Harrison returned for three days, preoccupied and nervous, then went back to the home office. Eddie came by in the evenings, and Lucin looked forward to his visits. The hour or so he spent with her at the end of each day was very peaceful, almost meditative. George called her in twice for fittings, Bryan questioned her about her program for the February show, James tried to keep her focused, the situation with Tami still rankled, and looming like a storm on the distant horizon, was the visit from the Japanese. Lucin struggled to handle the growing pressure. On the evening before the scheduled arrival of Harrison and Serata Onoshi of Nagata Industries, she sat on the deck overlooking her garden seeking the serenity she customarily found there. James came around the corner carrying two cans of Guinness.

"Want to be by yourself?"

"Not where you're concerned, James. You're the only person I'd want near me right now, and I need your company."

"Sound judgment," he grinned, walking into the kitchen for glasses.

"Only two cans?" she asked.

"Aye," he replied, returning to the deck, and pouring the brew. "I wouldn't want ya all sexually flustered and carnally exhausted for yer meetin' tomorrow. I thought one pint each would be safe."

She smiled. "So now you want to be safe around me?"

"Perish the thought," he said, taking a chair beside her. "I treasure bein' at risk. It's your safety I'm tryin' to make sure of, me darlin' and fair."

She reached over and rubbed the back of his neck. "I could never feel anything but safe around you, James."

"Now that's a grand compliment, that is. Thank ya, Lass. Are ya ready for to-morrow then?"

"God, James, I don't know what I'm ready for," she sighed. "This all seemed like such a good idea when I told Harrison to leave it to me, but now I'm not so sure. Let's face it, I was angry and I wanted to show off. Tomorrow, Harrison is going to arrive with these bigwigs, and here sits hotshot Lucin with his career in her hands. I'm an idiot!"

"Now you're insultin' me," James protested. "I don't consort with idiots."

"Well, I am. Look what I've gotten myself into!"

"Aye. A position to accomplish a great deal for your husband's livelihood and your personal relationship with the dear lad. How's your Japanese comin'?"

"I don't know that either. Eddie hasn't exactly been teaching me the language. He claims that would take too much time and be very difficult. He's been sort of hypnotizing me."

"Hypnotizing you?"

"That's not quite right. Regressing me might be a better term. I don't understand it, but I feel as if the young Japanese girl from my visions or dreams or whatever you want to call them, is nearby. It's strange. Eddie says everything is going well and I shouldn't worry."

"Well then, you shouldn't. Drink your Guinness."

Lucin looked at the glass in her hand as if she'd just discovered it. "Oh," she re-plied, and took a long pull. "Thank you, James," she smiled. "You're very thought-ful."

"Ah, there's that darlin' smile. Me poor heart can beat again at the sight of it. Sure, an' I though ya might be so far down in the bottomless pit of self-pity, that there was no savin' ya."

"Jimmy, me boy," she grinned, 'tis a wonder that ya can walk upright with all the blarney you're carryin'."

"A lesser man would drop to his knees under the strain of it," he chuckled. "What can I do for ya then to help you prepare for your grand ordeal?"

She slid her chair against his and leaned her head on his shoulder. "You do it al-ready, James. You love me."

"Aye," smiled James Mathew O'Doud as he patted her knee. "I'd be a fool not to."

Lucin spent the night in the garden house, fully prepared not to sleep a wink. She went out like a light. Mama-*san* and Moon Blossom flickered through her dreams, Grandmother Iona whispered in her ear, Eddie came and went, and sometime, dur-ing the darkness of the day, she settled. Morning found her rested and at peace. She was drinking green tea at the kitchen table a little before eight, when Harrison phoned.

"Hi, Luce," he said, and she could hear the tension in his voice.

"Good morning, Harrison. How are you?"

"I'm okay. I just called to let you know what's going on."

"What's the schedule?"

"I'm at the airport now. My plane arrives in Kaycee at noon. Onoshi and his people are due around twelve-thirty. James will drive us from the airport to their hotel, then to the office, then to the site, then to an early dinner. After that, we'll be out to the house."

"So I can expect you around eight?"

"I guess. Are you sure you want to do this?"

"That's not the question you're asking. You want to know if I *can* do it. The answer is yes. It is my place to do it. You are my husband. To offer you support is my duty."

"See? There you go. You don't even sound like you."

"Harrison, all will be as it will be. There is only fate. Even though you don't trust yourself right now, do me the honor of trusting me."

There was a moment of silence. "Alright," he sighed.

"Good. Try to relax. Nothing you do or say today can win them over. Onoshi will make up his mind regardless of what happens between you. This visit is a politeness only. This evening let him dictate the pace of things. Once you come here, stop attempting to convince him of anything. Put business away. If he wants to talk, talk. If he wants to be silent, be silent. Allow peace to happen."

"I don't understand."

"You don't have to. Just go with his flow. Under no circumstances press him for a decision. You must appear to put all of this in the hands of the gods and be at rest with it."

"Christ, Luce! This is all too weird!"

"I know it must seem so to you, but it really isn't. Try and relax, Sweetheart. Just do what you need to do with him and stay cool. Once he is here, pull back a bit and give him emotional and psychic space. I'll talk with him."

"He doesn't speak English."

"That's fine."

"His interpreter is pretty good though … oh, they just announced my flight."

"Have a good trip, relax, and know that I love you."

"I love you too, Luce. See you tonight."

"Yes, you will," she replied, and hung up.

The rest of the day was a steady pace of activity. Lucin stopped by George's and picked up the clothes he'd designed for the occasion. A visit to *Nails!* and a half-hour with Jolee made her laugh and got her feet back at least close to the ground. After a late lunch of broiled tuna and a spinach salad, Lucin spent the next hour on her hair, pulling it up on top of her head and securing it with a massive amount of hairspray and several inlaid chopsticks, allowing a strand to fall casually in front of each ear. She labored carefully over her make-up, lightening her entire face a bit, accentuating the natural oriental shape of her eyes as much as possible, applying subtle shades of green shadow and liner.

The hibachi was waiting on the deck, set up the evening before, and she checked it over to make sure nothing had been forgotten. In the pot on top went water and the large bottle of sake Tami had given her. Beside it on a small lacquered table sat six cups and four flasks. She spaced four chairs in proximity as well as four large kneeling pillows. At around six-thirty all was ready. Lucin turned on the misters to cool and refresh the garden, lit the charcoal fire, and went inside to dress.

First came the underblouse. In the palest green silk, with wide sleeves, it went on like a kimono and stopped just below her waist, tying in the traditional wrap-around style. Then came the overblouse. In light green raw silk, with sleeves reaching almost to her knees, it had a slightly wider neckline to allow the underblouse to show. Next were the pants. In a dark green silk that appeared nearly black, they were snug around the hips with wide, pleated legs giving the impression of a skirt reaching to the floor. Last was the overmantle. In medium green heavy silk, it went over her head and onto her shoulders hanging nearly to the floor. The rear was a single panel with a standing crane in a circle embroidered across the back in raw silk thread, matching the light green of the overblouse. Open at the sides, the front was overlapping panels and wrapped like a kimono. The shoulders were overlaid in broad padded scallops creating wings that reached six inches past each arm, giving the formidable impression of great width. The overmantle was belted by an *obi*, a wide stiff sash the same color as the pants. To this Lucin added white split-toed socks and the customary straw-soled sandals. She looked in the mirror. Masculine. Definitely masculine. Nearly samurai in nature. The hair and make-up retained all the necessary femininity, as would her attitude, but there was an under-layment of strength and power. As she walked about the room, Lucin noticed a difference in her carriage and could feel another presence moving with her. Smiling, she kneeled on a pillow and patiently waited for her husband's arrival. When the phone rang, James was on the other end.

"Twenty minutes," he said.

"*Ah, so desu,*" she replied. "*Arigato goziemashita,* James-*san.*" She hung up, relaxed, and went into that long ago garden.

The sound of the limo arriving by the garage pulled her back, and Blossom came with her, wisping around and within Lucin as unseen smoke. Confident and unhurried, she rose to her feet and straightened her overmantle. Through the window she could see Harrison and three Japanese men walking toward the garden. All were wearing gray suits, two of the men in their thirties and slender. Between and in front of them was an older man, squat and dense, obviously their leader. He and Harrison walked side by side. Neither of them spoke. They stepped up on the deck and walked toward the rear of the house. As they neared the corner, Lucin-Blossom exited her bedroom, pulled the *shoji* closed, and faced them. The surprise on Harrison's face was palpable.

"Mr. Onoshi," he stammered, "I'd like you to meet my wife."

As Onoshi struggled to control one eyebrow, Lucin bowed low from the waist, holding it until he, through politeness, was forced to return it. He bobbed. His two helpers each gave her a quarter bow. Lucin ignored them and focused only on the old man.

"*Konbanwa,* Onoshi-*san. Yokoso oide kudasareta,*" she said. "Good evening. Welcome to my house."

Harrison's mouth was open, and Onoshi hesitated for a moment. This was obviously not what he had expected either. The tiniest of smiles flickered across his lips. He bowed again, more deeply this time and spoke to her in Japanese.

"Good evening," he replied. *"I am honored to be here. Your husband seems to be out of breath. Please, what shall I call you?"*

"So sorry, my husband is seldom without speech. If it pleases you, call me Lucin-*Blossom. Please excuse my humble house and garden and sit while I prepare sake."*

"Your garden and house are exquisite. It is my pleasure to be here," Onoshi stated, looking at her intently. *"You have sake?"*

"Very, yes, Onoshi-san. *A leader of your power and experience must be at least a six-flask man. May I have the honor of pouring for you? Sake by a garden at the end of the day is a true blessing from the gods, is it not?"*

"Yes it is, Lucin-*Blossom-san. I had not expected to be so blessed this evening,"* he smiled.

"There is a bath also, if you would care to relax further. It is humble and totally inadequate, but you are, of course, more than welcome."

"You are too kind. Although the travel and business of this day have indeed left me weary, I must gratefully decline your generous offer."

"As you wish. Would you care for a chair, or would you like to sit in a more civilized manner?"

"A pillow, please," Onoshi chuckled, motioning Harrison and the aides to sit. All of them took pillows, Harrison struggling a bit with his and openly staring at his wife as if he had never seen her before. Lucin poured sake from the bottle into four flasks on a tray, then served each a cup from flasks designated for them.

"So," said Onoshi, as if she and he were the only two people on the deck, *"will you join us in a flask,* Lucin-Blossom-*san?"*

"Thank you for your kindness, Onoshi-san, *but I must gratefully decline. If I were to drink a flask with you, my knees would get weak, I would get silly, and all of us would be embarrassed! I would bring great disgrace on my family for the next ten generations!"*

"A lady as lovely as you bringing disgrace to anyone, is beyond imagination" he said. *"You are Japanese?"*

"In my ancestry and my heart, yes," Lucin confessed, her eyes downcast and looking away.

"You speak our language beautifully, and with ancient grace. I am surprised."

"In truth, as am I," Lucin replied. *"As we speak, kami and spirits help me to do so. I do not understand, I only accept."*

"Acceptance without understanding is very rare in a, uh ..."

"Barbarian?" she offered, looking him boldly in the eyes.

"Yes," Onoshi replied. *"So sorry. It is not my intention to offend you. Please forgive my stupidity and lack of manners."*

"It is nothing if not the truth, Onoshi-san,*"* Lucin smiled. *"You have spoken openly and honestly with me. I am honored by your candor. May I also speak frankly with you, Sire?"*

Onoshi bowed low, with heavy import. *"Please do. It brings me great gratification that you would ask."*

"I am a barbarian, Onoshi-sama, *as much a barbarian as any other westerner. I have been raised in this place, in this culture. Only recently has it come to my attention that my ancestors were anything else other than barbarians. This knowledge has changed my life. It has put me in the posi-*

tion of being able to see two sides of a stone at the same time. This man before you is my husband. I am bound to him and will not, cannot, betray his confidence or his wishes. Please understand that it is not my desire to influence you in any way to his will. I would never insult you or him in such a manner. I will simply tell you this: he is, in his own way, a man of extreme honor. He has only one face, Onoshi-sama. He speaks with only one tongue. Whether you trust him or not is, of course, your affair. However, he is worthy of your trust. Please forgive me for being so direct in my words. Doubtless it comes from my barbarian influences."

The squat man drained his sake and stared at her for a moment. "When I first saw you," he said, "your clothing brought to my mind the samurai of days past. I wondered where your swords might be. It would seem your Katana is behind your teeth. I dare not speculate at the location of your Wagasashi."

Demurely averting her eyes as she chuckled, Lucin filled his cup with fresh sake. Onoshi motioned for one of his underlings to fill the other cups and gazed into the garden for a time. Lucin waited quietly as she knelt beside him. At length he spoke.

"This stone I see before me, growing so artfully from the earth. It is special, is it not?"

"Oh, very yes, Onoshi-san. It was a gift and has great meaning for me."

"It is lovely. Does this stone have a name?"

"It is called 'The Waiting Courtesan', Sire."

"Did you name this stone?"

"No, Sire, I did not."

"As I suspected," he laughed. "You are much too wise to name a stone after yourself."

She joined him in his laughter. "I am what I am, Onoshi-sama."

"Does your husband know what a lucky man he is?"

"No, Sire. At least not yet."

"I would like to be a beetle in the bamboo of the bedchamber when he finds out, Child," Onoshi chuckled. "Will you dance or sing for us this evening?"

"Alas no, Sire, for I croak and stagger and would embarrass my husband."

"We would not want that," Onoshi teased. "Perhaps if we could recall other times and other places, I would be in a position to enjoy more of your company."

Lucin smiled. "Ah, so desu. But then you would have to give the Mama-san at least one koban."

"So much?!"

"But, Onoshi-san," Lucin replied demurely, her eyes downcast, "has it not always been true that one only recieves what one pays for?"

The old man threw back his head and laughed. "Very good, Lucin-Blossom-sama! In your case, perhaps two koban would be a small price to pay for such wit and beauty."

Lucin bowed. "And in your case, Sire, Mama-san would have to watch me closely so I would not give away her profit." They sat smiling at each other for a moment, then Lucin spoke again. "Now is the time when the evening belongs to you men. It has been my pleasure to meet you and be graced by your kind conversation, Onoshi-sama. If you will excuse me, I will await your needs within."

"Lucin-Blossom-san," he bowed, "it has been my honor to spend time with such a delightful woman as yourself. Do not concern your mind with the outcome of my visit. You have made it wonderful. Your duty to your husband is well fulfilled. You are excused."

She bowed deeply to him and turned to Harrison. "I'll be in the house, if you need me," she said, and retreated behind the shoji into her bedroom. There, backlighted by an oil lamp, she knelt on a pillow as was customary, her waiting silhouette cast upon the glowing screen.

223

THIRTY-THREE

Step carefully
On the path that appears clear.
Pitfalls lurk
Unanticipated.
My heart stumbles.

LUCIN SAT BEHIND THE SCREEN for less than half an hour, until the meeting broke up. Only a few words were spoken and she was not summoned to serve. When she walked back onto the deck and looked toward the garage, the limo was gone. She took a few moments to pick up the cushions and collect the sake, then returned inside. Carefully she removed her clothing and make-up, brushed out her hair, and slipped into a white cotton sleeping kimono. She walked to the main house to wait for Harrison.

Sitting at the kitchen table with a small glass of brandy, still inhabited by Moon Blossom, she mused over the events of her meeting with Onoshi-*san*. Lucin was so engaged when Harrison stalked through the door. Smiling, she rose to greet him. He glared at her.

"Jesus Christ, Luce! Have you lost your mind?"

Feeling as if she'd been slapped, Lucin sank back into her chair. "W-what?" she stammered.

"What the hell *was* that? I bring home the most important possible client of my entire career and I find you dressed up for Halloween! In case you haven't noticed, this isn't Japan. And then ... and then, you start spouting off Japanese at the guy and behaving like some kind of servant. My wife! *My* wife is nobody's fucking servant, Lucin. Not *my* wife! Nobody's! And there you are, bowing and scraping on your knees for that sonof-a-bitch as if you were his personal waitress! If I had wanted a goddam waitress, I would have married a goddam waitress! The next thing I know you're laughing and kissing up to that asshole like some kind of Japanese call girl! And then ... and then, you go inside and listen at the door. Christ! Your shadow was on the fucking screen while you eavesdropped! He saw it. He barely said another word, not there, not in the car, not at the hotel, nothing! I have blown this account, I have wasted a huge amount of the firm's money and resources, and I'll be lucky if I can even find another job after I lose this one!"

Lucin, emotionally crushed and bleeding, stared at the tabletop for a moment and collected herself. She regarded Harrison from under lowered lashes. "Of course you are quite correct in your anger," she murmured, bowing slightly. "The events of this evening are entirely my fault. Very yes. So sorry. I am entirely to blame. Please forgive me. My only thought was for you."

"Christ on a crutch!" Harrison shouted. "Knock off the oriental bullshit, will ya? I'm fucking sick of it!"

Lucin rose to her feet. "Alright," she flared, "I'll knock it off if you're fucking sick of it. Let me tell you what I'm fucking sick of. I'm sick of not having a husband at home to spend my time and my life with. I'm sick of being married to a man who has not the slightest idea of what's important in *my* life. I'm sick of empty beds and empty rooms and empty hearts. I'm sick of being in a situation where the only man in my life who makes any effort to understand me is my husband's driver! I'm sick of *that*, Harrison, and I am fucking sick to death of you expecting my world to revolve around *your* goddammed law firm and *your* goddammed career!"

Lucin drew breath, and launched again. "You want to know what else I'm fucking sick of, Harrison?" she spat, advancing on him from around the table. "I'm sick of offering support and getting none in return. I'm sick of being the only one in this relationship with the slightest idea that it is screwed up. And I am sick of your pompous judgments on my behavior. A Halloween costume?! That *Halloween costume* and what I did with it, may be the only reason you'll get your precious contract, you ungrateful shit! I don't expect you to understand this. Hell, I don't expect you to understand *anything*, but the way I treated Onoshi paid him the highest possible compliment. Speaking to him in his own language, serving him, placing my shadow on the screen so he would know I was there, *at his service*, told him I cared about him and that I cared very much about *you*! If you had bothered to take the slightest interest in a culture five thousand years older than your own, you pompous ass, you would have known that. The smartest thing you've done throughout this entire ordeal was to trust me, and you're too goddammed ignorant and self-centered to even begin to realize it. The way I treated Onoshi showed him how much I believe in you, how much I trust you, and how much I care about your business!" Nearly panting, she stared at him from a distance of three feet.

Pale and unable to look directly at her, Harrison took a step backwards. "Uh …"

"Uh, my ass!" Lucin replied. "I am going upstairs and take a bath. Then I am going to lie down in *our* bed. I am not going to retreat to the garden tonight, Harrison. I am going to sleep in *our* house. I don't know where you're going to sleep, but it damn sure is not going to be anyplace near me! I may or may not love you, but right now I definitely do not *like* you. Not one little bit. Call me sometime and apologize, but don't hurry. I'm tired of being insulted." She looked at him for a moment, shaking slightly, and calmed herself. He started to speak.

"Don't say anything," she growled. "Not one fucking word. Just get out."

Harrison stared at her back as Lucin climbed the stairs. Halfway up she stopped and turned. "By the way," she smiled, "being a Japanese call-girl, as you so sensitively put it, has its rewards."

As she walked into the bedroom, Lucin heard the kitchen door slam. She crossed to the bed, sighed, sat cross-legged, and waited to cry. In a few moments, she felt Moon-Blossom's arms encircle her and, laughing, eased back onto the pillows. There in the darkness, they held each other until Lucin fell asleep.

Groggy and muddled, Lucin lurched into the kitchen at around nine the next morning to find James fussing with the waffle iron. Realizing her night kimono could have been wrapped a bit more demurely, she ignored it and flopped into a chair. James grinned at her.

"Sure, isn't it nice to see you this morning. When do ya plan on waking up?"

"Coffee, O'Doud," she yawned. "And be quick about it, or you're fired."

"In a good humor, too," he laughed, moving to the pot. "And showin' a grand bit of thigh and cleavage, I might add. And don't be threatenin' me with me job, Lucille. I don't work for you. I work for that grand and glorious lad that is your husband."

"He around?"

"No. The last time I saw him, he had his tail between his legs departin' the limo at the airport. That was about two o'clock this mornin'."

"Got out of town, huh?"

"Aye. I suspect he thought it was for his own good," James grinned, placing a cup of coffee before her.

"You heard?"

"With me ear pressed against the door like that, it was hard not to."

Lucin chuckled. "I was pretty hard on him."

"Do ya care?"

"No," she replied, sipping from her cup. "God, that's good."

"At almost eighty dollars a pound, it ought to be. Waffles comin' up."

"Waffles?"

"Sure. With fancy maple syrup, whipped cream, and a strawberry or two."

"What's the occasion?"

"We're celebratin', me Darlin' and fair," James answered, pouring batter onto the iron. "Since it's a bit early in the day for Guinness, I thought waffles might do. How's your coffee?"

"More, please. What are we celebrating?" she asked, waking up a little and scratching her ribs while yawning.

"The acquisition of Nagata Industries as a client of Mr. Montgomery's law firm."

"What?!"

"That's the impression I got driving the heathens back to their hotel," James smiled, adding coffee to her cup.

"Really?"

"I told you once I spent time in Japan. I don't speak the language much, but I understand a little. The head guy thought you were alright. I believe he's gonna do the deal. Bein' the nasty old bastard that he is, he just may not tell your husband for awhile."

"James, that's wonderful!"

"That he's doin' the deal, or that he's not gonna let Harrison know?"

"Yes," she giggled. "Harrison could use a good sweat."

"Well, he's got one goin' right now. You knocked the pins out from under the lad last night, not that he didn't deserve it."

"Do you think I was too rough on him?"

"Do you?"

"No," she smiled, "I don't. It wasn't like me, though. I lost my temper."

"Not true," James said, putting the waffle on a plate. "You *found* your temper, Lucille, and a grand find it was, too."

"Thank you," she dimpled.

"You're more than welcome," James replied, taking a small pitcher of syrup out of the microwave, and slipping the waffle inside. "So, that's why I thought a bit of a celebration was in order," he continued, moving to the fridge. Lucin stretched as she watched him set the syrup, a small bowl of strawberries, and a can of Reddi Whip on the table and return to the cooking waffle.

"Hmmm," she grunted.

"Hmmm, what?" asked James, as he started the microwave, and put the second waffle on a plate.

"We have strawberries, James."

"Aye. I'm aware of that," he answered, placing the waffle in front of her and returning for the one still in the microwave oven.

"We like strawberries, don't we, James?"

"That's true."

"We have a history with strawberries, huh, James?"

"That we do," he replied, sitting at the table with his plate

She shifted in her seat and batted her eyes at him. "It just seems to me, that with all these strawberries and all this whipped cream, these two waffles are sort of a waste of time."

"The syrup's hot. Try some."

"Where's Stephanie?"

"Due back any moment."

"Liar," she smiled, slowly shaking the can of Reddi Whip. "Want some whipped cream, James?"

"I'll dispense it meself," he stated, looking rather hunted.

Lucin took a slow bite of strawberry as she continued to leisurely shake the can. "Suppose I accidentally got some of this whipped cream on me, James? You'd help me get off, uh … get *it* off, wouldn't you?"

"Sweet Mother," he complained, holding his head in his hands.

"I mean," Lucin continued, her eyes large and round, "If some accidentally got on you, Jimmy, I'd do almost anything I could to help. Honest I would."

"Eat your waffle, ye foul temptress," he grinned, reaching for the syrup.

"Are you absolutely sure about that?" she inquired.

"No, but I think it might be best at the present time."

"Okay, Jimmy," she sighed, squirting a small dollop of whipped cream on her finger. "I guess you know best." She took the Reddi Whip on her tongue, then leaned over and licked it onto his chin. "So, how ya doin' O'Doud?" she whispered, her lips just touching his. "All relaxed and comfortable?"

227

James dropped the syrup.

After breakfast, Lucin walked upstairs for a shower, enjoying the glow that always seemed to show up when James was around. Under the pounding spray she fed it a little, letting it grow into something golden and warm. Toweling off, she had an inspiration, and sat nude on the bed, shivering slightly as she made a phone call.

"Nails, this is Jolee. Help ya?"

"Hi, Jolee, it's Lucin."

"Hey, Sweetie! How ya doin? Got a cuticle emergency?"

"No, nothing like that. I was just calling to see what you were up to after work today."

"No plans. What's up?"

"Let's have a drink or three."

"Who is this really?" Jolee asked.

"It's me," Lucin laughed. "Honest!"

"Sweet Jesus! You wanna party?"

"Well ..."

"Well nothin', Girlfriend. I got no appointments after two today. I'll go home, clean up, and meet you here at the shop at four. Wear somethin' that stimulates the imagination. We'll hit Westport or the Plaza or both, and have 'em cryin' in their beer! We gonna make happy hour happy, Sweetcakes!"

At five minutes after four, Lucin, her hair in a ponytail, wearing thong panties, a light lavender silk t-shirt that reached to mid-thigh, high-heeled sandals, and nothing else, parked the Jag beside Jolee's yellow Mustang and walked through the front door of *Nails!*

"Damn, Sam!" grinned Jolee, looking Lucin up and down, "whatever you're looking for oughta sure as hell find ya!"

"You, too," laughed Lucin, eyeballing Jolee's white tank top and short red denim skirt.

"It pays to advertise," Jolee admitted, shaking her butt. "Even free drinks don't come free. Let's get out there among 'em, Sweetie. It's time you were appreciated!"

Over the next four hours they were in three clubs, never paid for a single drink, and enjoyed a steady procession of refreshments. With the libations came behinds to marvel at, waistlines to laugh at, lines to smile at, and enough offers to keep both of them busy for three months. They found a number of the men, from college age to early sixties, interesting, but the only one they both thought was really appealing bore a marked resemblance to James. Both the ladies thought that was hysterical. During the infrequent lulls, Lucin caught Jolee up on the latest with Tami, Harrison, George, and everything else.

At a little after eight, Jolee peered owlishly around the room and announced that she had to go home.

"Already?" Lucin blinked at her.

"Yes, 'cause I need to stop drinkin' and I won't if I don't go home. I think you're a bad influence on me."

228

"Me?!"

"Yes, you" Jolee said.

"I wasn't the one who patted that blond guy on the butt," Lucin protested.

"You couldn't reach him when you tried," laughed Jolee. "I just picked up where you left off!"

"God!" Lucin exclaimed, leaning back in her chair and looking around. "So many men. So little time. Is this fun or what?"

"C'mon, Sweetie," grinned Jolee. "It's time to go."

"I think I need a Guinness," Lucin observed.

"A Guinness?"

"Yep. When I feel like this I'm usually drinking a Guinness."

"Feel like what?"

"Uh ... aroused."

Jolee looked at her intently. "You mean horny?"

"That's it," Lucin blinked. "Horny."

Jolee cracked up. "Okay, fine," she giggled. "We are outta here."

"No Guinness?"

"Not a chance. I don't want you on my conscience. You drink a Guinness or two, and one a these ol' boys is gonna give you some whisker burn and play hide the salami. Then tomorrow you're gonna be pissed at me. You are as drunk as you are gonna get. C'mon, stand up." Three minutes later they were on the sidewalk heading for the parking lot.

"But what if I wanna play hide the salami?" Lucin asked.

"Not on my watch, Wanda," Jolee chuckled. "I am not gonna feed a rookie to the sharks. Somebody has to save you from yourself, and that would be me." They walked in silence for a moment, then Lucin looked at Jolee.

"Thanks a lot," she said.

"For what?"

"For going out with me."

"I wouldn't have missed it for the world, Sweetie. I didn't have to spend a dime, and the offers were better than usual. I bet shitfaced, you'd be funnier than a bent crutch! We gotta do this again sometime."

"Okay," agreed Lucin. "Anytime. I really enjoyed myself. I feel like a girl!"

"You are a girl, Dummy," laughed Jolee, unlocking her Mustang. "A lot of men thought so too. A *lot* of men. That had to make you feel great."

"It did," Lucin giggled, getting in the car. "It really did."

"I never could understand those women who dressed up, went out, then complained 'cause some guy hit on 'em," said Jolee.

"I like it," Lucin said, leaning her head back on the seat. "It makes me horny."

Jolee grinned. "Ready to slide down that banister now?"

"I bet I could," Lucin laughed. "Do you know what my great grandmother told me?"

"What?"

"She said that the only two things without limit were femininity and the ways it could be exploited."

"Grandma sounds like a pretty together lady."

229

"Maybe I should exploit my fenmimn … femininity," Lucin stated.

"Couldn't hurt," Jolee agreed, pulling into her parking area. "Can you drive okay?"

"Oh, sure. All I have to do is straighten up. I hate to, but I can. Let's do this again."

"Lucin, you're a hoot. It was great to see you damp and havin' a good time. Say the word, and we're suckin' on free drinks again, Kiddo. Now get out of my car and drive home carefully."

"God, I hope James isn't there," Lucin replied, opening the door. "He'll make fun of me."

"James loves you, y'know."

"I know," Lucin smiled. "I love him, too. Is that alright?"

Jolee smiled. "Oh, yeah," she said. "It's just fine. Goodnight, Sweetie."

Lucin stood up and shut the door. "Thanks again, Jolee. I feel really good."

"Be careful, Girlfriend," Jolee replied, and drove out of the lot.

Lucin walked to the Jag and fished the key out of her purse. As she was about to open the door, she noticed that Tami's shop had all its lights on. Tami. The thought of him made her a little angry and sharpened the glow that had been growing in her belly all evening. Standing there, she trembled a bit, and pressed her thighs together, feeling the ripple soar up through her chest; and her nipples harden against the silk shirt.

"*What the hell*," she thought, and walked to the door, her throat thickening as she approached the shop.

Just as she walked through the doorway, half the lights in the front room went out.

"Well, that's a fine welcome," she said.

Tami came hurrying out from the rear. "Lucin? Is that you?"

"Just me, Mr. Asaruka, stumbling around in the dark."

"I'm sorry," he laughed, walking to greet her. "I had no idea anyone was out here."

"I just came by to pick up my car, and noticed your lights were still on. Thought I'd say hi."

"It's my good fortune that you did," Tami smiled, and Lucin felt the heat rush to her low back and up her spine. "I have tea in the back," he continued, extending a hand. "Would you like some?"

"You are very kind. It is my honor to take tea with you," she replied, taking his hand. "Lead on."

In the dimly lighted back room, Tami poured two cups and placed them on a dark table in front of a low futon loveseat. "Please," he said, and Lucin sat, relaxing in spite of the length of her dress. Tami joined her. They sipped in silence for a moment. Lucin smiled at him.

"You're off the hook."

"The hook?" he asked, smiling slightly.

"Uh-huh," she said, swiveling to face him, her knee touching his thigh. She could sense a change in his breathing and feel the change in hers. "I've decided that the night you delivered The Waiting Courtesan should be left alone. I will not question you about it." She sipped her tea, attempting to keep her focus in her head and not elsewhere.

Tami chuckled and shifted a bit, increasing the pressure of their touch. "That's wise," he swallowed. "It was only a night."

"So is this, Tamiko-*san*," Lucin murmured, leaning toward him and allowing her leg to slide up over the top of his thigh. "Only a night of no importance. It is here and will soon be gone. What transpires this night is as fleeting and temporary as the darkness that would conceal it."

Tami looked at her and dropped his hand to her bare leg, stroking her gently with his fingertips. "Your tongue is honey, Lucin-san," he murmured, caressing her upper thigh with his palm, "sweet and wet and warm."

"As is my Jade Gate, Tamiko-*sama*," she replied, putting down her cup and panting slightly as she separated her knees. "It waits for your Peerless Pestle," she continued, stroking his lower lip with her thumb. "Let us begin our journey to the Fire and the Torrent. Let us join in the Little Death this unimportant night."

He drew a sharp breath with the words and brushed her mons with his hand. Lucin issued a small moan and clamped his hand between her legs, pleasure and need rippling up her spine. She leaned forward, her forehead pressing into the hollow of his neck. He lifted her face and kissed her, his tongue with a life of its own. She sighed and melted into him, her hand seeking his manhood, grasping, stroking, as her pelvis thrust of its own accord.

"*Iye*," he protested, tearing himself away from her. "*Iye! Iye! Dozo, iye!* No! No! Please, no!" Tami surged to his feet and stood staring away from her, head down, his body shaking. "*Sumimasen.* I'm sorry."

Lucin fought to keep her balance in this reality. Her head swimming, she pulled at the hem of her dress. "*Iye? Nan desu ka? Nanigoto da? Wakarimasen?* No? What is it? What's going on? I don't understand?"

Tami turned to face her, his face a mask of confusion and pain. "*Kinjiru. Gomen nasai, dozo ikinasai. Ima, isogi!* It is forbidden. I am sorry, please go away. Now, at once. Hurry."

Lucin rose to her feet and became very calm. "Alright," she said, "I will, but I'll return. I want an explanation for this, Tami, and when I come back, you better goddam well give it to me!"

It took Lucin almost thirty minutes to drive home. Windshield wipers don't work on tears.

THIRTY-FOUR

Elusive understanding
Whispers in the mist.
I try,
I try.
Even acceptance is pale.

EXHAUSTED both emotionally and physically, Lucin staggered into the house as if through a fog. Tami's rejection made her feel like a fool, a rejected fool, and she dragged herself up the stairs under that unrelenting weight, her heart actually aching from it.

She sat numbly on the bed for some time, rocking slowly back and forth, unable to collect the thoughts rumbling through her head. Her tub beckoned with warmth and peace, and she crossed to the bath on stilted legs with wooden feet that seemed far away. She ran water, sitting motionless on the side of the tub until it was full. Sighing, she rose and began to take off her clothes. The cell phone rang from her purse in the bedroom. She lurched back to the bed and answered. It was Kennedy Paige Hartrick, crying.

"I can't stay here anymore, Lucin," she sobbed. "I want to come home. Please let me come home!"

"Sweetie, what's the matter?"

"I hate this place. I'm the littlest kid here, the teachers are mean, everybody treats me bad. I wanna come home!"

"Settle down, Kaypee. Breathe slowly and try to relax your tummy. Have you talked to your mother?"

"She doesn't care! She never cares about me! She says I have to stay here. She's paid all this money so I can't come home!" The child fell back into sobs. "I hate this place. I hate it!"

"When did you talk with her?"

"About five minutes ago, alright?" the girl snarled. "She says I can't leave. She won't come get me."

"Kaypee, Darling, I don't know what I can do."

232

"*You* could come get me."

"I can't do that, Sweetie."

"Why not?"

"Because I'm not your mom. You and I both have to do what your mom says."

"You could come get me if you wanted to."

"No, I can't, Honey. I really can't."

"If you wanted to, you could!" the child wailed. "If you really wanted to, you could!"

"Kaypee, I cannot interfere between you and your mother. As much as I love you, I have no right to do that."

"Yes, you do. You do because I want you to! I wanna come home. I hate this place! Please, Lucin. Please!"

"Sweetheart ..."

"*You don't love me! You never loved me! If you did, you'd come get me, but you don't, you don't!*"

"Kaypee, that's not true!" Lucin protested.

"*It is too true! It is too! You're just like my mom! You don't care either!*"

"Sweetie, please ... just listen for a minute."

"*I hate this place, I hate my mom, and I hate you, too!*"

"Kaypee! Kaypee, listen ..."

Lucin sank to the floor beside her bed and leaned back against the mattress, holding a dead cell phone in her hand. Bath forgotten, she pulled the bedspread down over her shoulders and cried. She awoke just before dawn, stiff and aching, lying in the fetal position, the cover wet with tears.

Lucin was sitting at the kitchen table, staring at a cup of coffee, when James, clad only in a ratty old maroon flannel robe, schlepped barefoot into the room.

"Sweet Jesus!" he exclaimed with a start, "you're up! Well, it had to happen sometime," he grinned. "Now that you've seen me in me skimpies and flimsies, there'll be no hope for your poor husband, I suppose."

Lucin shifted her gaze to him for a moment, then began to quietly laugh. "James Mathew O'Doud," she chuckled, "I love you."

"Of course ya do," he replied, opening his arms and turning in a full circle. "What's not to love?"

"Hug," she said, rising shakily to her feet.

She clung to him, her massive Irish rock, as the waves broke over her, as the storm lashed at her, as the tempest pummeled her. She clung to him, taking comfort and strength from his power and gentleness. She clung to him and let it all come, the frustration, the helplessness, the tears, the anger. She clung to him in need, in desperation, in fear, in sorrow. And best of all, he clung to her, for all those reasons and more of his own, he enfolded her, protected her, shared with her and, in his way, needed her at least as much as she needed him.

When it was over between them, each of them knowing that it would never be over between them, they sat, his arm about her back, her head on his shoulder, and watched the kitchen turn golden with the sunrise.

"My coffee's cold," she complained, snuggling against his neck.

"I don't have time for your personal problems right now," James murmured. "I'm not wearin' any socks."

"Ooh."

"Now don't be getting' all excited, Lucille. I haven't had me shower yet either."

"Want me to help?"

"Would ya?"

Lucin thought for a moment. "Yes, I would," she said, and kissed his cheek.

"Alright," he whispered, his lips less than an inch from her ear. "Stand up and I'll pat your lovely backside, then you can make some fresh coffee and whip up some eggs and milk. That'll be a big help. When I get back from me shower, I'll fix breakfast."

Lucin stood and turned her back to him, sticking out her butt. "Tease," she said.

"Aye," James replied, "that ya are. It's part of your lovely charm." He kissed her on the bottom and headed for the shower.

"That's a dreadful thing," James observed, sipping his third cup of coffee. "The poor child. Feelin' so bad and not understandin' why you can't just come and whisk her away from it all. Musta been very hard for ya."

"I'd like to throttle her mother," Lucin replied with a grimace, nibbling on a piece of cold toast.

"That'd make everything all better," James grinned.

"Now Kaypee hates me!"

"Naw. She just thinks she does because you didn't come to her rescue. She'll get over it. Kids hate people they love all the time. Don't be so hard on yourself."

"I don't know what to do."

"Butt out, that's what ya do. You get in the middle of this, everybody loses."

"Easy for you to say," she smiled.

"Aye, it is. I have the advantage of bein' ..." The phone rang. James picked it up. "Montgomery residence ... well, top of the mornin' to ya, Mr. Asaruka!"

Hearing the name, Lucin began to shake her head no, and mouth at James that she was not there. He grinned at her.

"Sure," James continued. "I think I hear her in the kitchen, just a moment." He pressed the mute button and looked at Lucin. "Tami wants to talk to ya," he said.

"Dammit, James, I don't want to talk to him. I'm not here!"

"Are ya sure?"

"Yes, I'm sure!"

"Tami? ... she's on her way. Be just a minute. Have a nice day." He placed the phone on the table between them, blew Lucin a silent kiss, and nearly skipped out of the room. She could hear him chuckle as he entered the hall.

Lucin looked at the phone as if it were a snake. At length she gingerly picked it up.

"Hello?"

"Lucin-*san*. We must meet. I wish to explain my actions of last evening."

"Really?" Lucin snorted. "I thought perhaps an apology might be in order."

"My conduct does not require apology, only explanation."

"Is that right?"

234

"Yes. The *effect* my conduct had on you requires apology, and for that I truly apologize. It was not then, and is not now, my desire to hurt either of us in such a cruel and unfulfilling manner. I am very sorry for any embarrassment or injured feelings I may have caused. Please do me the honor of allowing me to explain."

Lucin paused for a moment. "Okay," she said. "Go ahead."

"No," Tami replied with a small chuckle. "I have already lost too much face to have such a conversation over as impersonal an implement as the telephone. If it would not greatly offend you, might I come by this afternoon? Perhaps we could sit beside your lovely garden and I could then tell you some things I feel you need to know."

"What time?"

"Around the three o'clock hour?"

"Very well."

"Thank you, Lucin-*san*. Your are very gracious."

"I will not make tea."

"That would be best. Perhaps I will bring a cool bottle of some lovely plum wine I have access to from time to time."

"Fine."

"Excellent. Thank you very much, Lucin. Until three, then."

"Until three."

"*Domo.* I will count the moments until we meet once more."

Lucin put the phone down and glanced around the empty kitchen. "*James!*" she yelled. "*Your Irish ass is mine!*"

From behind a closed door down the hall, came the shouted faint reply. "*Promises, promises, ya great tease!*"

Until around one, Lucin busied herself with straightening the house and garden for Tami's visit. It was a hot day and the misters kicked on and off with regular frequency, cooling the area and making the plants and stones truly beautiful. Ignoring the pull of the garden, Lucin showered and dressed in medium length, gray cotton shorts and an oversized peach cotton blouse. She applied no makeup, took little care with her hair, and attempted to look as un-Japanese as possible. When Tami arrived, she was sitting in a lawn chair, legs crossed ankle over knee, on the deck. Although she felt her heart beat quicken, she did not rise or even look directly at him until Tami reached her location.

"Good afternoon," he said, holding out a bottle. "Thank you for allowing me to visit. I have brought the wine."

"Have a chair," Lucin replied, rising to her feet and maintaining distance in spite of herself. "I'll get a couple of glasses and a corkscrew."

"Perhaps a cushion?" Tami enquired.

"Okay," she answered. "Whatever makes you comfortable."

"You're very kind," Tami bowed, smiling slightly.

Feeling totally transparent, Lucin went inside.

"This wine," Tami said, after they'd each had a sip, "is actually from China. A friend imports one or two cases a year and is kind enough to give me a bottle now and then."

"It's fine," Lucin answered.

"Very well," Tami acknowledged rather coldly. "Let's get to it. First I'd like to again express my apology for the effects of the events of last evening. So sorry."

Lucin shrugged. "Whatever," she said.

"Hostility is a poor substitute for humbleness, Lucin," Tami grunted, and gazed up at her. She felt pressure on her chest and breath rush from her lungs. Her shoulders sagged and she leaned back in her chair.

"When I tell you," he continued, "that I am sorry for the effects of last night, I am sincere. I treated you very badly. I should never have embarked upon such a journey with you. It is my weakness. You are a lovely woman, Lucin, in so many ways, and you have come very far. I, seeing and knowing you and these things, became selfish in my desires and did you a great disservice. I ask not to be excused, but to be understood. From the first moment I saw you, I wanted you. Not only for what you are, an extremely attractive woman, but for who you are, the person of power and strength and heritage you are discovering yourself to be. I found it amusing to be desired by the woman you were when you first encountered me. I find it immensely gratifying to be wanted by the woman you are becoming. I have succeeded in resisting my desires for some time. Last night, when my desire was compounded by yours, I succumbed. I am sorry. It should not have happened. It was my responsibility and my failure."

"God, the Spirit, Karma, the Force, whatever you care to call the power that drives the universe, indeed does work in mysterious ways. Existing simultaneously here are many worlds. The physical, the emotional, the spiritual, the mental, the karmic, the world of the living, the world of the dead, and many more combine to create our reality, or the lack of it. Time is an illusion of the physical, the physical an illusion of the mental, the mental an illusion of the spiritual and so on. There can be no reincarnation, because none of us dies. There can be no past lives, because there is no time. There can be no future because there is only the *now*. There can be no *now*, because we only exist in the memory of events. There can be no memory, because only the *now* can possibly be real."

He looked at her and the consternation on her face. "Confusing, huh?" he grinned.

"Yes," Lucin replied, feeling very heavy in her chair.

"Not unless you try to understand it," he smiled. "Make no comparisons, make no judgments, delete the need to understand. Once the need to understand is released, acceptance can enter. Acceptance conquers all. Expectancy and anticipation cannot stand against it. I do not ask you to believe. Belief is not important. Dogma is not important. Only acceptance is important because only acceptance will free you to assign importance with your will. All else is folly."

"I don't understand," Lucin said.

"Good," Tami laughed. "Understanding is a lie. I will tell you some things. You may do with them what you will. That is your business. If you choose to accept them, it is simple. If you choose to attempt to understand them, you will be continuously frustrated. If you choose to disregard them, that's fine, too. They are what they are and do not require your belief or understanding to sustain themselves. None of us is that important."

"You are alive in this place and this time to continue a journey. There is not a destination to your journey, nor will you ever arrive anywhere. There is only the journey. On this journey you have encountered many people. Me, James, Harrison, Jolee, the young girl and her mother, Onoshi-*san*, the man who teaches you skating, and many others. All of us are also on a journey and at this point our paths have crossed. We have the opportunity to learn from each other, to grow from our mutual contact, and to assist each other, even if we seem to only get in each other's way. And all of us, *all of us*, have met elsewhere and will meet again. Perhaps not in these bodies, perhaps not with these personalities, but we go on and on, sometimes together, sometimes not, but always for the possibility of mutual benefit."

"From time to time, as in your case and mine, we also need the assistance of ones from places other than this. Your great grandmother, for instance. Look what she has done for you. Look what you did for her. The balance is always maintained. Mama-*san*, Moon Blossom, Izumi-*san*, all have assisted or are assisting you on your journey. Have they not come to you? Have they not had effect on you? Have they not been real to you?"

"Yes, certainly."

"Did they require you believe in them?"

"No," Lucin smiled. "They definitely did not."

"Did they need your understanding to be real?"

"No. Just acceptance."

"Exactly," Tami grinned, patting her on the hand. "Just acceptance. You were raised to be a Christian, were you not?"

"Of course."

"In your Bible, it tells how God created woman from the rib of a man, correct?"

"Yes."

"Assuming that is true, can you understand how that could possibly have happened?"

"No," Lucin laughed.

"Do you think that God is diminished if you cannot understand how it happened?"

"No."

"If you choose not to believe it happened, does that diminish God?

"No."

"Then we can assume that God does not require your belief to continue to be God."

"Correct."

"Can we also assume that you do not have to understand God for God to be real?"

"Yes."

"So, if a Christian cannot understand God, and may not believe everything happened the way it is said to have happened, how can God possibly be real to that Christian? What does it take for that to happen?"

"Acceptance."

"And if we believe or not, if we understand or not, is God still God?"

"Yes!"

"Give the good lookin' lady a cigar!"

"My head is spinning," she laughed.

"Good," Tami grinned. "I'm almost done. Now to the events of last night. I should not have behaved in the manner in which I did, because it is still too soon. For me to have become involved with you would have been as totally unacceptable as if Izumi-*san* had come to Moon Blossom before Mama-*san* had agreed it was time. It is not done. If anything of such a nature is to occur between us, it cannot be allowed to happen until you are released from your lessons with Mama-*san*. Once that happens, we are free to do as we see fit. There is an order to these things. I nearly made a terrible mistake. I am sorry. I can only plead weakness."

Lucin sipped her wine. "I suppose I should be flattered."

"I don't know about that," Tami laughed, "but *I* certainly am."

"I mean," Lucin continued, "you were about to fling yourself into the face of the entire cosmos, just to take a swing at l'il ol' me."

"You're not going to let this go, are you?" Tami smiled.

"Not for awhile. I'm pretty pissed."

"I can see that. I just wanted you to know that I wasn't playing some sort of game with you."

"Maybe now it's my turn for games," Lucin smiled. "Someday when Mama-*san* gets out of the way, we might get together, Tami, and rock the cosmos. Maybe, maybe not, but I know one thing for sure."

"What's that?"

"I'll be the one who decides. I'll let *you* know."

He looked at her steadily. "I'll be around," he said.

"I'm sure you will, but not anymore today. Take a hike, Asaruka. Maybe I'll be in touch."

She watched him walk away and began to quietly weep. How much more was she going to have to accept? Harrison gone, James more or less off limits, Tami impossible because of some kind of karma or something, and now, even little Kaypee out of reach.

Jesus.

Or whoever.

THIRTY-FIVE

Sorrow and joy
Are but a whisper apart.
What shall I do
With my sorrow
But search for joy.

FOR THE NEXT SEVERAL DAYS, Lucin drifted. Harrison didn't call, Kaypee didn't call. Skating became the only anchor in her life. Daily she went to the rink, practicing with a vengeance, sweating on the ice, working herself to the point of exhaustion. Bryan noticed one morning and skated over to her after a group lesson. He moved into her path forcing her to stop.

"This is supposed to be fun," he smiled.

"It is fun," Lucin panted.

"Doesn't look like it. Looks like work. Looks like you're punishing yourself."

"That's ridiculous, Bryan!"

A five year old wobbled by and Bryan smiled at the little girl. "You're angry, Lucin, and you're taking it out on the ice. Half a lap from you and we need the Zamboni. You're fighting your edges, you're stomping around out here like a buffalo, and you're not doing yourself one damn bit of good!"

Lucin stared at him for a moment, anguish in her eyes. "Bryan, I've got to work!"

"Great! Then work, but do it constructively, not destructively. If you're gonna blast all this energy around, let's use it to your benefit. Work with the ice. Don't fight with it."

She looked at her skates for a moment, then dropped her shoulders and relaxed her knees. "Help," she pleaded.

Bryan slipped his arm around her shoulders and laughed, guiding her off the ice and onto a bench. "It's what I live for," he chuckled. "You have a program coming up. For this program you will need music, a costume, and choreography. You need to decide what you want to do, and I need to create a routine that will both challenge you and show you off to best advantage. Does any of this ring a bell?"

"Yes," she smiled.

"Really?"

"Yes," she grinned.

"That's nice. Perhaps we should consider directing some of this energy of yours to that end. Whatcha think?"

"You're right."

"God! Those are my favorite words," he laughed. "Say 'em again."

"You're right."

"Yes! More!"

"You're right, you're right, you're right, you're right!" Lucin giggled in exasperation.

"I am, aren't I? What a perceptive woman you are! Have you decided on a costume?"

"I have a costume."

"You do?"

"Uh-huh. Music, too."

"Why haven't you told me?"

"Because I just this moment decided what I want to do."

"Well, give. What? What? What?"

"Nope. I need to show you."

"Must be serious."

"It's a little intense."

"Alright. I've got a free half-hour this afternoon at three. Be here in costume with your music and we'll see whatcha got. Okay?"

"Okay," Lucin replied, rising to her feet.

"See ya then," Bryan said, and glided back onto the ice.

Driving home, Lucin noticed she was smiling.

After lunch, she transferred her music from CD to cassette tape and went upstairs. Freshly showered, she applied makeup in nearly theatrical proportions, struggled into her body stocking, made sure the seams were straight on her tights, slipped on a lightweight trench coat and loafers, took the garment bag out of the closet, her hat from the shelf, and was back at the rink by two-thirty. The ice was nearly deserted. She sat on a bench and put on her skates, sliding dark brown covers over the boots. In the bathroom she slipped into the double-breasted, pinstriped jacket costume, dropped the hat down over one eye, and looked in the mirror. She couldn't stifle her grin. Hat in hand and again wearing the trench coat, she walked back out to the rink and crossed the ice, stepping into the booth where the sound system was housed. Only three or four skaters were out, plus Bryan finishing up with a student. Young men were filtering in, perhaps in anticipation of hockey, and sitting around on the bleachers. It seemed she might have a small audience. Instead of making Lucin uneasy, she was surprised to find the possibility of onlookers excited her a bit. She popped the tape into the cassette player and turned her attention to Bryan just as he sent his pupil away. He looked at her from down the ice.

"You're back," he shouted.

"You said three," Lucin replied.

"Okay, Hotshot" he grinned. "Show me what you got."

Swallowing around the sudden lump in her throat, Lucin pushed the cassette play button, dropped her trench coat, perched the hat rakishly low over her eyes and took to the rink in long confident strides. Just as she reached center ice, the sound of Joe Cocker singing "You Can Leave Your Hat On" echoed over the sound system, and Lucin began to skate. Avoiding anything that might make her slip or fall, she moved with the music, selling her sensuality, shaking her bottom, showing off to Cocker's croaking blues. About a minute into the song, the hockey players began to applaud and cheer, standing and stamping their feet. Embarrassed, Lucin skated toward a grinning Bryan, spiraling slowly around him until she came to a stop next to his left side, the tip of her chin resting on his shoulder.

"So whatdaya think, Big Boy," she purred, bumping her eyebrows under the hat. "Like my outfit?"

Bryan looked at her from a range of three inches, completely deadpan. "Is this new?" he enquired. Lucin grinned.

"My God," Bryan continued, "that stuffy bunch at the Carriage Club has never seen anything like this. You look terrific! We are gonna do such a job, there'll be at least four divorces within twenty-four hours of your program. I will choreograph something that you can really sell, Lucin! We are going to shake these sonsabitches to their shoes! The costume is perfect, the music is perfect, and you are perfect. Ha!"

"You really like it?"

"I love it. We will scandalize the entire Club. Christ, do they deserve it!"

"You don't think it's too much?"

"It's fine. It's better than fine. Another minute from you, and none of the hockey guys will be able to bend over far enough to lace up their skates," he laughed. "You look great!"

Smiling, Lucin skated back to the booth and put on the trenchcoat. Boos and shouts of protest issued from the grinning hockey bunch, and she waved at them across the rink. One young man proposed marriage on the spot. Bryan skated over to join her.

"I have a copy of your music at home. I'll get started on editing it right away. How do ya feel about selling some sex?"

"As long as it doesn't involve the police, I'm in," laughed Lucin.

"Great. You will slink, you will shimmy, you will shake and you will strut. This is gonna be a real good time, Lucin. Good for you! I gotta hit the john and get ready for the next class. Thanks for coming by. I love it! You'll need more time with me than just your regular lesson. I hereby volunteer. We'll work it out, okay?"

"Okay," Lucin beamed.

Replaying the events of the afternoon over in her mind on the drive home, Lucin was almost joyful, happy with how everything had gone. Her cell phone rang.

"Hello?" she smiled.

"Lucin?"

"Yes?"

"I thought so! Lucin, this is Sheila Hartrick. Kennedy Paige is back from skating camp, and I found this phone in her bag. I'm just going to throw it in the trash. Kennedy Paige is *my* daughter! You leave my daughter alone, do you hear? You just leave my daughter the hell alone!"

Lucin walked into the kitchen feeling as if the weight of the world was on her shoulders. Drained from the emotional roller coaster of the day she sat, staring at the tabletop, equally sad and angry. The pleasure and excitement of her meeting with Bryan was all but eclipsed by the call from Sheila. Kaypee hated her, and now Kaypee's mother had all the ammunition she needed to make sure the girl never got close to Lucin again. In an effort to support the child and satisfy her own needs, Lucin had effectively isolated herself from any contact with Kennedy. Giving Kaypee the cell was out of line. She'd behaved like an idiot, and now she would have to pay the price. Nearly in tears, she looked up as Stephanie entered the room carrying a Federal Express letter packet.

"Hi, Lucin," she said, placing the package on the table. "This came for you a couple of hours ago."

"Oh," Lucin replied numbly, pulling herself back from the edge. "Thank you, Stephanie."

"Are you okay?"

"I'm something," Lucin smiled. "Excuse me. I guess I'm feeling a little sorry for myself at the moment. I'll be alright. Thanks."

Stephanie looked concerned. "Anything I can do?"

"No, Sweetie, I don't think so, but I appreciate you asking. Why don't you take the rest of the day off. It's after four. I'll dig up something for dinner myself."

"You sure?"

"I'm sure," Lucin replied, turning her attention to the packet.

"Thanks, Lucin. I'll see you tomorrow."

"Have a good night, Steph."

Inside the heavy cardboard was a thick parchment envelope sealed with wax. Lucin broke the seal and removed two sheets of equally heavy paper, edged in gold. The first sheet was hand written in Japanese. The calligraphy was beautiful to look at but meant absolutely nothing to her. The second sheet, also an example of the calligrapher's art, was in English. She quieted the trembling of her hand and read the message.

Dear Lucin Montgomery,

Please allow me the honor of expressing my most humble thank you to you for the warmest of receptions you extended to me upon my recent visit to your lovely home and garden. I dislike the adventure of traveling, but your most welcoming expression made my entire journey worthwhile. Your extension of effort to make me feel comfortably at home in the midst of my traveling to a foreign place was certainly surely appreciated hugely, and much more worthy than my humble visit required. I find you enchanting beyond my best expression. Your dedication to your husband and his concerns is admirable beyond expectation, and you are to be congratulated highly for your attention to duty. I very enjoyed my visit with you and your wonderful humor. Please accept my highly deserved gratitude for the undeserved honor you showed me. If others in your husband's company are even slightly as considerate and understanding as you have shown yourself to be, I have become convinced that Nagata Industries has chosen well and will prosper in your country. The wine was excellent. I will count the moments until we meet again.

Sincerely,
Serata Onoshi

Tears in her eyes, Lucin read the letter three times. She was looking around the kitchen, as if seeing it for the first time, when the phone rang. Her hand was trembling again as she lifted it to her ear.

"Hello?"

"Luce? Can we talk?"

"Hello, Harrison," she sighed with relief. "Yes, we can talk."

"Uh ... have I ever told you that I'm a fool?"

"You've mentioned it," she smiled.

"Well, I'm sure getting tired of proving it. Onoshi went for the deal, Sweetheart. He went for the deal!"

"Harrison, that's wonderful!"

"I got a letter from him today, confirming the thing was on. In the letter he said that you were the final factor that made him decide."

"Really?"

"Really! He said that if my wife would go to the effort she went to just to make an old man comfortable, he was certain that I was worth his trust. He went for it, Luce. He went for it!"

"Congratulations, Harrison," she laughed. "I'm very happy for you, I really am."

"You did it, Luce. You did it."

"I'm sure he'd already made up his mind."

"You did it. Hon, I am *so* sorry I came down on you as hard as I did. I mean I'm sorry I came down on you at all! Uh ... I mean, you were right, you were exactly right about the whole thing, and I should have just listened to you and trusted you and I didn't, Luce, I didn't. And then I jumped all over you and treated you like shit and I am *so sorry* I behaved like that, and I miss you, and I love you, and ..."

"Harrison ... *Harrison!*"

"Yeah?"

"You're prattling, Harrison. Don't prattle. Big time attorneys sometimes ramble, but they never prattle."

"Yes, Dear," he said meekly, and she could hear his grin.

"That's better," she chuckled. "Now, when are you coming home?"

"I'm off to Japan again tomorrow for at least a week, probably more, then back here for awhile, then to Kaycee to start the ball rolling again. I probably won't see you much for the next six weeks or so, then I'll spend most of my time in Kansas City. I'm sorry."

"So am I. I was looking forward to letting you make up with me."

"Sounds nice," he replied.

"I had a little more in mind than just nice."

"Uh ... okay," he stammered. "Look, Sweetheart, I've got a million things to do. I gotta go. I'll call you from Japan and let you know better what's going on, alright?"

"That's fine, Harrison," she replied, concealing her disappointment. "You take care of Onoshi-*san* and call when you can."

"I will, Luce. You did it, Baby! You did it! We're on our way now."

"I'm glad, Harrison. I'm very happy for you."

"Thanks. Gotta go. Love you."

"Take care."

Lucin sat for a few moments, then sighed, picked up Onoshi's letter and rose to her feet. Upstairs in her dressing room she stripped for a shower, then turned and went into the bedroom. Sitting on the bed, she picked up her phone.

"Hi, Jolee? ... Lucin. Fine, just fine. Busy tonight? ... Well, I thought we might go out for dinner and drinks, my treat ... I need a celebration ... then get me in the mood! ... Sure it's a challenge ... Let's see whatcha got, Girlfriend ... something low and short ... No, I'm not kidding ... Let's go for it! ... I need to lift some spirits and lift my spirits ... Great! ... I'll pick you up ... See ya!"

Letter in hand, Lucin walked back into the bath, dropped the letter into the sink, picked up a candle match, and lit a corner of the parchment. She stood by the sink as the heavy paper was reduced to ash, then washed the residue down the drain. There were some things Harrison didn't need to know, she thought as she turned on the shower. Hell, there might be a lot of things he wouldn't need to know.

THIRTY-SIX

Understanding
Escapes me.
Peace
Eludes me.
What do I want?

AS SUMMER GAVE WAY to fall, Lucin became more deeply immersed in herself. She spent a considerable amount of time at the garden, watching the seasonal shift create evermore austere effects on the color and texture of the plant life, coming to appreciate the flux of autumn more than she ever had before, recognizing the subtle facets that grew and manifested before her. In many ways, appreciation of the changes occurring in the garden gave the impetus for more changes within herself.

Harrison spent very little time at home and a large amount of time at the new offices. As the Crown Center staff grew so did his obligations and, while he was now at least living in their house, his sixty to seventy hour work week left him little time at home for more than sleep. His commitment to the job and Nagata Industries was total, and his hectic schedule also had an impact on James. As the firm became busier so did O'Doud's position as driver, and Lucin sometimes didn't see James for days on end. Harrison's work, James absence, and the fact she had severed ties with Tami, left Lucin short of male influence. She turned more and more to skating to prepare for her upcoming program, and to Jolee, who was also without James, for evenings out and relaxation. When Jolee was too tired or busy to go, Lucin went alone, watching the people, enjoying the subtle and not so subtle attention she received from men, having fun being a girl. While she was not exactly looking for male companionship, she was looking for men, and the exposure and appreciation she so enjoyed. By the middle of October she was out, usually by herself, three or four nights a week. It was something to do.

Preparing for happy hour one afternoon, she dressed in a deep red silk and wool blend sheath, dark stockings, and a black suede belt with matching three-inch pumps. Draping a dark gray leather coat over her arm, she walked downstairs into the kitchen. At the table sat James Mathew O'Doud behind a cup of coffee.

"James!" she nearly shouted, striding toward him. "I haven't seen you in ages!"

James rose to his feet and opened his arms. "Ah, Lucille, me darlin', sure and you're a sight for sore eyes."

She moved into his embrace and he kissed her on the cheek. "Don't ya look fine, then," James grinned, lifting an arm over her head and twirling Lucin in front of him. She giggled, enjoying the spin.

"My, my, my," James continued, "you could stop traffic on the freeway in that dress, Lucille. Where are ya off to?"

"Just going out for happy hour."

"Well, you've sure made my hour happy," he smiled. "It's a real treat to see ya."

"Thank you, kind Sir," she dimpled, realizing how much she'd missed spending time with him. "Are you through for the day?"

"Things got slow and himself set me free."

"Off to Jolee's then?"

"I'm afraid not. The dear lass is sufferin' a head cold or some such, and denied me the joy of her company. Claimed she wasn't fit to be seen."

"Her loss is my gain," Lucin grinned, stepping back to James' side and slipping an arm around his waist in an affectionate hug. "O'Doud, sure and don't ya know that I'm missin' ya, now."

"Aye, and not a bit more than I miss you," he replied returning the hug. "Can I get ya some coffee?"

"During happy hour?" she teased.

"Well, what would ya like, then?"

"Stoli on the rocks with two olives, if you'll join me," Lucin replied, taking a chair by the table and looking at his eyes. "Will you join me, James?"

James regarded her for a moment before he spoke. "I believe I will, Lucille. It'll be my pleasure."

"I hope so," she said very quietly. "Mix the drinks, Jimmy me boy. You have no idea how thirsty I am."

Stoli and ice from the freezer, glasses from the cabinet, olives from the fridge, and James was at the table with the drinks in less than two minutes. He sat. Lucin picked up her glass, swiveled to face him allowing her knee to touch his, and leaned forward.

"What'll we drink to?" she smiled.

"Saints preserve us," James muttered, feeling the electricity of her leg.

"I know," Lucin said, extending her glass. "Let's drink to secrets."

"Secrets it is," James replied. The glasses clinked and they drank. After a moment of silence, Lucin spoke.

"So what are you up to this evening?"

Feeling the world rushing by at an alarming rate, James struggled to collect himself. "Oh, I don't know. Maybe I'll go to Clancy's for awhile."

"Or you could stay here for happy hour with me," Lucin smiled over the rim of her glass.

"Aye, I could do that I suppose," he replied, halfway between excitement and resignation.

"You could also pour me another drink. This one seems to be empty already."

James threw back his vodka and escaped to the counter. While he poured and added ice and olives, he could feel her eyes on him. He sat and handed Lucin her glass. Never looking away from his face, she turned toward him again and slowly crossed her legs. Her nylons shouted a whisper through the room.

"Sweet Jesus," James shuddered. "That is one of the sweetest sounds in the world."

Lucin sipped her drink and smiled. "Let me tell you about another sweet sound, James. It's the sound of me saying 'yes'." She stood, leaned down to him until her lips nearly touched his, and took his hand. "Tell the truth," she breathed. "Wouldn't that be a sweet sound?"

James could feel his heart throb in his ears. "Aye," he answered. "That it would."

"Yes, James," she whispered. "Yes."

Neither of them spoke as she led him to the stairs. She began to climb, but James stopped. Lucin turned to face him at eye level.

"Are ya sure, then, Lucille?"

Lucin put her arms around his neck and leaned into him, full body, kissing him deeply and with great longing. When the kiss was over, she left her lips against his.

"Now, O'Doud," she whispered. "Right fucking now."

They climbed three more steps before James' cell phone rang. A minute later, he was gone, on his way to the office to take Harrison to the airport to meet a couple of Japanese arrivals.

Shaking with rage and crying with frustration, Lucin slumped on the stairs, her head in her hands. "Harrison, you sonofabitch!" she spat through her tears. "If you're going to leave me alone, then *leave me the hell alone!*"

Lucin, thick and heavy from a very restless night, hit the rink early the next morning, working to both punish herself and to practice her routine for the coming Carriage Club show. Kaypee was there and she ignored Lucin, just as she'd done the four or five other times Lucin had encountered her at the rink since Sheila Hartrick had discovered the secret sister cell phone. As before, Lucin could feel Kaypee looking at her, but the child would not meet her eyes or allow any sort of contact. Because of Sheila's warning, Lucin could make no overtures toward the child.

Sweaty, depressed, and feeling slightly sorry for herself, Lucin lurched into the kitchen around eleven. The phone rang.

"Hello?"

"Lucin?"

"Yes?"

"Oh, I am so glad it is you. I detest those dreadful message machines. This is Arleen Creighton. We met at Sheila Hartrick's neighborhood association drudge?"

"Of course!" Lucin smiled. "Mrs. Creighton ... uh, Arleen, how nice of you to call."

"It is thrilling, isn't it?" the older woman chuckled. "Occasionally I phone myself for the sheer joy of hearing from me."

"It *is* good to hear from you. I enjoyed the time we spent together very much."

"As did I, Child. I wonder if you would do me the honor of dropping by for lunch and a short visit, just the two of us?"

"Of course. I'd be delighted, Arleen. When?"

"Say, an hour and a half from now?"

"Oh. Uh ... of course."

"I realize it's on very short notice and extremely rude of me, but I have found that as I have gotten older, I quite enjoy being rude. So much so, that I sometimes forget and am rude to people to whom I really do not want to be ... rude, that is. Please, forgive me."

"Naturally," grinned Lucin.

"Good. I'm two blocks west of you, the most outrageously overbuilt mausoleum on the entire street. You can't miss it. Come to the front door. If you don't, my maid will have nothing to do all day. Allow her to announce you. It makes her feel important and presents her with another opportunity to despise me."

"I'll do anything I can, Arleen."

"Dear child. Come see me. Goodbye."

Intrigued, Lucin, dressed in cotton twill slacks, a chambray shirt, a light windbreaker and running shoes, and walked the quarter mile or so to Arleen's under a crisp October sky. The home appeared as if a small English estate had been imported to Kansas City. She moved up the mossy flagstone walk to a front door surrounded in climbing ivy and delicately graced with a brass knocker the size of a hubcap. Lucin lifted the knocker and let it fall. A moment later the portal was opened by a small dark woman with long black hair, wearing a maid's uniform. She glared at Lucin.

"Jace?"

"Mrs. Creighton, please. Lucin Montgomery calling."

"Pleece, cohm een." The woman shut the door and walked away. In about three minutes she returned, looking self-satisfied.

"Meeses Craytone weel see jew naow," she said and walked away again. This time Lucin followed. The trail led through a large hall or two, down a flagstone and brick breezeway, and finally stopped in a spacious glass and screen aviary populated by upright twisted tree branches, dozens of finches in all colors and types, one dark blue Hyacinth Macaw on a metal perch at the far end of the room, a few live plants, and Arleen Creighton at a table near the entrance. The maid walked away without a word. Arleen smiled.

"Watch where you step," she said. "The only place safe from finch shit is this table and an area about five feet around it."

Lucin made her way to the table and sat across from Arleen. "Birds," she said.

"Do you know birds?" Arleen inquired.

"I know that's a Hyacinth Macaw. A friend of my father's kept one when I was small."

"Yes, it is," Arleen agreed as she poured tea. "Lapa was my husband's bird. He's nice enough, but a bit standoffish since Ellis died. I expect Lapa is around sixty or so. He'll outlive me. I don't see Rufus."

"Rufus?"

"A Triton Cockatoo. Rufus? Rooofus!"

There was a squawk and a white parrot about sixteen inches tall came walking out from behind a table halfway down the wall. He stopped and regarded the women for a moment, then a lovely yellow crest rose from the top of his head.

"Don't *make* me come over there," he said, and began to swagger in their direction.

Lucin laughed. "Did he say 'don't make me come over there'?"

"That's my boy," Arleen smiled. "Rufus is thirty-seven. I've had him since he was about eight months old."

Rufus looked up at her from the floor beside Arleen's chair. "Hey, Baby," he said. "Give us a kiss."

"Oh, alright," Arleen replied, and extended her hand. Rufus climbed aboard and she held him to her face as the bird put his beak against her lips and made loud smacking sounds.

"He's wonderful," giggled Lucin. Rufus turned toward her and began to bob his head rapidly up and down.

"Hey, Baby," he said, and began to laugh, extending his yellow crest as he stood on one foot, waving the other in the air.

"That's amazing!" cried Lucin, thoroughly captivated.

"He won't do a thing if I ask him to," shrugged Arleen, "but when he gets in a mood to show off, he's a pistol."

"I been workin' on the railroad," said Rufus, then he flapped from Arleen's arm to the floor and began to waddle away, whistling the theme from The Andy Griffith Show with only a couple of mistakes. Lucin watched him climb a large potted branch several feet distant, ruffle his feathers, and perch on the tallest spire.

"Never can say goodbye," stated Rufus, then turned his back on the women.

"Ellis and I had no children," Arleen said, "so I lavish far too much attention on that bird. He is my constant companion here at home. I supplement my instinct to mother in other ways from time to time. One of those ways is to meddle in young people's lives. Yours, for instance."

"Mine?"

The maid returned with a magnificent salad, a variety of breads and cheeses, and tableware. After she left, Arleen forked some of the greenery into a bowl and placed it on a low bench. The macaw and cockatoo came over and began to munch from the bowl as Arleen served Lucin and continued.

"Yes, your life," she smiled. "You know, I spent some time with your husband recently."

"Harrison?"

"Indeed. His firm is handling the affairs of some Japanese company, I believe."

"Nagata Industries."

"Of course. They are purchasing some land not far from the sports complex to construct a facility of some type. I own a small tract they need for an airstrip that I refused to sell. Your husband can be a very persuasive man."

Lucin smiled. "So you sold?"

Arleen laughed. "Of course not," she said. "I leased it to them for a ridiculous amount and some company stock. I don't need the money. It just gave me the opportunity to be a bitch. Harrison worked so hard to convince me to sell. He was really quite entertaining. A very earnest young man. I suspect his dedication to his work is extreme."

"Yes, it is."

"I also suspect that you spend much of your time alone."

"I do."

"So you've taken to going out in the evenings."

Lucin bristled a bit. "So?"

"So indeed. Even these mindless little finches flitting about in this room know something you need to learn, my dear."

"Arleen, what's your point?"

"Even these finches know enough to not shit in their own nests."

Lucin squared her shoulders. "And I don't, is that it?"

"So it would seem. Now before you get all upset and storm out of here, let me say some things. I couldn't care less what, or for that matter, *whom* you do, Dear. It is none of my business, just as surely as what, or whom, I do is none of *your* business. Unfortunately, most of the denizens of the circles in which you and your husband must exist are meddlesome, small-minded busybodies whose collective mission in life is to help someone else be wrong, especially if that someone is new to the group. You and your husband are new and you are an exceptionally attractive woman. The Sheila Hartricks of this world would love, dearly love, to dish dirt about you. Keep in mind that it is not necessary that you commit indiscretions, you need only place yourself in the position where you *could* commit indiscretions."

"The whispers are rampant, Lucin. They have filtered to my ears from many directions. You go to clubs alone. You go to bars alone. You and your husband are apart most of the time. You have constructed your own house on the property. You ice skate. You have a friendship with your driver. You have a friendship with your manicurist. You are stepping out of your station, which is probably the most serious sin of all. Combine all that with the facts that you do not join, you do not gossip, you do not seek approval, and you do not play golf, and you are unfair game! My God, woman, you don't even have any children! These women are scared to death of you. What we fear, we hate."

"This society in which you live has a myriad of rules that have mostly evolved from fear. Fear of outsiders, fear of failure, fear of being found out, fear of having to perform, fear of not measuring up to our own publicity. These women stand in a big circle and tell each other how wonderful they are. Because you do not join them in their circle, because you do not participate in their desperate desire for status and the status quo, they are afraid of you. What they are afraid of, they attempt to bring down. If they can damage you, they will also damage your husband. He would be the icing on the cake. He makes more money that most of their husbands, he *has* more money that most of their husbands. If they can get to you, they will get to him. Their husbands will look better and so will they. The push and shove politics among the upwardly mobile, the 'right' people, are backstabbingly vicious."

"I don't care what they think of me."

"Of course you don't. In their tiny minds, that is the biggest sin of all."

"Fuck them!" Lucin flared.

"Indeed," Arleen smiled. "I can understand your anger, and please know that I am not accusing you of anything. I do not require your guilt to validate my innocence. I find you to be a delightful woman with a real mind and a lovely heart, but you must understand some things. The biggest of these is very simple. Get away from your nest before you shit! If you want to go out for happy hour, go someplace other than where you've been going. If you want to attract the attention of men, make sure to do it outside your social circle. Use your head, Child! Your conduct reflects directly on your husband, and these idiots will blow it totally out of proportion. It can ruin your marriage, it can ruin his career, it can ruin your life. If you wanna screw your garbage man, good luck and godspeed, just don't fuck the fellow in the goddam driveway!"

"I know more about how you are feeling at this point in your life than you believe I do, Lucin. You are angry with the world right now, and angry people make mistakes. You feel misused, abused, and confused. When you feel like that, it is time to pull back and center yourself."

Rufus squawked, and relieved himself on the branch. Arleen smiled.

"If you continue to expand on your present course of action in the manner in which you are currently conducting yourself, my child, you are going to be tremendously sorry. Now, I have said what I needed to say. Whether you have heard what you needed to hear or not, I don't know. Either way, I'm done. My dear Lucin, I said what I said, not for your benefit, but for my own. If you gain benefit from it, so much the better."

Lucin stared at the tabletop, attempting to move through her anger and into understanding. Arleen munched her salad and smiled, awaiting awareness or explosion. In the midst of it all, Rufus flapped his way to the back of Lucin's chair and planted several loud cockatoo kisses on her right ear.

"Thanks, Rufus," laughed Lucin, "I needed that."

Rufus bobbed up and down and raised his yellow crest.

"Never can say goodbye," he observed.

THIRTY-SEVEN

There are many paths
Leading to the mountain,
And still we may never arrive.
Each step contains victory.
Tomorrow is never grasped.

WHEN LUCIN RETURNED HOME, she sat on the deck for a time trying to dredge up some useful thoughts from her visit with Arleen, but the garden wouldn't let her. It kept sucking her into contentment rather than contemplation. She went inside and showered, then walked to the bathhouse and immersed herself to the earlobes in the tub, a cold glass of Guinness sweating on the table beside her. Arlene was right. As long as she and Harrison had to move in the slice of civilization required by his position and her association, she had better get her act together. As always, it seemed she must defer to Harrison.

Was she committed to that kind of life? Was she even committed to him? A year ago, back in Philadelphia, any other course was not only unthinkable, it was inconceivable. All her training and association since infancy had prepared her to be a wife to someone like Harrison. There was no alternative ever presented to her. Even in college, when she was supposed to learn and grow and think, she was still given no true options. Her peers, her family, her *universe*, for God's sake, kept her firmly on the path of business wife. Had she not come to Kansas City she would have never strayed. But she *did* come to Kaycee, and Harrison brought her here, away from her conditioning and comfort, away from her family and his, away from the dull quagmire of duty and responsibility. No Junior League, no Young Matrons, no sorority, no teas, no charities, no fundraising drives, no gossip with lifelong associates, no wasting of time passed off as the responsibility of station to those less blessed by either birth or condition.

Life without Harrison was not unthinkable, it was merely unconsidered. What would she do without him? Money was certainly not a problem. Her family had plenty. For that matter, she supposed, *she* had plenty. Her life had been such that she had never needed to call upon any of her own financial resources, but they were there. Thanks to her father, she was well provided for. Enough money, while certainly not a problem, was not a solution either. What would she do? Bon-bons and soap operas? Charities and fundraising? Work? She had her degree in English Literature, a lowly bachelor's, which qualified her for absolutely nothing.

That was really it. She had spent her entire life being highly trained to choose the right type of staff, manage the correct household, make sure the toilet paper was neatly folded into a point, and remember the names of her husband's important associates. A servant without the honesty of employment or the validation of children, bound to a husband who wanted her to be exactly what she'd always been. God! James Mathew O'Doud was more man in a moment than Harrison had been the entire time she had known him. Was Harrison, who she had seen as the rule, the exception? Was James less unique than she believed?

If Tami was right, then this move to Kansas City was a cosmic opportunity for her. James, Kaypee, Eddie, Arleen, Sheila, Jolee, Harrison, even her mother, were all intertwined in this great experiment they'd inflicted on each other and themselves — this one immense opportunity for growth that encompassed all they knew, all they believed, all they assumed they wanted, and all they thought they needed. If that was the case, there was always much more going on than any of them were aware of. An interplay of entwining purpose and destiny that encompassed everyone in the most unseen of webs, delicately spun by a neutral spider-god with compassionate eyes and a fateful smile, who watched but did not really care.

It was up to them. We decided. Not some benevolent god, not some wrathful deity, not some all-knowing universal presence. Them — and her. It was up to her to assign importance in her world, up to her to grow and develop in her own way, up to her to do what she thought was best for herself.

For the first time in her life, Lucin felt the slightest slipping of the mantle of duty that had cloaked her all her years. For the first time, she felt the excitement of possibility stirring beneath the burden of probability. For the first time, she sensed she really could have what she wanted. Now, what the hell did she want?

She left the bath, slipped into a heavy terry kimono, and padded into the kitchen, not exactly hungry, but needing a snack. Some peanut butter on a couple of crackers seemed good, and she walked around the garden house, munching and trailing crumbs. Clicking on the spotlight above the blue vase, she sat regarding it for a time. The glaze was so beautiful, so exquisite. The color so deep and intense, she could not take her eyes from it, even when the delicate shades of blue began to run and shift. As she watched, the blues muddied and separated, ran and pooled, dripping and trickling down the sides of the pottery, cluttering and confusing its beauty, changing and releasing its texture.

How must that long-ago potter have agonized over his art, dripping on the glaze, caressing the surface with color. What to do? When to stop? How to trust the order of things unknown and unseen? How to sense when to fire the vase, that instant when the color was at its peak, the clarity most perfect, the texture exactly right. How to find the courage to assume the ultimate responsibility.

But that is truly the task, she realized, watching the colors coalesce before her into the mysterious and familiar beauty of the vase. When to start, when to stop. That's always the task. Timing is everything. Knowing what you want is just the beginning. The courage of action and non-action and the wisdom of when to start and when to stop make whatever it is happen.

Feeling more burdened, yet strangely light, Lucin walked to the main house and dismissed Stephanie for the evening. Sitting with a hot cup of green tea and enjoying her solitude, Lucin rolled her discoveries about in her head, attempting to appreciate and not analyze. Everything Tami had told her, contradictions included, was true. The universal truth was that there was no universal truth.

Feeling both adrift and anchored, apprehensive and accepting, she even found it possible to smile when Harrison walked through the door.

"Hi, Sweetheart," she said, noticing he appeared to be more haggard than usual. "Are you okay?"

He crossed to her and took Lucin tenderly in his arms. "God, Luce, I'm so sorry," he whispered. "Your mother's dead."

They flew to Philadelphia that evening and Lucin plunged into the emotional and physical whirlwind that is the death of a parent. Harrison stayed with her for five days, being as supportive as he knew how to be, between visits to the home office. He returned to Kansas City right after the funeral service.

The shock of her mother's death, compounded somewhat by its suddenness and her mother's relatively young age of fifty-nine, caught Lucin completely off guard. The two women had never, even when Lucin was a child, been very close. Even though they were not friends and had dissimilar interests, the mother's passing was difficult for her daughter.

The funeral was huge and endless. The graveside caravan of mourners stretched for blocks, the police barricading intersection after intersection so the vehicles might stay together. When the long afternoon was finally over, Harrison went straight to the airport and Lucin was left to face the throng of well-wishers, distant cousins, and curious kin that descended on the house. Her mother's mother held court in a corner of the immense living room, accepting tribute and sympathy with all the self-satisfied, aloof smugness of Don Vito Corleone. Drink of all types abounded. Buffets bristled and groaned under the gluttonous cacophony of a cruise ship fantasy. Lucin, dressed in a simple black suit, sat in an armchair as far as she could get from the throng and wished everyone would just get the hell out.

She thanked those who stopped by for their wishes of hope and consolation, listened to tired stories of her mother's girlhood and school days, was hit on by two of her mother's friends, and finally escaped to the kitchen to avoid screaming aloud. A couple of the assistant caterers were sitting at the table. The two young men bolted to their feet.

"Relax," Lucin smiled. "I'm just looking to get out of the crush."

They stood nervously looking at her.

"Sit," she said. "Eat something if you like."

"Our boss would get pissed ... uh, upset if he found us sitting with you."

"Your boss works for me. I'm *his* boss." Lucin prowled through both the immense refrigerators, then turned back to the two young men. "Either of you old enough to buy booze?"

"I am," said the shorter of the two.

"Good," Lucin replied, reaching into a pocket of her jacket. "What's your name?"

"Jimmy."

"That's appropriate," she smiled, extending a hand to him. "Jimmy, here's twenty dollars. I want a four-pack of Guinness in cans, cold. You may keep the change. Get it here in less than fifteen minutes, and there's a twenty-buck tip in it for you. Clear?"

"My boss wouldn't want me to leave," he replied, eyeballing the twenty.

"As I said before, your boss works for me. Go."

Jimmy grinned and headed out the door. Lucin turned to the other young man.

"What's your name?"

"Gary, Ma'am. Gary Bailey."

"Well, Gary Bailey, you are going to sit here at this table with me and do your best to tell me your entire life story before Jimmy gets back."

"I am?" he grinned.

"You am," Lucin assured him, sitting down. "Start talking."

Jimmy was back in less than thirteen minutes. Lucin gave him an extra twenty, and handed one to Gary also.

"What's this for?"

"Entertainment fee, Gary," Lucin replied, pouring a Guinness into a tall glass and taking three long swallows. "You guys bring any ham?"

"Yes, Ma'am," Jimmy said.

Lucin took another long pull at the Guinness. "Well then, Jimmy, me darlin' and fair, throw me together half a sandwich with mayo and mustard and a bite or two of chips or potato salad, and I'll dine in here with you two fine lads, while that bunch in the other room chews their way through the crab puffs and caviar."

The two young men, obviously unused to being treated as equals and totally fascinated by Lucin in so many ways, bent to their task and within a very short time Lucin was halfway through the sandwich and most of the way through the Guinness.

"Uh, Ma'am?" said Jimmy.

"Ma'am ... God," smiled Lucin. "Yes?"

"We really gotta get back out there and check the tables and stuff."

"Fine. Thanks, boys. You've helped me a lot this afternoon. I am ready to return to the fray. Go do your jobs."

Grinning, they both thanked her and left. Lucin finished the sandwich and the glass, poured herself another pint and carried it back into the living room. She almost made it back to her chair before she was intercepted by her grandmother.

"Lucin," the old woman hissed. "What are you drinking, beer?"

"God, no," Lucin stated. "This is not, nor should it ever be called, beer, Grandmother. This is Guinness."

"Well, it certainly looks like beer to me!"

"Of course it does," Lucin replied, taking a long slow swallow.

"There are two bars open on the ground floor, Lucin. I suggest you get some wine or a mixed drink, and put that glass away! The very idea. Your mother was buried today!"

"Grandmother, I like Guinness and right now I need a little Irish courage."

"Irish courage?! Young lady, I don't think I even know who you are anymore."

Lucin smiled. "You never did, Grandmother, and your daughter didn't either. Neither do I, but I'm learning. The sad thing is, I never knew my mother, and now it's too late. You taught her to act her way through life, to play a part, and she did it very well. She passed that on to me and it damned near took. Had I stayed here, it would have."

"What are you saying? This is utter nonsense!"

"I'm sure you believe it is, Grandma. Your mother knew better and so do I. I'm reasonably sure that my mother knows it too, now."

"What?! You sound like you think your mother's death was some sort of blessing!"

"Not for you, not for me, but for her? You bet," Lucin replied, and drained her glass. "Excuse me," she said, and began to walk away.

"Where do you think you're going?"

"Back to the kitchen. My glass is empty."

"Young lady, you come back here!"

"I don't think so," Lucin smiled. "Not ever again."

Lucin was two steps from the kitchen when she turned at the sound of her name. It was her mother's attorney and old family friend, Granville Walton. Nearly seventy and small in stature, he was dressed in the traditional black. Lucin had never seen him clothed any other way. He walked to her with stooped shoulders and a slight limp, his bald head reflecting light from the chandelier.

"Considering the circumstances, it is so good to see you, Lucin," he smiled.

"And you, Granville," she replied, resting her glass on a table and taking both his hands.

"Can we talk?" he asked.

"Of course," she said. "Come with me to the scullery."

He followed her into the kitchen and waited as she retrieved the last two pints from the fridge.

"Granville," Lucin smiled, "I have two of these left. I do not need to drink both of them. You must save me from myself. You must have one."

"Guinness?" he replied. "Of course! I don't care for beer, but Guinness is another matter." She poured and he continued.

"I know this is a rather delicate time, but life goes on, as they say. The reading of the will is to be in about two weeks. Will you be here?"

"No. I expect to stay for another few days, but then I'm going home."

"I suspected as much. I overheard your confrontation ... uh, conversation with your grandmother." His eyes twinkled over the rim of his glass. "Rest assured, your interests are well protected. Nearly everything will go to you."

"Sell it," she said. "With the exception of a few things I'll send home before I leave, sell it all. The furnishings, the jewelry, the artwork, all of it. Find my grandmother a townhouse or something, make provisions, if they have not already been made, for her welfare, and get rid of everything."

"There are a few small allotments for other distant relations, clubs and organizations, the staff, things like that."

"The staff, did she take care of them well?"

"Ah … as well as could be expected, I suppose," he hedged.

"Triple it," Lucin stated. "Whatever it is, triple it, and continue their salaries for six months, or until they have found employment, whichever comes first."

"That's very kind of you," Granville smiled.

"They deserve it," Lucin replied. "When I return to Kansas City, I will not be back. We can do all this from a distance, can we not?"

"Of course. I will see to it. I must say, Lucin, that your rather rash response to all this seems to me to be in your best interest, and I understand fully your motivation."

"I take that to mean you approve?" she grinned.

Granville drained his glass, and sat it on the countertop with some authority. "Get out of town, Kiddo," he beamed. "It ain't big enough for you and your grandmother."

"That's exactly what I intend to do," she laughed.

"Good," he replied, patting her on the arm. "I'll be in touch." He turned to go, then stopped and faced her. "You know, Lucin, you remind me very much of your great grandmother, Iona. That is to your credit. Now there was a lady who knew how to be a woman, and a woman who knew how to be a lady."

"Why, Granville, what a nice thing to say!"

"Must be the Guinness," he smiled, and went through the door.

THIRTY-EIGHT

Whatever steps are taken,
I place my feet.
Whatever sights are seen,
I direct my eyes.
Only I am responsible.

"I KNOW IT'S NOT A LOT OF TIME TO PREPARE," he said, "but we want to have the party while the whole Japanese contingent is in town. The ground breaking is that Friday afternoon at three. The celebration will begin that evening at eight."

Lucin sat with Harrison in the study shortly after dinner on her first evening home. Turning all the nuts and bolts of divesting herself of her mother's estate over to Granville Walton and the flight back to Kansas City had left her nearly numb.

"We can't exactly call it a Christmas party," Harrison went on. "A third of the staff are Jews and there will be at least ten upper level Japanese and their families relocating as plant management. A 'holiday celebration' sounds rather noncommittal. What do you think?"

"I think you have only a little over a month until the first Friday in December and that is a very short time to put a thing like this together," Lucin replied. "How many guests?"

"Employees and spouses only, no children. We're not at full staff yet and won't be for several months. Counting the Japanese, a few peripheral people we must invite because of their station, some city bigwigs and politicos, no more than five hundred if everyone comes and brings a guest. Probably closer to three hundred."

"I'd plan for six hundred, if I were you."

"Six hundred?"

"Yep. This is a big deal. Wives will all want to come. The singles will bring dates to impress them. Not a politician will show without an entourage, the Japanese must have attendants and assistants for 'face', and some people will just invite more than they should to show off."

"Jesus."

"Are you serving dinner?"

"I don't know."

"Don't. You can't possibly keep that much tasteless chicken hot on the plates. Go with buffets and finger foods so you can include Japanese stuff on the menu. Sushi, noodles, rice, sashimi... Also, make sure you stock sake and plum and rice wines at the bars. You should probably have at least four bars, by the way. If they get drunk, they'll have fun. Where are you going to have the party?"

"I thought in our building. I've already talked with Crown Center Properties. We can use the atrium area."

"Good. It's large and very open, it has that huge balcony overhanging the main floor, plus there are lots of restrooms and facilities. Make sure the holiday decorations do not include any direct reference to Christmas, Santa Claus, or any other specific. How 'bout entertainment?"

"Do we need entertainment, too?" Harrison asked, his eyes appearing to glaze over a bit.

Lucin smiled. "No, but you do need music. People like to dance and it's nice ambience. I'd consider a ten piece big band that's versatile enough to please people in their thirties. This is Kansas City. Kansas City is known for great music. You need to get in touch with a good party planning organization tomorrow and get this thing moving. Five weeks isn't much time to put it all together."

"Uh ..."

"Uh?"

"Uh ..." Harrison smiled. "I was wondering if you could possibly, I mean ..."

"You want to dump all of this off onto me, is that it?"

"I don't know if 'dump' is the right word ..."

"Sure it is. Dump is exactly the right word."

"Well ..."

"Harrison, I have a life. I'm in the middle of a bit of a crisis of my own right now."

"I know, Luce, but you're so good at this kind of thing and ..."

"Don't patronize me, dammit. I don't like it! I didn't say I wouldn't do it, I *will* do it, but here's the deal. You don't bitch about the budget, you don't hassle me for details, you don't pry about the progress, and you don't look over my shoulder. You give me the name and number of somebody on your staff that will have all the information I need to get this done and you stay the hell out of my way. If I take it on, you're out."

"Well, naturally I'll want to know how things are progressing."

"Nope."

"No?"

"Perhaps I didn't make myself clear. Let me try again. If I do this, you have nothing to say about it. Nothing. You show up just like everybody else, walk in, have a good time, and leave. If I am going to put a huge party together on this kind of notice and make it work, I answer to nobody but myself. All I need from you is who to call for information and who to call for money."

"Geeze, Luce, I don't know."

"No deal."

"Now, wait a minute."

"Nope. No deal."

She stared at him and he squirmed under her gaze. "Christ," he grimaced. "Who are you and what have you done with my wife?"

"Your wife is right here," she smiled, softening a little. "Make up your mind. I'll have to start on this early tomorrow. It's my way or the highway, Cutie," she grinned.

"Shit," he laughed, dropping his head. "Alright, alright. You got it. It's your baby. I'll stay out of the way."

"I mean it, Harrison."

"I know you do. You've got a deal."

"Good. I'll get rolling first thing tomorrow morning after I call Mother's attorney."

"Oh. That's uh …"

"Granville Walton."

"Right. You sure about that, Luce? He's gotta be a hundred years old. We have a lot of good people out there."

"Granville's fine. He knows this family better than anyone. He was Mom's lawyer for over forty years. Besides, all he has to do is sell the stuff."

"Sell the stuff?"

"Yep. Houses, land, cars, furnishings, personal property, business property, stock, all of it."

"You're selling out?!"

"Everything."

"Christ, Lucin, do you think that's wise?"

"It is for me."

"The taxes are gonna eat you alive!"

"There'll be plenty left."

"Well, yeah … but it's just not good business to sell off everything like that!"

"I'm keeping some of the artwork. Everything else goes."

"God, Lucin! Please think about this!"

"I have. I don't want to own all that stuff. I don't want to have the weight of it on me. I do not want the responsibility of those jobs and properties and things around my neck. I've told Granville to drop ten percent or so below market and divest me of all of it as soon as everything is probated. As it is, it will probably take two years for it to happen."

"You are going to lose millions!"

"Can't lose what I don't have. I'm going to make millions. What the hell do I need more money for?"

"What about your grandmother? Where's she going to live if you sell the family home?"

"Wake up, Harrison! It is not, and never was, a family *home*. It is the family *house*. I have no love for it, no need for it, no desire for it. My grandmother will live in a condo, or an assisted living village, or wherever she chooses. She will not want for anything except, perhaps, status quo. Status quo is fucking *over*."

Harrison stared at her for a moment, then shrugged. "And not just in Philadelphia," he said, looking away. "It would seem that status quo is over elsewhere, too."

Feeling a little sorry for him, Lucin smiled. "It would seem so," she replied.

Leaving Harrison staring at the wall, Lucin went upstairs for a long bath, then directly to bed. She was asleep before he came up; he was gone before she awakened. After a breakfast of melon, coffee, and a bagel, Lucin phoned Granville, a caterer, a party planner, and George.

"Darling!" he bubbled, "I was just fantasiz ... thinking about you, you delicious thing! So sorry to hear about your mother. Were you close? Come see me and we'll just gab and gab!"

"That's why I'm calling, George," Lucin laughed. "I need something special."

"Sweetie, *you* are something special. Whatever it is, just go nude! Nothing poor George could ever do would be able to compete with that! Ha! Ha! Oh, Christ, my wit! Hurry, hurry, you Lu-SIN-full thing. I salivate awaiting your arrival! Ta!"

Lucin grinned all the way to the Jag. As usual, the door flew open before she could ring, and George, wearing a bright yellow wind suit and green sneakers, swept her inside. His head was shaved.

"Black velvet pants, knee boots, a white silk blouse, and a short cape!" he gushed. "My, my, my. Kiki the Cossack reborn! I love it almost as much as I love you, Darling. Shout Russian at me and I shall have to go lie down where I can be alone! Terrible about your mother, Dear. Espresso?"

Lucin gawked at him. "George! Your wonderful hair!"

"I know. I shaved it all off just yesterday. Ringworm."

"What?!"

"I lie!" he crowed, fanning himself. "God, it's such fun! The looks on people's faces. No, Sweetie, no ringworm. Just time for a change. I think I'm going to grow one of those horrid droopy mustaches and wear lots of black turtlenecks and glare at everyone all the time. Very chic! Maybe I'll buy a ferocious Pit Bull and name him Pussy. Ha!"

"George, you are amazing," Lucin laughed.

"Oh, I am, aren't I," he agreed, steaming milk. "And you, you bad little girl, what have you been up to, as if I hadn't heard the drums in the night."

"Drums? What drums?"

"Oh, the ones that began playing when you and that brazen sweetheart Jolee began flaunting yourselves all over Westport and the Plaza. The same drums that got louder when you began hitting three or four happy hours a week all by your lonesome."

Lucin glared at him. "Don't believe everything you hear, George."

"Oh, I don't, Dearest. I believe very little of it, I just enjoy hearing it, that's all," he commented, placing two cups of espresso on the bar. "Now drink up and don't think badly of me. I could never think badly of you. I don't care what you do, Lucin. I'm just sorry you can't do it to me!"

"Lots of rumors, huh?"

"If I took all the men you supposedly have been out with and laid them end to end," he gushed, "I wouldn't be able to sit down for a month!"

Coffee nearly came out Lucin's nose. Switching gears as only he could, George continued. "So, what can I do for you, and please make it a challenge. The debu-*taunts* are driving me to distraction! I long to work for a woman of attribute."

"Okay," Lucin giggled. "In five weeks there will be a party for my husband's law firm. It is to celebrate their new offices here in Kaycee, the ground breaking for a new manufacturing facility out near the stadiums, the alliance between the firm, the city, and Nagata Industries of Japan, and to welcome various members of Nagata Industries to the Kansas City area. It is also a Christmas party that will be, instead, a holiday celebration. Five to six hundred in attendance, music, dancing, huge buffet tables, lots of liquor. I need a dress that is very sexy without being sleazy, very Japanese and still American, very showy and yet elegant."

"How soon do you require this masterpiece?"

"Four weeks."

"Child's play," George beamed.

"Wonderful! You're invited to the party, by the way."

"Marvelous. I love to hobnob. I will set the evening aside to eat, drink and be merry. And believe me, I've been Mary more times than you can count! How old was your mother, Dear?"

"Fifty-nine."

"So young. Heart?"

"Cerebral aneurysm."

"Ah. Any place, any time. Did you have a color in mind for this party dress?"

"I trust your judgment completely."

"So wise for such tender years," he smiled. "Here's some more wisdom for you. Growth seldom runs rampant, Lucin. It almost always has purpose. I suspect you lack purpose at this point in your life. You won't find it at happy hour."

"Suppose I told you to mind your own business," Lucin flashed.

George smiled. "Then I would. But you won't tell me that, Dear, because we have great affection for each other and you know I care about you."

Lucin looked at the countertop. "Yes, I do."

"Lucin, I am a forty-nine year old queer. A creative, funny, imaginative, person-able, HIV positive, faggot. I have looked for love all my life and never had a relation-ship that lasted longer than eighteen months until the last four years, and he has AIDS. All the pain in my life, all the denial, all the hurt, all the frustration, all the sad-ness, all the persecution, has been worth it. Do you hear me? It has been *worth* it to love and be loved by that wonderful person who I watch die a little more every day."

"I am not a tragic figure. I am a hopeful figure. I am hopeful for our future to-gether, and for my own if we can no longer be together. Love is hope, Lucin. Love is truth, love is beauty, love is life! Your girlhood is gone, Sweetie. I suspect that you never really had one. You will not find it in bars or wishful thinking or daydreams. You must decide what you want. Everything else is preparation. When you can commit to yourself, you can then commit to someone else, *whomever* that is. I am not telling you to be true to your husband. I am telling you to be true to yourself."

"I deal with so many frustrated women in my line of work. Mothers attempting to vicariously lead their lives through their daughters. Daughters that despise their mothers. Anorexic little twits, loudmouthed spreading matrons, pretentious Junior

Leaguers, trapped husband haters, women of all ages who believe happiness can be found in a bottle, or a bank, or a car, or a bed, or a house, or a dress. It's not out *there*," he said, waving his arms around the room. "It's in *here*," he continued, touching Lucin gently over her heart.

"You are not the same person I met on that fateful day at Mama's. You have grown so much. You shine, Lucin, you truly do. Know that. *Be* that. It has nothing whatsoever to do with morality or propriety, with old promises or withered licenses, with being faithful or steadfast, with adhering to rules or societal convention. Whatever you choose to do, if you do it with love, for love, and because of love, then you are going the right way. It has taken me almost my entire life to figure that out, and it is worth every mistake I ever made, except perhaps these shoes with this outfit." He grinned. "God, I am such a sleaze! How can you stand me, you slut?"

"Because you are such a wonderful sleaze," Lucin smiled, and leaned into him, wrapping her arms about his neck and kissing him on the cheek. George held her as the tears began.

Lucin cried for George, for her mother's squandered years and her own. She cried for Kaypee, for Harrison, for the sadness James felt about his daughter. She cried because duty cannot substitute for love and love cannot substitute for like. She cried because she knew Grandmother Iona only from the written word and *Mama-san* only from dreams. She cried because she had not cried for her mother and it was way past time. Through it all, George held her, caressed her hair, whispered meaningless comfort in her ear, and did not once ask her to stop.

When she eventually gurgled to a halt and released him, George poured her a glass of sherry and wrapped some ice cubes in a damp hand towel.

"Put these on your eyes," he smiled. "If you walk out of here like that, people will think I am an absolute beast!"

"God, George. I'm sorry. I don't know what's wrong with me. Maybe I need professional help!"

"We all do at one time or another, Sweetie. I go to this marvelous woman. A psychologist. She's done me so much good! If Ruby can't help, it's too late," he smiled. "I got to her just in time. I used to be hetero!"

"Why would I need her, if I have you?"

"Why would anyone need anyone, if they had me, Sweetie. And so many have had me, I can't remember them all! Don't rule it out," he said, moving to the door. "Ruby LaCost. If you ever need it, I'll give you her number."

"Thank you, George. You're a good friend."

"Just keep the money coming," he grinned, stepping to the Jag with her, "and the friendship never stops. I'll get to work on your party dress. Have it in three weeks or so. I'll phone if I need a fitting. Sorry about your mom. Chin, and everything else, up, Sweetie."

Lucin arrived back at the house about noon and found James exiting the kitchen door.

"James! Good to see you!" she shouted, walking over from the car.

"Ah, Lucille," he said, holding the door for her, and stepping back inside. "Are ya well, then? Sorry I am for the loss of your poor mother. Bein' an orphan is not an easy thing."

She looked at him blankly for a moment. "My God. You're right, James. I'm an orphan."

"Aye, ya are, Lass, and I'm sorry for ya."

"I never thought of that."

"Why should ya? Orphans are supposed to be children, not adults, but you're an orphan just the same. It leaves a great empty spot for awhile that's not good, but it's worse if ya don't know what it is."

Lucin looked up at him. "Thank you, James."

"Sure," he grinned. "I care about ya, Lucille. There's Guinness in the fridge."

Lucin grasped his neck and kissed him tenderly on the mouth. "That," she said, "is because I like you."

She kissed him again, more deeply and urgently. "That is because I love you," she smiled.

The third kiss was slow and sensual, warm and sexual, with ample tongue and full body contact. "And that," Lucin purred, "was for the interruption on the stairway." She licked his nose. "Go back to work, O'Doud, and try not to think about me." She walked toward the stairs.

"Saints p-preserve us," he stammered.

She stopped and turned. "Sure, and it's way too late for that, Jimmy," she smiled wickedly. "The devil's got us now."

THIRTY-NINE

I celebrate with joy.
I ache with sorrow.
I yearn for love.
I rejoice at reunion.
I live.

LUCIN SPENT THE NEXT THREE WEEKS dancing as fast as she could. The dealings with Granville Walton and the endless bureaucracy involved in setting the disposal of her mother's estate in motion, combined with the myriad tasks involved in planning and coordinating the holiday party for Harrison, plus the effort and time consumed in preparing and practicing her program for the show at the Carriage Club ice rink, left her no opportunity to ponder her situation or make any decisions about her personal life. She seldom saw James, she rarely saw Harrison, and had very little contact with anyone who wasn't an attorney, a caterer, a party planner, or her instructor, Bryan.

Lucin was sitting at the kitchen table one morning, examining a list of dishes available from a caterer and wondering how she got into this mess, when the phone rang.

"Hello?"

"Hello, yourself, you glorious girl!"

"George!"

"In the flesh, such as it is. Put away your vibrator, dry off, and whisk your succulent self over here to me, you sleek thing and let's have a lick at ... look, *look* at you. Am I terrible or not? Wear something awful so I may feel superior! Over and out! But then, I've been out for years ... oh, well. Tootles!" Grinning at the dead phone, Lucin pushed the caterer's list away and shifted her mental gears. She had been summoned by George.

As usual, George flung open the door as she reached for it and swept her inside. He was wearing a black velvet jumpsuit, white cowboy boots, an electric yellow bandana, and a full head of hair. Lucin gaped.

"Oh, stop!" he giggled. "It's a wig, Darling. It's always been a wig. I was bald by the time I was thirty!"

"I had no idea!"

"Of course you didn't, Dear. That's why I pay so much money for these dammed things. They're hand crafted of Swedish pubic hair, or some equally exotic substance, guaranteed to fool anyone but the young Swedish maidens from whom they were so ruthlessly plucked. My God! Sometimes I hear their screams in my sleep! Dreadful."

"George," Lucin laughed, "you are so full of shit!"

"Pooh on you, Dearest," he replied, eying her sweat suit. "How wonderfully tacky! I feel better already. Are you ready for your party ensemble?"

"It's done?"

"Of course. Remove that uniform for trailer park trash you're draped in so fetchingly and try it on. God, I hope you forgot underwear. It would absolutely make my day!" He walked to a nearby rack and unzipped a hanging bag as Lucin took off her sweatshirt and pants.

"Take off that tacky sports truss," George continued. "I have a bra for you here," he said, handing her one in black. "Slightly push-up, Darling. Cleavage is called for. Subtle, yet sensuous." As she slipped into the bra, he withdrew the rest from the bag.

There was a sheer black underblouse with a thin high collar and snug, but not tight, long sleeves. Next came black seamed pantyhose, and then the dress, a subtly tailored sheath. In deep red raw silk brocade, with a tone on tone pattern of lotus blossoms and a Mandarin collar, the dress deepened to black at the hem, which fell to just above the knees. Below the collar was a keyhole neckline, nearly round in shape, backed by the sheer black of the underblouse. Fabric covered buttons closed a slit on the right side of the skirt beginning at mid-thigh, and traveled upward to near the shoulder, then across the upper bodice, finally fastening the collar. Along the buttons and around the open keyhole, the material was edged in thin black piping with the deep red fading to black along the neckline. The sleeves were an abbreviated kimono style to the elbows, exposing the sheer underblouse beneath.

"My goodness, George … this is lovely," Lucin said.

"Very reserved, very American, very Oriental, and very sexy," he replied, holding out a pair of three-inch pumps in the same material as the dress, each with a covered button above the heel. "Pull your hair back with a pair of lacquered combs, then let it fall in well planned disarray. Some of the men at this party may never recover from the subtlety of your wickedness," he smiled.

"This brocade silk is amazing!"

"That brocade silk is nearly six hundred dollars a yard," George said. "When we dyed in the black, I thought my heart would stop!"

"It's perfect."

"I suppose it will do," he smiled, reaching for another garment bag. "It is, however, not all I have for you."

Lucin watched as he laid out a traditional kimono in delicate pale green silk, lined in white, with sleeves that reached all the way to the hem. Embroidered across the right breast and down the sleeve in even lighter green, was a dainty pattern of bamboo leaves. Next came a pale peach under-kimono of the same weight, a dark green under-kimono that was nearly sheer, and a peach underskirt as diaphanous as a breeze. The wide, stiff *obi* in heavy, raw silk, matched the underskirt in color.

"Oh, my," she murmured.

"It is my gift to you, Lucin," George smiled. "For all you are, and for all you will be. I celebrate having you in my life."

Lucin kissed his cheek and began to put her arms around his neck. George backed up.

"Hug me after you put your sweats back on," he said. "If you wrinkle that dress, I'll scratch your eyes out!"

That afternoon, Lucin met the party planner at Harrison's office building in Crown Center to look over the atrium for the last time. Harrison walked through the area once while she was there, but didn't see her. She said nothing. When she returned home, Lucin went to the garden house, showered, and spent an hour or so in the bath, luxuriating in the steaming water and watching leaden skies that promised snow but failed to deliver. Harrison returned home while she was bathing. They had dinner that evening and went to bed together. After a perfunctory kiss, he rolled over and went to sleep. She double-checked the party menu.

The next few days were chaotic. In the middle of the frantic last minute preparations for Friday's celebration, Bryan announced he wanted Lucin to do a run-through of her program in full costume at four Thursday afternoon. She arrived at the rink, hat in hand, at three-thirty. Sitting to don her skates, she noticed Kaypee practicing on the ice. The child ignored her. A minute or two after four, Bryan stopped Lucin's warm-up.

"All set?" he asked, smiling at her.

"I'm so stressed," she admitted. "I don't know if I'm ready or not."

"Well, at least you're dressed for it," he grinned. "Take another couple of minutes to loosen up and we'll do this thing. I'll get the kids off the ice and set up your music."

All too soon, Bryan shouted at her, and waved her to center ice. She stood there, alone, twenty or thirty adults and children looking on, and waited for the music.

The slightly out of tune brass opening blared through the speakers and she held her pose, hat cocked over her left eye, waiting for the slow blues piano beat to kick in. When it did, so did she, pushing off on her right foot in a crouch, bobbing her bottom up and down in rhythm to the beat, waiting for Joe to tell her to take off her coat. Like whiskey over gravel, Cocker's voice cut through the air and she was off, gloriously outside herself, totally absorbed in the moment, the music, and Joe. *She* was the one he sang to. *She* was the one he urged to take off her dress. *She* was the one who gave him reason to live. *She* was the one who could leave her hat on, and she *knew* it. Lucin strutted and shimmied, she stepped and shook, she worked it, she pushed it, she gave it up and got it back again. She sold it, every edge and pick, every bump and grind. Lucin Montgomery did exactly what Joe Cocker wanted her to do, and she loved it. So did everybody else in the rink. When she slid to a halt on her knees, tipped her hat back and grinned, whistles and shouts broke out, and Bryan looked like he'd just discovered teeth.

Laughing with joy, he skated to her side and lifted her to her feet, cheering. She hung on his neck, embarrassed and giggling.

"Damn, Lucin," he crowed, "you tore that up! You are one nasty girl! I'm gonna have to raise the difficulty a little. That was terrific!"

Sweating and joyous, she became the center of a small crowd of admirers. Over Bryan's shoulder she saw Harrison standing by the ice. He was staring at her. As quickly as she could, she separated herself from the group and skated over to him.

"Harrison!" she smiled, still panting from exertion, "what are you doing here?"

"I might ask you the same thing, Lucin."

"What?"

"I got a call at the office from some company called Origami, that said they could only provide five sushi chefs for the party. They wanted to know if that was alright. I called everywhere and couldn't find you, so I stopped here trying to avert some sort of disaster."

"It's no disaster," Lucin protested. "Five will be fine. I'll call them as soon as I cool down."

"Cool down?! I should think you would. What are you playing at? I walk in here and see my wife, *my* wife, making an absolute spectacle of herself! My God, Lucin! There are bars that will hire you to do that kind of thing. Ice skates aren't necessary!"

"Oh, Harrison ..."

"Oh, Harrison, my butt!" he spat. "Look at you! You're less than half dressed, shaking your ass all over the place, behaving like some kind of cheap ... I don't know what! Jesus Christ! I don't know what you think you're doing, but it is over. Over! Do you hear me? This skating nonsense is finished! Get your clothes, cover up, and come with me. You are leaving!"

Lucin, suddenly very calm, looked at him. "I don't think so."

"You don't think so? *You don't think so?*! Well, I don't think that any wife of mine is going to be allowed to exhibit herself like a whore, that's what I think! What if some of my friends came in here and saw you behaving like that? Now you get your things and you ... *ow!*" he yelled and flinched, moving to one side and grabbing at his kidney. Behind him stood Kennedy Paige Hartrick.

"You leave Lucin alone!" she shouted. "She's my friend, and you just leave her alone!"

Red-faced, Harrison sputtered. "Lucin! Who is this child?"

"This *child* is my adopted sister," Lucin snapped, surprised to see Kennedy materialize behind Harrison, "and she has a wonderful idea. Leave me alone. You don't come into *my* world and yell at me. You don't invade *my* space without *my* permission, goddammit, and you don't have it! Get the hell out of here, get away from me, get away from this rink. You ever walk into *my* world and yell at me again, and I will find a way to *kick your ass*! Now get out or I'll have some of *my* friends throw you out!" She pushed off and glided back out onto the ice, Kennedy at her heels.

Lucin stopped and looked at the child. "Hey, Kaypee," she smiled.

"Who was that man?" Kaypee asked.

"Just my husband."

"He's a buttface!"

"Now and then, he certainly is," grinned Lucin.

"You said some bad words," Kaypee observed.

"You're right," Lucin confessed. "I did."

The child thought a moment. "That's okay," she said. "Sometimes I do, too."

"You know what I'd like to have, Kaypartner?"

"What?"

"I'd like to have a hug. I've really missed you."

"I missed you, too," the girl sniffed.

For the second time that afternoon, Lucin dropped to her knees on the ice. This time was sweeter by far.

FORTY

Ages apart,
Bound with threads
Unaffected by time,
We are one.
There is only now.

WHEN LUCIN GOT HOME, she went straight to the garden house. Unusually calm, she prepared some egg drop soup and ate it along with a bagel and cream cheese. After dinner the bath beckoned and a thirty-minute soak relaxed her nearly to the point of sleep. She took some time to go over last minute details, attempting to determine if she'd forgotten anything of importance for the holiday party, drank a Guinness, and went to bed early with the red lacquered box. Her sleep was warm and deep.

The next morning she placed a few phone calls to make sure everything was on track for the party, then went to the rink for a couple of hours trying to clear her mind. When she got home, James was in the kitchen eating a peanut butter sandwich.

"Ah, Lucille, me darlin'," he grinned, "I must tell you how much I enjoyed your display on the ice yesterday."

"You saw it?" she asked, blushing slightly.

"Aye. I was driving your dear husband. I followed him inside and stood back in the reception area. I viewed your performance through the glass. It was an exhibition with little inhibition. I loved it. You are very good."

"Thank you, James," she smiled.

"Sure, and ya don't skate too bad, either."

"Thank you again, James," she dimpled.

"It looked to me like you and himself had a few words."

"We did."

"It also looked like the young Hartrick lass throws a pretty mean kidney punch."

Lucin laughed. "She was trying to protect me. She called Harrison a buttface."

"Ah," grinned James, "from the mouths of babes. Your husband is nearly over the edge. Everything he's worked so hard for is almost here and he's scared to death something is going to happen to screw it all up. The dear boy is in a bit of a state."

"He treated me as if I were some kind of tramp!"

"Take it easy, I'm not defendin' the lad. Anyone who treats you badly has a serious problem with me. I'm just makin' observations."

"I know, James," she sighed. "I'm sorry."

"Well, it was a treat to see you stand up to the darlin' lad, and another one to see you and little miss Kaypee back together again."

"Did Harrison say anything in the car."

"Not a word. He was too busy sulkin'."

"Good for him," she grimaced.

"And now, I have to be makin' tracks," he continued. "I'll be drivin' back and forth from the airport all day, or to the ground breakin', or to hotels. Your husband wants me to bring you to the party tonight, and keep an eye on you."

"What exactly are you supposed to save me from?"

"I'll be fortunate if I can save meself, as far as you're concerned," laughed James.

"You're as safe as you want to be, Jimmy," Lucin teased.

"I give up," James chuckled.

"When is Harrison going to the party?"

"He'll be goin' down early from work. What time would ya like to arrive?"

Lucin thought a moment. "It starts at eight ... around nine, I guess. I'm certainly not going in early just to stand around and fuss over everything. I'd much rather hope for the best and arrive fashionably late. I'll be dressed and ready to go anytime after eight-thirty."

"Why don't ya wear that outfit with the hat? That would make a hell of an impression at the festivities."

"You want to get me in trouble, James?"

He moved close to her. "Naw. Lucille, me darlin', I want ta get ya, sure and there's no doubt about that, but not in trouble."

"No?" she asked, looking up at him and biting her lower lip.

"No," he said, lifting her chin and gently kissing her on the lips. "That is because I like ya. This," he continued, "is because I love ya." He kissed her again, letting some of his power move between them, unleashing a little urgency. "And this," he went on, swinging her up in his arms and holding her with the ease she'd use to lift up Kaypee, "this is for the other day." He began a slow deep kiss that lasted across the kitchen, up the stairs, through her bedroom and to the bed. When he pulled away, Lucin's mouth felt hot and bruised, her knees were weak, and she hung in his arms like a marionette.

"The next time ya start somethin' with me, Lucille," he whispered, his lips grazing hers, "let's make damn sure there are no interruptions." He released her and she fell two feet onto the mattress.

Lucin gasped and watched him walk away from where she sprawled on the bed. "See ya around eight-thirty, Sweetheart," he said, not turning around. "Wear something pretty."

Mid-afternoon, Lucin gathered up her two new garment bags, make-up and essentials, and went to the garden house to prepare for the evening. She enjoyed a long hot shower, slipped into a heavy terry kimono, and walked aimlessly around the house for a while, thinking about the party. Nervousness started to niggle at her, and she crossed to the vase, peering at it from about two feet, enjoying the richness of the colors and the crispness of the glaze. There, in the sheen of the glowing finish, she saw her reflection. Startled, she flinched and stepped back.

What?! Why should something as normal as her reflection on a shining surface frighten her? Simple. It wasn't normal. In all the time she had looked at the vase, never before had she seen herself in it. The vase drew her eyes again, and she watched her blue-tinted image appear on the porcelain ... not arrive as she did when she moved in front of it, but appear, gradually forming as if rising up through the glaze. Her vision fuzzed a bit, her head throbbed, and she could hear her heartbeat. A slow ache, somehow comforting, grew behind her forehead and she felt as if she didn't need to draw breath, but merely relax and let the air move through her. She gazed at her image for a while, until she realized her eyes were closed. Opening them, she could still see herself in the porcelain, calm and serene, accepting and expectant. Shifting awareness to her body, she nearly shook herself, pulling carefully back from wherever it was she had gone. A glance at the clock showed she'd lost nearly an hour. Time to get ready. She stretched and smiled, feeling very comfortable about herself and with herself. The party would be fine.

Taking the advice George had given her, she pulled her hair up and back, and secured it with two Japanese combs lacquered in black and deep red. Gently she pulled a curl down in front of each ear and a short one over her left eyebrow. Carefully applying a little more makeup than was usual, she accented the shape of her eyes, lifting them up and out toward the ends of her brows, augmenting their oriental heritage. She put on the hated pantyhose, adjusting and re-adjusting until the seams were straight. The black bra came next, its push-up design raising and deepening her cleavage. Over that went the sheer black underblouse, the delicate collar snapping in place at the back of her neck.

On a whim, she found her grandmother Iona's ivory crane pendant, adjusted its length on a piece of black silk cord, and hung it about her neck against the sheer black of the blouse and the swell of her breasts. She slipped the dress over her shoulders and fastened every one of the forty-two tiny buttons from mid-thigh to the center of the collar. That completed, she slipped on the pumps, added a pair of plain antique ivory stud earrings, and walked over to a mirror. The effect was wonderful. Suzy Wong goes to America by way of Japan. The dull white of the pendant against the sheer black, framed by the keyhole neckline below the mandarin collar, was the perfect finishing touch.

Lucin stared at herself. So American. So Japanese. The dress seemed to emphasize both. If she wanted to see Lucin, Lucin was there. If she wanted to see Lucin-*san*, she was there too, each overlaying the other, as if she were a double image, two superimposed people looking back at her through the eyes in the mirror. Warmth crept through her torso and the dull ache returned behind her forehead. Two people *were* looking back at her from the mirror. She staggered a bit, but held her ground as Moon Blossom smiled at her.

272

"*Konnichi-wa*, Lucin-*san*," Blossom said. "*Please do not allow yourself to be frightened. I hope you are feeling well?*"

"*Konnichi-wa*, Blossom-*san*," Lucin replied, bowing slightly. "*So sorry. This occurrence frightens me somewhat, but I could never be afraid of you, my sister.*"

"*Your words are very kind, Lucin-san, and as lovely as your impeccable dress, but we are much more than sisters, very yes. You and I, we are the same and yet not the same, wakarimasu ka?*"

"*Sumimasen*, Blossom-*san, wakarimasen. I am sorry, but I do not believe that I truly understand.*"

In the mirror, Blossom shifted her stance, and Lucin could hear the rustle of silk on silk. The young woman smiled and spoke. "*We are each other in different places and different surroundings with different experiences,*" she said, "*but we are each other, as surely as rain is rain, wherever it falls, and sunlight is sunlight, whatever it touches. I understand this because it is acceptable in my reality to do so. You have difficulty because, in your reality, this is not an accepted occurrence.*"

"*Gomen nasai*, Blossom-*san, so sorry, but this is difficult for me,*" Lucin confessed, looking at the double image in the mirror.

"*Relax your heart, release your mind, take peace in the truth, and remove all need to understand,*" Blossom said. "*Our lives are now one, in you, to do with as you will. You have come a long way and are deserving of your own choices and decisions. What we were, I give to you. What we are, we give to each other. What we shall become, you give to me. Know we are one, and one we are.*"

Lucin felt the warmth increase in her torso and spread up her neck to her forehead. The pain disappeared and she felt herself expand and fill. As she watched the mirror, the two images shifted and lost focus. When the mirror cleared, she saw only herself. New memories of Mama-*san* flickered across her mind, as well as many other things she had never seen, places she had never been, people she had never known, events she had never witnessed. The collage whirled and spun, flashed and flickered. A lifetime scrolled across her mind in seconds, then gradually settled, to be called upon as she would will it. In the mirror, she saw tears streaming down her face.

"*Ah, so desu*, Blossom-*san*," she said aloud. "*Now I remember. Now I understand. Oh, very yes.*"

Make-up repaired, Lucin arrived at the main house kitchen just as James pulled in the drive. He walked inside and looked at her.

"Sweet Mother," he said, nearly choking. "Lucin, it's a vision ya truly are. The loveliest woman I have ever laid me tired old eyes upon."

"Thank you, James," she smiled. "Kind and wonderful words from a kind and wonderful man. There is no one in the world I'd rather hear them from than you. That's a gorgeous suit, by the way, and you wear it very well."

He looked at her for a moment, his eyes shining, then shook himself. "Uh … are ya ready then? Should we be going?"

She shrugged the short fox jacket Harrison had given her over her shoulders. "Why wait, Jimmy me boy?" she grinned. "Let's get Cinderella to the ball."

James escorted Lucin into the building and stopped at the bank of elevators just outside the atrium. She looked at him with a raised eyebrow.

"We're goin' upstairs first," he said. "The cloakroom is on the balcony level. You can check your coat there and make your grand entrance down that long sweepin' staircase to the floor of the hall. Since I can't keep ya all to meself, I want everybody to enjoy ya."

"Good idea James," she grinned, stepping into an open elevator. "I may as well go for a big first impression. I certainly have nothing to lose."

"Let me have your wrap. I'll check it for ya and hang on to the ticket. I'll be around all evenin'. You've been made my responsibility. When ya want to leave, just look for me and off we'll go."

"Thank you, James. It's nice to be looked after," Lucin replied, slipping out of her fox as the doors opened on the balcony level.

"Oh, I don't think that'll be a problem," James chuckled, taking the fur. "I expect you'll be looked after, and at, a lot this evenin'." He walked away to the coat check and Lucin looked over the site.

Above the atrium floor on the other side of the balcony, a big band played and several couples danced in an area surrounded by tables. A bar did brisk business in the corner. The place was festooned with delicate white lights and silver streamers, accenting the blue of the indirect lighting. Below her in the atrium, several banquet tables, covered in a staggering array of foods and dishes and graced by servers and chefs, catered to a never-ending progression of partiers. Some were seated at small tables strewn casually about the floor, many more stood in groups, networking and noshing, and the volume of conversation was considerable. On one side was a sushi bar, manned by five chefs filling orders. Nearby, a buffet with prepared sushi, sashimi, condiments, sticky rice, and soups drew a crowd. As Lucin had predicted, at least six hundred people milled about the spacious hall.

Kansas City's mayor, looking as though she was fresh from the desert southwest, stood in the middle of her entourage, talking with a developer and his minions, smiling and dismissing all lesser supplicants. Several other city officials, business people, entrepreneurs, and office seekers worked hard at being seen, table hopping and glad handing their respective ways about the room. In the far corner stood Harrison in the company of the city manager and a school board member, deep in earnest conversation.

"Well," said James, materializing at her elbow. "Are ya gonna stand here all night, or are ya gonna knock these hustlers on their ass?"

"My Grandmother Iona told me that the only two things in the world without limit are femininity and the means by which it may be exploited. Let's go for the ass, Jimmy," she grinned, taking his arm. "Walk me down."

"Sure," he laughed, guiding her toward the staircase. "Might as well get me fifteen minutes of fame."

The room, large and busy, was nearly silent by the time they reached floor level. Every eye in the place found Lucin as she descended the stairs. A slight smile on her face, her carriage flowing and graceful, she moved beside James in an aura of easy femininity that was immensely sexual and compelling. James felt it flow from her in quiet waves, turning heads, stopping conversations, moving eyes toward her. The men were as fascinated as the women were upstaged. Nearly all of them were curious.

"My God," James whispered. "You just grabbed this place by the balls!"

Lucin chuckled. "Don't stray too far, O'Doud," she grinned, kissing him on the cheek. "You could be next." She winked at him, turned on her heel, and walked toward her husband. Harrison appeared numb.

"Darling," she smiled as she reached him, taking his hand and offering her cheek to be kissed. "How is the party?"

"It seems fine," he said, pulling himself together. "I believe you know Councilman McGrath from the club?"

"Of course," Lucin replied, taking the councilman's hand. "Good evening, Sir, I hope you're having a good time."

Silver-haired, well tanned and sixty, the councilman looked down at her from his six foot four inch height. "Lovely. Absolutely lovely."

"Good," Lucin smiled.

"I was referring to you, Dear," he continued, still holding her hand. "You are, without a doubt, the loveliest woman in the room. And you, Harrison, are without a doubt, the most fortunate man."

Harrison ignored the comment and turned to the short heavyset man on his right. "Lucin, this is Arthur Payne," he said, as the councilman squeezed her hand and finally released it. "Arthur is a member of the Kansas City school board."

"A thankless job, Mr. Payne," Lucin said, offering him what was left of her hand now that the councilman was finished with it. "I admire your courage."

"And I admire your, uh … gown, Mrs. Montgomery. You look very, ah, beautiful this evening. Very beautiful indeed," he said, unable to keep his eyes from her cleavage.

"Please," Lucin purred, "Mrs. Montgomery seems so formal. If we are to be friends, call me Lucin."

"Only if you'll call me Arthur," he quipped.

"That's better," Lucin smiled, taking back her hand. "We're more than just acquaintances already. Are you enjoying yourself, Arthur?"

"It's a fine party. Harrison says you planned it?"

"Harrison is too modest," she smiled, taking her husband's arm. "It was all his idea. I just offered a suggestion or two. If you gentlemen will excuse me, I see an old friend across the way. I must say hello."

"Reluctantly," rumbled Councilman McGrath, his eyes roaming over her body.

"Thank you," she replied, and kissed Harrison on the cheek. "Have a good time, Darling. Don't talk business all night, now. I'll catch up with you later." As she walked away, Harrison felt both his companions exhale.

Moving through the room, exuding restrained sexual confidence, a hundred eyes on her every step, Lucin closed the gap between herself and Arleen Creighton. Arleen saw her and welcomed Lucin with a slow rolling chuckle.

"Well, well, well, my dear," Arleen beamed, "if ever there was a ball with a belle, you are certainly she. This crowd would have taken less notice of an earthquake. Good for you! If you got it, you may as well flaunt it, and you have it in abundance, Darling."

"Too much?" Lucin asked.

"On over ninety per cent of the women on this planet, yes. On you … just right. Sensual, sophisticated, sexy and sensational. You look wonderful." Arleen peered at Lucin intently for a moment. "There has been a change in you, Lucin. You are more than you were. I sense something has arrived. A homogeny of sorts."

"Yes," Lucin smiled. "Perhaps someday I'll tell you about it."

FORTY-ONE

Desires and wants
Surround me as
Butterflies on the wing.
Too elusive to capture,
Too delicate to grasp.

ARLEEN JOYOUSLY DISHED various dirt on some of the guests as she and Lucin scanned the crowd. Several men and women stopped by to say hello to Arleen and get a better look at Lucin. The two women, each in her own way, played to the throng, having a great time. During a lull, a familiar voice cut through the babble.

"My god, can you believe it! My two favorite women side by side. I'm so excited, I'm nearly incontinent!"

George, wearing a forest green tux with a red turtle neck and matching red patent pumps, wafted toward them, martini in hand.

"Maturity before youth," he gushed, kissing Arleen on both cheeks.

"George, you dog," she beamed. "I haven't seen you in months. We absolutely must gossip this evening."

"And we shall, dear lady. A tongue as sharp as yours deserves me for a whetstone!"

"Is Samuel with you?"

"Alas, no. He was feeling a bit under the weather and decided not to come." George replied, with just a faint flicker of sadness. "But look at *this*," he continued, kissing Lucin. "Darling, you are absolutely ravishing! As well you should be. You're wearing me! The rest of these cows simply can't compete. Ha!"

"Thank you, George," Lucin grinned.

"Thank me? I am your *slave*, Sweetie. You are the marble to my Michelangelo! It's women like you who make me wish my gene pool had a diving board!"

"George," Arleen laughed, "you are the most honest man I have ever known."

"The trick with honesty, as you well know, Leenie, is to dispense it only for those who are prepared to appreciate it. My God, there's the mayor! How horrid!

Something must be done about her wardrobe before the old warhorse self-destructs! Ta, Girls. I shall accost both of you again before the night is through."

"God, I love that man," Arleen said, watching George flap away, her eyes shining. "So bright, so talented, so sad."

"And so brave," Lucin murmured.

"Yes," Arleen agreed, then shook herself. "Well, you don't have a drink, and I certainly need one. Shall we mosey to the nearest saloon for some red eye?"

"Let's," laughed Lucin, and they walked toward one of the bars.

Their stroll led the two women past the foot of the staircase. As they neared it, the tone of the crowd changed and Lucin looked up to see Serata Onoshi and his entourage descending the stairs. She stopped. Arleen noticed the group.

"Find me later, Dear," she said. "You're on."

With Onoshi were seven or eight other men. As they walked down the stairway, the room became nearly quiet. The mayor and several council members hustled over along with a few business people and, of course, Harrison. As he neared the floor, Onoshi noticed Lucin. His stern visage eased into a tiny smile and he turned in her direction. She returned his smile and waited, her hands folded in front of her. He approached to within a respectful six feet and bowed slightly.

"*Konbanwa*, Lucin Blossom-*san*," he said. "*Good evening.*"

"*Konbanwa*, Onoshi-*sama*," Lucin replied, bowing deeply with great respect. "*It brings me joy to see you again. I must offer you my humble thanks for your very kind and considerate letter.*"

"*The letter was nothing except the truth. Pardon my asking, but did you show it to your husband?*"

"*I did not, Sire. I thought it best that it remain between us.*"

Onoshi chuckled. "*It would appear then, that you and I share a secret.*"

"*Very yes, Sire,*" she smiled. "*Something we must keep behind the hedge of our teeth.*"

"*Fear not, Child. I am very good at keeping secrets.*"

"*Do you have many secrets, Lord?*" Lucin asked, wide-eyed and enjoying herself.

"*Very many,*" Onoshi responded, allowing himself to look stern. Then he smiled. "*But, unfortunately, only one with you. May I offer you my humble compliments on your dress. You look very beautiful this evening.*"

"*Thank you, Sire. It is very kind of you to say so. Forgive my excessive rudeness, Onoshi-sama, but there are many people of importance that wait to meet you. I feel they are resentful of the time you are spending on only me.*"

"*I am sure they are, for such is their nature. Barbarians have little understanding of patience or beauty, neh?*"

"*It is true, Sire, but what is to be done? They are what they are and there is no changing that. So sorry.*"

"*Alas no. You are very wise, Lucin Blossom-san. Will you, perhaps, join us later this evening for sake?*"

"*Who knows what the gods have in store for us, Lord,*" she answered demurely, lowering her eyes.

"*You are truly a treasure, Lucin-sama,*" the old man laughed. "*My nephew said you were, and he could not have spoken a larger truth.*"

"*Your nephew, Sire?*"

"He lives in this country and has spoken of you to me. He is here at this function, I believe. I invited him. Perhaps you and he will see each other this evening. He has great admiration for you. Now I must attend to the reasons for my visit and conduct my affairs. So sorry. Will you excuse me?"

"Of course, sire. What else is there of importance except duty. It is good to see you. I will count the moments until we meet once more." Lucin bowed low to him.

Onoshi returned it in a perfunctory manner and turned his back, answering the call of duty.

A stir went through the crowd as Onoshi turned away from Lucin and she sensed a curiosity directed at her as she began to walk away. Good. Let them be curious, let them wonder. It is best to keep Barbarians off balance, neh?

The party continued. Lucin was approached by several people wanting to introduce themselves, seeking position within her company. She found it amusing. So did George.

"They're pissing themselves to get next to you," he observed. "You have become an item, you bad girl. That exchange with the head Japanese fellow has them standing on their dicks! God! This is so good, my nipples are hard. How 'bout yours, Sweetie?"

"Getting there, George," she laughed.

"Oh look, there goes your husband. He actually appears as if he's going to get something to eat. Things must be progressing well."

"If you will excuse me, George, I'm going to go make contact with him. We haven't really spoken all evening."

"Go on, Darling. Put a little shake in it, Dear. It pays to advertise."

Harrison was back near the Japanese contingent, serving himself from a table that contained both sushi and American finger foods. As she approached, she noticed he was spreading a glob of wasabi on a cracker. The fluffy green Japanese horseradish looked harmless. She stood beside him.

"I wouldn't do that," she said.

He looked at her. "What?"

"I wouldn't do that. I wouldn't eat wasabi on a cracker."

"Why?" he snorted. "Am I breaking some big Japanese taboo?"

"No, not at all, it's just that ... never mind Harrison," she smiled. "Just remember that I warned you. Go ahead and do whatever you think best."

Not taking his eyes off her, he popped the cracker in his mouth and began to chew. In just seconds, tears leapt to his eyes, his complexion reddened, and he gasped for air.

"Cheezus!" he shouted around a spray of cracker crumbs and wasabi.

As Harrison flapped about and drank anything he could find, Lucin stepped to the coffee service and quickly opened three packs of sugar. She got his bloodshot attention as he keened and flailed.

"Sugar," she said, trying not to laugh. "Put it on your tongue and leave it there,"

Snorting and wheezing, Harrison did as she advised, and hung on to the side of the bar, tears streaming from his eyes, his face nearly purple. The Japanese looked at him impassively as he struggled.

"In a few minutes sip the sweetest wine you can find. You'll be alright."

"Wha diden yew teh me wha tha wa?!"

"I don't know. Maybe I hoped you'd just trust me." She turned and walked away.

Lucin had taken only a few steps, when she felt the warmth of a hand on the small of her back. She turned, but there was no one there. The warmth spread up between her shoulder blades. She looked around and her gaze was drawn upward to the overhead balcony. There, wearing a black suit, tie, and shirt, his hair loose to his shoulders, stood Tamiko Asaruka. The nephew! He smiled and saluted her over the railing with a glass of wine. Unable not to, she smiled back. The warmth spread up to her neck and down under her bottom, between her legs, and up into her belly.

Instantly she was wet. Instantly her nipples were erect. She grasped her lower lip between her teeth, clamped her arms across her chest, and tried to look away from him. His lips moved and she heard his whisper in her ear.

"All is well, Moon Blossom. All is right, Lucin. There are no barriers, there are no restrictions. Whenever you are ready."

She could feel the orgasm coming, uncoiling between her legs, and fought to tear her eyes from him. They watched each other as it happened, as she locked her knees and trembled with the effort of staying on her feet. Rigid and panting through her nose, she struggled with it, trying to hide what was occurring. With her will and against her will, the spring snapped and she came. In the middle of six hundred partiers, she came. Standing on the polished floor of the atrium, surrounded by business people and politicians, friends and hangers-on, Tamiko Asaruka thrust his way inside her and hurled her over the edge.

When it passed its peak, she lurched twenty feet to a chair and sat as it receded, willing herself to be still as the ripples pulsed through her, afraid her dress was wet, frightened that someone would notice. She looked to the balcony, but Tami was gone. My God. If he could do that without touching her … she leaned back and tried not to shake.

A few moments later, she noticed Harrison walking in her direction. Feeling stronger and in control, she stood and went to him. He glowed.

"Are you alright?"

"I'm better," he said, speaking slowly and carefully. "Damn, Luce, how could you let me eat that stuff?"

"What was I supposed to do, slap it out of your hand?"

"Of course not, but you could have said something!"

"I did say something, Harrison. You chose to take it as a challenge instead of accepting it as advice."

"I looked like a fool in front of the Japanese!"

"That is not a new event. They pretty much think you're a fool anyway."

"What?! Goddammit, Luce, all I'm looking for here is a little support!"

"No, you're not. I have supported you every step of the way for years. When I start to exercise a little of my own will, when I begin to discover more of what I want from life, when I start to make my own way and my own decisions, you become threatened and paranoid. You don't want my support, Harrison, you want my obedience! Sweetie, that ain't gonna happen. You don't tell me what to do, how to act, where to go, what to be! I need *your* support, especially now with so many changes going on in *my* life, and I don't have it. You can enjoy and celebrate the changes in me and benefit from them, or you can continue to believe I'm not entitled to an identity of my own. Those are your choices."

"That's ridiculous!"

"No, it isn't, Harrison. I have run your household, sucked up to clients, taken care of details, stood demurely in the background, and been the perfect business wife for years. Then I pull the Nagata Industries thing together for you, and you attack me. I make this whole gathering possible, at *your* request, to support you and your business, and you don't even say thank you. I re-do the servant's quarters into a lovely house and garden, and you couldn't care less. You see me skate, something I work very hard at and do very well, for the first time in your selfish, narrow life, and do I get the slightest encouragement from you? The smallest compliment? No! Instead, you as much as call me a whore! Do you have any idea how close we are to being *over*?!"

"What?!"

"You heard me. You are running out of chances, Harrison. You may have already run out. I haven't decided."

"Jesus Christ, Luce!"

"Don't treat me like I just said something that makes no sense. It *does* make sense. It makes sense to me, and right now, Buster, I am a hell of a lot more important to me than you are! Say goodnight, Harrison. I'm leaving." She spun away from him and began to look for James.

"Before we go any farther," said James, reaching over the seat back and rummaging around in the rear of the limo, "I got somethin' for ya." Lucin sat in the front seat beside him and accepted a tall glass. James produced a pint of Guinness, popped the top, and poured it straight down the middle.

"There ya are, Lucille. It's been a hell of a night for ya, and I thought a little Irish might bolster up your saggin' whatever."

Lucin laughed. "I'll have you know, James Mathew O'Doud, that my whatever does not sag!"

"A figure of speech, Darlin'. I've seen your whatever and it appears to be quite pert."

"I thank you, and my whatever thanks you."

"So, how are ya then," he asked, easing out into traffic.

Lucin took a long pull of the pint. "I don't know. There were some surprises tonight, that's for sure."

"Himself certainly seemed surprised when he took a bite of whatever that was that bit back," James chuckled.

"Let's not talk about Harrison."

"Whoops. Gone that far, has it?"

"About as far as it can."

"I noticed Tami at the party tonight," James ventured.

"So did I," Lucin replied.

"Aye. I noticed that, too."

Lucin grinned. "There's not much you don't notice, is there, James."

"Not much."

"You even noticed that a little Irish would do me good," she grinned, taking another drink of her Guinness.

"Aye, that I did."

"What about a lot of Irish, James?" she teased, sliding toward him on the seat a few inches. "If a little does a little good, then a lot ..."

"Be careful, Lucille," he cautioned. "I meant what I said. The next time we start this thing up, we finish it."

She tilted the glass back and drank the last of her pint. "There," she said. "The little bit of Irish is all finished. When can we start on a lot of Irish?"

James looked at her as he pulled up beside the house. "Are ya sure, then?"

"Yeah, Jimmy, I think I am."

"Well, not tonight," he replied, patting her on the leg. "I've got a lot of drivin' to do. Why don't we talk about this tomorrow."

She leaned over and kissed him lightly on the lips. "And you," she smiled, rubbing noses, "why don't you think about it all night."

Thirty minutes later, Lucin climbed out of the shower in the garden house and toweled dry. She stretched out on the futon, pulled up the goose down coverlet, and sighed. James and Tami wafted through her mind. Either way, she couldn't go wrong, she thought. The difficulty was, which way could she go right?

FORTY-TWO

On the path that has no end, do not dismiss the fellow traveler.
Always there are lessons, always there are teachers.
Always there is more to learn.
I have become.
I am becoming.

LUCIN'S NIGHT WAS HAUNTED by visions as Japan of yesteryear came to her. Columns of marching Samurai, strange sailing ships at harbor, old friends from another place and time, mountain paths, immense castles, twisting streams, paper and wood houses, earthquakes and fires tumbled through her dreams in an endless overlapping tapestry of metaphysical memory that left her emotionally spent and partially awake before sunrise. She lay on the garden house futon, staring upward into the gloom, as shadows of her night chased each other into the darkness. Not quite conscious, not quite asleep, tendrils of jasmine incense teasing her nostrils, she hovered on the thin edge of awareness and slumber.

"Be at ease, Child."

"Mama-*san?*" Lucin asked, lurching to one elbow and peering into the dark.

The old woman chuckled from her position kneeling at the foot of the futon. "You were expecting the Emperor?"

Lucin struggled to rise. "Mama-*san!* Welcome to my house. Let me get you a pillow. Would you like some tea?"

"Calm yourself. You cannot serve me in this place, for I am not truly here," she said, and Lucin knew it was *honto*, the truth. "You have spent a restless night," the old woman continued. "Many things have come to you. These are to be expected as you and Blossom-*san* become one in this life."

"I saw her reflection in my mirror," Lucin said.

"*Hai*," Mama-*san* smiled. "How else can one see oneself?"

Lucin returned her smile. "*Wakarimasu*, Mama-*san*. I understand."

"I have released Blossom-*san*, Child. She has served me well and now has her freedom. You, too, have served me well. You are now also free. The disgrace brought on your ancestors by the courtesan who took her life in Yedo is expunged by your actions. You have sought honor, you have welcomed your ancestry, you have freely accepted what you are in your search for who you are. You have done these things from the pure motive of discovery and you cherish what has come to you. I leave you to who you are and what you will become. I am here, Child, to say good-bye."

Hot tears rose in Lucin's eyes. "Mama-*san*, don't leave me!"

"It is time. You no longer need me."

"I do, Mama-*san*! I do need you!"

"You do not."

"But I *want* you, Mama-*san*."

The old woman smiled and bowed slightly. "You have the memories, you have the knowledge, you have the skills, you have the heart. You will have what I am to you and what you are to me with you always. I also need to be free to continue my journey. In giving you your freedom, I receive mine, *neh?*"

"*Ah, so desu*," Lucin smiled through her tears. "Now I understand."

"Of course you do. You always understood duty. I go, Child. Rest beneath your covers for a time and know that I will count the moments until we meet once more."

Suddenly very sleepy, Lucin fell back onto the futon and rolled to her side, the quilt around her neck, a pillow firmly between her thighs.

"I will count them too, Mama-*san*," she whispered. "Oh, very yes."

It was nearly ten before Lucin woke for the second time. As she dressed, the memory of Mama-*san's* visit ran dream-like through her head. Decisions had to be made, action had to be taken. She must now rely on herself to do what was best for her, and upon Blossom for the understanding and knowledge to get on with their life. Frightened and excited, she entered the kitchen of the main house. Stephanie was cleaning a head of lettuce at the sink.

"Morning, Steph."

"Hi, Lucin. I just made a fresh pot. Can I get you a cup?"

"With cream," Lucin smiled. "Thanks, Sweetie. I appreciate you."

Stephanie blushed. "That's awfully nice of you to say."

"I'll do more than that," Lucin grinned. "You just got a thirty percent raise, Kiddo, retro-active to December first."

Stephanie spun around, dripping water on the floor. "Really?!"

"Yes, *really*!" Lucin laughed.

"Uh … thank you!" Stephanie stammered, drying her hands. "That's gonna make a big difference!"

"Just the start of the differences around here."

"That's so nice of you!"

"Well, give me a hug and get my coffee or you're fired!"

After she finished her second cup, Lucin went into the library and sat with some heavy linen stationery and a fountain pen. For the next few minutes she carefully composed an invitation. After addressing the envelope and sealing it with wax, she picked up the phone and made two calls. Stephanie was cleaning crumbs out of the toaster when Lucin walked back into the kitchen.

"Drop what you're doing, Steph, I have a couple of errands for you. First, deliver this invitation. I'm not sure where you'll find him today, but find him and hand deliver this to him. Second, at around four-thirty, stop by the florist and pick up a small package, then drop by the Origami Japanese restaurant in Crown Center. They'll have a tray for you. Bring the tray and the package directly back here and put them in the fridge in the garden house. I'll be there, but please don't disturb me. Okay?"

"Sounds mysterious."

"You have no idea. Use my Jag to run the errands. That is all you have to do for the balance of the day. Take tomorrow and Monday off. I'll be unavailable through tonight. No calls, no contacts. I am not here. Clear?"

"You bet."

"Great. The keys are in the Jag. Scoot."

After Stephanie left, Lucin went through a ritual cleaning, straightening the garden house, dusting, changing the bed linen, fluffing the pillows and such. She placed a large rice mat on the floor in front of where the vase stood and wrestled a low table onto the mat. On the table went an oil lamp and a small brazier stocked with charcoal sitting atop a marble tile. She placed a shallow cedar box filled with smooth flat stones beside the table and arranged sticks of incense artfully upon the stones. Lucin then turned on the small overhead spot and centered the vase in its light. Kneeling pillows went on each side of the table, screens were moved to create an intimate atmosphere, and two more oil lamps on stands were positioned to cast shadows on the screens. Perfect. She then turned to her shower and bath. An hour later, as she was drying and slipping into a white cotton night-kimono, Lucin heard Stephanie arrive and depart.

In the bedchamber, Lucin pulled her hair loosely up and secured it with combs, taking little care with its appearance. She lightly oiled, then re-dried her body, dabbing just a touch of rose oil at the base of her throat. Moving into the kitchen, she turned up the thermostat a bit to counter the cooling night and walked to the fridge. Lifting out the florist's package, she reached into the box and scattered a couple of handfuls of rose petals around the table in the living area and across the futon and floor in the bedchamber. She lit the oil lamps and extinguished all the electric lights, save the spot on the vase in the living room.

Back in the bedroom, Lucin lit a single oil lamp, dropped her robe, and carefully slipped on the delicate peach underskirt. The feel of the fragile fabric on her bare body was like cobwebs. Over the skirt went the sheer dark green underkimono, tied carefully with waist strings. Next came the heavier underkimono in pale peach silk, also tied with strings, and finally the fully lined, light green overkimono. Lucin adjusted its line and wrap, then secured it in place with the wide *obi*, dyed to match the underskirt. Finally she slipped the thick white *tabi* on her feet and stepped into her straw-soled sandals. Holding her arms at waist level so the trailing sleeves of the kimono would not touch the floor, she walked back into the living room carrying the earthenware *cha-no-yu* vessel containing the implements of the tea ceremony. She placed it on the table, opened it, poured the dusty green tea powder into its correct container, closed the lid, lit the charcoal in the tiny brazier and went into the kitchen to fill the small iron kettle.

While in the kitchen, she retrieved the package from Origami and returned to the living area with it and the kettle. The kettle went on the brazier. On the table she put a compartmented lacquered tray containing small amounts of tuna, bonito, squid, shrimp, sticky rice, soy sauce, pickled ginger, and *wasabi*. On a tiny dais in the corner of the tray was an orange, delicately sculpted into the shape of a rose. Simulating dew, one petal had been graced with a single drop of honey. She lit the incense, placed a white porcelain bowl filled with fresh water and a white cotton towel on the table, kneeled on a pillow, sat back on her heels, allowed her mind to approach the void, and began to wait.

The vase told her he was coming. It pulsated gently through the room as if the air pressure was fluctuating. Lucin opened her eyes and carefully arranged the skirts of her kimonos for the most artful effect. She placed her hands delicately in her lap and anticipated his knock. When it came, she bade him enter and kept her eyes downcast as he stepped into the room. Only when he was completely inside and the door closed did she speak.

"Welcome to my humble house and the *Cha-no-yu*, Lord," she bowed. "If it pleases you, do not speak until the ceremony is completed. This is not a night for words. You may place your outer garment on the hook beside the door. There are sandals to replace your shoes on your right. If you would care to, sit across from me, please."

He glanced around the room, the vase holding his gaze for some time. Carefully he hung up his coat, removed his footwear, and sat behind the opposite side of the low table. Lucin waited a moment for him to settle in. She indicated the tray of food and rice, the lantern light reflecting nicely off the colors of the fish and condiments. He shook his head no, looking at her intently. She did not meet his eyes. They sat in silence for a moment until Lucin bowed again, and began.

With studied slowness and gentle grace, she carefully removed the cover of the earthenware tea caddy and placed it aside. Using one hand to hold her kimono sleeve inches above the tabletop, she lifted out the handleless porcelain cup and placed it on the table. Deftly, and with extreme focus, she used the delicate bamboo spoon to lift just the right amount of green tea powder from its willow bark vessel and placed it in the cup. She could feel his eyes on her as she lifted the bubbling kettle. With the same graceful precision, she poured the perfect amount of water into the cup and replaced the cast iron vessel on the brazier. Removing the bamboo whisk from the tea caddy, she demurely beat the tea powder and steaming water into the desired blend.

Lucin added one spoonful of cool water to the mixture, bowed to him again and, two handed, offered him the cup across the table. As he took it, she felt an energy pulse and fleetingly looked at him for the first time. His face was a study in concentration. He lifted the cup to his lips and drank. Once, twice, thrice he sipped, and it was empty. She felt the room shift with the power of the event and sensed a change in his posture as he finished the tea. He offered her the cup and she took it, their fingers briefly touching. She felt her diaphragm tighten and heard breath flow from his nostrils. The vase surged at them, and for an instant the room seemed full and thick. The sensation left as quickly as it came, and they both found their balance.

Again, she observed the ritual of the *Cha-no-yu*, mixing the green powder with the steaming water, each movement choreographed to a fraction of an inch. Again, he drank the liquid. Again, when he passed the cup back their fingers touched. Again, the flux claimed the room for an instant, anticipated and appreciated by both of them.

When she passed him the third cup, as was correct, he sipped from it and handed it back, encouraging her to drink. She sipped. The hot liquid traced a path directly to her low belly and settled there, trailing warmth downward, ever downward toward the juncture of her thighs. She shivered from it, allowing it to grow, expecting the familiar desire to rise through the heat.

Carefully, oh so carefully, she prepared the fourth cup. When he returned it to her after drinking and she consumed the last half of the tea, the liquid flashed down the already prepared path, its heat growing as it went. It tumbled into the existing glow and concussed through the center of her womanhood. Her nipples rose against the fabric of her kimonos, dampness seeped between her thighs, and she felt as if a velvet-covered tuning fork were vibrating inside her. The sensation she had expected to receive was so inconsequential compared to the one that arrived, it was without consideration. This was not some itch in search of a scratch. This was the joyous anticipation of a certainty. The expected and deserved culmination of a long wait. Outcome was not in doubt.

Images flashed at the edges of her vision, fragmented flickers of smooth skin and warm secrets from other places in another time. Erotic pulses of awareness and understanding foamed and bubbled through her as the tuning fork sang and sizzled. She struggled to remain serene and controlled facing the creation of another cup, her hand shaking slightly as she reached for the spoon. The vase held the room in its cobalt grasp and, for a brief moment, time was suspended.

As was absolutely correct, he politely refused the preparation of a final cup and so did she, her fingers trembling with relief. Collecting herself, she ritually washed the cup with the clear water and dried it with the cotton towel, then returned all the components to the earthenware caddy and replaced the lid. The *Cha-no-yu* was complete.

She bowed to him, and he to her. Lucin reached for the carved orange rose and removed a delicate petal, offering it to him across the table. As he ate it, for the first time that evening, she looked directly at him and could see the room reflected in his eyes. He finished the petal and removed one for her. She ate, enjoying the moment and the vibrations inside her. From her thighs to her breasts, she hummed with the power of who she was and the certainty of what was to come. The wait was over. It was time.

Plucking the petal containing the drop of honey, she placed it on the brazier and they watched as the heat consumed it, sending the scent of orange rippling through the room. A tiny tendril of honey smoke ascended to the rafters. They watched it together, until it disappeared. Sighing at the loss of such beauty, Lucin rose to her feet. She took his hand and led him into the bedchamber. He regarded the room and a small smile graced his lips.

"Sit," she said, indicating the futon.

He did, and looked at her in the light of the single oil lamp, his eyes shining.

"It was beautiful," he murmured through his smile. "How did you remember all that?"

She lifted the red lacquered box from its resting place, sank to her knees beside him, and placed the box on the floor next to the futon.

"Oh, Harri-*san*," she said, "you are going to be surprised at how much I remember. Very yes."

Nearly three miles away, as he prepared his evening meal, Tamiko Asaruka smiled.